LETTER FROM A RAKE

SASHA COTTMAN

Chapter One

LONDON, 1817

At three o'clock in the afternoon, on the eighth day after her arrival in England, Miss Millicent Ashton made up her mind. She wanted to go home.

The snide remarks had begun the moment she and her mother entered Lady Elmore's spacious drawing room.

'So that's what an Indian elephant looks like,' whispered a blonde miss by the window. She leaned in close to another girl, who giggled.

'I wonder if she gives free rides.'

Millie knew the cruel taunts were aimed directly at her.

In the other homes they had so far visited, she had managed to perfect the art of removing her coat and sitting down in one motion. With luck, she was usually able to seat herself in the corner of a couch and hide partially behind the skirts of her mother.

Unfortunately, this time Lady Elmore had greeted them at the drawing room door and Millie had suffered the humiliation of being presented by her mother in the middle of the room, where of course everyone could take in Millie's ample frame.

While the two older women remarked on how cold the weather

was in England compared with India, the first of the whispers began.

The giggling misses' barely concealed mirth earned them both a steely stare from Millie's mother, who ushered her daughter to a couch to be seated next to their hostess.

Millie's heart sank. Now everyone in the room could see her. As Violet took the seat beside her, Millie gave her mother a half-smile, silently regretting her mother's need to make a statement.

For the rest of the two-hour visit, she sat quietly between the two women, taking the occasional sip of her black tea and politely refusing to partake of the delicious array of cakes Lady Elmore's servants had laid out on the low table before them.

With her hands folded in her lap, she focused on the pain of her thumbnail boring deep into her palm. She would poke her own eyes out before she would show any kind of response to the cruel taunts.

She retreated into the comfort of her own private thoughts, slowly and methodically naming the fjords of the Norwegian coast-line, and when she was done, she started on Finland. Nothing soothed her mind more quickly than attempting to tackle mental tongue twisters.

When her mother finally began making her farewells, Millie was lost somewhere in the far frozen north of Scandinavia.

A whispered 'Millie, we are leaving,' roused her.

With a well-practised curtsy, she politely thanked Lady Elmore and followed her mother to the front door. Hands clasped tightly in front, she kept her gaze firmly fixed on her gloves.

After attending several of these events since their arrival in London, she had learnt the painful lesson of what would happen if she risked one last glance around the room of vipers. At Mrs Wallace's house earlier in the week she had caught several of the girls puffing their cheeks out at her as she left. One had even managed to poke out her tongue before smothering the action with a well-timed cough.

As soon as the carriage door closed behind them, she turned on her mother.

'That is the last of those horrid things you drag me to; next time you can go on your own,' she snapped, stamping her foot for good measure.

Violet Ashton let out a sigh. 'And what am I to tell the ladies of London society when my highly eligible daughter does not accompany me on these outings?' she replied.

'Tell them you have locked me in my room for swearing, or better still tell them that I went mad and you had me put me away in Bedlam.'

She crossed her arms, glared out of the window and continued.

'If they want to see me they can pay the keeper a coin. I barely know these people and yet they choose to judge me purely by sight. Not one of those simpering misses has attempted to speak to me. No, they would rather just make fun of a newcomer; well, it's the last straw.'

'Don't say it,' her mother replied.

'Say what?'

'"I want to go home to India, I hate this place, all the people are horrid and it's cold." If I hear those words from your lips one more time today, I swear I shall get on a boat myself and go back to India just to get away from you.'

Violet pulled her coat tightly around herself and let out a tired sigh.

'Honestly, Millie, my ears cannot take many more of your complaints. Don't think I don't know how unkind those girls are, but you have to remember you pose a threat to them and they don't like it. They are trying to bring you down to their level. You just have to rise above them.'

Millie sat staring at her mother, too stunned to speak. For the first time since their arrival, she was lost for words. How could she possibly be a threat to anyone?

Finally, she shook her head. 'How am I a threat to those girls, Mama?'

Violet gave a knowing smile and nodded her head.

3

'You are from a good family; your father and uncle are powerful men and you come with a sizeable dowry. A lot of those girls have only their passing beauty to catch a potential husband and most men want more than that,' she explained.

Millie scowled. 'Yes, but most men want a slender, elegant wife who stays out of their way,' she replied, knowing she would never be that sort of woman.

Her mother laughed. 'Where on earth did you get such a silly notion from? Have you ever seen me shy away from your father? And believe me, I have never been thin in my life.' She leaned forward on the leather bench and brushed her hand gently over Millie's cheek.

'Darling, you will find that different men are attracted to different things. Some will find you a little unusual because of your foreign upbringing and not to their taste, but I assure you there will be someone who finds you the most enchanting creature he has ever laid eyes upon. And when he discovers the witty, intelligent girl that you are, he will give thanks you have come into his life.'

She tucked a wayward lock of Millie's chestnut-brown hair behind her daughter's ear before adding, 'Of course, you will have to stop complaining about England for him to have a chance to appreciate your finer qualities, but I am sure you will soon overcome your aversion to the place; everyone does eventually.'

'Apart from the French,' Millie muttered, knowing she was testing her mother's patience to the limit.

Violet sat back in her seat and rubbed her temple. She had complained of a throbbing behind her left eye before they'd arrived at Lady Elmore's and Millie knew from the pale colour of her mother's cheeks that one of her serious headaches was imminent. As soon as they reached home she would retire to her room and have a long afternoon sleep, leaving Millie once more alone to amuse herself.

Her mother's words of advice still hung in the air. Violet was right, of course; Millie would have to make peace with her new home but, as for the other matter, her mind was wracked with doubt.

4

No one in London would think her wonderful or stunning. It would take a special man to look beyond the obvious and see the real Millie Ashton. From what she had seen of London society so far, she doubted that such a man existed anywhere in England.

As the carriage made the short journey to their new home in Mill Street, Millie continued to look out the window. The cobbled streets of London were a stark contrast to the dusty streets of Calcutta, the city where she had been born.

Instead of the hot windy streets full of people, animals and hand carts all attempting to make progress through the oncoming traffic, London was the picture of ordered civility. The few people walking on the streets of St James made their way on stone pavements, not in the middle of the road. And there were no cows wandering lazily in and out of the street stalls and markets.

Millie sat back in her seat and, closing her eyes, tried to recall the cries of the *khonchavala*, as they walked the streets of her home city peddling their many wares.

Once they'd reached home and were inside, Millie quickly handed her bonnet and coat to her maid. The house call had been long and trying, her temper was frayed and she knew if she stayed near her mother for a minute longer, harsh words would be exchanged and the whole day would be a complete shambles.

She brushed a kiss on her mother's cheek, wished her a speedy recovery and with purpose headed downstairs in search of the kitchens.

Millie was sitting in the big wooden cook's chair with a mug of hot sweet tea, slowly chewing on one of Mrs Knowles' mawa cakes when she saw her brother Charles' head appear around the kitchen door.

Stepping into the kitchen, he was greeted by the Indian born Mrs Knowles with a respectful 'Namaste'. He bowed in return, before turning to his sister.

'Thought I might find you in here. How was the visit to Lady Elmore's?' Charles asked, as he stopped near the kitchen table.

His gaze drifted to the plate sitting next to Millie at the end of the table. A single cake sat alone among the scattered crumbs.

'Oh dear, that bad?' he replied, running a hand through his sandy blond hair.

Millie wiped her mouth with a cloth napkin and slurped down the last of her tea. Small tears formed in her eyes and she bravely blinked them away. Rising from the chair, she managed to maintain her composure for the seconds it took for her to fall into her older brother's embrace.

He wrapped his comforting arms around her and held her close.

'They called me an elephant,' she said as the tears found their way to her cheeks. 'None of them wanted to talk to me; they just sat and giggled behind their hands. They were simply horrid.'

Charles stroked her hair and planted a kiss on the top of her long brown locks.

'Millie, you just have to give them time, let them get to know you, and I promise things will get better. Not everyone here is horrible. You will have lots of friends in no time. We've only been here a week, you cannot dismiss all of London just yet,' he said with a sigh.

Millie sniffled back the tears and took the handkerchief he offered.

'I know, I know; Mama says exactly the same thing, but—'

'But what?'

'London isn't what I was promised. Where is the sophistication, the elegance? So far all I have seen are drawing rooms full of small-minded harpies,' Millie replied, pulling out of his embrace.

Charles shook his head.

'I hope you are not setting your mind against our new home?'

She shrugged her shoulders. 'It's just that I had hoped London might be a bit more cosmopolitan. I know many of the English in Calcutta tended to be indifferent to the rest of the country, but I suppose I expected a little more from all that I had heard of England. It is harder to find my feet here than I had expected.'

'But, you have to admit, it's not all been bad. You cannot tell me you have not enjoyed shopping for new clothes, Millie. I have twice tripped over piles of boxes in the front hallway,' Charles replied.

'No, the shops are simply wonderful. I have never seen anything like them. I am sure one could shop for days and not venture into the same store twice,' she replied, grateful for the change in topic.

'Good and what about the museums? I know you have a long list of galleries, gardens and castles you wish to visit.'

Her spirits rallied at the idea as she looked at her brother and nodded. They were both going to have to find their way through the maze of London society in the oncoming months.

'Thank you, Charles. You are possessed of the happy knack of finding the good in every situation. I can always rely upon you to pull me out of a miserable mood. And you are right; I shall ask Papa if he will take me to see Lord Elgin's Greek marbles when he next has some spare time. I hear they have moved them to a new display room.'

'Good. You could ask him on the way to the party tonight,' he replied.

A wave of nausea came over her. Whether it was as a result of the large number of spiced cakes she had eaten, or from the realisation that tonight her family were to be guests of honour at a 'Welcome home' ball, Millie couldn't tell.

Millie thanked Mrs Knowles for the cakes and headed for the door. As he passed the table, Charles snatched up the last remaining mawa cake, stuffed it into his mouth and followed his sister from the room.

Chapter Two

Millie peered through the window of her family's carriage as it drew up outside her uncle's brightly lit house later that evening. Ashton House might not have been the largest house on Green Street, but it certainly was the most elegant.

Four huge stone columns rose high above the street, forming an arched portico. Black iron gates on both the side arches meant entry to the house could only be gained from the arch facing toward the front of the street. Those foolish enough to choose this side of the street on which to walk were forced to negotiate a narrow path between the columns and the road.

Millie thought it rather outrageous that one of her father's ancestors had been able to steal the public footpath from the front of Ashton House.

'They widened the street after the house was built,' her father noted.

Millie glared at him. James Ashton had an uncanny ability to know exactly what his only daughter was thinking at any moment. When she was young, she had thought it a fun game when he told her what she wished to eat for supper.

Now, as she grew older, Millie found herself having to maintain a distance from her ever-observant father. Though she knew it didn't take any special insight to see how unhappy she had been from the moment they had docked in damp, grey England.

Her parents had talked about returning home for so many years, London had taken on an almost mythical status. Then one night her father cheerfully announced that he had accepted a senior post there with the East India Company and they would all be leaving Calcutta in six months. Her shock at the sudden news contrasted sharply with the light she saw shining in her mother's eyes as her father made the announcement.

Later, when she passed the door of her parents' room on her way to bed, she witnessed them sharing a passionate kiss. As they drew apart, she saw a huge smile on her father's face. When her mother whispered to him 'Thank you darling; this is the greatest gift you have ever given me,' Millie knew her life in India was at an end.

In the weeks that followed, she realised she had never seen her mother and father so happy. After seeing her parents' loving embrace and the giddy excitement her mother had displayed when the first of the packing crates arrived, Millie had vowed not to tell either parent how devastated she was about the impending change in their family address.

It was now almost a year later and she still found it hard to believe she had seen the monsoon rains for the last time.

'Kindly stop reading my mind, Papa; it's not polite,' she replied, her mind returning to the present.

'Well, stop thinking so loudly and I won't be able to,' her father chuckled.

The carriage came to a halt in front of Ashton House and James Ashton stepped out and on to the pavement. He helped Violet and Millie down, leaving Charles to follow behind them.

Inside Ashton House, James' older brother and his wife warmly greeted them. Married for fifteen years, the Viscount and Viscountess had sadly not been blessed with children.

'Violet, Millie,' Lady Ashton said brightly. 'I am so pleased to see you; I have been waiting for this night for such a long time.'

She placed a warm kiss on Millie's cheek and gave her a hug. 'I love your silk gown; it matches your nose ring. You will make quite an impression in London society, my dear,' her aunt remarked.

Millie raised a hand and touched the tiny sapphire-studded ring which she wore in her right nostril.

'Thank you, Aunt Beatrice, you don't think it makes me look too foreign? Mama has been trying to get me to take it out since the day we left Calcutta,' she replied. Her pale blue gown with gold edging on the skirt had arrived earlier that morning from the modiste; it matched the colour of the sapphire to perfection.

Lady Ashton nodded her head. 'I love it, but you may want to listen to your mother's advice; the *ton* can be a rather close-minded lot when it suits them. Not everyone will see you as interesting and exotic.'

'I am beginning to understand what you mean,' Millie replied.

Lord Ashton slapped Charles heartily on the back.

'My boy,' he laughed. With an empty nursery in Ashton House, his nephew would be the eventual heir to the Ashton family title.

'Remind me to send you the bill for his schooling,' replied James, with a grin.

The two brothers shared a playful wrestle while the rest of their respective family members watched. Violet seemed to be the only one who did not find the whole brotherly exchange the least bit odd.

'Nothing changes,' she sighed. 'From the first time I met James, I noticed the two of them could not keep their hands off one another. Always slapping, hugging and wrestling.'

'Yes, well, we do have a bit of catching up to do, my dear,' replied her husband, his head tucked firmly under his older brother's armpit. The two men both grinned like naughty schoolboys. The joy of being reunited with his younger sibling shone brightly in Lord Ashton's eyes.

Millie had a sudden vision of two little boys running wild through the fields of Kent, laughing as they went. Her father had related many stories of his joy-filled childhood at Ashton Park to Millie and Charles as they grew up.

Years later, when they were grown and the Ashton estate was facing financial ruin, her father had gone to restore the family fortunes across the other side of the world, leaving both Oscar and England behind.

Lord Ashton released James from his brotherly embrace and turned his attention to Violet. Pulling her into his arms, he gave her a tender kiss on the forehead. 'I am so glad to have you home, my lovely sister; you spent too many years away from us, too many.'

Hot tears stung in Millie's eyes as she watched her uncle hold her mother as if he would never let her go.

Until recently, Oscar Ashton had been merely a name on a treasured letter from a far-off land, but here and now, he was all too real. All flesh and human emotion, wrapped up in the spitting image of her father.

She felt the gentle pressure of her aunt's hand on her upper arm and turned to see Lady Ashton gulping down air as she vainly attempted to stifle her own tears.

During the blissful, ignorant years of her young life, Millie had never understood that her parents had been painfully separated from their families. Although India was her home, for James and Violet the stay on the subcontinent had been twenty years of sacrifice and longing.

Now, with her father's endeavours and skilful management, the family had made enough capital to return to England and re-establish themselves and their children at the pinnacle of London society.

Millie drew a handkerchief from within her gown and dabbed at her tears.

'To think I wailed over leaving my horse behind. What a dreadful, selfish daughter I am. I should be happy that my parents have finally come home, yet all I can think of is my own miserable self.'

Her aunt put a comforting arm around her.

'My dear girl, you have nothing to be ashamed of, so don't be too hasty to punish yourself. Your mother tells me your first week has been a bit of a trial. We all have to remember that England is a foreign country to you, Millie, so none of us should expect you to settle in here straight away. Your parents might have returned home, but now you are the one who has left her homeland behind and begun a life abroad.'

'Thank you,' Millie replied, finding a smile for her aunt. 'You are kind.'

Lady Ashton's failure to provide her husband with an heir must have been a painful humiliation for her. Yet, from the moment James and Violet had arrived back in England, she had done everything to make them and their children feel welcome.

She gave Millie a hug. 'Nonsense; that is what family is for, my dear. If you need an ear to bend with your problems, I would be more than happy to lend you mine. It's hard to be an outsider in the *ton* if you are not born into it. Now, dry your eyes; I want to show you and your mother how beautiful the ballroom looks before the rest of the guests arrive.'

An hour or so later, Millie stood alone to one side of the crowded ballroom reflecting upon her aunt's words. As the other guests huddled in small, friendly groups, she felt the sting of being a true outsider.

Earlier, she had made several turns of the elegant ballroom with Charles, both smiling with pride as the other guests admired the beautiful silk wall hangings their father had brought back from India. The four large multi-coloured panels were hung on the walls in pairs on either side of the French doors at the rear of the ballroom, affording new arrivals a full view of them from the top of the staircase.

'They will serve as a constant reminder of where the Ashton family's salvation came from, when it came so very close to the edge of ruin,' her father had said when he commissioned the works from the local weavers in Calcutta. Now, as she stood looking at her favourite panel, which depicted a view of the Hooghly River from Fort William, it occurred to her that the silks were a visual representation of all that her parents had sacrificed.

When their uncle came and dragged Charles off to meet his friends, Millie declined the invitation to join them, preferring to spend some time on her own. Considering that apart from the Ashton family she knew no one else in the whole of London, this was an easy feat.

'What a crush; I didn't think there were that many families in town at this time of the year,' observed a young, fair-haired woman who stopped at her side. 'Though I ought not to complain; at least it keeps me from Lord Ashton's supper table. My mother says if she sees me near it once more this evening she will have my lips sewn together.'

Millie turned and after taking in the petite pink roses on the bodice of the slender girl's muslin gown, gave her a wan smile. After the miserable day she had endured, another figure-obsessed miss was last on the list of things she needed.

A spark of mischief glinted in the other girl's eye.

'Of course, if you and I just happen to be deep in conversation and stroll slowly by the said table of delights and I lose one of my slippers and...'

'Your hand reaches out to the table to steady yourself,' replied Millie, quick on the uptake.

'At which point, my hand accidentally touches one of those delicious apple and cinnamon tarts...'

'Then you could only be held to acclaim for your good manners. Since you had touched the food, you could hardly leave it on the table for another guest to eat.'

The other girl giggled, before painting a determined, serious look on her face. She took hold of Millie's hand, and gave it a gentle squeeze.

'You know you are right, absolutely right,' she replied. A grin threatened at the corner of her mouth, but to Millie's delight, her new acquaintance managed to keep it valiantly at bay.

'It would be saving my family from the most outrageous of scandals. Why, I should receive a standing ovation the moment that tart touches my lips.'

Millie closed her eyes and sagely nodded.

'I should think a medal would be struck in your honour; my uncle would see to it. For eating that one tart, whilst saving your good self from falling, was truly a feat of wonder, and it should not go unrewarded.'

A snicker escaped the other girl's lips, followed by the most unladylike of snorts.

Both girls bent their heads and tried to capture their laughter in their hands.

Millie let out a sigh of relief.

Real girls did exist in London society.

'Lucy Radley,' said her new friend, her pale green eyes sparkling with tears of mirth. She extended her hand with all the elegance of a queen.

'Millie Ashton,' Millie replied, dropping into a curtsy.

As she rose, she saw the smile had disappeared from Lucy's face.

'Ashton, as in Lord Ashton's niece?'

Millie nodded.

'Oh, no. How embarrassing. You are one of the guests of honour and here I am telling you how to steal food from your uncle's table. You must think me the height of rudeness; I am so terribly sorry,' Lucy said, as a patch of red appeared on both cheeks.

Millie took the opportunity to make a thorough study of her evening gloves. If she was ever going to see what sort of girl Lucy truly was, now was the time.

'I am sorry, but your apology is simply not good enough, you shall have to be punished for such a grave transgression,' she replied haughtily.

'Yes?'

Millie raised her eyes and with a look of gravity worthy of an Old Bailey judge, she passed sentence.

'I am afraid there is nothing else for it, the sentence must match the severity of the crime. Lucy, you shall have to become my new best friend.'

A look of relief crossed Lucy's face, followed swiftly by a well-executed expression of feigned horror.

'It was only a tart, I had no idea the punishment would be so harsh. Couldn't you just transport me to the colonies?' she replied.

Millie laughed; her instincts about Lucy had been spot on.

They were meant for each other.

'Now, let us visit that supper table,' commanded Millie, rubbing her hands together with glee. She had just made her first friend in England and it was time to celebrate.

Lucy gave her a short bow and waved toward the table. 'Lead on.'

Later, after polishing off several of the delicacies gracing Lord Ashton's table, including two of the apple and cinnamon tarts, Millie and Lucy retreated to a far corner of the ballroom.

Fortunately, they managed to find an empty space near some open doors and immediately found relief from the heated crush. Millie had expected a few people to be interested in meeting her family due to her father's position at the East India Company, but the three hundred or so guests crowded into the ballroom left her stunned. The room itself was lost in a sea of bodies and humming conversations.

'I have never seen so many people in one room,' she said. Then turning, she pointed her face toward the doorway and allowed a gentle cold breeze to ruffle her hair. She shivered. After a lifetime of the heat of the subcontinent, the English winter would forever be a novelty to her.

'The weather was always too hot and steamy to have this sort of number at a social gathering in India. Without room to fan themselves in the heat, ladies would simply have fainted dead away.'

'Now, that would make for an interesting evening, though it might stop your aunt and uncle's guests from ever returning to Ashton House,' Lucy replied.

Millie nodded her head. 'Yes, well, from my short time in London, there are few people I would like to meet for a second time. Present company excluded, of course.'

'Thank you,' Lucy replied with a smile.

Millie watched as Lucy's gaze now drifted from her and tracked slowly across the room. Lucy then rose up on her toes and attempted to peer over the heads of the other guests.

'Who?' Millie enquired.

'Who, what?' Lucy replied, as her gaze continued to roam the room.

'Who or what are you looking for?'

The thought that her newly found friend might have already tired of her company crossed Millie's mind. Perhaps her instincts about Lucy had been wrong. After a week of bitter disappointment in the land of her heritage, the thought of being unceremoniously abandoned in the middle of a party was close to all she could bear.

'If you have someone else with whom you have made a prior arrangement, I shall understand. I did attach myself to you without notice,' she added.

Lucy turned, and with a reassuring smile on her face, shook her head.

'I'm not going anywhere without you, sweet Millie, so there is no need for you to be alarmed. I am simply looking for my brothers. They're supposed to be attending this evening's festivities and as usual they are late. I am eager to introduce you to them. David is wickedly amusing, and Alex is just...'

'Just what?' Millie replied.

Lucy screwed up her nose.

'Well, let me put it this way: all the girls are in love with him, and all the boys wish they were him. If he weren't my brother I am certain my father would have him at the top of his list of suitable husbands for me.' She screwed up her nose once more. Alex's magical spell clearly had little effect on his sister.

Millie wondered how long it would be before her own parents started talking to her about finding a husband. Charles had to marry soon; it was expected of the future Viscount, but she prayed she would be allowed a little time before the question of marriage was raised for her.

She hoped that before then she would have found a way to return to India.

She was still having an almost daily argument with her mother as to whether she was too old to have a debutante season. That at least kept the subject of marriage at bay. With any luck she would be able to convince her mother that the notion of a twenty-year-old debutante was ridiculous and she would be spared that particular form of public humiliation. The idea of being presented to London society alongside a group of rake-thin, younger debutantes made her feel ill. With her curvaceous figure, she could not possibly compete with any of them for the eye of an eligible bachelor.

No matter what her mother said, Millie held grave doubts about her chances of making a love match. How many times this week had she heard that English gentlemen only liked slim-figured girls: no curves, no breasts? Of course, once the *ton* discovered that thanks to her father's efforts abroad, she now came with a sizeable dowry, her stakes in the marriage market would lift significantly.

Every fortune-hunter in the country would find her a delight. They would overlook her many faults until she finally relented and selected one of them as her husband. She would then be free to spend the rest of her life regretting her decision while her spouse frittered away her fortune and shared his nights with someone else.

She knew the same fate might well await her back in India, but at least she would be home, and far away from England.

Leaving her brother behind would be the hardest break of all, but she had come to realise that she did not belong and never would. It would be best if she went home and did not remain to embarrass him.

A recent visit to the tailor on Bond Street had resulted in a daily display of Charles' new, well-cut wardrobe. While the new clothes made him look more handsome than ever, she worried that the change would go deeper than just his attire.

It would be a terrible pity if the influence of his new friends and expected future title took away the very things that made him uniquely Charles Ashton.

'Stay true to yourself,' she murmured.

'Pardon?' Lucy replied. But before Millie could respond, something caught Lucy's attention and she shot up her arm and began waving madly toward the staircase at the top of the ballroom.

'Hello! We are over here,' she called out.

Millie smiled; Lucy really was a breath of fresh air.

She looked and saw two young men standing on the landing at the top of the stairs. They were peering out over the crowd in the direction of Lucy, who continued to wave at them. Upon seeing the girls, the man nearest to them raised his hand and gave a friendly wave.

'The one with the black hair is my oldest brother, David. The fair-haired one next to him is Alex, known to all and sundry as Alexander the Great,' Lucy explained.

As the two men made their way down the stairs and into the ballroom, Millie saw the immediate impact that the arrival of the Radley brothers had on the gathering. For every step they took, someone hailed them. Handshakes flew out from the crowd; their backs were slapped by everyone and a chorus of cheery greetings rose ever higher in pitch.

She wondered which of them had been wielding the sword when the dragon had been slain, so rousing was the reception these two young men received. They seemed more like all-conquering heroes returning from a dangerous quest, enjoying the spoils of victory, rather than a couple of *ton* lads arriving at a private party. Any moment now, she expected the crowd to hoist them high on its shoulders for the whole world to laud.

How intoxicating it must be to be so popular, to wield such power.

Lucy's brothers slowly made their way through the thronging mass. Finally, Millie got her first real look at the Radley brothers and her heart stopped.

David had been leading the way through the crowd, but as they drew closer to the girls, the crowd thinned a little and Alex was able to walk beside his brother.

As he appeared from behind David, Millie thought she must be imagining things. No mortal man could be that good looking.

Not merely handsome, but breathtakingly beautiful.

A pile of blond hair sat ruffled atop his head. At first glance it appeared not to have seen a comb or brush for many a day and yet it was perfect.

He looked as if he had recently rolled out of bed, thrown on his evening clothes and headed out to the Ashton party.

His cravat, against all fashion dictates, was tied loosely around his neck, but in such an elegant way that was clearly by design. His red and gold striped double-breasted waistcoat fitted tightly to his long, lean muscular body. As Millie's gaze took in the magnificence of Alex's evening clothes it was obvious that every piece of clothing on his body was of the finest cut and fabric, the touch of a master tailor evident in this pinnacle of casual elegance.

Her eyes drifted lower to the highly polished black Hussar boots which clung to his calf muscles. She took a deep breath and tried to turn her head away, but found herself unable to.

Or was it unwilling?

The instant she saw the deep green of Alex's eyes, she knew he was dangerous. When his soul-piercing gaze landed upon her, she felt a cold shiver of premonition run down her spine.

Millie gave a quick glace over her left shoulder to see who had caught his eye, but found herself facing a dark green velvet curtain.

There was no one behind her.

When she looked back at the approaching Adonis, she realised his gaze was locked firmly on her, a look of puzzlement etched upon his face.

She looked toward Lucy, but could not catch her eye. Her friend was busily attempting to paint a look of annoyance on her own face, whilst glaring at her approaching brothers.

'Oh no, I can see this is not going to end well,' Millie muttered, feeling her face turning red. She took two steps backward, but found herself hard up against the ballroom curtain.

'I need to get away from here', she said under her breath, beginning to panic.

Horrid girls were bad enough, but disapproving brothers were another matter entirely. With his eyes trained upon her like a hunter stalking his prey, she knew she would not be fortunate enough to escape unscathed.

From the look on his face, Millie deduced Alex was not happy to see her standing beside Lucy. Was it that the perfect brother did not like his sister associating with those who were less than godlike? It would not be the first time since arriving that she had been judged by others because of her looks.

Lucy shook her head. 'You can't leave yet; you haven't met my brothers. They will be delighted to meet you, I am sure of it,' she replied. 'Once I have finished boxing their ears, that is.'

Millie grabbed a handful of the heavy green curtain. For an instant, she toyed with the idea of hiding behind the voluminous fabric screen and making herself invisible, but she knew that would be ridiculous. Escape was impossible.

With every step, he drew closer to her, his gaze never leaving her face. Trapped by his stare and unable to flee, she steeled herself for the humiliation she knew she was about to endure.

'I was beginning to wonder when you two miscreants would finally arrive,' Lucy said, letting out a huff of displeasure. 'Where have you been?'

The two men exchanged a knowing grin.

'See, I told you she would be cross with us,' David replied and nodded to his brother.

'I don't know why. We are only late because Mama asked us to call in at home and pay our respects to Great Aunt Maude. You can hardly blame us for that, Lu,' Alex replied, never moving his gaze from Millie.

Millie blinked hard and with great effort tore her eyes away from his magnetic stare. She looked at Lucy, who gave Millie a pained look of embarrassment in return. Millie's heart went out to her.

'Sorry,' Lucy muttered as her hands fell to her sides. 'How is Aunt Maude? Mother has been so worried. She only came out tonight because Maude finally agreed to the doctor visiting.'

David reached out and pulled his sister into a forgiving hug. She wrapped her arms around him, and hid her burning face in the front of his evening jacket.

'It's all right, Lucy, Maude is fine. The doctor was leaving as we arrived, and he said it was just exhaustion from the long trip south. A few days' bed rest and she will be gadding about town before we know it.'

He placed a gentle peck on his sister's cheek, before his hand went slyly to her hair in a well-practised move. Lucy flinched and struggled to break free of his embrace. She took a step back before reaching out and giving him a solid punch on the arm.

'Oooh, you are a bad one, David Radley, and don't think for one minute I won't tell Mama it was you who fussed with my hair,' she laughed, wagging her finger at him. David stood rubbing his poor offended arm.

'Sharp right, Lucy; ever considered bare-knuckled boxing?'

Millie stifled a laugh. With an older brother herself, she knew the price of a brotherly hug was always a well-timed ruffling of the hair. David Radley, it would appear, was another exponent of the art.

Another spark of hope flared; warmth did exist in the cold heart of London society. She immediately liked David; he was just like her own brother Charles.

Her gaze returned to the other Radley brother, Alex, who was slowly looking her up and down, and appeared to be taking stock. She gave him a smile and prayed that her social death would be a mercifully quick one.

He gave a short bow and held out his hand.

She had not anticipated that move. It took a moment for her to unclench her right hand and offer it to him. He captured her hand and held it firmly.

She looked down and saw that her fingers had disappeared under his palm. She sucked in a shallow breath and bit her bottom lip. The sooner this was over the better.

'Alex,' he barely whispered. He bent and placed a kiss on her glove.

She felt his hot breath through the glove's fine cotton and a second shiver went down her spine.

He lifted his head and stared once more into her eyes. If death had come at that moment, she would have welcomed it. For if

Helen of Troy's face had launched a thousand ships, Alex Radley's eyes could have burned them all, such was their power.

They stood silently staring at one another, until David cleared his throat in a none-too-subtle manner.

Alex waved a hand in his brother's general direction. 'David,' he muttered.

Still held by the smouldering power of Alex's gaze, Millie gave a small nod of her head.

She heard a sudden indignant huff and Alex disappeared, then David and Lucy took his place.

Millie snapped back to reality.

She realised that, with one arm draped loosely around his sister's waist, David had used his other hand to give his younger brother a hard shove to one side.

Out the corner of her eye, Millie could see Alex standing nearby, staring daggers at David.

Fortunately for David, Alex could not stare at two people at once, and so his silent punishment lasted only momentarily before Alex resumed his keen observation of Millie.

She looked down at her hand, and was surprised to see it still on the end of her arm. She was certain Alex had taken it with him, so tightly had he held it within his grasp.

'Sorry; he does lack a certain amount of social finesse at times – you would never think he was a duke's son,' David said, returning his brother's filthy look in kind.

Millie raised her eyebrows and looked at Lucy.

'So, it's Lady Lucy?'

Lucy looked surprised. 'Oh, sorry. I assumed you knew who the Radley family were, but of course since you have only just arrived in England, that was a rather silly presumption on my part. Our father is the Duke of Strathmore. There are the three of us here, as well as Stephen and Emma, who are both still in the schoolroom. I always make a mess when it comes to the formality of introductions.'

David gave a polite bow.

'Mr David Radley; pleased to make your acquaintance. This

blond buffoon here is the Marquess of Brooke, much to the shame of our family.'

'Shut up David; you don't even know her name,' Alex snapped.

Millie saw Lucy and David exchange a look of surprise at this display of temper from their brother.

Lucy stepped away from David and took hold of Millie's hand. 'This is Miss Millicent Ashton, Viscount Ashton's niece, recently arrived from India. Her family are the guests of honour for tonight,' she explained.

David must have seen the anger simmering on Alex's face and rather than taunt his brother further, he gave Millie a wave and a smile.

'So, you are Charles' younger sister?' he asked. 'We met your brother on Monday at White's; your father was completing the paperwork for him to become a member.'

Millie let out the breath she realised she was holding. 'Yes, Papa plans to have him admitted to all the right clubs as soon as possible. He and my uncle are grooming Charles for the day when he eventually comes into the family title.'

'And you were born in India?' David asked, as his gaze locked on her nose ring.

She smiled, grateful for his polite questioning; it gave her something to contemplate while Alex stood silently to one side staring at her. For her part, she kept her eyes facing forward, her gaze locked firmly upon a small freckle above David's right eyebrow. His blue-green eyes reminded her of the colour of the sea.

'Yes, I was born nearly two years after my parents and brother arrived in Calcutta; I have lived all my life on the subcontinent,' she replied.

It was the first time since she had arrived in England that anyone had asked her about her own life. The usual queries, more often than not, pertained to Charles's plans for his future.

Lucy smiled as the conversation began to smooth over the awkward earlier greeting from Alex. Millie ventured a shy smile in her direction. Her new friend appeared to be as keen as she was for this friendship to survive its first night.

'Miss Ashton finds our weather a bit of a challenge. She is not used to the chill of London in March,' Lucy offered.

At that moment, the orchestra began to warm up for a quadrille. Millie glanced over towards the dance floor and saw various couples joining hands and finding their places. She wished she were among them.

She turned back to continue speaking to David, but instead found Alex once more taking up her whole field of vision. He reached out and grabbed her by the hand.

'Dance with me, Miss Ashton,' he said, and began to drag her towards the dance floor.

She whipped her head around and caught a brief glimpse of David and Lucy staring open-mouthed with surprise, before she lost them in the crowd. Alex pulled her swiftly through the throng, which parted for him easily, as it had done on his arrival.

As he strode hurriedly towards the dance floor, she was compelled to run to keep up with him.

With all her attention focused on holding up her skirts and running, Millie did not realise Alex had stopped until she ran straight into him.

'Ooof', she exclaimed, as her wrist twisted painfully out of his grasp.

He turned and from the expression on his face, he looked as if he had been struck by lightning. She heard him suck in a deep breath and swallow, almost as if he were in pain.

He closed his eyes, nodded his head and then, reaching out, seized her by the hand once more. 'Come on, they are nearly ready to strike up the tune,' he announced.

He turned his back and continued to forge a path through the party guests, towing Millie behind him and stopping only once they had reached the dance floor, where he quickly let go of her hand.

He breathed heavily in and out several times and Millie feared he was about to have a convulsion. To her surprise he took an even deeper breath before giving her an abrupt bow, to which she responded with a curtsy. Since they were in a public place, there was little else she could do.

When the music began, Millie offered him her hand, but Alex stood rooted to the spot.

A flash of fury sparked its way through her brain. He had rudely stared at her, dragged her through a crowded ballroom and now he was refusing to take her hand for the dance.

For Millie, things had been bad enough when Alex had her cornered by the door, but now they stood in the middle of the dance floor, where everyone could see. Out of the corner of her eye she could see the other dancers had begun to take notice.

'Lord Brooke, please. I beg of you, take my hand and let us either join the dance or leave the floor. I don't know what sort of game you think you are playing with me, but your behaviour is boorish and I have had just about enough.'

She saw his lips begin to move, but no words came out of his mouth.

She silently counted to ten before letting out a deep sigh of frustration.

'Very well, if that is how you wish to behave I shall leave you here. Good evening, my lord.'

She turned, and with her head held high, walked away.

'You horrible conceited man,' she muttered through gritted teeth.

If she had looked back, she would have seen Alex still standing alone in the middle of the dance floor, staring after her, a pained look on his face.

At the edge of the crowd, she found Lucy and David.

Poor Lucy's eyes were full of unshed tears and her bottom lip was quivering. Millie took hold of Lucy's hand and gave it a gentle squeeze.

'It's all right, Lucy; I don't dance that well anyway. You and the rest of the party have been spared that unnatural spectacle at least for this evening. You should be grateful for your brother's lack of manners,' she said, giving Lucy a reassuring smile.

Lucy nodded. 'Thank you,' she replied, as the first tears began to roll down her cheek. Millie reached out and wiped one away. The poor girl had stood helpless while her brother humiliated her new friend in front of all the guests at a party.

'Please don't cry, Lucy, no harm was done,' Millie said.

The dance continued and the remaining dancers were compelled to work their way around the inconvenient obstacle that the motionless Lord Brooke presented to them.

Other guests soon began to take note and comment on the odd human centrepiece which was the Marquess of Brooke. To his credit, Millie felt David Radley held his temper rather well, but finally it was clear he too had endured enough of his brother's outlandish behaviour.

'Excuse me, ladies, but I need to go and speak to my fool of a brother before he causes the family name any further disgrace,' David said as he walked away.

As the girls and a growing number of party guests looked on, David stormed on to the dance floor and took hold of Alex's arm. The brothers exchanged a few sharp, angry words before David marched Alex across the ballroom and out into the rear garden.

As they passed by, Millie could see the look on David's face was one of pure rage.

Lucy let out a small cry of despair and gripped Millie's wrist

'Millie, I had better go after them; something must be terribly wrong with Alex. Please believe me when I say he has never behaved like this before in his life. He can be impetuous at times, but I don't know what has come over him tonight.'

She kissed Millie on the cheek.

'I promise that if you come and visit at Strathmore House, I will make sure he is not at home and if he is, he will be on his best behaviour.' Lucy's gaze followed her brothers as they disappeared through the door and out into the night.

'I have to go,' she said urgently. 'My parents are here tonight and they will soon hear about Alex's behaviour toward you. If I don't go and separate my brothers, my father will have them both by the ear and marching out the front door. If I go now, we may still be able to salvage this evening.'

With a growing sense of unease, Millie watched as Lucy picked up her skirts and headed quickly for the French doors.

Her spirits sank, knowing she would have to make the trip to the Duke of Strathmore's house, no matter how much she dreaded it.

If her new friend had to suffer the embarrassment of having dozens of pairs of eyes watching as she followed her brawling brothers outside, then paying Lucy a social call the next day would be the least Millie could do.

'Millie, Mama wishes to speak to you.' She turned and saw Charles standing behind her, shaking his head. She swore under her breath, pushed past him and went in search of her mother.

When she reached her mother's side, it was obvious whom her mother blamed for the whole embarrassing spectacle; the look on Violet's face said it all. Then, seeing her father, Millie turned and started toward him, but he shook his head and pointed in the direction of his wife.

'But I haven't done anything,' she silently pleaded with him.

'Mama,' she said, as she stepped in front of her mother, with her back to the assembled guests. If she was to be on the end of an undeserved scolding, then let her mother face them as they strained their ears to overhear.

Violet took hold of Millie's hands and pulled her in close.

'What was all that about?' she snapped.

Millie sighed and shrugged her shoulders.

'I honestly do not know, Mama. I met Lucy Radley earlier in the evening; she seemed sweet and introduced me to her two brothers. When they arrived, the Marquess of Brooke just stood and stared at me; even his brother accused him of being rude. The next thing I knew, he had dragged me across the ballroom and pushed me on to the dance floor.'

'Where he then refused to dance with you?' her mother replied, her eyebrows lifting in a clear display that said she was not convinced of her daughter's innocence in the matter.

'Yes, and it was very embarrassing,' Millie replied, hurt at her mother's obvious mistrust. 'Do you think I staged the whole thing to get sympathy?' She pulled her hands away from her mother, not caring that their exchange was being observed.

Violet closed her eyes and sighed.

'What am I going to do with you? I am at my wits' end, Millie. I don't know what happened between you and Lord Brooke, but this nonsense stops right this minute, do you hear?' She wagged her finger at Millie for good measure, which brought on a flurry of whispers from the eavesdroppers behind her.

'For the rest of the evening you will stay by my side, and you will smile and make small talk with anyone who is good enough to speak to you. I will not have you ruin this evening for the rest of the family.'

A reply formed on Millie's lips, but Violet shook her head, indicating that the discussion was at an end. Millie knew exactly where she stood in her mother's graces.

'Yes, Mama,' she replied, taking her place at her mother's side.

'Good,' Violet said as she smiled at the other guests.

For the next half an hour Millie watched dancing couples as they waltzed through a succession of popular pieces. Charles even ventured an appearance with their Aunt Beatrice on his arm.

Millie stood smiling as Charles and Lady Ashton took the floor. His lips moved slowly as he counted out the steps and Lady Ashton, gracious as ever, tried to hide her discomfort every time he stepped on her toes.

'You shall have to start on your dancing lessons again, now that we have been introduced to London society,' her father murmured in her ear. Millie kept her gaze on the dancers, but it was no use; James Ashton was reading her mind again.

'If it's of any comfort, I understand the Duke of Strathmore has taken his son to task, and Lord Brooke will not be troubling you any further this evening, my dear.'

'I wish you would tell that to Mama,' she replied.

Her father put his arm around her shoulder and squeezed. 'Once this dance set is over, your uncle will be making a speech, then we shall be going home. After your visit to Lady Elmore's this afternoon and tonight's unpleasantness, I think you have suffered enough for one day.'

Millie gave him a tight smile; at least someone in her family believed she was not the one to blame for the scene on the dance floor. The thought of going home and tucking herself into bed sounded like heaven.

Her father was right; of all the days they had been in residence in London, today had definitely been the worst. At least now all she had left to endure was a long, boring speech from the head of her family and this day would finally be at an end.

To her surprise and delight, she discovered her Uncle Oscar was a keen and skilled orator. When the orchestra took a supper break, he called the gathering to order and gave a lively and often emotional speech welcoming his brother and family back to England. Millie, Charles and their parents stood together and accepted the heartfelt welcome from the head of their family.

'You just watch the invitations come flooding through the door from first thing tomorrow,' James remarked to his wife. As her parents exchanged a smile, Millie could see the light in her mother's eyes. She had never seen her so happy.

Having one of the most eligible bachelors in all of England as her son would ensure Violet's name appeared high on the guest list for the most exclusive parties and events for the forthcoming season.

Millie caught her mother's eye, and the edge of her mother's smile wavered. If anyone was going to be the proverbial fly in the ointment, it would be her chubby, troublesome daughter.

'Yes, well, I didn't cause this evening's little scene. You can blame that on Lord Brooke,' she muttered to herself. For the first time in her life, Millie felt a distinct distance growing between her mother and herself.

If a young man had treated Millie in the same fashion at a function in Calcutta, she knew her mother would have been across the room and having serious words with him in an instant, but not here, not in London. The rules were different; people did not say what they thought in public, but instead whispered about you long after you had gone.

As she continued to listen to her uncle's speech, Millie's gaze roamed the room, eventually settling on a tall, stern-faced gentleman off to one side. She felt the hairs on the nape of her neck move and stand on end. The man held the hand of a dark-haired woman who wore the same disapproving look.

When the gentleman leaned in close to the woman and whispered something quickly to her, the woman looked behind the man and, turning back to him, gave him a nod.

It took a minute or two for Millie to realise why the couple had caught her attention. As she looked behind the woman, she saw David and to the side of him, Lucy. Both were standing stony-faced, listening to Lord Ashton's speech.

She noted the similarity between the Radley siblings and the older couple, and now, looking at how closely they were all standing to one another, felt it safe to assume the gentleman and the dark-haired woman were in fact the Duke and Duchess of Strathmore.

Her gaze now drifted to a lone figure standing slightly to one side of the Duke. Over the Duke's right shoulder, a pair of eyes stared straight at her.

The Marquess of Brooke.

It was clear to Millie that when the Duke had gathered his family together to hear Viscount Ashton's speech, he had made Alex stand behind him so their host could not see him.

She would have preferred that he had sent his ill-mannered son home, but she knew the scandal that would have caused.

Alex moved slowly away from his family and found an empty space in the crowd. He now had a direct line of sight to her. She tore her eyes away from him and looked down at her gloves.

Charles leaned in close and whispered in her ear 'Lift up your head, Millie, and give them all a smile, you look thoroughly miserable. Please don't spoil this evening; you know how important it is for all of us.'

He took hold of her hand, and gave it a gentle, reassuring squeeze. She smiled. Good old Charles.

Raising her head, she looked back into the crowd, well away from where Alex was standing, only to find her gaze once more falling upon him. He, consistent with form, stared back at her.

He smiled and she felt yet another cold chill run down her spine. The Marquess of Brooke had somehow managed to work his way across the ballroom and now stood on the opposite side of the room from his family.

Calling on all her reserves of stubbornness, she willed herself to keep looking out over the gathering, a brittle smile painted on her face.

She tried in vain to study the nearest of the Indian wall hangings, taking in the intricate floral pattern around its edge, but it was no use. The spark she had felt on the dance floor now began to flame into a small fire of angry resentment.

Fed up and despondent at her first disappointing week in London, and now the intended victim of a twisted game played by a rich brute, Millie decided enough was enough.

If he thought she would simply allow him to carry out his stupid vendetta without her retaliating, then he was in for a nasty shock.

Why can't you leave me alone? There have to be plenty of other young women you could tease. If you think you have found an easy target, you are sorely mistaken. I am much stronger than you think.

She gave a laugh and nodded her head toward him.

Someone had to stand up to the likes of Alex Radley, and Millie Ashton had never been one to shy away from a fight. Though he didn't yet know it, the Marquess of Brooke had met his match.

Chapter Three

He couldn't be certain of the exact time, but the one thing clear in Alex Radley's mind as he watched the dawn's first light creep slowly across his bedroom floor was that he had not slept a wink.

For some inexplicable reason, the Angel of Fate had decreed his life was not complicated enough and had decided to throw Miss Millicent Ashton into his path for good measure.

Stretched out, chest down, with one arm hanging lazily over the side of the bed, he contemplated the events of the previous evening and their likely repercussions.

The moment he had set eyes upon her, Alex knew he was in trouble. Her effect on him was both immediate and violent.

He liked women and enjoyed the pleasure of their company, both in the ballroom and the bedroom, but never before had one of them grabbed his attention the way Millie did. Grabbed it and then held it in a vice-like grip.

He remembered striding through the crowd with his brother, cheerfully greeting their many friends, ready for a full evening of laughs with David.

As soon as they arrived at the party, they had spotted Lucy over in the far corner of the ballroom and made a beeline for their sister. The next thing he knew, his body had sprung to life in a roar of heated lust as he set eyes upon the most exquisite creature he had ever seen.

The blood had rushed from his head to his heated loins, rendering him incapable of meaningful speech.

Unable to move, he'd thought himself on the verge of passing out. All he could do was stand and stare at the luscious sight before him as he fought with his body. In the middle of a crowded ballroom, he had felt his manhood twitch once and then stand resolutely to attention.

Standing in shock, he had been at a loss as to what he should do. At first, he tried kissing the poor girl's hand and trying to talk his body into behaving, but that had failed.

And just as his raging erection threatened to punch a hole in his trousers, his brother had lost his temper and shoved him to one side.

Tears had welled in Alex's eyes at that moment. In a state of complete agony, he then came up with the brilliant idea of trying to dance with Miss Ashton, believing that if he could make his body think of dancing then it would calm down and he could regain control. He had barely made it to the dance floor. Of course, as soon as he faced her on the dance floor, he knew what a huge mistake he had made.

Talk about trying to stare down the devil.

He let out a sigh and rubbed his eyes. The whole evening had been an unmitigated disaster for him from start to finish. He had managed to insult his host, offend a guest of honour and anger his father all in the space of an hour.

The highlight of the evening had been when David dragged him out into the garden and berated him for his dreadful behaviour. Away from the delectable Miss Ashton, Alex's body had calmed down enough for him to be able to see straight.

'What the devil was that all about; how could you do that to a girl you have only just met? You know the rules: you toy with the innocents a little, allow them to fall in love with you and then let them down gently. Instead you publicly humiliated Lucy's new friend, whose uncle just happens to be our host. What has come over you?' David demanded.

David listened while Alex explained his predicament. Then he shook his head.

'I have never heard of anything so absurd in my entire life. She is pleasant enough to be Lucy's friend, but she is certainly no diamond. There must be a thousand prettier girls in London for you to make a fool of yourself over.'

After punching his brother hard on the arm, Alex turned to see Lucy appear outside on the garden terrace. She had been crying and he knew he was to blame.

He and David had shared a brief panicked look. What was he to say to his little sister? 'Sorry Lucy, you don't mind if I lust after your new best friend, do you? Excuse my manners, but as my blood is currently pooled in my loins I am unable to make polite conversation.'

His mind had deserted him and gone completely blank.

When David explained it away as a muscle spasm in Alex's back, Alex had put on his best contrite face, and given a heartfelt promise to make things up to Millie.

Lucy had accepted David's offer of a dance and gone back inside when the Duke appeared through the French doors and angrily demanded an explanation for his son's actions.

Knowing his father would not believe the story about a bad back, Alex had been compelled to tell the truth. His father had berated him. 'Stop behaving like a callow youth and control your lust, young man; you are not thirteen years old. Do you have any idea how embarrassed your mother is? Lord knows what I am going to tell her.'

After agreeing that the back-injury lie was the more socially acceptable explanation, Alex had remained out in the garden until he felt he could face the gathering once more.

For the rest of the night, he had not been able to get near Miss Ashton to apologise, and in the cold light of morning he realised that was probably not such a bad thing as every time he had caught her eye from across the ballroom, his body had begun to harden.

Standing behind his father during Lord Ashton's speech, he could see she was distressed. He had embarrassed her in front of the entire gathering and then she had been obliged to stand alongside her family as a guest of honour in the centre of the room. When he managed to catch her eye at one point he offered her an apologetic smile, but that only appeared to anger her further.

'What a mess,' he said as he rolled over on to his back and pulled the blankets up to cover his head. He longed to stay in bed and get some much-needed sleep, but of more pressing importance was working out how he could apologise to Millie without getting too close.

Closing his eyes, he saw her face and those stunning blue eyes. They were the deepest blue he had ever seen, and put to shame the delicate sapphire nose ring she wore.

His mind's eye drifted lower and he thought of Millie's breasts full, plump and so ripe. How wonderful it would be to touch them, to run his tongue over her peaked nipples.

He sat up in the bed, and threw back the covers. Staring up at him from between his legs was the hugest morning erection he had ever seen. He blinked at the sight.

He counted to three, and called forth the image of his old Latin master Reginald 'Tuppence' Groat from Eton.

'Think of the warts on old Groat's nose, think of the warts,' he muttered, as he watched his body submit to his will.

'Bloody hell, why didn't I do that last night?'

He flopped back in the bed and rubbed his face. He had made a complete fool of himself last night, but worse than that, he had humiliated an innocent young woman in front of a huge social gathering. And if there was one thing Alex Radley had a deep-seated fear of, it was any form of humiliation. Considering what he had done to her, he was genuinely surprised at how well she had maintained her composure.

Most other young society debutantes would have dissolved in a flood of tears and gone running to their mama. The look Millie

Ashton had given him during Viscount Ashton's speech could have frozen the Serpentine.

Accepting that staying in bed would resolve nothing, he pushed back the blankets and scrambled quickly across the floor to where his dressing robe lay across a chair.

He tied the belt and after opening the bedroom door, went to rouse his valet. Although the sun had barely risen above the horizon, he knew he had to be dressed and out of the house as soon as possible.

Before he did anything else today he had to make amends with Miss Millie Ashton.

Chapter Four

M illie cursed herself for having allowed Lord Brooke to make a fool of her.

As she woke the following morning, she felt like a kitchen cloth after it had dried several hundred dishes. Utterly wrung out and spent.

Life for her in England was becoming unbearable. She had tried to make friends, but apart from Lucy no one wanted to know her. Instead, she had been mocked and ridiculed.

Things had been bad enough over the past week and just when things had started to look a little more hopeful, Lord Brooke had walked into her life and racked her misery level up several notches.

He was breathtakingly handsome, and there was no doubt in her mind that he not only knew it, but exploited his looks for all they were worth. It was such a pity that he was the brother of the only girl in London with whom she stood any real chance of forming a friendship.

She could imagine that for him, life had always been easy. He had never had to work to make friends or be accepted. Women would literally throw themselves at his feet. His kind ruled the *ton* like the gods they thought they were.

She let out a tired sigh, and sat up in bed rubbing the crust of sleep from her eyes. The tonic Mrs Knowles had prepared for her when she arrived home from the party had certainly done its job. Millie had slept the sleep of the dead.

'How could he possibly get a thrill out of making a spectacle of me? What an arrogant...'

She stopped herself as the door to her bedroom opened and her maid, Grace, entered.

Millie forced a smile to her lips and hoped Grace had not overheard her early-morning mutterings.

By all accounts the sweet young girl had many friends in other big households. It would not do for her to be telling tales of how foul-mouthed Millie Ashton was running down one of the most eligible bachelors in London.

'Good morning miss. I hope your horrid headache of last night is gone. Your mother was ever so worried about you; she would not let me dress you for bed,' Grace said, opening the wardrobe and taking out a smart morning dress.

Millie silently thanked her mother, who, upon realising the foul temper her daughter was in, decided it was best to play lady's maid herself when they got home. The little white lie of a post-party headache now meant Millie would be compelled to stay at home for a day or two.

'Thank you, yes, my head feels a lot better,' Millie replied.

It was only her heart which ached so desperately.

'I won't need the morning dress today, Grace; I won't be venturing out. Mama and I were going to visit my new friend Lady Lucy at Strathmore House this afternoon, but our outing will have to be postponed until I feel well enough. I shall only need a dress for staying at home. One of my old dresses should suffice. I hope that later in the week, when I am feeling better, we shall call upon the duchess and her daughter.'

Grace gave her a look that said she knew more about last night than she was prepared to admit.

'Very good, miss,' Grace replied. She hesitated for a moment then, appearing to think better of saying anything else, put the morning dress back into the wardrobe.

Please do not speak of last night, Grace, please just pretend you know nothing about it. I shall die if you say anything.

When Grace turned from the wardrobe with a cheery smile on her face, Millie counted her blessings. A few days at home, quietly working on her new scenic London tapestry, would do her the power of good. At the very least it would mean she could complete the top tier of St Paul's Cathedral and perhaps make a start on the rest of the streetscape. The thought of stabbing a needle into something also held a certain appeal in her current state of mind.

She watched as Grace busied about the room, putting away Millie's dress from the party and then selecting a simple day gown for her to wear. Grace hummed a happy tune as she went about her work, a stark contrast to the constant miserable condition in which Millie currently found herself mired.

This is ridiculous. I am usually the happiest, most cheerful person in the place. Granted, I am also the loudest and at times the feistiest, but I have never been like this before in my entire life. When have I ever sat silent and let others walk all over me? Never.

She shook her head. This had to stop. She had to find a way to live in England without going mad. The rest of her family were settling in well; they had put their lives in India behind them and moved on. Until she could find a way out of England, she would have to do the same.

With her elbows propped on her knees, she cupped her chin in both hands and stared at the bedclothes. If the solution to her problem was so simple, then why did she feel so sad?

Because I am not being true to myself. How can I become one of them? I will always be different. I have lived my entire life on the other side of the world. It has shaped who I am and how I perceive things, I cannot change that no matter how hard I try.

This is why I must go home.

A real headache began to pulse in her head.

To fit into London society, she would have to change, but in her heart, she knew that would be asking the impossible. She would never be quite like those who had been baptised in the font of St Georges, Hanover Square. London society dictated how you were to behave and if you operated within those boundaries, you would be safe. You would be protected. If you did not, then the rules ensured that you were ostracised and punished.

She swore under her breath. Last night now made perfect sense. How stupid could she have been not to have seen it?

She was too different from the other girls of her age; she stood out as an oddity, and society in the form of Lord Brooke had made itself clear. Her kind were not to be tolerated; she must either conform or experience more of this public censure from the likes of him and the twittering misses.

'A light in the dark,' she murmured, remembering the humiliation of the dance floor.

'Pardon, miss?' Grace replied.

Millie forced a half-smile. 'Nothing; I have just had a bit of an epiphany.'

Grace screwed up her nose.

'Shall I get you something for it?'

Millie laughed aloud, grateful for Grace's unintended jest. 'No, thank you; I am fine. An epiphany is when you get a good idea,' she explained.

At least the next time Grace heard the word she would understand it and, unlike herself, no one would hold her up to ridicule.

'Actually miss, there is something I could get for you, it's downstairs. It arrived early this morning, but I didn't want to disturb you. I could go and bring it up for you if you like,' Grace replied with a shy grin.

A raised eyebrow was Millie's first response. Then, seeing the little dance which Grace was performing on the spot, she realised the something downstairs must be good.

'I shall go down shortly and see what it is; you don't have to run delivery errands for me, Grace. You are a lady's maid and should not be made to fetch and carry.'

Grace bounced one last time and clapped her hands excitedly together.

'Oh, I couldn't help it; they are so beautiful and I did have a footman carry them upstairs. Please miss, he has been standing outside the door holding on to them now for ages. Can he bring them in?'

Millie rolled her eyes and laughed; Grace's unbridled enthusiasm was so infectious that Millie quickly leapt off the bed and hurried to open the door.

Fortunately, the footman in question had had the good sense to put the heavy glass box down while he waited. As she opened the door, he bent down and picked it up.

'Flowers, oh my, but who could have sent them? I surely don't deserve such a wonderful gift, but they are a lovely surprise,' Millie said. She stood back from the doorway and allowed the footman to carry the large box containing the flowers into her room. He placed it on the top of her chest of drawers, turning it so she could see the card.

Grace gave him a wink and ushered him swiftly out the door.

Millie stood back and surveyed the magnificent blooms.

'I know what the white flowers are; they are obviously roses, and those behind them are orchids,' she said, pointing to the tall white flowers at the back of the arrangement.

'But I'm not so sure about the blue ones. Are those forget-me-nots?' she asked, stepping forward and touching the tiny, delicate buds.

'Yes miss, and those other blue ones are love-in-the-mist; how romantic. So nice to see that a gentleman knows his flowers,' Grace observed.

Millie silently enjoyed the flowers, all the while knowing she was teasing poor Grace, who was doing her best not to snatch the card from the arrangement and read it herself.

Finally, Millie reached in and took out the card. 'Miss Millicent Ashton; how terribly formal,' she said, turning the card over. She looked at the back and pursed her lips when she saw that it was blank. She handed the card to Grace who turned it over several times, searching for the elusive message.

'I thought when someone sent you flowers, they were supposed to come with a message, or at least a note to say who they were from. How am I meant to send a thank you card if I don't know who sent them?' Millie asked.

Grace stared down at her hands and muttered, 'You must have met someone at the ball last night who liked you. Perhaps you made an impression on a certain gentleman who might like to make your acquaintance again.'

She gave Millie a hopeful smile before turning to fiddle with the hairbrushes on the dressing table.

Millie looked at her name written in plain bold ink on the card once more. She smiled.

Of course: Charles had sent them, he must have called in to the florist early in the morning when out riding with their father and, being in too much of a hurry, had forgotten to sign the card personally or pen a quick note. 'What a thoughtful brother,' she said, as she pulled a single white rose from the arrangement.

At the dressing table, Grace let out a cough worthy of a stage performer and promptly dropped a hand mirror. Millie saw a flush of red appear on the young woman's cheeks. Grace stood staring at the mirror as it lay where it had fallen on the carpet.

As it was, they were in luck. Hand mirrors made in India were designed to survive falls on to a stone floor, so the glass remained intact in its frame. Millie bent down, picked up the mirror, and placed it back on the dressing table. Then she stood and stared at her maid until Grace was forced to raise her eyes and meet her gaze.

'Grace Brown, whatever you know about these flowers, please tell me now; if my brother did not send them I need to know who did.'

Grace bit her bottom lip and let out a sigh.

'Sorry miss, I know I shouldn't be talking about things which don't concern me, but a carriage arrived early this morning after Mr Ashton had left and while your brother was out riding in the park. The man from the carriage delivered them to the front door. I know it was early, because Mr Stephens, the head footman, was still downstairs having his breakfast.'

Millie's eyes lit up. What sort of person would deliver to the front door of a grand house, and at that time of the morning? Deliveries were always to the rear; every shopkeeper and tradesman from Calcutta to London knew that golden rule.

She looked at the flowers once more.

'But what if the person who delivered the flowers was not from the florist; what if they were someone who is used to being received at the front door of good homes?' she muttered.

Whom had she met last night who would give her such a beautiful gift, and so early in the morning? She shook her head; there was no one she could remember from last night who would do such a thing. The only person she had made any impression on at the party was the odious Marquess of Brooke, and he was not likely to have sent her such a generous offering.

Millie held the single rose in her hand up to the light which streamed in from the window.

'How peculiar, but not to worry; they are absolutely lovely and no doubt in time I shall find out who sent them,' she said, putting her nose to the petals and taking a deep breath.

Later, when she was dressed and seated in front of the mirror, watching as Grace worked to fashion her hair into a simple stay-at-home style, a thought struck her.

She looked into the mirror and addressed Grace's reflection.

'When the flowers were delivered, you said they came from a man who arrived in a carriage.'

'Yes miss, they did,' Grace replied, picking up another hairpin and placing it into Millie's hair.

'What sort of carriage was it? Did you get a look at it?'

Grace shook her head.

'No, but Joshua, the footman who took the flowers, would have seen it; he came out into the street and spoke to the driver. He didn't half get into trouble from Mr Stephens for it. Told him he should have sent them around the back and that it wasn't proper to park in the street; said next they would be delivering the milk and leaving it on the front step.'

So, my mysterious flower-sender, you are definitely not used to using the servants' entrance. Don't think that just because you didn't sign the card, I will not find out who you are. You have set me a puzzle, and I like nothing better than solving puzzles.

When Millie was finally ready for a day spent indoors, she sent Grace downstairs to seek out the footman who had accepted the delivery. She was intrigued by the mysterious delivery man and knew that the answer she sought lay with the markings on the carriage.

When Grace returned she gave Millie a piece of paper with a hand drawing of the crest Joshua had seen emblazoned on the side of the carriage.

'Well done, Grace; now we just need to find out to whom the family crest belongs,' she said. The first place she would start would be with her mother.

With the piece of paper tucked into her pocket, she knocked tentatively on Violet's sitting room door. She had been dreading this encounter all morning, and was surprised to see her mother rise from her chair and greet her with open arms.

She held Millie in a warm hug and cooed gently.

'My beautiful girl, my darling daughter, I am so sorry for last night. It wasn't your fault and I should not have been so hasty in judging you. Your father says it was all the Marquess of Brooke's doing and you were not to blame. Horrid boy; I shall box his ears the next time I see him.'

Millie giggled at the thought of her mother assaulting a leader of the *ton*. She wrapped her arms tightly around her mother's waist and enjoyed the welcome relief as Violet rubbed Millie's back. She hoped one day to be as fearsome a mother tiger as Violet; no one would dare hurt her children.

Her mother released Millie and stood back giving her a smile. 'How are you feeling this morning? I was pleased to see that you slept late. I know you thought I was fussing last night when I made you take that sleeping draught, but you certainly needed it.'

Millie shrugged her shoulders.

'Truth be told, I am not feeling too poorly, just a little wrung out. I have had the chance to think about things this morning, and I've decided that last night will not happen again; from now on I will not let people upset me that way. The next time some fool grabs me by the hand and tries to drag me through a crowd, I shall bite his hand until he lets go.'

Violet raised her eyebrows and shook her head. The threat that Millie would sink her teeth into the flesh of London's young men was perhaps taking things a little too far, but her mother understood her meaning.

Millie tactfully changed the subject. 'Did you happen to see the flowers I received?'

Her mother gave her a knowing smile; nothing happened in the Ashton household without her mother being the first to know. The servants in their home in Calcutta had been completely at a loss to explain Violet's ability to outwit them until they discovered she had used the long boat journey from England to learn to speak fluent Hindi.

'They were lovely, darling, and presumably very expensive, because not only is the edging on the box pure gold, but the orchids are out of season all year in England. Someone's hothouse had an early visit from a St James Street florist. What did the card say?'

Millie gave her a wry smile. Her mother knew everything about the flowers, including what was – or was not – written on the card; in fact, she was certain that most of the household knew its contents long before its intended recipient had first set eyes upon it.

With Violet being the best chance she had to find out about the carriage and who had sent the flowers, she decided to humour her mother and play along.

'Surprisingly, the card was blank; just my name was printed on the front. I would have thought if someone had made the effort to send me flowers, they would have at least put their name on the card. To tell you the truth, it is all a bit of a mystery, but I have found a clue which may help.'

Violet slowly raised her eyebrows, and a smile formed on her lips.

'Yes?' she replied.

'One of our footmen got a look at the carriage which delivered the flowers and he kindly drew me a picture of the coat of arms which was emblazoned on the carriage door.'

She pulled the piece of paper from her pocket and waved it slowly in the air.

'Now I just need someone to help me to identify whose coat of arms it is.'

She let out a heavy sigh and looked down at the paper.

'I expect I shall have to wait until Papa comes home; if I am lucky he may be able to assist me.'

Violet let out a girlish squeal of delight and in an instant snatched the paper from Millie's hand. Then she froze. She looked at the paper she held in one hand, while her other went slowly to her lips. She opened her mouth, but instead of the apology Millie expected her to offer, Violet let out a roar of laughter. Mother and daughter stood looking at one another before dissolving into fits of laughter.

'Oh, I can't believe I just did that. I spend every waking moment trying to teach you ladylike manners and then I go and do something like that; I must be the worst mother in the entire world,' Violet laughed.

As the tears rolled down Millie's face, she wagged a finger in Violet's direction. If any of the servants had walked into the room at that moment, they would have been aghast at the sight of the two Ashton women doubled over, holding their aching sides. It took several minutes for the spontaneous silliness to calm down, after which Millie and her mother embraced once more. Millie gave her mother a kiss on the cheek.

'I am sorry Mama. I have been so selfish since we arrived, thinking of my own concerns. It was only when I saw you and Papa at Uncle Oscar's last night that I realised how hard all those years away from home must have been for you. How much you must have missed your family and friends. I promise I shall try and make a better effort to fit in from now on. Maybe last night's unpleasantness was a dose of karma coming back to bite me for my selfishness.'

Violet shook her head. 'It's not all your fault, my dear. I know it's been hard, and I don't think I have helped things by being so absorbed in trying to catch up with everyone in such a short time. How about we agree to put this first week behind us and start to find our feet more slowly? You just need a little time.'

Millie smiled, grateful once more that her mother was a rational woman. How rational she would be when Millie took the boat back to India and did not return would be an entirely different matter, but that was for the future.

'You know I don't subscribe to all that karma business, but there may be something in what you say. First, let me have a proper look at this paper,' Violet replied.

She examined the piece of paper Millie had obtained from the footman more closely. On it was drawn the rough outline of a shield, and within the shield was what looked like a horse with a crown above it. Under the horse was a series of three four-pointed stars.

Violet hummed knowingly. 'Well, your karma might be up to something because if I am not mistaken, this is the coat of arms of the Duke of Strathmore. And if this was the crest on the side of the carriage which delivered those beautiful flowers, then I think someone might have decided to send you an apology.'

'But no note; just the flowers,' Millie replied, still perplexed. Without knowing who in the Duke's family had sent the flowers, she didn't know whether it was an apology from one particular person for his boorish behaviour, or an apology on behalf of someone else who was embarrassed by that particular family member.

Why did everything in London have to be so complicated? A simple 'Sorry I was a complete ass last night; can you please run me through with a sharp sword and I will die the painful death I deserve,' would have been sufficient. Now, with the unsigned card, she was back trying to discover other people's motives. She swore.

'Millie, you are going to have to do something about your fish-wife's mouth,' Violet said with a shake of her head.

'Sorry.'

'Of course, now that we know where the flowers came from, we can politely pretend we never received them,' her mother said, screwing up the piece of paper and throwing it into the fireplace. Violet tucked a wayward curl of her long dark hair behind her ear and examined her fingernails.

Millie felt a subtle change in the air. Violet was right. As the card had not included the name of the sender, Millie was under no obligation to pen a note of reply. Unless the person who had sent the flowers appeared on the Ashtons' doorstep, there was nothing else for her to do. The lovely flowers would adorn her bedroom for as long as they lasted, after which she would use the glass box for displaying her favourite books and trinkets.

An apology that had not really been offered was one that did not have to be accepted. Nor did it have to be acknowledged. She knew it was a petty stance to adopt, but the memory of being utterly humiliated the previous evening still burned brightly. And since Violet knew a great deal more about the intricacies of *ton* society than Millie did, she knew she had received the best advice regarding protocol.

She headed back to her room feeling confident and relaxed, but as soon as she opened the bedroom door and saw the flowers, her thoughts turned to Lucy and with that, her confidence evaporated.

It was simply not possible to act as if she were indifferent. Someone would eventually ask her about them and the moment they did, she would be obliged to say how delighted she had been to receive them.

'I hope you were from anyone but Lord Brooke,' she whispered as she breathed in the exquisite scent of the white orchids. Mr David Radley seemed a decent enough man and it would be far less complicated if the flowers were his way of apologising on behalf of the entire Radley family.

Chapter Five

M illie spent the rest of the day quietly working on her
tapestry. She had found a perfect spot in front of a window
in one of the upper-level sitting rooms. The morning light allowed
her to sort the various skeins into the shades of white and grey she
would need as she began the painstaking task of recreating the
dome of St Paul's Cathedral in wool.

Her mother had offered to take her shopping on the second
morning after the party, but she was content to remain at home.
Lucy had sent a note offering her sympathies after receiving word
that Millie was still suffering the effects of the long sea voyage from
India. At some point Millie and Violet would have to call on the
Duchess of Strathmore, but for the time being, the ladies of the
Ashton household would not be making any social calls, nor
receiving visitors.

Millie was still working in the sitting room later that morning
when Grace entered carrying a delicate array of white rosebuds,
wrapped in a sapphire-blue ribbon. Millie looked up from her
tapestry frame and seeing the flowers, stopped mid-stitch and let
out a sigh.

'I don't suppose they came with a note, did they?' she asked.

When Grace shook her head and replied that the card had been the same as the first, Millie stabbed her needle into the fabric and sat back in her chair. 'Same form of delivery as yesterday?'

'No miss; these came via a delivery boy from the florist. When he came to the rear entrance of the house, Mr Stephens asked who had sent them, but the lad said he didn't know. He did say it was a young man who had placed the order, and it had gone on the Duke of Strathmore's personal account.'

She held the flowers up to the light from the window and examined them, running her fingers over the silk ribbon.

'Well, whoever he is, he certainly likes blue. Maybe he wants them to match the colour of your eyes, miss. Shall I put them in a vase for you, or would you like me to leave them here so you can look at them?' Grace said.

'Thank you, Grace. Would you put them next to the other ones in my bedroom, please; I don't want the whole house seeing them,' Millie replied.

After Grace had left the room in search of a large enough vase to hold the flowers, Millie sat staring out of the window. Two days in a row, someone from Strathmore House had sent her flowers, each time with no note, just her name on a card. At least now she knew for certain that it was a young man who was placing the orders; one who, as Grace had noted, had a penchant for the colour blue.

She sensed the hairs on the back of her neck moving. What had Grace said about the gentleman who was sending her flowers liking the colour of her eyes? She thought back to the events of the party and her heart sank. She had been a fool to hope it had been David Radley sending her the lovely gifts.

The obvious answer was far less palatable, as was the notion that the flowers were not meant to be an apology and hence the reason for the card being blank.

She crossed her arms and pursed her lips. Only one of Lady Lucy's brothers had stood and held her gaze for any length of time; only one would know that her eyes were the deepest of dark blues.

Her father had always said her eyes were the colour of a perfect sapphire because she was a true jewel of India. She had worn deep blue ribbons in her hair all throughout her childhood, believing that she was the reincarnation of an ancient Hindu princess. Millie loved the colour of her eyes. It angered her to think someone could try to use them to cause her pain.

Yesterday's flowers were no accident, no; they were merely a way for him to get to her while she was at home. By sending her blue flowers, and then the blue ribbons, it was his sly way of saying that he had taken in all of her physical features and would, over time, show her just what he had seen and what he thought of her.

With his initial public humiliation of her now achieved, he was shifting the game into a more subtle, more personal form of attack. And since the Marquess of Brooke had taken his time to examine every inch of her ample curves, she knew he would have made a mental inventory of all her shortcomings. She wondered when the first piglet or ham hock would arrive.

Millie closed her eyes and the corners of her mouth began to crease. Letting her head fall back, she let out a long and wicked laugh. The conversation with her mother had done her a power of good. She would accept the flowers and enjoy them, and she would proudly wear the blue ribbon in her hair. Let him spend his father's money on sending her lavish gifts.

'I am not sure if Mrs Knowles can put half a side of beef to good use, if he sends me one. I don't suppose he realises that in my part of the world, cows are considered to be sacred. Stupid boy,' she chuckled.

Since discussing her lack of ladylike manners with her mother, Millie had promised to curb her use of foul language. Now, after enjoying a good, hearty laugh at Lord Brooke's expense, she took a deep breath and congratulated herself on her restraint. Not one foul word had passed her lips.

'Thank you, Lord Brooke, the flowers were lovely.'

She pulled the needle back out of her tapestry and calmly went back to work, pushing all thoughts of Alex Radley from her mind.

With the third morning came the third beautiful bunch of flowers and as with each of the two previous deliveries, the card only had Millie's name on it.

Later that afternoon, she stood staring at the three arrangements now crowding the mantelpiece and smiled. She could not fault his taste; they were all truly exquisite. This time, the flowers were a mix of little white flowers and lavender in a blue china bowl. Running her finger around the rim, she noted the colour of the flowers.

'You are cheating, Lord Brooke; any fool could tell you lavender is not blue, but purple. I shall have to take you to task if you are going to start changing the rules of battle,' she observed.

There was a knock on her door and a moment later Charles's head appeared. Seeing the flowers, he gave her a smile. 'So, he has not given up yet?'

She smiled. 'His father's pockets must be bottomless. I was just thinking of how I could get him to send me jewellery. Anonymously, of course, which would mean I could only wear them at home, but I am sure I could live with that.'

'Or take them to the pawnbrokers in Exchange Alley; I would be happy to do so for a small fee,' Charles replied as he leaned back against the door frame.

Millie eyed a cushion on a nearby chair and wondered if she could hit him with it from that distance. 'What is the purpose of your visit, dearest brother? I can't remember the last time you set foot in my bedroom. Are you just arriving home from somewhere or heading out?'

He cleared his throat. 'It's been three days since the welcome home party and I think it is time I took you out for a stroll in the park. You can get some fresh air and stretch your legs. You must be going mad being cooped up here at home.'

She saw his eyes make a sly sideways glance to the clock nestled between the vases of flowers on the mantelpiece.

'It's nearly five o'clock and the best of society take over Hyde Park at that time every day without fail. The only thing which would keep them from setting out would be a storm blowing in from the Atlantic, and since the day is fine, it's high time the Ashton siblings joined the fray. Put on your coat, Millie, grab your gloves and I shall await you downstairs. Don't be long, old girl,' he said.

Charles stepped away from the door and disappeared.

Millie sighed. Why did big brothers have to be so bossy? And why did they have to be so right about what little sisters needed, for that matter?

Of course, Charles was right, she had spent three pleasant days at home and now it was time to get out and face London society once more. She could not hide away forever in her father's house.

'Old girl? I am this side of one and twenty,' she muttered as she rang for her maid. If she went out without allowing Grace to pull her coat out of the cupboard and fuss over her hair, she would never hear the end of it.

Chapter Six

Twenty minutes later, Millie and Charles were walking down Union Street, heading toward Hyde Park. The wind had died down but the sky was still overcast. Although the sun had not managed to make much of an appearance, at least it wasn't snowing or raining. Millie had yet to decide which of the two forms of English weather she disliked the most. At least the monsoon rains of India had been warm.

'Stephens says we will get more snow tonight,' Charles said, stuffing his hands in his coat pockets.

She smiled at him. She could not have cared less about the weather; it was just good to be out with her brother, walking the streets of London. Numerous barouches and curricles passed them by, all of which, by the look of their passengers, were also headed in the direction of the park.

'Does he have bunions?' she replied.

Charles stopped and gave her a quizzical look. 'What?'

'Stephens; you said he told you we would get more snow tonight. Remember how Nishant would tell father the rains were coming because his feet hurt?'

He laughed. 'Oh yes, and how many times did we have to listen to him complain for days until it finally did rain? He was no weather vane, Millie, just a daft old man who thought he ran the house servants.'

'Didn't he?' she replied.

From first thing in the morning to last thing at night Nishant had bustled about the Ashton family home in Calcutta, giving orders to servants and the Ashton children alike.

Charles shook his head. 'No, he was a remnant of the previous family who'd lived in our house, and he had nowhere else to go. When we arrived from England, Father didn't have the heart to make him leave. The other servants seemed to respect him, so he stayed. Ash was really the head servant, but he wouldn't have dared say anything.'

A warm grin spread across his face and he laughed once more. 'For over fifteen years Ash worked under a man who had no right to be in our house. Father even paid them both the same wage. I suppose Ash had nothing to complain about, Nishant had a home and it all seemed to work. When Nishant died, Ash simply took over the role he had spent all those years understudying.'

Charles took hold of Millie's hand and gave it a squeeze. They continued into Dean Street, then crossed over Park Lane and entered the park via the main gate.

Cold though it was, everyone seemed to be prepared to ignore the freezing temperature and venture out for his or her daily promenade. Millie had never seen so many carriages in the one place before; her gaze followed the seemingly endless line as it slowly snaked its way in and through the park.

Noticing that many of the carriages were marked with family crests and arms, Millie looked to see if any of them bore the markings of the Duchy of Strathmore. When, out of the corner of her eye, she saw Charles following her gaze, she turned and gave him an innocent smile.

Everywhere she looked, there were people. In London society it was obviously of vital importance to be seen at this hour, no matter what the weather.

The long rows of flowerbeds stretched into the distance. How anything living could survive in this weather amazed her. A few rose bushes were still managing to flower along the edge of the paths, but the rest of the beds were covered with a thick layer of straw. She imagined that come spring, a riot of colour would erupt from beneath the straw and fill the flower beds. She thought that perhaps she might remain in London long enough to see Hyde Park in all its glory.

As they walked, Charles pointed out the newest models of carriage, promising her a ride when he had purchased his new means of transport.

'Papa keeps telling me I need to get a decent buggy to get around town in, something with a sleek line. Something like that one,' he said, pointing to a shiny black phaeton being drawn by a pair of magnificent matching greys.

Millie lifted her eyebrows. Their father had taken to poring over the daily news sheets every morning, checking the advertisements for the latest phaeton while pretending to be catching up on news from the subcontinent.

'I don't know who is more pathetic. The pair of you can be so childlike,' she laughed.

'Though he does insist that he will be the first to take it into the five o'clock crush, as he wants to make certain that everyone knows Mama is back in town,' Charles said, as he keenly eyed off yet another a shiny new phaeton.

Millie cleared her throat. He was so caught up with the prospect of a new horse and carriage that he had completely missed her comment. It was obvious to her that he was taking to his new role of future viscount with gusto; Uncle Oscar had called earlier that day and invited him to watch proceedings from the strangers' gallery at the House of Lords. When the time came, Charles would take his place in the house.

She hoped that day was many years from now; the prospect of both her father and uncle being gone was not something she wished to consider. Charles deserved time to enjoy being an English gentleman before he took over running a town house and a sizeable country estate. Of course, by then he would likely have a wife and a brood of children.

She looked up at him; he had the same little smile on his face he had been wearing since the day they arrived. London was all a big exciting adventure for him. In a few months when the season began, he would be ready to take on the *ton*.

She caught his infectious smile, happy in the knowledge that he would be a success in his new home.

Charles suddenly stopped and turned to her.

'Don't hate me,' he said.

He pointed his head in the direction of a group of people who were making their way down the gravel path toward them. Millie saw a hand wave in their direction, followed by the sound of a cheery hello.

It was Lucy Radley, accompanied by her two older brothers.

'You rotten cad, you could have given me more warning,' Millie spat out.

He put an arm around her and pulled her close.

Returning Lucy's wave with a hand held high, he whispered into Millie's ear. 'You wouldn't have come if you knew they were going to be here. I know you won't make a scene while Lord Brooke attempts to apologise to you in person. You are not the only one who suffered as a result of the other night. I understand Lady Lucy was most aggrieved on your behalf. Let her brother attempt to make amends.'

Millie sucked in a deep breath and puffed out her cheeks. Although this encounter had been inevitable, she still intended to have words with her brother when they got home.

The plans for her grand revenge had included preparing a whole series of witty and cutting remarks. Now, as the Radley siblings approached, she found her mouth had gone dry and her wit had abandoned her.

Don't cry, whatever you do, don't cry. The second he says anything untoward, you feign a headache and ask Charles to take you home.

She would have been the first to admit that hers was not amongst the greatest battle plans in the history of warfare, but on the field of conflict, she had to use the weapons at her disposal. The delicate female with a sudden headache was a tried and true tactic, however feeble it was.

Lucy let go of David's arm and hurried ahead of her brothers. Reaching Millie, she threw her arms around her and exclaimed. 'I am so pleased to see you. I have been out of my mind with worry. Your mother said you were still tired from the trip, but I thought perhaps you had come down with some terrible tropical disease.'

Millie shook her head. 'No, I was just tired from the long voyage and getting used to this London weather,' she replied. She gave a quick upward glance to the grey heavens.

'Besides, if she was going to come down with a tropical disease she would have done so before she got to London. We don't tend to have too many of them here,' David offered as he and Alex stepped up to stand beside their sister.

He reached out and took Charles by the hand. 'Thanks.'

Charles gave him and Alex a brief nod. Then he bowed to Lucy. 'I am sorry my sister has not been well enough to visit, it has taken her a little longer than expected to regain her health.'

Millie forced a smile to her face for Lucy's benefit as she quietly steadied her temper for the moment when Lord Brooke eventually spoke. Perhaps his plan was to stand silently in the group and not say anything, but she doubted that David and Charles would grant him that indulgence. The brothers had obviously arranged this meeting to allow Alex to offer his apologies. Now all that remained was to see if he could manage to speak to her without causing further offence.

She steeled herself.

Alex cleared his throat and took a tentative step forward.

The other men fell silent.

And poor hapless Lady Lucy went and made a mess of the whole thing. Before anyone could stop her, Lucy had grabbed Millie firmly by the arm and begun to march her off toward the Walnut Trees Walk.

It was not completely her fault. No one had bothered to mention to Lucy that the apparently chance meeting with the Ashtons in the park had a purpose. As her friend dragged her away from the group, Millie looked back at the dumbstruck men. She gave them a tiny wave goodbye but saw to her disappointment that Lord Brooke had started to follow them.

Lucy began talking at a hundred words to the minute, of which Millie only understood about one-third. Every second sentence bounced to a different topic. She talked about her family, their trips to Scotland, frogs and Roman history. She had just started rambling on about the Great Fire of London, when Millie stopped her.

'Slow down, slow down, I cannot keep up with your train of thought,' she pleaded.

A look of horror appeared on Lucy's face.

'I'm sorry; I can't seem to help it. I just start and my mind runs so fast that my lips struggle to keep up. Oh, please don't go away, Millie; I have been waiting every day for you to get well again so I could see you. After meeting you the other night, I knew you were special, that you were different. And I know my brother embarrassed you, but please don't...'

She burst into tears.

Millie looked back and saw Alex close behind her, a look of deep concern on his face. With one long stride he reached his sister, flung his arms around her and hugged her tight. She buried her face into the lapels of his coat as great sobs wracked her body.

Millie was mortified.

'It's all right, Lucy,' he murmured into her ear.

Charles and David caught up with them.

'What happened?' Charles asked, his voice edged with disapproval.

'I just asked her to slow down; I couldn't keep up with what she was saying.' The look on her brother's face told her he did not believe her. Millie was angry with Lucy's brother and now she had taken it out on poor Lucy.

'Your sister's version of events is accurate,' Alex replied. 'Miss Ashton simply asked Lucy to slow down; she didn't say anything else. I heard her.'

He continued to stroke Lucy's hair.

'Miss Ashton, rest assured it was not your fault. Lucy has been on edge for days now and she became a little overcome with excitement at seeing you again. If anyone is at fault here, it is me,' Alex said.

Millie was dumbfounded.

The Marquess of Brooke had just performed two miracles in under a minute. He had spoken at least a dozen words to her and he had actually said something nice. She checked the miracle count and found another one to add to the tally. He had defended her.

Where was the bully from three nights ago who had stood smiling as he humiliated her, and who was this kind, caring brother now holding Lucy in his arms?

Just remember how he smiled at you after he mocked you on the dance floor. This is all part of his plan. He saves you from looking like a shrew so you cannot take him to task.

Lucy waved a hand toward Millie and pulled away from her brother. 'He's right, she didn't say anything wrong. I just got a bit upset. It is so good to see you again, Millie.'

Lucy wiped the tears away from her eyes with the back of her hand and took several deep breaths in an attempt to compose herself.

Millie pulled a clean white handkerchief out of her reticule and offered it to Lucy, who sniffled back her tears and accepted it. She gave Lucy a gentle rub on the back and whispered an apology. It might not have been her fault, but she still felt badly that her new friend had been reduced to tears by something she had said.

A collective sigh of relief went around the little gathering as Lucy rallied and managed a smile for them. Millie felt Charles' gaze fall upon her and knew she had to be the one to make the first approach. With his sister in tears, she could not expect Alex to offer her an apology.

'So, do you come to the park each day, Lord Brooke?' she asked her nemesis.

He nodded his head, and looked away.

'Yes, we do come most days,' David replied. 'We have not been out much this week as my brother has had a bad back and been unable to walk any distance.'

As if on cue, Alex rolled his shoulders and placed a hand in the small of his back.

David gave Alex an approving nod. 'You may recall he was experiencing some difficulty at the party the other night. I thought he was all in jest, until he explained to me that he was in absolute agony, the poor chap.'

A bad back? Sounds more like a rather convenient lie to me. But if that is what you wish to pretend, who I am to question you? Just don't think you are getting away without rendering a proper apology, Lord Brooke.

She counted to ten before painting a concerned look on her face and stepping in close to Alex.

'I am so sorry that you have also been unwell, Lord Brooke. It appears to have been an unfortunate week for both of us. Pray tell me, how did you manage to injure your back?' she asked.

Alex shot her a look of surprise and she heard him swallow deeply. He was rattled; good. Why should she be the only one feeling uncomfortable at this moment? However, she felt a pang of disappointment, as it appeared Lord Brooke was going to transpire to be an unworthy adversary. Arrogance was bad enough, but if it was coupled with stupidity or even worse, laziness, she would retire from the battlefield. There would be no honour, or fun, in besting him if that was the case.

David stepped forward, but Millie shot him a look which stopped him in his tracks. She was prepared to be polite, but Lord Brooke would have to fend for himself. One false move on anyone's part and she was ready to turn on her heel, walk back to the main gate, and go home.

'Riding in the park,' Alex replied. 'I…' At that moment, his gaze drifted over her head and he raised a hand and waved.

As she turned to see who had captured his attention, Millie was certain she heard Alex whisper 'Thank God.'

A barouche with its hood folded down had turned into the head of the drive and entered the park. Seated in the carriage were two women. She squinted and could just make out the Strathmore family crest on the side of the carriage.

'That's Mama nearest to us and the lady on the other side of her is our Great Aunt Maude,' Alex explained.

'Maude shouldn't be out in this cold weather, but Mama could not talk her out of a visit to the park today,' added Lucy. Out of the corner of her eye, Millie saw Charles and David exchange a quick glance.

When David cleared his throat and made mention that he had been remiss in not introducing Charles to his mother or aunt, Charles developed a sudden interest in the general wellbeing of the elderly Aunt Maude and suggested they should make haste and catch up with the slow-moving carriage.

'Come on, Lucy, Mama will wish to see you' David said, taking his sister firmly by the hand.

As the others headed toward the carriage, Alex turned and gave Millie an elegant bow.

'Would you allow me to accompany you, Miss Ashton? I am sure my mother would like to make your acquaintance; she has heard a lot about you from Lucy.' He offered her his arm and for a moment, she was tempted to tell him what he could do with his miraculously discovered manners, but she knew it would only disappoint her mother. She gritted her teeth and placed her arm in his. 'Good,' he replied and they set off, following the others.

Millie hoped the Duchess of Strathmore was more like David than like Alex in her treatment of newcomers. She was pleased to discover that instead of a fearsome society matron, the woman sitting in the curricle was a pure delight. As soon as the group approached, the Duchess registered the distressed look on Lucy's face, and called out to her footman to let down the steps.

The Duchess did not fuss over Lucy; rather she spoke in a firm but tender way to her daughter. However, Millie did begin to suspect that quite a number of people were aware of the 'chance' meeting between the Ashtons and the Radleys in Hyde Park that afternoon. The arrival of the Duchess of Strathmore's carriage at that very moment did appear to be rather fortuitous.

After a short talk, and some head nodding on Lucy's part, matters were resolved. Millie managed to catch snippets of the conversation, during which she heard the Duchess tell Lucy to slow down and not suffocate her new friend. This was followed by some sage advice, counselling Lucy to allow Millie to get a word in edgeways.

Alex stood quietly by her side as they waited for his mother to finish with his sister. Then David introduced Charles and the obligatory pleasantries were exchanged all around.

While her brother chatted with the duchess, Millie tuned her ears to listen to Alex's breathing. Every so often, he appeared to struggle with his breath. It would catch in his throat and the muscles in his arm would firm just a little. He would then suck in a large amount of air and appear to hold it. She turned to him after he had done this several times, and she could see a look of pain on his face.

Perhaps he really had injured himself; he certainly appeared to be suffering from some mysterious malady.

I hope he was not telling me the truth, now that I have vowed to dislike him for eternity.

Her musings were disturbed as both David and Charles stepped aside and Alex brought her forward to meet his mother. He gave his mother a bow, to which she responded with a regal nod of her head. Millie saw them both exchange a grin and realised the formalities were for her benefit.

'Mother, may I introduce Miss Millicent Ashton, daughter of Mr and Mrs James Ashton, lately of Calcutta, India. Miss Ashton, my mother Lady Caroline Radley, Duchess of Strathmore,' Alex announced.

He released Millie from his arm and she dipped into her best curtsy. 'Your Grace.'

When she rose, the duchess held out a hand and as Millie accepted it, she was drawn into a warm embrace. She felt a flush of red come to her face as the duchess placed a kiss on her cheek.

'Miss Ashton, I am so pleased to finally meet you. Lucy has not stopped talking about you since the night of the ball at your uncle's house.'

Millie shot a glance at Lucy, who was staring at the ground as she dragged her slipper through the stones at her feet.

'It was a pleasure to meet Lucy and I am sorry I have not been well enough to visit in the subsequent days. I think Lucy and I have much in common,' Millie replied. Lucy's head shot up and a smile lit up her face.

The Duchess smiled. 'I am afraid Lucy can get a touch over-wrought when she finds a new friend, and some girls find her behaviour a little difficult to comprehend.'

As Millie looked at Lucy, she realised how alike she and her new friend were. She could understand why the simpering misses would avoid Lucy, despite her connections.

'Thank you, Your Grace. I knew I liked Lucy the moment I met her,' she replied. Then, turning to Lucy, she held out her hand. 'You seem to like a lot of things which I would not expect a duke's daughter to be interested in. You have not once mentioned fashion, or which of the young gentlemen you think is the most handsome man in London. In fact, come to think of it, you sound just like me, only you speak faster.'

Lucy flipped up a stone at her feet and kicked it under the carriage.

'I would bet a week's worth of pin money that you know all the oceans and seas and could point them out on a map with your eyes closed. Though I think I could give you a run for your money when it comes to the Scandinavian fjords,' Millie said.

Lucy laughed.

'Millie, I do like clothes and hats; it's just that I want to talk about other things. I like jewels, but I want to know where they came from and how they were formed, not just look at them and think they are pretty. I know, for instance, that sapphires come from India and I was hoping you might tell me about them,' Lucy replied.

The duchess put a hand to her lips and gave a delicate cough.

Lucy's gaze settled on the jewel in Millie's nose, before she turned away and gave Alex a quick look. He smiled at his sister.

What a coincidence that the man who likes blue would just happen to have a sister who mentioned sapphires.

Millie smelled a rat, but she was not going to spoil the mood. Lucy appeared to be happy. Charles and David were both smiling, as was the duchess. As for Lord Brooke, well, he kept mumbling something under his breath, but he was also smiling.

Even Great Aunt Maude, sitting wrapped up in thick woollen blankets to ward off the cold, was smiling.

'Since you are well again, Miss Ashton, I shall send a note around to your mother inviting you both to an early afternoon visit at our home tomorrow. I did not get much of an opportunity to catch up with Violet when we attended the party, and I have been most anxious for us to become reacquainted. We were both debutantes in the same year, and she was a good friend of my late sister's.'

The duchess gave a nod of her head towards David, who briefly touched his fingers to his heart.

'Now Lucy, I think you should come home with me and get a cold compress for your face. We have dinner with the bishop at Fulham Palace this evening and you do not want to be arriving with puffy eyes. I am certain Miss Ashton's brother will not keep her long in the chilly climes of the park, as she has been unwell.'

Whether the duchess's last comment was an observation or a direction, Millie was unsure. Lucy did as her mother bade and climbed up into the carriage, taking the seat next to her elderly aunt. She gave them a half-wave as the carriage lurched forward and they drew away from the group.

With Lucy out of the way, Charles and David wasted no time in addressing the real reason for their visit to the park. As the Strathmore carriage rolled away, Charles and David spotted a spanking new phaeton at the end of the line of carriages. Making hurried promises to return as soon as they could, they dashed off to take a closer look.

'They are not even attempting to be subtle,' Alex observed.

'No,' Millie replied.

'Unfortunately, since they have left us with no chaperone, we cannot stray too far from here. We will have to be content to walk the length of the driveway and try to avoid badly driven vehicles.'

He took her hand, but rather than place it in the crook of his arm, Lord Brooke simply held it as they began to walk. She did not know if it was a deliberate solecism on his part, but she found it odd; it was almost as if he were attempting a public display of ownership.

'You must realise that today's meeting was prearranged,' he said, without looking at her. 'I asked your brother to bring you here as soon as you were well enough to be out in society once more. I, too, have been anxious to see you again.' He stopped and drew in a ragged breath.

He turned to her and she could see his face was a study of serious intent. 'I am so sorry for the way I behaved toward you at the party; my behaviour was inexcusable and boorish. Please accept my deepest and most heartfelt apologies for the pain I must have caused you. My only defence is that I was in agony and not thinking clearly. I am grateful that David rescued me before I turned your night into a total disaster.'

'You did,' Millie replied, adamant that he would not get off so lightly for his churlish behaviour at the party.

'Pardon?'

'You did ruin my whole night. You humiliated me in front of hundreds of other people and you continued to stare at me for the remainder of the evening. Since then, you have sent me three magnificent floral arrangements, without having the decency to sign your name or even offer an apology. Correct me if I am wrong, but I take it they did come from you?'

Alex nodded his head. 'I am apologising now.'

'Very well then, your apology is accepted, Lord Brooke. Please let go of my hand,' she snapped.

'No. Not until you tell me how to get into your good graces,' he demanded.

She stopped mid-stride and attempted to snatch her hand back, but he held it firmly. She gave him a hard stare, knowing she could not afford to create a scene in such a public place. What was his game? He had made his apology and she had accepted it. He should have politely steered her in the direction of her brother and said nothing more.

He stepped in closer and spoke so only she could hear. 'Please; I need to know how I can make this up to you. I need you to—'

'Need me to what?' she interrupted, raising her eyebrows.

Alex looked over her shoulder, seeming to search the landscape for an answer. She heard him take a deep breath and swallow before he spoke.

'I need you to like me. I like you. I know I was a complete ass at the party, and I am terribly sorry. I did not know what to do or how to talk to you. To be honest, I still don't know. You have taken me completely by surprise.'

Millie's world tilted on its axis and she blinked as she waited for it to right itself. But instead, it stayed exactly where it was, slightly off-centre and a little out of focus.

Now it was her turn to struggle for air and be utterly lost for words. She shook her head; this could not be happening. She reminded herself that he was Lord Brooke, the man she had spent the past few days intensely disliking. His only redeeming feature was his lovely sister. Why should he care about what she thought of him? Her mouth opened and closed twice, but nothing came out.

He smiled at her and his whole face lit up. His magnificent green eyes sparkled.

Oh god, you are so beautiful. Is this how you hold sway over everyone: break them down and then make them like you? This is going to end badly, I just know it.

'Did you like the flowers?' he asked, skilfully turning his smile to a shy grin. 'I chose them especially for you, to match your stunning blue eyes.' He chuckled. 'Though I expect you will take me to task over the lavender; it was the closest thing to blue the florist could find this morning. He was struggling to find summer flowers in the hothouses, so again I will have to beg your forgiveness.'

Her heart leapt. He had not been sending the flowers to hurt her; rather, he had been trying to apologise in his own odd, clumsy way. She found his lack of finesse strangely appealing. How this god of a man could make a mess of a simple apology was beyond her, but he was obviously earnest in asking for her forgiveness. She had been wrong about other people before, but she still sensed he was holding a great deal of himself back.

'Hey ho, you two,' David called out, as he and Charles returned. 'All sorted?'

Alex and Millie continued to stare silently at one another. 'Hello,' David tapped Alex on the shoulder. His brother's head snapped around and David took a step back, hands held up in surrender. 'I was just trying to get you to come back to the real world. May I remind you that you are standing in the middle of the mad hour in Hyde Park?'

'Not to mention that Miss Ashton's brother is standing two feet away, wondering why you have hold of his sister's hands,' Charles added. Millie looked down and saw that Alex was holding not one but both of her hands. She stared dreamily at them, thinking how perfectly they fitted within his grasp.

Then she remembered who he was, and slowly withdrew her hands. He was being nice to her for no other reason than his concern for his sister. If he could not make peace with Millie, then she would find it impossible to visit at Strathmore House and Lucy would never forgive him.

She stepped back and gave a nod of her head. 'Yes, Lord Brooke and I have settled our differences; you can tell Lady Lucy that everything is fine. I shall speak to my mother about arranging a visit to see her as soon as possible.'

Her heart silently accepted that as she meant nothing to Alex and never would, it was now safe. He was a marquess, someday a duke; men like him did not fall for unfashionable girls like her. They barely noticed them. He would marry one of the diamonds of the season; in fact, he probably already had a fiancée or at least an unspoken understanding with someone.

She and he would be friends, nothing more, and if their friendship made her life within the *ton* a little easier, she would join the long list of his admirers, however reluctantly. She turned to her brother, who offered her his arm. As she took it, she sighed. 'I think I should like to go home now, Charles; I am feeling a touch weary. Do you mind if we leave?'

Charles and the Radley brothers exchanged a brief farewell and he escorted Millie out of the gate and on to Park Lane. They were at the corner of Union and Mill streets, away from the crowds of the park, before he finally spoke. 'So how did it really go? Did you manage to sort things out, or did you just reach some form of détente for the sake of Lady Lucy?'

His words barely stirred Millie from her thoughts. 'Hmmm?'

She stepped off the pavement, and began to cross the street. Charles took a firm hold of her arm and steered her clear of a flower cart as its driver lost control of the reins and the horse and cart suddenly backed up.

'Pay attention, Millie; you can't daydream and walk across a busy street at the same time. You'll get us both run over if you do, and I for one will not appreciate it,' Charles chided her as he guided her safely to the other side of the street.

'Sorry, I did not see the cart,' she replied. Her mind was still full of a certain young man's eyes, his smile and a declaration that she had taken him completely by surprise.

He is a friend. We are friends. He is Lucy's brother and he is —

She felt a hand on her back firmly pushing her forward. She took a step and followed it with another, then another, until her toes hit a stone edge. Millie stopped and looked up. They were home.

Charles was halfway up the front steps and the look on his face was one of bewilderment and frustration. He pointed to the front door and motioned for her to follow him. When she turned her head and looked back down Mill Street, her brow furrowed; she had no recollection of having walked the last block to their home.

She called out to him, 'Well?'

'Can you please come inside? I don't particularly like you bellowing at me from out in the street like some early morning orange-seller,' Charles replied.

He threw his hands up in disgust, turned on his heel and marched into the house.

She shrugged her shoulders. Lifting her skirts, she ascended the steps in the most graceful manner she could muster; Millie was fast learning that in London, you never knew who was watching.

❦

'That looks good, am I ready?' Alex asked impatiently as his valet stood giving Alex's evening clothes one final inspection.

'Nearly done, my lord; I just need to straighten your cravat,' Phillips replied, as he stepped forward and tucked in a wayward inch of neckcloth.

Alex counted slowly to five because he could never be bothered making it all the way to ten. After returning from his successful mission to apologise to Millie, he was now eager to go out and celebrate with David. It had been a very long week; his usual social habits meant he didn't normally rise until close to midday, but over the past few days he had been up early every morning in order to visit the florist and organise flowers for Millie.

He knew full well she had not believed his story about a bad back, but she had accepted his apology, and that made the days of getting out of bed at an unholy hour all worthwhile.

'Come on, we will be late and all the good tables will be gone,' his brother shouted from the hall outside Alex's bedroom. Alex laughed. David would have shaved, bathed and dressed in his usual expedient manner and accepted his own valet's first attempt to have him ready.

'Shut up and finish your drink, I won't be long,' Alex yelled in reply. His grooming always took a long time when it came to a night out on the town. Phillips would spend hours getting Alex's clothes perfect, his hair smooth and his cravat tied with mathematical precision. The Marquess of Brooke would be the most immaculately turned-out aristocrat in London tonight; Phillips would see to it.

Phillips gave a bow. 'May you have a pleasant evening, Lord Brooke; I shall await your return.'

'Thank you, Phillips; don't wait up for me, as I expect this will be a late one,' Alex replied as he admired himself in the mirror.

'Handsome devil,' he chuckled.

The door closed as Phillips took his leave.

A few minutes later, Alex wandered out from his bedroom. He looked at David, who gave him a nod. Alex's hand went to his perfect head of blond hair and gave it a good rub, leaving it elegantly messed. He then set to work on his cravat, pulling the last knot out and tucking the loose end into the top of his shirt. A quick check in the downstairs hall mirror confirmed that he was happy with his handiwork and ready to go out.

'All right; where are we off to first?' he asked.

David picked up a walking cane from the hall stand and handed it to him.

'Brook's for dinner and a drink or two, then on to White's as I have a small wager to settle. Where we end the evening and with whom is anyone's guess,' he replied, his face sporting a wicked grin. Alex laughed; when David had that look on his face, he knew they were in for a long night. Tomorrow they would be nursing well-deserved hangovers and vowing never to do it again. That, of course, was until the next time they ventured out on the town.

'Just don't leave me somewhere like "The Bloody Bosun's Mate"; you have no idea how much money they won from me the night you took me there,' Alex said.

'As I recall it was you who strolled into the bar and announced loudly that you would take on all comers in a game of cards. You lost less than a week's worth of your allowance and then complained for months,' David replied, slapping Alex on the back.

'You should be grateful that we managed to avoid going to Fulham Palace for dinner.'

Alex rolled his eyes. Many an evening had been spent listening to their uncle lecture Alex about the pressing need for him to take a wife.

'Remind me again of the benefit of having the Bishop of London for a relative?' he replied, as they stepped out into the street.

David laughed. 'Free weddings at the church of your choice. Now do come on, my precious petal, the night is young and we are far too sober.'

Chapter Seven

W hen Millie woke the following morning, it was with a sense of contented calm. For the first time since she had arrived in London, she looked forward to calling at someone's home. The note from the Duchess of Strathmore inviting her and Violet to visit had arrived at the house not long after she and Charles had returned from the park the previous evening.

She smiled when she thought of Lucy, picturing how she would have begged her mother to pen the invitation and have it delivered as fast as possible. Then again, it was more likely that the duchess had prepared the note well in advance of the peace talks in the park and was just waiting for the opportunity to send it on its way.

Fortunately for all concerned, Millie and Lord Brooke had managed to patch things up. She had convinced herself that they could now meet and be indifferent to one another; he was simply the older brother of her friend, nothing more.

She rolled over and snuggled down further under the blankets. It would still be icy cold outside; Stephens had been right when he had forecast a snowfall overnight. The clock on her bedroom mantle chimed six.

'So much for sleep,' she muttered.

She poked a toe tentatively out from under the blankets and shivered. 'I swear this place is closer to Iceland than the maps say.' She took a deep breath, counted a quick one, two, three and flung back the bedclothes.

Ever grateful that the previous owner of their house had decided to spend a small fortune on modern plumbing, she headed for her bathroom. Running water was one of the real advantages that she could concede living in London had over Calcutta. As she went about her morning ablutions, she called for Grace to set out one of her new winter dresses.

'The pale blue one, with the cream lace on the bodice if you please, Grace; it goes with my grey coat and hat. Mama and I are visiting the Duchess of Strathmore and her daughter today.'

Even with the sound of the running tap, she could still hear the feigned gasp of delighted surprise from her maid. Grace would have known all about the visit since the previous afternoon. The whispers would have no doubt started downstairs the moment the letter addressed to Mrs Ashton had been hand delivered by a footman in the Duke of Strathmore's livery. Why else would Grace be in Millie's room, wearing a smile two feet wide, a full half hour before she was normally due to arrive?

Stepping out from her bathroom, fresh and ready for the day, Millie returned Grace's smile; today was going to be a good day. She did not care how cold it was outside; let the arctic winds throw all they could summon at her, because nothing was going to spoil her mood.

'At least you won't have to meet that wicked Lord Brooke when you visit at Lady Lucy's house today,' Grace noted as she buttoned up the back of Millie's dress.

'Why not?' Millie replied, attempting to sound uninterested in the man who had been the centre of her dreams for the whole night. Grace moved to the dressing table and picked up a hairbrush. She stood quietly waiting by the chair while Millie took a seat in front of the mirror.

'Well?' Millie asked Grace's reflection in the mirror. The young girl's cheeks turned a bright red and she shook her head, clearly annoyed with herself.

'Oh, sorry miss, I had promised Mr Stephens I wouldn't spread any more tittle-tattle, but sometimes I can't help myself. I open my mouth and it just comes out,' Grace replied.

Millie turned on the stool and faced Grace.

'Grace, there is nothing to be sorry about. If you didn't keep your ear to the ground, how would I find out half of what goes on around here? Besides, I am relying upon you to be my second pair of ears and eyes when the season begins. I am going to need all the information you can gather from the other ladies' maids when we attend the big society balls. Just as long as you only tell it to me, no one else, understood?'

She could make her maid swear to secrecy, but she reasoned it was perfectly acceptable to use the titbits of information which happened to come Grace's way. Her mother had made it very clear that the *ton* was not just about who you were or who you knew; it was very much about everyone's secrets.

Grace began to hum and Millie could see she was wool-gathering.

'Grace.'

The young maid snapped out of her daydream and began quickly brushing Millie's hair. Her mistress sat silent for several more seconds before letting out a sigh and reaching up to take hold of the hand wielding the brush.

'Grace, you were about to tell me about Lord Brooke and why I won't be seeing him at Strathmore House,' she said, trying to maintain her good humour.

Grace looked at her blankly, and then Millie saw her eyes light up with realisation.

Grace clicked her tongue. 'Sorry miss. Well, you see, Lord Brooke doesn't live at Strathmore House anymore.'

She leaned in closer and whispered in Millie's ear, 'I heard from another girl who works in another house that his father threw him and his brother out. She said that they were always getting drunk and coming home at silly hours and making an awful noise.'

Millie's toes curled up in her slippers. This was exactly the kind of wicked gossip she wanted to hear.

'Really? How dreadful,' she replied, making sure she looked deeply concerned.

Grace nodded her head.

'Well, last summer the duke found Lord Brooke asleep on the floor in the front hall at eight in the morning. Even the footmen couldn't rouse him. His father said enough was enough and made him and his brother pack their bags. Can you imagine that, a duke having to scrape his son up off the floor?'

Millie was not about to tell Grace the mess Charles had made of himself on numerous occasions in the past few years. Only she was privy to that piece of information. And that was only because her bedroom window was the easiest for her drunken brother to climb through without being in danger of falling and breaking his stupid neck. He still owed her for the many times she had held his head over a bucket while he lost the contents of an evening's wild drinking.

'So, Lord Brooke and Mr Radley took up rooms in Bird Street,' Grace said finishing her story.

A pair of blue eyes stared back at Millie as she looked at herself in the mirror and held her own private conversation with her reflection.

When I visit at Lucy's house, Lord Brooke will not be in residence. Good. I am sure it will make things easier for me and also for him. Good. Yes, it will be much easier for everyone.

Damn.

How was she supposed to charm him into being her champion in the shark-infested waters of the *ton* if he was not going to be around to see how good a friend she was to his sister?

She chastised herself for thinking of using Lady Lucy in such a cold and calculating way. It was wrong of her to see Lucy as the means to her devilishly handsome and very popular brother, especially when Lucy Radley happened to be the only friend she had in the whole of London.

She had no cousins on her father's side, and only once on the long voyage from India had her mother made any mention of her relatives in Northamptonshire. There appeared to be a dark cloud over that side of the family, so she had not pressed her mother further on the subject. Apart from her uncle, there had been no one else to greet them the morning their ship berthed at the East India Docks.

Besides, it would be fun to have a friend who knew that the Romans had built Hadrian's Wall. There were times she despaired of the females her own age. All they could think of day and night was how they were going to sink their claws into some unfortunate bachelor and his bank account.

After she had finished dressing and dismissed Grace, Millie retrieved a large teak box from under her bed and placed it on the table by the window. There were no flowers from Lord Brooke this morning, which left her oddly disappointed. It would have been nice to know he still thought enough of her to send them at least one more time after she had reluctantly accepted his apology.

She wondered how many other girls in town had received flowers sent by the Marquess of Brooke three days in a row. The first one personally delivered to the front door. If the count was more than one, she did not wish to know. He had sent them because he wanted her to like him and that was all the detail her private fantasy required. Logic and reality could kindly call in at the house next door.

'Another bunch of white roses would have been nice; I quite liked them, especially the buds,' she said to herself, opening the box and examining its contents. Inside lay her most prized possessions. She had refused to set foot on board the ship bound for England until she knew for certain that the box with its gold silk lining was safely in her cabin. She smiled as she ran her fingers over the leather-bound books which sat tightly packed in the box. Adamant that not one of them was going to be abandoned, she had packed and repacked them until she had managed to squeeze them all in.

A small red book caught her eye. She gently prised it out of the box and stared at the cover. For most other girls it would have been an odd choice of gift for a new friend, but she knew it would be perfect.

In one of her other travel trunks she found a beautiful red silk scarf and wrapped the book in it. Her mother had decreed that she must unpack completely by the end of their second week in England, but most of Millie's things were still in the trunks in which they had arrived from India.

'Perhaps next week I will empty the large one,' she said to herself.

By the time their carriage pulled up outside Strathmore House, Millie was half out of her seat and holding on to the swinging strap in order to steady herself. Her mother took hold of Millie's other arm and made her sit back down.

'Wait until the carriage has come to a complete stop, my dear. We would not want you to have an accident, especially since you are likely to land on me.'

Millie shot her a dirty look.

'Mama, that is uncalled for and unkind,' she snapped.

She did not need reminding of how much she weighed, especially from her mother. Violet shook her head. 'I was not referring to the little bit of extra padding you are currently carrying, young lady, I meant that the fabric of this dress crushes if you so much as look at it.'

She looked at the mulberry silk dress Violet had chosen to wear. It was far more elegant than the gowns she had worn to other homes, and it left Millie wondering whether her mother was apprehensive about their visit.

'But since you are so sensitive on the subject of your figure you could do something about it, such as taking dancing lessons. I hear Lady Lucy is having one today; I may speak to her dance master and see if he can fit you into his weekly schedule. Your Aunt Beatrice was going to speak to one of the patronesses about procuring vouchers for us for Almack's Club, so you must work at improving your waltz.'

Violet adjusted her gloves before continuing. 'With the season a few months away, now is the time to master those tricky steps and be light of foot for the young gentlemen who will be clamouring to fill your dance card.'

A footman opened the door of the carriage and as soon as she had followed her mother out on to the pavement and finished arranging her skirts, Millie looked up at the house in front of them.

'Huge' and 'stately' were the first words which came to mind. Strathmore House took up nearly half the block, and was twice the size of the elegant houses either side of it.

'The Duchy of Strathmore is one of the oldest titles in England; it dates back to somewhere in the fourteenth century. When your father refers to someone's family as being an old family, this is what he means,' Violet explained.

The huge Portland stone columns which imposed themselves upon the streetscape spoke silently of great wealth and power. Millie made a mental note to ask Lucy how big the house was so she could calculate how many times her old home would fit inside.

'If there is one friendship I would wish very much for you to carefully nurture and cultivate, it is this one,' her mother whispered, as she stepped forward to brush something invisible off Millie's coat.

Millie's eyes lit up with delight.

'Why, Mama, if I didn't know you better I would say that you sounded like an unashamed social climber.'

Her mother pursed her lips.

'I shall remind you that I am the daughter of a viscount and your father is the brother of one. When you have those sorts of family connections you are already at the top of the social ladder, my darling.'

Violet gave her gloves and silk skirts one last inspection.

'As such I know the intricacies of the *ton* and how best to ensure that my daughter gets invited to all the select parties and balls in the forthcoming season. I might have been away for twenty-odd years, but let me assure you, the rules have not changed one iota. Millie, you are either in with the right people or you are out and believe me the walls of the *ton* are thick and heavily fortified against the outsider.'

'I was only in jest,' Millie replied, as her mother turned and headed up the front steps to the door.

'I wasn't,' Violet coolly replied.

ꝫ

'Oh Millie, you shouldn't have,' Lucy exclaimed as she accepted the silk-wrapped gift. When she took the scarf away and saw the little red book, her eyes nearly popped out of her head.

'Mama, it's a book about Genghis Khan, and it has such beautiful drawings. Look at this one; you can see how that man's head has come clean off.'

Violet shook her head slowly. 'I am so sorry, Caroline; I did not realise Millicent had selected that particular book to give to your daughter. Please let me take it back and I shall choose something more suitable.' She held out her hand, but Lucy hugged the book tightly to her chest and glared at her.

The Duchess of Strathmore laughed. 'Violet, my dear, you have no idea how alike these two are. I don't think you will be getting that book back any time soon.'

Millie shot Lucy a victorious look. She knew exactly the kind of book Lucy liked. If she had given her a book of poems, Lucy would have accepted it graciously and then more than likely pitched it out the window at the first opportunity.

'There are some even more gruesome pictures in it toward the back, but they may be best viewed later,' Millie offered.

On one of the few port stops they had made on the long sea voyage from India, Millie had dragged Charles to a local town square and found a dingy bookshop that sold all manner of strange publications. While she had busied herself with dead Mongolian warlords, Charles had managed to find some pictorial publications with undressed women in them. Millie had noted that he made a point of hiding those particular books when they were back on board the ship and would not let her read any of them. Her generous brother had even paid for all of her many purchases in the town that day. All she had to do in return was not mention the existence of the naked-lady books to either of their parents.

She smiled when she thought of how sheltered Charles had thought she was. The day when she finally mentioned to him that she owned not one, but two copies of the *Kama Sutra*, and had done so since she was sixteen, was one worth remembering.

'I was hoping that my two eldest boys would be here this afternoon; Alex at least promised to call in and pay his respects. Unfortunately, I suspect he and David were out with friends last night and have forgotten the time. Alex often makes it over on a Wednesday for Lucy's dance lesson in the late afternoon,' said the duchess as she handed Violet a cup of tea. Violet smiled at her, and the two women settled down to catch up on twenty years of *ton* gossip.

Lucy gave Millie a look of resigned disgust. Then she leaned over and caught her mother's eye.

'Would it be all right if Millie and I went upstairs to my room, Mama? That way you and Mrs Ashton can talk in peace without worrying about our sensitive ears.'

The duchess raised her eyebrows and looked at Violet, who nodded her approval. The sooner the girls were gone, the quicker they could get on to discussing the real scandals of the past two decades.

'Yes of course, my dear,' the duchess replied.

An hour later, the girls were sitting on the floor in Lucy's bedroom, flicking through the pages of some fashion books.

'I didn't think you were interested in fashion, Lucy?' Millie said, as she piled the books on top of each other.

Lucy gave her a sly smile.

'I noticed that you picked them up as soon as you got in here.

Admit it, Millie, you and I are just the same; we like both bonnets and bayonets.'

'And bloody barbarians,' Millie giggled.

'Sometimes, I wish I could ride through Hyde Park and lop off a few heads. Granted, it might get me barred from Ascot and all the good at-homes, but I think it would be worth it,' Lucy replied.

Millie shook her head. 'Remind me not to get on your bad side.'

Lucy laughed her best manic laugh, before gathering up her skirts and using the edge of the bed to pull herself to her feet. Millie watched as she went to the dresser and pulled open the bottom drawer. Lucy took out a pair of plain slippers and after removing the pair she already had on her feet, she put them on.

Millie looked at the clock and scowled. Was there some particular time of the day at which young English ladies changed their shoes, she pondered? Perhaps the other slippers simply hurt her feet and these new ones were her favourite comfortable pair.

She turned to see Lucy smiling at her. 'I have a dance lesson this afternoon, remember? These have a smooth sole for gliding gracefully across the dance floor. Well, that is the theory anyway.'

Millie began to pack up the books. Her first visit to Strathmore House was now coming to an end; she hoped it would not be her last. 'I have really enjoyed visiting today; thank you for inviting me,' she said, offering Lucy a grateful smile.

Lucy's face fell. 'Oh, you are leaving? I thought you might stay for a bit longer,' she replied. She reached out and, taking Millie's hand, helped her to her feet. 'I have another pair of slippers which are perfect for dancing.' She looked down at Millie's less than dainty feet and frowned. 'Well, even if you just come and watch me for a while. Please stay,' she pleaded.

The touching plea brought a tear to Millie's eyes and at that moment she prayed that no matter what the future brought, she and Lucy would be firm friends forever. She beamed as her heart filled with joy.

'I would love to stay. I am having the best fun, and even if I just sit and watch you practise, I am sure I will pick up on some of the finer points. Mama will wish to go home shortly, but I shall ask her to let me stay and meet your dance master; I am certain she will agree. If she sees that I am showing any interest in brushing up on my dancing skills, she will happily send the carriage to collect me later.'

Lucy twirled around on the spot and gave Millie an elegant bow. 'If you speak to Mr Roberts, he might even be able to find a time in his schedule to give you lessons.' She let out a gasp. 'Or, even better still, we could combine our dance lessons and you could come here every week,' she announced excitedly.

Millie's left eyebrow lifted slightly. 'I could do that, unless of course your Mr Roberts is far too exclusive for the likes of me. Who knows, he may only take on the finest of lead-footed ladies.' They both giggled.

Chapter Eight

It might have been a bitterly cold day, but Alex Radley did not feel it. Mired deep in self-inflicted pain, his brain was incapable of taking in much of his surroundings. The blinding light of the sun filled his entire field of vision.

His bare hands were stuffed into the pockets of his unbuttoned coat, which flapped about in the icy wind, allowing the cold to pierce his shirt and chill his skin. With his body already in such a painful state, it was unable to register any further discomfort. It could snow for all he cared.

As he made his way on foot to his parents' house, every step he took was agony. His eyes were like two tiny slits in his face, barely allowing him to see the path in front. Crossing North Audley Street, he did not bother to look left or right; he merely stepped into the road. The way he felt at that moment it would have been a blessed relief to be run over by a large mail coach.

When he first woke that morning, still in his evening clothes, Alex thought he had swallowed his shirt. It had taken several minutes to realise that the large cloth-like thing filling his mouth was actually his tongue.

He had thought of crying off making the arduous journey of

half a mile, but if he did, it would mean having to deal with David. After the humiliation he had suffered at the hands of his older brother the previous night, this enforced death march was the far more pleasant option.

'Fool,' he muttered, as his feet hit the pavement. His nauseous stomach threatened to wreak revenge with every step. 'I cannot believe he told everyone about what happened with Miss Ashton. How am I ever going to face them again?'

'Oh dear,' a voice said, and he turned his cat-like eyes to the sound. An arm came gently around his shoulder and by straining to focus he was able to see the pained look on Hargreaves the family butler's face.

He had reached Strathmore House, and with any luck, salvation.

'My lord, I gather you are feeling rather poorly this morning, because you certainly do not look at all well. How about you come inside, before either of their Graces set eyes upon you; the last thing I think your head needs right now is the soothing sound of a lecture from your parents,' Hargreaves said. Alex attempted to nod, but as his head was on the verge of falling off, he thought the better of it. He was content to allow Hargreaves to guide him around to the rear entrance of the house and down into the household kitchens.

Once inside, the family cook plied him with tea and a greasy bacon and egg sandwich. It was her famous hangover cure. The tea helped to stop the pounding head and the sandwich took care of the acid burning the bottom of the stomach.

Alex sat quietly on a chair, nursing his second cup of tea and praying that no one from the upper household ventured into the kitchens while he was there. If they did, it would only be a matter of minutes before he received the summons to either his father's study or his mother's sitting room for a none-too-subtle reminder of his station and responsibilities.

Meanwhile, the kitchen staff went quietly about their tasks, treating him as if he were no more than a cat perched on a stool. They knew he was there, but no one would speak to him. If they did then it meant he had been in the kitchens and they could not deny having seen him. He managed a weak smile as he thought of this strange below-stairs rule, which afforded protection to all those who abided by it. If they pretended he was not there, then he had never been there.

The only person exempt was Cook; she ruled the kitchens during the day and only relinquished control when the family chef took over for a dinner party, and then under sufferance.

'You really have made a mess of yourself, my lad. I have not seen you this bad in a very long time; it is a wonder you made it over here at all. Mr Hargreaves tells me you walked,' she said, placing a cold, wet towel on Alex's face.

He closed his eyes and took hold of her arm to steady himself. 'Oh, that is good, thank you Cook. You always take such good care of me; I truly don't deserve it.'

She chuckled. 'You are one of god's poor creatures and I hate to see them suffer; besides, I didn't say the towel was clean,' she replied. Even in his delicate state, Alex could see the joke and he laughed.

Gingerly.

Taking the cloth from his face, he handed it back to Cook, who wiped her hands on it and threw it in a nearby basket of dirty washing. He took a deep breath. He was beginning to feel human again.

'You'll live,' Cook said, giving him a gentle pat on the arm.

He watched as she took a freshly baked batch of scones out of the oven and stacked eight of them carefully stacked on a fine china plate, which was then placed on a cotton-covered tray next to a collection of jams and a pot of cream.

One of the kitchen maids hauled a large kettle off the fire and filled an elegant teapot with hot water. She pulled four matching cups and saucers from the kitchen dresser and arranged them next to the teapot. It was apparent his mother was entertaining visitors at home.

Alex downed the last of his tea and then sat staring at the tea tray. Why had he come here today, when he could still be lying unconscious in his own bed? He swore and in an instant Cook had picked up a wooden spoon and rapped him over the knee. 'Not in my kitchen, my lad. I don't care how poorly you are feeling. If you want to use that sort of language then you will have to go upstairs and out into the yard.'

Alex sat shamefaced, looking at his knee, which now hurt more than the rest of his body.

'Sorry Cook, I just remembered who the visitors are and why I was supposed to be here today,' he replied. He let out a sigh and silently berated himself for having got so terribly drunk last night. After David had drunkenly revealed Alex's sexual response upon meeting Millie Ashton, he should have gone home and got some sleep.

Instead, he had stormed out of the Silken Slipper Club, the laughter of his friends still ringing loudly in his ears, and found the nearest public house in which to drown his sorrows. He had fallen in with a bunch of sailors whose ship had just arrived in port following a rough sea crossing from the West Indies.

If the sailors had thought they could drink this foolish young man under the table, they were sadly mistaken. Alex had offered to fight the bar, but instead they convinced him to pay for their drinks.

'Gentlemen and scholars,' were the last words he remembered slurring at some fellow who had a large gold ring through his nose, before he'd managed to stagger home and pass out.

He looked down at his hands and saw they were shaking. He really had made an awful mess of himself.

'I most certainly will not make a good impression in my current condition,' he lamented.

'No, and you smell like the bottom of a brewer's barrel,' Cook replied tartly. 'If I were you, I would forget about seeing the visitors and find a spare bed to crawl into. Lord Stephen has gone out for the day, so his room will be empty. I shall have a word with Mr Hargreaves and make sure you are not disturbed.'

She took the empty cup from Alex's shaking hands and placed it on the table.

'While you get some sleep, I shall get one of the footmen to locate Lord Stephen's valet and ask him to help clean you up in an hour or two.'

Alex nodded, and thankfully his head stayed on his shoulders. He slid slowly off the stool and after stealing a stray scone, headed upstairs in search of his younger brother's bedroom and, he prayed, some sleep.

᪥

After Violet had made her farewells and thanked Lady Caroline for the invitation, she went home, promising to send the family carriage back to collect Millie later that afternoon.

As soon as her own mother had turned and gone back upstairs, Lucy dragged Millie into a large ballroom which ran off one side of the main front hallway.

Millie stood in awe as she surveyed the size of the ballroom; the ballroom at Ashton House could have easily fitted into it and then had space left over. When Lucy took her by the hand and pulled her toward a second door, Millie gave her a quizzical look.

'I thought you were having a dance lesson in the ballroom?' she said, as Lucy opened another door and stepped into a second room.

'I am,' Lucy replied, as she pulled Millie through the doorway. 'This is the winter ballroom; it is too small to practise in. We will be using the summer ballroom.'

As soon as she saw the size of this second room, Millie's jaw literally dropped. Strathmore House was so huge it contained not one but two enormous ballrooms.

The summer ballroom was the largest room Millie had ever seen in a private home. It could have housed two of her uncle's ballrooms. When Lucy let go of her hand mid-way across the floor, Millie stopped and looked up. Above her soared an ornately decorated ceiling, so high it gave the illusion of stretching to reach to the heavens.

'Gosh,' she murmured.

From across the other side of the room she could hear someone practising on a piano.

A smile came to Lucy's lips.

'I must go; Mr Roberts does not allow my lessons to run over time. He has several more lessons after me.'

She gave Millie a wave and hurried across the floor to meet up with the dance master.

'There are some chairs over there if you want to sit and watch,' she called out, pointing to several chairs against the wall at a midpoint of the room.

'Thank you; I might just have a look at this magnificent ceiling before I come over to watch, if that is all right?' Millie replied.

Lucy glanced up at the ceiling and shrugged her shoulders. She had lived in this house all her life, so the roof of the summer ballroom was nothing for her to get excited about. Then a smile appeared on her lips.

'You do know your Aesop's fables, don't you? Let's see how many of them you can identify before you check the answers,' Lucy called out, laying down a challenge.

'If you read the writing which is upside-down at the top of the picture, it will give you an obvious clue, and if you still don't know the fable, the answers are in order on the two main wall panels in the middle of the room. Good luck.'

Millie was captivated by the ceiling and she took to the challenge of examining the amazing baroque artwork with relish. The ceiling was decorated with a gilt grid, and in each section, a variety of animals and people enacted a series of ancient fables on a coloured background. Every so often smaller pictures of laughing cherubs, unicorns and angels had been painted between the stories. Whoever had commissioned this ceiling certainly had a liking for filling up every inch of available plaster with colour.

In the first section she was delighted to see a fat white goose sitting on a golden egg. 'That one is easy,' she said.

As she slowly made her way around the room, gazing up at the ceiling, she identified the more famous of the fables, including the tortoise and the hare and the boy who cried wolf. Having guessed those without checking the answers, she continued across the floor.

She was busily staring at a picture of a beautiful woman and a cat, trying to recall the story, when the pianist struck up a waltz. She looked over and saw Lucy and Mr Roberts begin to dance. Millie smiled when she saw how graceful a dancer Lucy was, and reminded herself to ask for Mr Roberts' card so her mother could speak to him about lessons.

She turned from the dancers and resumed staring up at the ceiling. As she listened to the music, her eyes slowly closed and she began to sway in time.

Alex was immensely proud of himself. He had managed to slip into his parents' house and have a solid three hours' sleep in his younger brother's bed, and only a handful of servants knew he was here. And not one of them was about to reveal the whereabouts of the future head of the family to anyone. All those who worked in the households of the *ton* knew that the Radley family was one of the best employers in England and when the servants of an estate were promptly and well paid, they made sure to protect their future livelihoods.

He stood at the top of the stairs and peered over the balcony. A few hours ago, he would not have been able to accomplish such a simple task, but his head was now clear. The front entrance was empty, so he made his way downstairs. His plan was a simple one. Quietly open the front door, close it, go around the block and arrive at the front door once more.

He had borrowed a shirt from Stephen's wardrobe, grateful that his brother had had the good sense to sprout tall and large in his fourteenth year. The shirt fitted him well enough.

Stephen's valet had helped make him presentable. After a hot towel and a quick glide over his stubble with a cutthroat blade, Alex finally admitted he looked more like his usual self. Though as he sat and stared into his brother's mirror, he realised there was little he could do about the dark circles under his eyes. The nights he had spent in fitful dreams of Miss Millicent Ashton, followed by the drunken indulgence of the previous evening, were reflected back at him in his tired and drawn face.

'I look a million years old,' he muttered to himself as the valet took the shaving bowl and brush back to the washstand.

Certain that no one was about downstairs, he began to cross the tiles of the front entrance, a cheery greeting and a ready-made story on his lips for any family member he might encounter before he made it out on to the street. Strathmore House had over thirty rooms and the Radley family were forever losing each other both upstairs and down. Alex fancied his chances. But just in case anyone did happen to be in the vicinity of the front door, he slowed his steps so as not to make a sound with his boots.

As he opened the door, he heard music coming from the summer ballroom. He stopped and turned toward the source of the music. Odd that someone would be in the ballroom playing the piano. Then he remembered it was Wednesday; Lucy had her dance lessons on a Wednesday afternoon.

He also remembered he had promised he would come and watch her practise. That had been the excuse he had given Lucy for coming today, his original intention being, of course, to arrive some time earlier to arrange a purely coincidental meeting with Miss Ashton. He felt he still had more apologising to do before she truly forgave him.

As it was now late in the afternoon, Mrs Ashton and her daughter would be long gone, but at least the journey would not have been a complete waste of time if he managed to sit through Lucy's dance lesson. Spending time with her would ensure he was firmly back in her good books.

Taking a deep breath and painting on a relaxed smile, he walked through the door of the winter ballroom. By the time he made it into the summer ballroom, he had managed to turn the stilted walk into a casual stroll. One would have had to look closely at him to know that he had been at death's door only a matter of hours ago.

Once inside the summer ballroom, he crossed the floor, making a beeline for the row of chairs along the wall. There he could sit in comfort while he watched Lucy and the dance master as they worked their way around the ballroom floor, finely tuning her already excellent skills. She was an accomplished dancer, but in the heavily fought battle to secure a good husband, Lucy was leaving nothing to chance. With her first season the prior year considered a failure, he knew she was determined to shine brightly from the very first ball after Easter.

A movement to his left caught the corner of his eye. He turned and stopped dead in his tracks. There in the middle of the ballroom was the curvaceous and utterly luscious Miss Millie Ashton, eyes closed, swaying in time with the music. Even though she had her back to him, he felt an instant response to her presence. He licked his lips and swallowed deeply.

What is it that you do to me?

He stood transfixed for a moment, watching her hips as they moved. She was the most sensual creature he had ever seen. Totally uninhibited and lost in the music, she was so unlike any other girl he had ever met. She danced purely for the joy of it.

She laughed and he felt his heart take flight and soar. Was this love? Whatever it was, he had never felt such a strong attraction to another human being in his life. If she was a siren come to lure him to his fate, then he stood ready to throw himself overboard at her command.

A hundred mothers with their doe-eyed daughters in tow found a way to fortuitously cross his path every week. And it was the same surprised squeal of delight that they gave every time. How wonderful it was to make his acquaintance, and how much they looked forward to meeting him at whatever social gathering they intended to waylay him at, thus allowing him to see how delightful Prudence or Primrose was. He was always polite when he met the mothers, reserving the gentle crushing of hope for those private moments at the end of the dance for the hopeful young misses.

Compared to the other girls who were constantly thrown in his path, Millie was a true revelation, a balm for his jaded soul. As the music continued, a strong desire to reach out and touch her nearly overwhelmed him. His breath came in short gasps as he watched her body swaying to and fro. He craved nothing more than to be able to walk up to her, place his arms around her waist and sway along with the music, just holding her.

When she opened her eyes and turned towards him, the unbridled happiness he felt told him this girl affected him on much more than just a primal level. The sense of her essence went all the way to his heart. He smiled and gave her a small wave in greeting.

Her eyes locked upon his face and as they found focus, her smile disappeared and she let out a horrified squeal. Her cheeks turned bright red and her dancing came to a sudden halt. Alex felt his heart sink; he had frightened the beautiful wild bird and her colourful display was over. 'Oh, how embarrassing,' she whispered. 'I had no idea you were standing there. You must think me a complete fool.'

He strode across the floor and as he reached her, he stopped and gave her a bow. She might not dance like that again in public for fear of ridicule, but one day he would ask her to show him all her rich plumage, a private display just for him.

'Good morning, Miss Ashton,' he said. 'I loved the way you danced; you are naturally at one with the music.'

She smiled and Alex found himself smiling right back at her. They stood standing smiling at one another, just as they had done in the park. For a man who prided himself on his suave demeanour it was utterly pathetic – and he could have done it all day.

'It is nearly three o'clock,' Millie replied, as the red on her cheeks subsided. 'You look as if you have just got out of bed, Lord Brooke.'

'Alex,' he replied. 'Just Alex.'

He could see she was examining him closely and knew that the circles under his eyes would give him away. 'You look like my brother Charles after he has been out to an all-night Diwali party,' she replied. Her smile turned a little sly and crept to the corner of her mouth. 'You have not injured your back again, have you, Your Lordship?'

Alex shook his head and wondered if she would ever let him forget the little white lie he had told.

If she knows my back is fine, I dread to think what she made of my performance the other night. No wonder she was still angry with me.

'You would not be mocking me, now, would you Miss Ashton?' he chided her gently. 'I can honestly tell you I look a thousand times better than I did several hours ago, but yes, I am sorry to say the rings under my eyes and my late arrival are both due to an over-indulgence in all manner of spirits. One would think that at nearly three and twenty I would know the point at which to stop imbibing, but unfortunately I am yet to develop that quantum of good sense.'

Millie laughed and then quickly covered her mouth with her hand. 'I am so sorry; I should not laugh at you when you are in such a delicate state. I know my brother Charles would consider it extremely poor form on my part.' She looked at him sheepishly, and he was powerless to do anything but laugh. 'I was just enjoying the magnificent ceiling you have in this room; I hope my dancing did not frighten you. I do tend to let myself get carried away with the music at times.'

Alex sighed. 'Fat babies,' he replied.

'Pardon?'

He looked up towards the ornate ceiling. 'I was going to have it whitewashed at one point when I was younger,' he continued.

She still had a confused look so, raising his hand, he pointed to one of the richly painted scenes, hoping she would understand him.

'Up there – the fat gold babies and the angels and all the scrolling work. I used to think it was an absolute disaster. I swore that when I eventually took over this place I would have the lot painted over.' He waved a hand about as if holding an invisible paintbrush. 'I even considered putting in a false ceiling. To me it was just an unholy mess of colour and silly animals with more gilt than you could poke a stick at; I couldn't abide the sight of it.'

'Cherubs,' she corrected him. 'They are not fat babies, but magnificently painted angels and cherubs. This ceiling is absolutely stunning; I love it. Though I can't see much scrolling work, unless you are referring to the witty clues as to which fable is which.'

Alex looked more closely at the ceiling and squinted. The squiggles and scrolls remained as they had always been to him. Indecipherable.

Damn, I forgot they were letters, not decorations. This could be really awkward. Now what was the fable about the cat and the woman? I used to know all of them by heart.

He silently cursed the long-dead Greek philosopher.

'Yes, but if you look closely you will see that some of them are armed with bows and arrows. So, they are not as innocent as they would have you believe. Look at that one over there,' he said, pointing to a cherub which appeared to be biting a unicorn. He raised his eyebrows, confident that he had proved his point.

He hoped she had not noticed his sleight of hand in changing the subject.

'My brother David and I used to spend hours in here finding all the wicked ones and believe me, there are quite a few of them. It was only when I got older and began to appreciate the whole magnificent tableau that I knew my family would never allow me to put a brush to anything in this room.'

'Philistine,' Millie muttered.

'Former philistine, thank you Miss Ashton,' he replied with a grin. He motioned toward the chairs. 'Shall we sit and talk, while we watch Lucy dance to perfection?'

She gave him a nod and, taking hold of his arm, allowed him to escort her across the floor, where they took chairs side by side. He had been out of bed for less than an hour, but Alex was grateful to be able to sit and rest his head against the wall. They sat for a few minutes, silently enjoying one another's company while Lucy and Mr Roberts waltzed and laughed their way around the dance floor.

'He is very good with her,' Millie observed.

'Yes, I think it part of his contract that all the young women he teaches fall in love with him,' Alex replied, his gaze fixed on the dance instructor.

'You don't seem to mind, though,' she replied.

He shook his head.

'Because I know him to be the most happily married man I have ever met, apart from my own father, of course. His wife used to be a dancer with a French troupe, and believe me, there would be few women able to hold a candle to her.'

He glanced at Millie and gave her an easy smile. With her there was nothing staged or forced, he could relax and be himself. He shifted in his seat. Whether it was as a consequence of his hangover he couldn't be certain, but Alex was relieved to discover that his body had decided to cooperate. There would be no embarrassing repetition of their previous meetings. He tapped his feet on the polished wooden floor, confident in the knowledge that if he put his mind to it, he could take matters with Millie quickly from budding friendship to something possibly more.

'Are you going to take lessons with Mr Roberts? He is the best dance instructor in London,' he asked, before instantly regretting his remark. He winced. 'How rude of me to cast judgement on your dancing abilities, when I was the one who refused to dance with you at the ball. By the way, I am still deeply sorry for the other night; every time I think of it, I cannot believe I did that to you. You were well within your rights to abandon me on the dance floor.'

She laughed.

'My waltz is about the same as your tact, Lord Brooke: terrible. So yes, I shall be speaking to Mr Roberts about taking some lessons with him.' She gave him a more serious look before placing her hand briefly on his jacket sleeve.

'Thank you for your second apology, but it is not necessary; I think I made you suffer enough in the park. Though I must admit to missing having fresh flowers delivered each morning. I shall have to ensure you insult me again soon, so you can buy me some more.'

He closed his eyes, grateful that she did not bear him a grudge. He could name a long list of other young ladies who would not speak to him again if he had done the same to them. And therein lay the difference with Millie; she was the master of her own mind. She had decided to overcome her anger and forgive him for his stupid transgression. It did not escape his notice, either, that in her long, chestnut-brown hair she wore the blue ribbon he had so carefully chosen for one of his floral apologies. He smiled when he thought of her wearing a gift he had sent.

They sat quietly for a few more minutes, during which Alex boldly reached over and took Millie by the hand. He knew he had crossed the line of social politeness, but with the way she made him feel, he was prepared to take the risk. Millie looked down at his hand as it covered hers, but made no comment. Alex took comfort in the fact that she did not attempt to pull her hand away.

'I could help with your lessons,' he offered. 'If you take lessons here with Lucy, then I can come over and partner you when Mr Roberts dances with my sister. Would you consider that acceptable?'

The responding smile which lit up her face gave him hope. When a bashful glow appeared on her cheeks, it took all of his strength not to reach over and touch her face.

'I would have thought a gentleman such as you would have far better things to do with his time than to indulge my desire to learn to waltz,' she replied.

'It would help ease my conscience,' he replied, knowing it was only a small part of his reason for wanting to spend time with Millie.

She nodded her head. 'That would be lovely, thank you Lord Brooke.'

'Alex,' he found himself replying. 'You must call me Alex; only servants and shopkeepers call me Lord Brooke. My friends, and I hope to number you among them, call me Alex.'

Friends – who was he fooling? There was no one else in his wide group of friends whom he wanted to kiss, only her. Those plump, rosy lips were made for kissing, and once the thought had entered into his mind, Alex found himself thinking of little else. She might be his sister's new friend, but he was beginning to find it increasingly difficult to see her in such a disinterested light. Just sitting next to her stirred his whole being into life.

'All right, Alex,' the object of his desire replied. 'We are of similar age, so I don't expect my parents would object if I used your Christian name when we are not in a wider social setting.'

Alex felt his breath catch and he let out an involuntary groan.

'Alex, are you, all right?' Millie asked, clearly concerned. 'Head or stomach? I find it is usually one of those two which brings Charles to his knees.'

Alex scowled, before remembering he had mentioned his hangover. He theatrically rubbed his temple; his suffering of the morning was suddenly worthwhile.

'Head,' he lied. 'I thought my head was coming good, but it is beginning to pound once more.'

He curled his toes up inside his boots, as he stifled a laugh about which head was actually throbbing. David would no doubt have filled a whole afternoon laughing over that witty double entendre if he had been aware of Alex's current predicament.

'Is your brother in the same condition as you? I have not seen him here today, so I am assuming he is not possessed of as strong a constitution as you,' she said.

He slowly shook his head as anger replaced lust. 'I am not aware of the state of my brother's health this morning; we did not come home together last night. I heard his door close in the early hours, so he must have made it back in one piece,' he ground out.

Millie fell silent beside him and Alex sensed she was waiting for him to tell her more.

'If you must know, Miss Ashton, my brother and I are not on speaking terms at present,' he continued. 'We had a falling out last night and I left him at a club with some friends, while I went elsewhere.'

'Oh, I am sorry to hear that, I hope it's not too serious and that you will be friends again soon,' she replied.

Alex picked at a piece of fluff stuck on his jacket. It would be impossible to explain to her the reason for his current estrangement from David. Everyone in the *ton* believed that nothing would ever come between the two older Radley brothers and that for them to have a serious falling out would simply be impossible.

How very wrong they were.

'Yes, of course,' he replied without thinking, while his mind was occupied in designing horrid and bloody ways to kill his brother and successfully hide the body.

'So, when do you want to start?' she asked.

'Pardon?'

Millie shifted in her chair and turned to face him. He had not been paying attention and she knew it.

'Miss Ashton, I am not myself today and my manners appear to have stayed in bed, so once again I must apologise for my behaviour,' he said.

'Millie,' she replied with a smile. 'Actually, I think you have done remarkably well to come here and sit through Lucy's lesson. Charles would have pinned a note of apology to my door and taken to his bed for a week. For someone who prides himself on being an excellent pugilist, he can be a bit wet.'

Alex stifled a laugh. 'One must not speak ill of the self-inflicted near-dead, Millie,' he teased. He saw her eyes light up when he said her name, and the temptation to place a kiss on her lips nearly overcame him.

You are so beautiful; you are going to break more than one heart this season.

The season. Oh no.

It may be months away, but when the season hit its peak, London would be full of eligible young men and women. If he didn't begin a concerted campaign to claim her soon, he would be caught up in the crush of other bachelors vying for her attention and that simply would not do. This intriguing girl from the other side of the world was going to be his; the longer he sat next to her, the more he became convinced of it. A girl like Millie Ashton only came along once in a man's lifetime. He would be a fool not to seize his chance and make her his bride.

You are wool-gathering again, Brooke; speak to her before she notices.

'Next Wednesday, we shall rehearse while Lucy has her lesson. That, coupled with the lessons your mother arranges with Mr Roberts, should have you the mistress of the waltz in no time,' he said.

'Good; I look forward to it, though I think Mr Roberts will still ask for some form of payment, since we are utilising the services of his pianist,' she replied.

'Leave the light-footed Mr Roberts to me, Millie; I shall make sure he earns double his usual fee. We should aim to have you ready for your first public waltz at my cousin the Earl of Shale's ball on the first Monday in April. It is usually the Easter event, but they are having it early this year as Rosemary, his countess, is with child.'

He reached out and took hold of her hand once more. 'Enough about dancing and men with sore heads; what about you, Millie Ashton? I want to hear about your life in India, it must be so very different from here.'

They spent the next ten minutes talking about India and Millie's childhood. He questioned her at length about the long sea voyage to England, and how she must find the cold of London a sharp contrast to the heat of the subcontinent.

'Apart from the shock of realising just how cold snow really is, I think I have learnt to adapt to it rather well. It's the things I could not bring with me that I miss. I left all my friends behind, and my horse. Then there are the silly things I didn't realise I would miss, like the colour of the Hooghly River and the smelly, noisy spice markets.'

'London smells, if you had not noticed,' Alex replied, trying to make her smile.

Millie nodded her head. 'Yes, it does: damp and musty most of the time. Mother keeps promising me that it will be better in the summertime, but I somehow doubt that London will suddenly transform into an oasis of colour and sensual delight just because the sun finally manages to break through the clouds. With any luck I shall only have to endure one winter in England before I go home.'

He felt a cold shiver race down his spine. Did she just say she was planning to leave England?

'You are going back?' he asked, as a sense of overwhelming sadness filled him. How could she leave and not return? How could she leave him?

Because she doesn't know the first thing about you and if she did she would run a mile. What girl in her right mind would want to be wedded to an illiterate fool like you?

He swallowed, and tried to beat down the rising panic as it swelled within him.

'I am sure once you have seen more of the countryside and the beautiful spring flowers you will feel differently,' he replied.

She shrugged her shoulders and leaned forward to watch Mr Roberts instruct Lucy on a new dance. The sound of Lucy's laughter echoed throughout the room as she struggled to master the steps.

'That looks like fun,' Millie said.

Alex bit his lip in frustration. He was contemplating the loss of the one girl who had ever stirred his heart and she was making a quip about some trivial dance.

'It would be such a shame for you to leave before you really got to know and love the place.'

And me.

Millie shook her head. 'Our family came back to England to ensure there was an heir to the Ashton title close at hand. My mother was also keen to come home, though I never realised how much she hated it in India until we reached London.' Millie sighed. 'But it doesn't matter if I stay here or not. England has not exactly welcomed me with open arms. I would rather go home.'

For the first time in his life, it occurred to Alex that other people did not see England, and especially London, in the same way as he did. For Millie this was not home; her heart remained many thousands of miles away. He could not imagine leaving England, never to return.

'What if your family won't allow you to return to India? What will you do then?' he asked.

She turned and gave him a quizzical look, and he knew what she was thinking. What did it matter to him what she did with her life? She puffed out her cheeks and shrugged her shoulders once more.

'I don't know; I hadn't thought that far ahead, so please don't speak of it to anyone in my family. It was careless of me to have mentioned it at all. It's simply that the idea of going back keeps turning over in my mind. Perhaps this coming season will resolve things for me. Who knows? I may meet some dashing young man who sweeps me off my feet and carries me away to his castle in the Scottish Highlands,' Millie replied.

She gave Alex a friendly pat on the arm, but it did little to quell his growing uneasiness. Until she came to realise that her future was already sealed with him, she would not give up the dream of returning to India. He would have to make her see that she could be happy in her new home. And that he had a large and imposing castle at his disposal. Granted, it was in the lowlands, but it was a castle none the less. He would be more than happy to share it with her, along with his heart.

Finally, the music came to a halt and with her lesson over, Lucy walked over to greet them. Alex watched as his sister's gaze took in how closely he and Millie were seated, and he saw a disapproving look appear on her face. It was the same look she always gave him when one of her friends got a little too friendly with him. He had broken more young girls' hearts than he cared to admit and it had cost Lucy several friendships. The list of girls who had cried themselves to sleep over Alexander the Great was long.

He wasn't a fool, though. He knew full well that several girls had befriended Lucy in order to get closer to him. He understood the attraction he presented to the unmarried misses. What sensible girl would not use Lord Brooke's sister as a means to get close to the future Duke of Strathmore? Many had tried, and all had failed. Then he had met Millie. She had not thrown herself at him; there had been no batting of pretty eyelids in his direction or sudden swooning. She was different.

She had stood up to him in Hyde Park and called his bluff. She knew his back was not injured, but rather than make a scene, she had placed her friendship with Lucy ahead of her hurt feelings and accepted his apology. She was a newly discovered delight, and if Lucy thought he was about to take a step backward, she was seriously mistaken. Millie would be his, and Lucy was going to have to accept it.

'You are such a skilled and elegant dancer, Lucy,' Millie said, clapping her hands in appreciation. 'I must remember not to dance too close to you in future. That way no one can compare your light feet to my flat ones.'

Lucy laughed and took Millie by the hand, pulling her to her feet. 'Come, you must meet Mr Roberts, I have told him all about you and he is eager to make your acquaintance.' As Lucy walked arm in arm with Millie across the ballroom, Alex followed slowly behind, humming to himself. When Lucy did look back at him, he returned her wary look with a warm smile. He was too busy formulating a plan to woo Millie to allow his sister's concerns to bother him. Millie was the one he had to win over, and only after she had fallen in love with him and accepted his suit would he dare to share his humiliating secret with her.

'Did I mention that we have a family castle in Scotland, Miss Ashton?' he muttered under his breath, making a mental note to drop it into the conversation at the next opportune moment.

Chapter Nine

The row between the Radley brothers continued unabated. David approached Alex several times over the next few days, but each time he attempted to speak to his brother, Alex held up a hand and gave him a firm 'Don't bother' before walking away.

He knew David felt guilty about what had happened at the Silken Slipper Club, and that it had been the brandy talking, but Alex still found himself unable to put the embarrassment he had endured that night behind him. David, his lifelong champion and protector, had exposed him to the scorn of the world. For the moment, Alex's pride was wounded and he was in no mood to forgive.

Seated on his magnificent midnight-black gelding as he joined the rest of the early morning Hyde Park riders, the Marquess of Brooke was the epitome of a young English peer.

Under his black greatcoat, his cravat was tied correctly, but far more loosely than the current fashion dictated. Refusing to conform to the strictures of the dandy set, he insisted his neckcloths be only lightly starched, allowing him full movement of his head when he rode. His tight buckskin breeches clung to his strong legs, showing every muscle to its best advantage. Below the knee, his riding boots hugged his calves tightly, the result of an elegant marriage of expensive English leather and a masterful valet. Neither dandy nor buck, Alex Radley dressed to suit himself and others were left to follow in his wake.

One of the benefits of being out of sorts with his brother, and therefore not out every night, was the newfound sensation of waking early and feeling well each morning. He smiled as he recalled the look of surprise on the stable master's face when Alex appeared in the yard just after dawn and ordered his horse be ready within the hour for an early-morning jaunt.

Watching as a steady stream of the *haute ton* arrived with their horses and grooms in tow, Alex pondered the events of the afternoon several days earlier. The time he had spent with Millie in the ballroom at Strathmore House had been a major revelation. She was the first girl who had made him question the way he lived his life.

He had lain awake on his bed for several hours after returning home, recalling every word she had said to him. The memory of his hangover still fresh in his mind, he had made the uncharacteristic decision to stay home for the evening, ignoring the raised eyebrows of his valet when he informed Phillips he would not be venturing out. When sleep finally claimed him, he had dreamt he was holding Millie, his hands on her hips as she swayed to the music from an invisible orchestra. It had been a long and sexually satisfying dream.

The snort of his horse and the stamp of its hooves on the hard-cold ground stirred him from his musings.

'Sorry boy, I know you didn't come out here to stand and watch everyone else get a good run down the Row. Time to stop wasting the morning,' he said as he dug his heels into the side of his mount and the horse set off at a light canter.

Further along the sandy track, he let his horse have its head and the beast responded by stretching out to a full gallop. The biting wind slapped against Alex's face and he blinked away the tears which formed in his eyes. He laughed with pure joy. It was marvellous to shake the cobwebs from his mind.

The sound of pounding hooves caught his attention and, glancing over his right shoulder, he saw another rider on a grey gaining on him. He spurred his horse on, intent on being the first to reach the unofficial finish line at the Lodge.

'Come on Brooke, my sister can ride faster than you,' the other rider bellowed.

Alex looked again and saw Charles Ashton drawing alongside on the grey.

'Bloody hell, Ashton, you ride like the devil,' Alex replied with a roar. He dug his heels in once more and leaned forward in the saddle.

Faster and faster the two horses raced. Over the sound of his horse's heavy panting, Alex could hear the cries of other park visitors urging him on to victory. With the blood pounding in his ears, he gripped the reins and urged his mount on.

He reached the Lodge a half-length ahead of Charles Ashton and, punching the air, let out a loud whoop of delight. 'Huzzah, the victory is mine!'

He eased back in the saddle and loosened the reins as his horse slowed from its gallop to walk. Charles drew alongside and offered Alex his hand.

'Well done, Brooke; first time I've been beaten in years. That's one determined beast you have there.'

Alex shook Charles's hand and looked down at his mount. 'From my father's estate in Scotland; I expect he has been champing at the bit to get out and have a good run.'

He threw his leg over the saddle and dropped to the ground. Charles followed suit. The sweat-soaked horses wandered off to the nearby grass, nuzzling the ice-covered ground in search of young grass.

'I haven't seen you in the park before. Do you ride here often?' Charles asked.

Alex shook his head. 'I am ashamed to say that this is the first time in months I have been up to make the early ride, but I promise henceforth you shall see me here every morning.'

Charles smiled. 'Excellent; then a rematch is on the cards. I nearly had you at the end.'

Alex picked up the reins of his horse as he and Charles began the long walk back along the track towards their grooms. He had to give Charles his due; he was a superb rider, much like himself. Fearless and prepared to let the horse have its head when it counted. Few other riders were willing to trust that their horse had as much hunger to win the race as they did. It was little wonder Alex never lost.

'So, who taught you to ride like a mad man?' he replied.

Charles stopped and fixed Alex with a hard stare. 'Necessity.'

Alex furrowed his brow. 'What?'

Charles sighed. 'I came across a leopard on a forest trail a few miles from our summer home one year. My horse took off like the wind, with me holding grimly on to the reins for my life. So now when I ride I just imagine that day and I am never beaten.'

Alex raised an eyebrow.

'Well, almost never,' replied Charles with a smile. 'What about yourself?'

'Rode like a reckless fool since the day my father first put me on a horse's back. I am sure he thinks one day I am going to come off and break my bloody neck, but it hasn't happened so far,' Alex replied.

They continued on the track back to the main gate and their waiting grooms. As he handed over the reins, Alex gave his horse one final pat on the neck.

'So, are you off home for breakfast?' he asked.

Charles shook his head. 'No, we eat early in our house. Millie was just wandering into the breakfast room as I left. She and our father are going to the British Museum this morning to see the Elgin marbles and if I know Papa, he will want to be there when they open the doors. I hear everyone is flocking to see them. Myself, I am spending the morning with my tailor; Mama says I need more evening attire for the season.' He gave a clear sigh of disgust. 'I don't think there could be anything more tiresome.'

'Quite,' Alex replied, attempting to sound disinterested. 'Well, I suppose I had better head home and see what is on the breakfast table. This fresh morning air has given me an appetite. Same time tomorrow, Ashton, and let's see how close you can get your nag to my fine steed.'

Alex bade Charles goodbye and he followed his groom out the main gate. But instead of heading home to Bird Street, he hailed a hack and headed up Park Lane. Leaning back on the leather bench, he began to formulate a plan. If there was one person in London who would appreciate a visit to the British Museum, it would be his history scholar of a brother Stephen. If they happened by pure chance to encounter a young lady and her father who were also visiting the museum that morning, he would claim it as the most fortunate of coincidences.

'I am pleased to see you happy,' Mr Ashton said as Millie smiled broadly.

Millie and her father had arrived at Montagu House, home of the British Museum, early. With a small tip to the attendant, they were admitted to the viewing room half an hour before the official opening time. With only a small number of people in the room, Millie was afforded an unobstructed view of a twenty-foot section of the Parthenon Frieze.

'They are stunning and I have been longing to see them since the day we arrived. Especially the Parthenon Frieze; I cannot believe they managed to ship over two hundred feet of it; it must have cost Lord Elgin an absolute fortune,' she replied.

The museum guide, who was accompanying them, gave her a patronising smile. 'The young lady need not concern herself with the vulgarities of money, as the British government now owns them,' he said.

Millie sucked in a breath and replied haughtily. 'And I expect since the government spent thirty-five thousand pounds on them, they will be staying in England permanently?'

The guide gave Mr Ashton a quick look, and he shook his head in response.

James whispered in Millie's ear. 'The man is only trying to do his job. Let him show us around for a little and then I shall pay him off. I am certain you know as much as he does about the marbles, but chances are the man has a family to keep.'

Millie nodded and gave the man a small apologetic smile.

'You were saying?' she said.

A carriage bearing the livery of the Duke of Strathmore stopped out the front of the British Museum in Great Russell Street and Alex and his brother Stephen got out.

'Remind me again why you are taking me to see the marbles when I have already seen them twice?' Stephen asked, as he hugged himself to keep warm in the bitter cold.

Alex sighed and rolled his eyes. 'Because, dear boy, you know all there is to know about these things, so I won't need the services of a museum guide,' he replied, waving his arm in the direction of the museum's front door.

'But I told you everything I knew at home and you memorised it; you never forget anything,' Stephen replied.

After arriving at Strathmore House following his ride in Hyde Park, Alex had roused his younger brother from his sleep and made him tell him everything he knew about the Elgin marbles. After a hasty breakfast he had bundled Stephen out of the house before anyone could enquire as to where they were going.

'I know, but Miss Ashton is here with her father and it would look odd for someone like me to be on my own at the museum at any time of the day, let alone at this hour. You, my boy, are the best excuse I could possibly have; what better way to impress a young lady than to show her how good a brother I can be?' Alex replied.

'You could have brought along David; Miss Ashton has already met him.'

The steely stare Alex shot his brother said it all.

Stephen stepped in close. 'Just so you are aware, I think Papa suspects something is amiss with you and David. Don't be surprised if he summons you both home and makes the two of you have it out. By the way, what is the problem?'

Alex put a friendly arm around his brother's shoulder. 'None of your business, imp. Now let's go inside, and just remember who will be paying your annual allowance in your old age. We wouldn't want you living in penury simply because you didn't help me to impress Miss Millicent Ashton, now would we?' he said.

The brothers exchanged a laugh, knowing full well that Alex could never refuse his youngest brother anything.

'Why do you want to impress her?' Stephen replied. The look on his face belonged to one who was yet to discover the delights of the opposite sex.

'Because I need to, and that is all you need to know,' Alex replied.

'Alright, but I want an onion pie and a hot chocolate after we have finished here. Actually, make that two pies, I'm very hungry,' Stephen replied with a grin.

'Done.'

&

Millie and her father had examined several large sections of the Parthenon Frieze before Mr Ashton finally gave the exasperated guide a large tip and sent him on his way.

'He has gone; happy now?' he said as the guide headed back to the front door.

'Thank you. It is hard to appreciate their beauty when someone is continually prattling on in your ear. Besides, it's a centaur, not a "man-horse",' she sniffed, pointing to a panel depicting a centaur and a Lapith in battle. Millie was very particular about the correct terminology when discussing matters of history and mythology.

Noting that the centaur was missing one of its arms, Millie wrinkled up her nose in disappointment. While Lord Elgin had claimed he wanted to preserve the marbles, it was common knowledge that in removing them from their original home, many pieces had sustained damage. Even if some day the British government gave the marbles back to their original owners, she doubted they would survive the long sea voyage. She pointed to a seated statute of a man which was missing its head. 'I thought marble was supposed to be white, like the Taj Mahal, but some of these are almost black.'

'It is dirt, Miss Ashton. You must remember the marbles were on the side of a Greek temple on top of a windswept mountain for over two thousand years,' a deep male voice murmured into her ear. She turned and was surprised to see Alex standing next to her. A smile found its way to her lips.

'Good morning, Lord Brooke,' she replied.

Alex gave her a bow. 'Good morning.' After shaking hands with Mr Ashton, he motioned for a young man to step forward.

'This is my brother, Lord Stephen Radley,' he said.

Millie looked at the young man and noted the strong resemblance to Alex. Lord Stephen gave a bow and then looked to his brother. Alex cleared his throat.

'As I was saying, the marbles date back to around four hundred BC, so one would expect them to have weathered somewhat over that time. But I am of the understanding some items were damaged during their journey here, especially the ones which went down with the brig *Mentor*; they spent nearly two years at the bottom of the sea.'

Millie's eyes widened with delight.

'I had no idea you were a man of the classics, Lord Brooke,' Mr Ashton replied. 'It is refreshing to meet a young man of your status who takes an interest in the ancient world.'

Alex gave a nod of his head. 'I feel it is important to obtain such knowledge and pass it on to young, impressionable minds.' He glanced in his brother's direction, as Lord Stephen let out a snort.

Lord Stephen scrambled around in his coat pocket, took out a handkerchief, and made a great effort to convince everyone present that he had a cold. Alex scowled at him before continuing. 'I see you do not have the services of a guide. I would be most honoured if you would allow me to accompany you around the room and enlighten you further on the history of the items on display.'

Millie looked to her father, who had an odd, almost bemused look on his face. 'Of course, Lord Brooke; never let it be said that I stood in the way of my daughter's enlightenment. And your brother's education is of paramount importance.'

Millie looked at Alex and as she beheld his magnetic eyes, she sensed a flash of heat coursing down her spine.

'May I?' Alex said as he offered Millie his arm. She stared at it for a moment as she caught her breath, then looked to her father, who nodded his approval. As she took his arm, the heat in her body continued to rise. If she hadn't known better, she would have sworn she was back in the steamy heat of Calcutta.

They continued around the room, but with the museum now officially open, the number of visitors steadily rose and obtaining a clear view of the marbles became difficult. Alex sensed an opportunity. 'It's a touch crowded in here. If I may suggest, perhaps Lord Stephen could accompany Mr Ashton around the left side of the room. He should remember most things I have taught him. At the same time, I shall walk with Miss Ashton toward the right. We can meet up in the middle at the East Pediment statues.'

Millie looked at her father.

Please, Papa. Please say yes.

He smiled and nodded. 'Of course, that makes perfect sense.'

She swallowed deeply, relieved to know her message had got through.

'Excellent,' Alex replied.

Making their way through the crowd, Millie noticed several other patrons looking at Alex and then at her. One society matron whispered to her companion as they passed by. 'Who is that girl? I have never seen Lord Brooke walking with a young lady before. The Marquess seems rather pleased with himself.'

Millie continued to stare over her shoulder at the women as they walked away.

'Here we are; something we can actually see,' Alex said, coming to a halt in front of a large marble head of a horse. Millie swung her head back toward Alex, but not quickly enough to see that he had stopped. She took one step past him, before he pulled her back close to him.

He placed a large, warm hand on her waist where it lingered for eternity. She looked up at his face and received another of his dashing smiles.

'Oh,' Millie sighed, unable to form a more eloquent response.

Alex chuckled. 'One day I will learn not to stop suddenly when I am with you. But I think this time I may not be the one at fault. Why were you staring at those women?'

Millie's cheeks flushed a deep red, while she silently prayed he had not heard them. 'I...I thought I had met them at a gathering earlier in the week, but I must have been mistaken,' she lied.

He raised one eyebrow for a moment, before nodding his head. 'Yes, of course'.

'The Selene Horse,' she said, looking past Alex. 'The detail on its facial features is quite magnificent. Papa and I stopped and looked at it when we first arrived. I think it might be my favourite piece of the entire collection.'

He reached out and rubbed his fingers under the horse's jaw.

'Not very responsive, this one; I think we have been sold a marble nag.'

Millie smiled and shook her head. 'Let us see how responsive you are when you are two thousand years old and have had your head chopped off.'

They grinned silently at each other.

Millie looked back to the horse. 'Though I still think it is sad that this is the final home of such a wonderful piece of antiquity.'

'You don't agree that the marbles should be in England?' Alex replied.

She clenched her reticule tightly in her hands and bravely muttered. 'No.'

Alex nodded. 'Good for you, Millie; I admire anyone who holds their own opinion on the matter. For myself, I think hacking the marbles off the walls in Athens was cultural vandalism of the lowest kind,' he said. 'And that Elgin nearly bankrupted his estate to do it shows a callous disregard for the wellbeing of his tenants and heirs.'

Millie twisted her reticule into a tight knot. Finally, someone else in London agreed with her opinion on the marbles. Her mouth opened in an O of surprise.

'You thought someone like me would naturally condone Elgin's actions? Rest assured, I spoke long and hard against keeping them in England. The Ottoman Empire has ruled Greece for hundreds of years and the Turks have never felt the need to destroy the ancient temples, so I don't see why an English earl should.'

Everything he said made perfect sense to her. To find that they agreed on such a controversial topic was a surprise. He took hold of her hand and gave it a gentle squeeze. When their gazes met, Millie was left in no doubt as to the peril which she now faced. She was hopelessly, irrevocably in love with Alex Radley and there was nothing she could do to save her heart.

When they re-joined her father and Lord Stephen, Alex regaled them with his impressive knowledge of the myths and gods of ancient Greece. As he spoke, other patrons and guides began to mill around him and finally Millie found herself part of a large, enthralled crowd. Watching the Marquess of Brooke holding court in the middle of the museum, she smiled proudly at him. He truly was Alexander the Great.

She barely remembered parting with Alex and his brother on the steps of Montagu House, and sat quietly in the carriage for the short ride home. Her mind's eye was filled with the image of a smiling Alex, while the words of the society matrons repeated themselves over and over in her head.

The Marquess seems rather pleased with himself.

As her father helped her down from the carriage, he gave her a knowing smile and kissed her on the forehead. She was in love with Alex; of course, her father could sense it.

Chapter Ten

On the evening of the Earl and Countess of Shale's Easter ball, Millie sat before her dressing table mirror and stared at her own reflection. She looked just as she had for the past few months, but something inside her had changed.

She smiled, remembering how Alex had tried to make good on his promise to give her a dance lesson. That hour, spent laughing with him as he invented new and outrageous fables to paint on to the ballroom ceiling had done little to improve her dancing skills.

'I shall just have to ensure I am in the ladies' withdrawing room when they play the waltz,' she consoled herself. It would not do to make a poor impression at the Easter ball.

Millie waited until her maid had finished with her hair before standing and walking over to examine herself in the cheval mirror which a footman had placed in the middle of her bedroom.

She stood with her hands held in a ladylike manner in front of her and then, with a coy smile on her face, she practised her curtsy. A young lady should always behave as if she were a little shy and unsure, her mother had instructed her. It gave the appearance of not being too forward.

'Or of having any intelligence,' Millie whispered into the mirror.

She turned and faced side-on to the mirror and her heart sank. Her hair was perfect, her pale silver gown made by one of the best modistes in London, but none of it could hide the curves which set her apart from the other young ladies.

She screwed up her nose in disappointment.

'If I may suggest, a spot of walking each day would soon have those pounds falling off you, Miss Millie,' Grace said, as she knelt down to straighten the hem of Millie's gown.

'You are right, Grace. Later this week you and I shall start going for walks around the nearby streets and some of the shops,' Millie replied.

She saw the look of disappointment on Grace's face. Her maid had clearly not counted on being dragged around London as her mistress tried to rid herself of her extra padding. 'That will teach you for coming up with such good ideas,' Millie teased. 'Besides, since Mama slipped on the ice in the rear court earlier today and is under doctor's orders to rest her ankle for a whole week, she will not be able to come walking or shopping with me. But you may choose the footman who accompanies us if you like. I am sure a suitable one will come quickly to mind.'

Grace gave a secret smile and the deal was sealed.

Just after nine o'clock, Charles helped Millie down from the family carriage outside the Earl of Shale's townhouse in Duke Street. The path out the front of the house had been cleared of snow, allowing the guests to alight from their conveyances without getting their footwear damp.

The dozen or so of the household staff who formed an honour guard up the front steps were decked out in black livery with gold helmets giving them the appearance of Roman Centurions. The four huge fire cages which burned fiercely either side of the front door helped to set the scene for Lord and Lady Shale's Ides of March-themed party. The guests of course were expected to overlook the fact that the party was too late for Caesar and just a touch too early for the Last Supper

At the top of the stairs they were handed a cup of hot honey mead. Standing sipping the warm liquor as the other guests milled around them, Charles and Millie exchanged a look of delighted expectation. The smoke from the fires whirled around in the night wind and the enticing scent of burning birch tree reached her nose. Inside her slippers, she wriggled her toes with excitement.

This was the kind of party and glamour she had been promised for so long. With any luck, she would have lots of wonderful stories to tell her bedridden mother in the morning. 'I can't believe this is the first party you and I have ever been to on our own. I know it is wrong of me, but I am glad Papa cried off to stay at home with Mama. Look at how amazing the outside decorations are; I do hope the inside is just as good,' she exclaimed.

Charles gave her a nod of his head. 'They are splendid, but I do think the centurions are rather relieved not to be wearing togas or sandals.' She looked at the nearest centurion and saw that his teeth were chattering. She and Charles exchanged a pained look. 'Poor chap; I do hope they have a large pot of coffee waiting downstairs for him,' Charles said.

Once inside, they were greeted by their host, who was dressed as Caesar, with the obligatory knife marks cut into the toga he wore over his evening clothes. He motioned them towards the ballroom, where they found Lady Shale splendidly reposed on a couch situated on a raised dais at the far end of the room.

She was playing the role of a heavily pregnant Cleopatra to the hilt. Every so often she would pull out a wooden toy snake and pretend to let it bite her. Her court of guests would let out a gasp of horror and beg her not to do it, and then roar with laughter at the end of her overly dramatic death scene.

'I wonder how many times she is going to die tonight?' a familiar voice spoke behind them. They turned to see a beaming Alex standing behind them, resplendent in formal black evening dress. After he and Charles had shaken hands, he took hold of Millie's hand and planted a kiss on her glove. He bowed and Millie felt her face begin to burn red as she returned his greeting with a curtsy.

As she rose, and their eyes met, she tried to give him her well-rehearsed coy smile, but found herself laughing when she saw him raise one eyebrow. The afternoon spent laughing as they danced around the Strathmore ballroom had formed a bond they now found hard to disguise.

'Well done, Miss Ashton, you shall make an excellent London debut this season,' Alex said, with a wicked glint in his eye. 'You shall surely impress all the pompous arses.'

Millie's eyes grew wide with horror and she glared at Charles. 'You didn't?'

Charles sighed, clearly disgusted with himself.

'He did. I beat him yet again this morning when we raced our steeds in Hyde Park. Every time we race, the loser has to confess to something embarrassing that they have done; your little swearing game was today's revelation,' Alex replied.

To alleviate the boredom on the long sea voyage, the Ashton siblings had devised the swearing game. This involved attempting to drop profanities into polite conversation without getting caught. The more profane the word the higher the point score. She imagined how embarrassed her brother would have been to admit to such a childish game.

'Bloody brilliant, if you ask me,' Alex said.

Charles turned to his sister. 'There is to be no point-scoring tonight, Millie; this is our first time out without Mama and Papa and you don't want people to take note of your untamed tongue. If Mama finds out you have been engaging in discussions of bloody battles, you will not be allowed out of the house for a fortnight. Brooke, I would ask that you don't encourage my sister to play a childish game which was devised out of sheer boredom. I am beginning to regret ever having told you.'

Millie sighed, knowing his words were no idle threat. Violet Ashton had of late started clamping down on her daughter's more unsavoury habits. It had already cost Millie a new hat and gloves in Harding, Howell & Co when her mother overheard her singing a rough sea shanty in the haberdashery section. No amount of pleading had worked and she had been banished to her room once they got home. Only her mother's desire to nurture the friendship between Millie and Lady Lucy saw Millie being allowed out later that day to visit Strathmore House.

'Yes Charles, I promise to be on my best behaviour and remain as near-invisible as I possibly can,' she replied.

'Except, of course, when you are dancing with me,' added Alex, in an obvious attempt to cheer her up. 'Then I expect the whole gathering to be watching and wondering who is the magnificent dancer they have in their midst.' He gave her one of his dazzling smiles and she smiled back at him, knowing that when she was with him, she could not stay sad for long.

'Modest, aren't you, thinking everyone will be staring at you?' she replied.

He laughed heartily and, taking hold of her hand, pulled her one step closer to him. Charles noisily cleared his throat, clearly displeased at the way Alex was manhandling his sister. Millie shot her brother a sharp look.

'May I remind you, Brooke, that we are in a public place, so I suggest you let go of my sister's hand, this instant,' Charles said. The threat might have been delivered politely, but Millie could see a familiar grey shadow pass over her brother's eyes. She attempted to move away, sensing Alex was in more danger than he realised, but he held firmly on to her.

'I was just making sure your sister has her dance card with her so I may add my name. That is of course if there are any dances still left to claim,' Alex replied, with all the charm of one used to getting his own way.

'Yes, well, you can mark her card from a tad further back if you don't mind, Brooke,' Charles bit back. Millie glared at him once more. To her mind, he was taking his role of chaperon for the evening far too seriously.

'Now, dear sister, will you please hurry up and offer your dance card so Lord Brooke can choose his dances. Then I shall help you to locate Lady Lucy'.

Remembering her promise to spend the evening with Alex's sister, Millie replied, 'Yes of course, dear brother.'

Alex let go of her hand and, reaching down, took hold of the ribbon of Millie's card. He examined the gold picture of the Sphinx on the front and then opened the card. From his evening jacket pocket, he withdrew a small pencil and offered it to her.

'Will you mark the dances I may have this evening, Miss Ashton?' he asked.

Her stomach fluttered with excitement. He wanted to dance with her in public.

'Since one could hardly call the travesty of a dance lesson I gave you last week as being sufficient to extinguish my debt for leaving you in the lurch at your uncle's party, I think it only fair I made amends in public.'

Her stomach sank. He was her best friend's brother and he was being kind. He would dance with her because he felt an obligation.

Oh well, it was nice while it lasted.

She would lock that moment of fantasy away with all the other ones she had created over the previous weeks. They were hers to replay in her mind when she lay awake in her bed at night. Her favourite one always ended with him telling her he loved her, and then taking her mouth with his in a fierce kiss.

If only he knew. Perhaps he did, and that was why he was so sweet to her. She knew he had hurt other friends of Lucy's, but perhaps because he knew she accepted things as they were, he felt no need to cause her pain. Fantasies were private and safe, she thought, and no one got hurt in them; well, only a little.

A bashful smile found its way to her lips. It was a nice touch, so typical of Alex at his best, that he was giving her the choice of dances.

'Make sure you include a waltz, I want to show everyone just how well we move together on the dance floor,' he added. His eyes sparkled with mischief.

'Lord Brooke, I doubt if you and I managed a full turn of the ballroom that afternoon, but since you are so insistent, may I suggest you place your name next to a waltz and then perhaps choose another dance?' she replied.

He stared at the card and she saw his brow furrow as he read the order of the evening. Then he sighed and offered her the pencil once more. 'I cannot choose; if I do I am sure I will get it wrong. Let's do it together, you choose the waltz and I shall choose the other one.'

Millie ran her finger down the list. She stopped at the first waltz and as she placed her finger on it, Alex took the pencil and placed a small tick on the line next to the dance.

He spent the next minute or so running his finger up and down the list, always going back to the one dance he had already marked. Then he placed a small line under the W in every other waltz.

"Just making sure I chose only one waltz," Alex noted.

He took an inordinate amount of time choosing the next dance. Each time he placed his finger on a dance he would look up at her. When he finally pointed to a quadrille and she smiled, he placed a tick next to it on the card.

For someone who was dancing with her out of a sense of obligation, he was certainly trying not to make it appear so. Alex was not only being kind, he was being thoughtful. She was doubly cursed.

'There you are; I have been wondering where you were,' Lucy called out to them as she managed to fight her way through the growing party crowd. Millie gave her a wave.

Out of the corner of her eye she saw Alex tuck the pencil back into his jacket pocket. She could have easily asked to borrow the pencil in case other gentlemen wanted to dance with her, but she didn't.

'Sorry we were late arriving; Mama insisted on reading me the riot act before we left,' Millie replied.

Lucy's eyes opened wide. 'So, you are here on your own; how thoroughly convenient. Our parents have also cried off, but I am pleased to say I did not have to push my poor dear mother down the front steps in order to do it.' Alex's eyebrows lifted in surprise and Millie shook her head as she gave Lucy a look of mock indignation.

'Our mother had a fall on some ice outside the house and has injured her ankle; I was nowhere near her when it happened, and it was in the rear yard,' she explained.

'I do hope she will make a full recovery; please send her my very best regards,' he replied. She looked at him, noting that he had an uncanny ability to change his behaviour to suit the moment. One minute he would be the fun-loving rascal known to his friends as Alex; the next he became the serious and very formal Lord Brooke. She had to admit that it was an admirable skill and one which she knew she sadly lacked.

With Millie Ashton, what you saw was pretty well what you got; as a result, she knew there would always be people within London society who would not accept her.

'Have you marked Miss Ashton's dance card yet, Alex?' Lucy asked. Her brother gave her a strange little smile and nodded.

'Good; then I can ask Mr Ashton to mark my card,' she replied and stepping up to Millie's brother, she boldly handed him her card and a pencil.

'Two please, if you will, Mr Ashton,' she said with a cheeky grin on her face. Charles gave her a bow and marked his name against the same two dances that Millie and Alex had chosen to share.

'There now all four of us shall be on the dance floor at the same time. Does that suit you, Lady Lucy?' Charles replied.

She gave him a gentle touch on the back of his hand and nodded her head regally. 'Excellent, thank you, Mr Ashton,' Lucy replied.

Charles laughed and looked at Millie. 'You two are so alike, it borders on witchcraft.'

Millie smiled and nodded her head. She knew exactly what he meant. She and Lucy would always be skirting around the edges of propriety. Often close to going over the edge, but somehow managing to pull back at the very last minute.

Lucy clapped her hands together and turned to Millie.

'Well, that was a good start. Now, if you can just get your brother to mark your card for one of the more boring dances, I shall do the same with Alex and David and then we will only have to find a couple of other young gentlemen who are prepared to offer us a dance, and our cards will be filled for the evening.'

Alex and Charles shared an uncomfortable look, after which Alex cleared his throat. 'About other gentlemen dancing with you, Lucy; remember what father said before we left. Either David or I have to approve any dance partners before they are allowed to put their names on your card. I expect Mr and Mrs Ashton also asked Charles to agree to any prospective dance partners for Miss Ashton.'

Lucy let out a tsk of annoyance, but held her tongue. Millie nodded her acceptance of the rules before Charles had the chance to add his piece.

'Good, then let the evening begin.' Lucy took hold of Millie's arm and dragged her off toward the largest group of party guests. Millie barely had time to wave goodbye to her brother and Alex before they disappeared behind a throng of people. She glanced at Lucy who had a huge grin plastered across her face.

'This is wonderful; none of our parents are here and all you and I have to do is make sure we avoid our respective brothers for as much of the night as we can. We are going to have a fabulous time.'

'So why didn't your parents come to the party?' Millie asked as they made their way toward Cleopatra's raised dais.

Lucy stopped and let out a giggle. After looking around to make sure no one else was within earshot, she replied, 'Mama and Papa had a huge fight an hour before we were all due to leave. Mama called him a thick-headed fool, as a result of which Papa refused to go to the party with her. Then she got angry and told him he could not leave her to go on her own.' Lucy sighed, but Millie saw a sparkle appear in her eye.

'Well, then Mama stormed off into her private sitting room, while Papa went to his study. Five minutes later he came out of his study and I heard the door of the sitting room open and close. At which point both Alex and David said we were leaving and made me get into the carriage.'

'So, your parents are at home having a blazing row? Millie asked.

Lucy gave her a knowing smile. 'No, they are at home making up after their argument, and knowing my parents, will be "making up" for the rest of the evening.'

Millie's mouth opened in a small O and then she closed it on a titter. 'I see. What on earth were they arguing about?' she asked.

'Scotland,' replied Lucy, who, having lost interest in the sexual exploits of her parents began to busily scan the room in search of eligible young men.

§

After several early dances, the gloss had begun to wear off the evening. Lucy had worn new slippers which pinched her toes and caused small blisters to appear on the sides of her feet. She hobbled over to a chair and toed the offending slippers off her feet. Millie took a seat next to her.

'Oh, that is so much better. There is no way I can get through the rest of the dances this evening. Especially now that I have taken these horrid slippers off, I can feel my feet beginning to swell,' Lucy complained.

'You could go in bare feet, but somehow I think that might be taking the whole Roman theme to an extreme,' Millie offered. Lucy sadly shook her head. There would be no more dancing for her this evening.

'I think the next dance is the first waltz. Shame about that, I shall have to stand your poor brother up,' Lucy replied. 'I hope he won't mind, but there is no way I can glide around the floor in these things.'

'I am sure Charles won't mind, I don't think he is all that enamoured with dancing. Besides, your feet have suffered enough for one evening; you don't need him stepping all over your toes with his big heavy feet.'

Lucy looked up and Millie saw a look of pain cross her face as Alex as he approached. 'You are not still upset with him over his row with David, are you?' Millie asked. Lucy shook her head. 'Since I don't know what their ongoing argument is about, I cannot hold either one of them to blame. But that is not what bothers me.'

She turned to Millie and took her by the hand.

'All I will say before Alex joins us is that you should take care with your heart, Millie. I should so hate to see you hurt.'

Alex arrived a moment later, sporting a large grin. He held out his hand to Millie and drew her to her feet.

'The first waltz is about to commence, and I believe my name is marked on your dance card, Miss Ashton.' He gave a brief, pleasant nod to his sister, noted her lack of footwear and turned back to Millie. 'Shall we?' he said.

She smiled as he gave her a bow, her second for the night. She curtsied once more.

'You really have got that deep curtsy perfected, Miss Ashton; it is worthy of a grand duchess,' he said.

She laughed. 'Practice, Lord Brooke, practice.'

He led her away towards the dance floor. 'Do you think we should have stayed with Lucy, or at least gone to find Charles?' Millie asked, concerned about leaving Lucy sitting alone.

He sighed and shook his head. 'No, she will be fine. She worries every time I dance with one of her friends, but rest assured, you have nothing to fear.'

As soon as the music began, Alex swept Millie into his arms and they began to move with grace and skill around the floor. She shook her head. How gullible had she been? Alex Radley was as light of foot and smooth a dancer as his sister.

His clumsy, awkward moves during their dance lesson had been an act. She looked into his eyes and saw they were full of laughter.

'I never said I couldn't dance, Millie. I just wanted us to have some fun while you practised,' he whispered.

'I should stomp on your toes in punishment,' she replied.

'Just bloody well try.' He tightened his grip and began to twirl faster with the music. All Millie could do was to hold on and try to keep up with him.

'You are a devil, Lord Brooke, but I shall give you two points.'

'Only two?' he replied.

'Yes, you can only score the maximum five swearing points if you use it with other non-players. Sorry, those are the house rules and they are set in stone,' she replied with a grin. 'And tell me, what weakness have you had to admit, Lord Brooke?'

He shook his head. 'None, I haven't yet lost. I would rather risk breaking my neck than face humiliation. Your brother could summon the devil and I would still outride him.'

She raised her head and from the look on his face, she could tell he wasn't in jest. She silently wondered how he would cope if ever he were faced with failure. Would he be of resilient enough character to survive?

He spun her into another tight turn and pulled her close for a second. 'Loosen your grip and enjoy the dance, I promise I won't let you fall,' he breathed in her ear. She relaxed and allowed herself to trust him, while he held her tightly and kept his word. She felt as if she were small again and dancing with her father around the rooftop garden of their house in Calcutta. Knowing he would never let her go and that with him she would always be safe.

Finally, the music slowed and Alex pulled her through one last turn. Then, as the dance ended, Millie found herself right where she should be, in front of her partner and receiving his gracious thanks for allowing him the dance.

'Shall I return you to Lucy?' he said.

She managed a nod while a huge smile remained on her lips. She had never danced like that before in her life. He was strong and skilful as a dancer, but it was the way he held her that was so thrilling. Her whole body pulsated heat and her heart pounded in her chest.

'I had better go and see how she is faring with those sore feet,' Millie stammered. At that moment, Lucy was in fact the furthest thing from her mind. She was too busy lamenting the fact that the next dance she had saved for Alex was not a waltz.

They walked slowly back to where Lucy sat. As they approached, Millie could see her friend's face was still glum. 'I shall leave you two to talk,' Alex said and took his leave. He wandered off through the crowd, leaving Millie to stare after him. When Millie turned back to Lucy, she saw her friend's sad gaze was still fixed on her brother's back. A sudden realisation hit her.

'Lucy, there is nothing to worry about. Alex and I are merely friends, nothing more. I am not so foolish to entertain the notion that he could ever be interested in me romantically,' she said.

Lucy nodded. 'I hope so Millie, I sincerely do. I love my brother dearly, but there have been times when he has behaved poorly toward my friends. I would be utterly devastated to lose your friendship because of something Alex did.'

Millie gave Lucy a gentle kiss on the cheek. 'You won't lose me.'

She stood up and took a deep breath.

'Now I must visit the ladies' retiring room; that dance has made my face rather flushed and I should like to cool down with a wet towel. Would you like to come with me?' she asked.

'No,' Lucy replied. 'My feet still hurt, so I will rest here until we are ready to go and get some supper.' Her gaze fell upon on a young matron who approached them from the other side of the room. A big smile appeared on Lucy's face and she called out a friendly 'Hello' to the woman.

'It's all right, Millie, you can go. I see my cousin Eve is here and she is always good for the latest gossip. I will catch up with you later, and I can introduce the two of you properly. Don't let my silly choice in slippers spoil your evening. You should circulate and try to meet some new people.'

'Very well then, I shall see you in a little while,' Millie replied, and went in search of the retiring room. She spent the next half an hour or so resting while quietly listening to all the developing gossip in the ladies' room. One of the household maids applied a cold towel to Millie's face and tidied up her hair.

After returning to the party, Millie took time to mingle with the other guests, exchanging small talk with some of Lord Ashton's friends who remembered her from the gathering at Ashton House.

When she finally grew tired of relating how different she found England from India, she wandered away from the crowd and found a small alcove in which to sit quietly on her own. She decided to seek her mother's counsel the next morning. She did not wish to drive a wedge between the Radley siblings, both of whose friendships she valued.

She stood and began to walk towards the main ballroom, intending to find Charles and see how his evening was faring. As she neared the end of the hallway, she noticed two girls standing with their backs to her. They were deep in conversation and so did not hear her approach.

'He only danced with her because she is his sister's friend. The silly thing is a fool if she thinks he likes her for any other reason. You know I am right, Clarice; no sane Englishman could fall in love with a girl who has a sapphire stuck in her nose,' the tall thin one scoffed.

'Don't be unkind, Susan; I happen to think Miss Ashton's nose ring makes her look rather exotic. But you are right; the poor girl wouldn't be the first to think that Lady Lucy was the path to her brother's heart. If she does, I fear she is in for bitter disappointment. Remember last year when Lucy threatened to become the most popular girl on the social circuit, and all because of her brother,' Clarice replied.

Millie shifted to one side, closer to a nearby doorway. If the two girls turned around at this instant, they would see her standing behind them and know she had heard their every word. She recognised Clarice as the daughter of the Earl of Langham, whose family home was close to her own. Violet had known the late Countess of Langham and the two girls had been introduced when Violet and the Earl had exchanged greetings on the street one morning.

For a moment she pitied Lucy; was it any wonder she was so keen to claim Millie as her friend? Still, she felt a huge sense of relief in knowing she had not confided her secret tendre for Alex to Lucy. Other girls might have laughed off a friend's having a soft spot for their brother or perhaps think it sweet, but she knew it would devastate Lucy. The truth being that Lucy did have good reason to be wary of Millie and Alex's friendship. She shook her head; why did it all have to be so complicated?

'Then she went and turned down two excellent marriage proposals just to spite us all,' Susan added.

Millie put a hand over her mouth, and stifled a gasp. Lucy had made mention of her romantic failures the previous season, but to hear them discussed in such a public place distressed Millie.

'Well, you can hardly blame that on her two dreamy brothers,' replied Lady Clarice. After the initial shock of hearing Lucy's personal life critiqued by strangers, Millie quickly warmed to Lady Clarice; she at least appeared to have a modicum of decency, whereas her friend only seemed intent on tearing Lucy's down.

Susan let out a sigh of disgust. 'Yes, well, I don't know about the other one, that Mr Radley, but Lord Brooke still has to be the most eligible bachelor in the *ton*. If he ever put his name on my dance card, I tell you, I would have the card mounted and placed in a gilt frame.'

'And displayed on your front door?' Lady Clarice replied with a gentle laugh. 'Come on, enough talk about men who we will never marry; let us go and see if we can find something decent to eat at the supper table.'

As Lady Clarice and her friend moved away, Millie remained near the doorway and mulled over their conversation. She looked down at her own dance card and smiled at the two ticks Alex had placed on it. It was charming the way he had made her choose the dances and point them out on the card before he would make his mark.

'Well, you may think Lucy a jilt and me a fool, but I have had the pleasure of dancing with her brother twice and he marked my card as soon as I got here,' she muttered. Of course, tonight might be the last time she danced with him, but at least she would have her precious memories.

'Who marked your card?' asked a deep, sensual voice.

She turned and saw that Alex had crept up quietly beside her. It was a habit of his she found both thrilling and unsettling. He was so close she could smell his cologne, and in an instant, she was transported back to the spice markets in Calcutta. She took a deep breath and closed her eyes.

'You are wearing essence of bergamot, if I am not mistaken, Lord Brooke. I didn't notice it when we were dancing,' she replied.

'Am I now, Miss Ashton?' he murmured. 'When did we go back to being so formal?'

Millie smiled. Calling him by his title made her feel hot all over and the bodice of her gown became constricting.

'I like to call you Lord Brooke; it helps to keep a respectable distance between us,' she lied.

'Not the way you say it, it doesn't. Besides, I don't think we had anything like a respectable distance between us when I held you on the dance floor,' he teased.

Millie flashed her eyes at him.

'How can you say such an outrageous thing?'

He chuckled. 'I love it when you try to be all prim and proper.'

'Why?'

'Because you fail so badly at it.'

Millie took her dance card and began to use it a fan. She felt the heat burning in her cheeks and ears. This flirting would be harmless if she weren't so in love with him.

He took hold of her arm.

'Where are we going?' she asked.

'I thought we might go and see if we can find a cup of tea. I passed the supper table on the way here and it looked rather good; my cousin Bartholomew always puts on a decent spread. I saw Lucy busily piling a plate with food. She and our cousin Eve had their heads together, plotting something as usual, I expect. I am surprised you are not with them.'

'Lucy wanted me to form some new acquaintances. We were going to meet each other at supper,' Millie replied.

Alex nodded his head.

'We could stop and say hello to Lucy, have something to eat and then go and find Charles. I haven't seen him for most of the evening. I expect you still owe him a dance at some point,' he replied.

She wrinkled up her nose.

'Lemonade will do fine; I am not that interested in English tea. I have not had a decent cup since I got here. The long sea journey must spoil the good leaf and our cook has not been able to find anyone in London who stocks our favourite tea,' she said.

'Really? No one in the whole of London has a supply of delicious Calcutta chai? How very surprising. I shall have to tell the man I get mine from that he is a fraud and have him publicly unmasked,' Alex replied with a chuckle.

Millie grabbed hold of Alex's arm and let out a gasp. 'No! You cannot have found proper masala chai here, we have been looking for weeks and no one has it. Even Twinings on the Strand do not stock it.'

A wicked glint appeared in his eyes and a sly smile grew upon his lips.

'Are you game, Miss Ashton?'

She furrowed her brow. 'Game for what, Lord Brooke?'

He gave a quick furtive glance around them to see that no one else could hear him and he leaned in close.

'My house is not far from here. We could steal away and have a cup of my chai impostor tea, then be back here before anyone notices we are gone. I know it's a wicked idea, but trust me you will come to no harm. You have my word.'

Her breath caught in her throat. Had Lord Brooke, the most handsome and magnificent man in the whole of the *ton*, just asked her to run away with him? Of course, it was only for a cup of tea, not a moonlight flit to Gretna Green, but to her ears it might as well have been. She turned and stared at him for just a moment as she mulled over his illicit tea proposal. He raised his eyebrows in an effort to add weight to his argument; and when his grin turned into a sultry smile she knew she was a lost cause.

'How on earth are we going to get out of here without my brother knowing I am gone?' she asked, ever aware of the practicalities of a situation.

His smile turned into a smug grin. Alex was certainly gifted with all the right smiles.

'May I remind you that the Earl of Shale is a dear cousin of mine, so this is not the first time I have been to this house? I have been to countless parties and family gatherings here over the years, so trust me when I say I can get us out of here without us being seen.'

Millie's heart thumped loudly in her chest; the thought of heading out into the night with Alex was intoxicating. It was also scandalous and completely mad, but it would make the most brilliant addition to her collection of Alex Radley fantasies.

She took one step forward before the rational part of her brain reminded her that if they were caught, she would be ruined. She remembered the solemn promise she had made to her mother earlier in the evening: to behave as if her parents were with her at the ball. For the briefest of moments, her sensible side won her over and she decided to say no. But, as she opened her mouth to politely refuse his offer, she saw the smile disappear from his face. He had sensed her hesitation. He leaned in once more and whispered. 'I promise no one will ever find out. It's only a cup of tea; I will not attempt to ravish you.'

Millie looked away. She knew he was doing the right thing by confirming the innocent nature of their little adventure, but she found his supposed words of comfort surprisingly painful. If only he knew how she felt; how she would give her soul for him to take her in his arms.

Then her rational self spoke once more. What if they did get caught? He would be forced to marry her. Then what? He would spend the rest of his days hating her for it. Men like Lord Brooke did not choose to marry girls like her unless they were compelled.

On that thought, her mind was made up. Her reputation would be safe; he would make certain they were not seen. He had as much to lose as she did if they were discovered. He would be the laughing stock of the *ton* if he were forced to take her for his bride. What was it he had said about never allowing himself to be humiliated?

'All right, yes, but we will have to make it a quick cup of tea and then come straight back to the ball. When I last saw Charles, he was headed into one of the sitting rooms talking to a chap about a pair of horses the man had for sale, but we can't rely on him staying interested for too long,' she replied.

'Good girl; I knew you would do it,' Alex replied, and the smile returned to his face. 'You could go and retrieve your pelisse from the ladies' cloakroom maid but that might raise suspicions, so I shall borrow an extra coat from the gentlemen's cloakroom and meet you back here shortly. But you should try to stay out of sight just in case any of our respective siblings come wandering by. I won't be long.'

He disappeared back into the crowd and made his way towards the cloakroom, and Millie took a seat on a plush gold couch in the small alcove behind her. Since the alcove was set back, away from the ballroom, she was out of sight of most party guests. As long as no one came looking for her, she reasoned she stood a good chance of not being seen before Alex returned with the coats.

Sitting alone on the couch, she felt her heart beating heavily in her chest. Looking down at her hands, she saw they were shaking. She took a deep breath and attempted to calm herself. 'I can't believe I am doing this; I must be mad. What if we get caught?' she muttered to herself. She was seconds away from calling the whole thing off and going back to the party when Alex returned, carrying two coats in his arms.

'Try and bunch it up as small as you can,' he instructed her as he handed over the fine wool coat. 'Then no one will see it and think you are leaving the party. If your dancing slippers get wet now, you will have to forget to put your outside shoes on when you leave and blame it on the snow on the road out the front.'

She looked down at her silver slippers with their fine white tassels and silently bade them goodbye. As soon as she set foot outside she knew they would be ruined beyond repair.

'Now, when we get to the hallway, I will go first, to make sure we are not seen, and then you can follow,' he said.

Millie did as he asked and folded the coat into a tight little bundle. She hugged it to her chest and crossed her arms. With luck, anyone she might encounter between here and outside would think she was cold and carrying a wrap for comfort.

Avoiding the majority of guests at the party was a surprisingly easy task; Alex and Millie strolled together until they reached the end of a long hallway, along which a number of doors were situated at various intervals.

'Ready?' he said, as he took one last look around. 'Just watch where I go and then follow; if anyone comes out of those doors, just pretend you were looking for the cloakroom to hang your wrap. I shall wait for you outside.'

He turned and started to make his way down the long hallway to the side entrance of the house. At the end of the hall, he stopped and looked back, making sure she had seen the way he had gone. He held up his hand and beckoned for her to follow, then passed through the door and closed it quietly behind him. With the coat held tightly in her sweating hands, Millie started after him.

About midway down the hall was the door to the ladies retiring room. If she could make it past that door and not be seen, she had a clear run to the exit through which Alex had just disappeared.

She slowly blew all the air out of her cheeks as she began the long walk down the hallway toward the exit door, knowing that if she went through it, she could stamp this evening as one of the highlights of her life.

Fortunately, the hall runner was a deep, luxurious Persian carpet, which muffled her footsteps. Inevitably, as one foot followed the other, the distance between her and the door to adventure closed. She could hear the music from the ball and the sound of shuffling feet as those currently occupying the dance floor made their way through another waltz. Fortunately, her card was not marked for this dance, so no one would be looking for her. The next dance she had on her card would be with Alex, their second for the night. It was a pity it was not a waltz, but she had promised the last dance of the evening to her brother.

We had better be back well in time for that. Charles will be looking for me.

The door at the end of the hallway opened and Alex poked his head inside. He silently mouthed, 'Come on.'

She took one look at the door to the ladies' retiring room and saw to her horror that the handle had started to turn. Someone was coming. In a moment they would be out into the hallway and she would be seen. Alex looked at Millie as she took one last look at the opening door and knew it was now or never.

She picked up her skirts and ran to him.

Chapter Eleven

As soon as she had cleared the doorway and was outside, Alex closed the door behind them. She spun around and put her hand to her heart.

'That was close,' he said, as he checked the side path to make sure no one else was having a private moment out in the darkness.

'That was fun,' she laughed, her eyes full of light. 'I never get to go any faster than a slow walk anymore; it's not considered lady-like. In fact, any sort of amusement seems to be off limits to young ladies in this town. I would be sent to my room for a week, just for running, if my mother saw me. I dread to think what she would do if she found out I was here with you.'

He pointed to the coat, still in her hands. 'You might want to put that on; it is rather cold out here. It could be a touch difficult to explain a chill to your mother if all you have done tonight is to attend a party in a well-heated house.'

Millie unfurled the dark blue coat and allowed Alex to help her put it on. His hands rested gently on her shoulders as she quickly did the buttons up on the front. When he stepped in a little closer, she began to fumble with the double brass buttons at the top.

'Here, let me help you,' he offered, as he spun her around to face him. 'I have a couple of these and they are the devil to work with if you don't have a valet or mirror.' He made quick work of the buttons, but allowed himself the indulgence of standing a little closer to Millie than he should.

When he was finished he took hold of her hand. He made another quick check of their surroundings, making sure they were alone, before guiding her down the dark pathway which ran behind the house. As they cleared the path and came out into the next street, Alex looked both ways. With his careful vigilance, they would be back at the party in no time, and no one would be any the wiser.

Apart from a hack dropping off a couple of drunken old gentlemen into a nearby house, Bird Street was silent and empty. Alex laughed. He was having a wickedly fun time.

'Nearly there; that is my house,' he said as he pointed out a tall, thin building on the other side of the street. They crossed the road, avoiding patches of ice and snow as they went.

As they reached the top of the front steps and faced the door, he quickly withdrew a key. Millie raised an eyebrow.

'We utilise the staff from Strathmore House during the day, so most evenings the only servants left are Mr and Mrs Phillips. Granted, it is a little odd, but my brother and I like the privacy it affords us,' Alex explained. He unlocked the door and ushered her inside. As she stepped across the threshold of his elegant town-house, Alex gave her a bow and she smiled.

'Welcome to my humble abode, Miss Ashton,' he said.

She held her head in the air in a regal fashion as she gave the vestibule of his home a brief examination.

'Yes, it is rather humble isn't it?' she replied.

Before he could stop himself, Alex grabbed her by the waist and swung her around. She let out a squeal and he suddenly remembered who she was and where they were.

'Oh. Oh, I am so sorry, Millie,' he gasped as he let go and set her down. 'I'm so used to doing it to Lucy when she gives me cheek that I completely forgot who you were for a moment.'

He stood shaking his head in disbelief. Not only had he stolen his sister's best friend away from a house party, but he had managed to manhandle her within a minute of having her in his house. What sort of rogue had he become?

'Well, you did say you would not try to ravish me,' she replied, as she straightened her clothing. 'You did, however, fail to mention that you would attempt to wrestle me to the ground.'

Alex searched for words to express his regret, but he could only manage another pathetic 'Sorry.'

Millie held her hands up in surrender. 'I give up; just tell me what you want from me?'

'What?'

'I have met pirates and pickpockets, Lord Brooke; Calcutta is full of them, but I have never been so openly assaulted for my treasures. Just tell me what you want and I shall hand it over. My gloves? Or my shoes perhaps, though they are a bit wet. I don't actually have much else on my person that is worth taking.'

He stared at her, unable to respond. Knowing that whatever he said at that moment, it would come out all wrong. Then, to his immense relief, she laughed and shook her head.

'It's all right Alex, I was only joking. I know you meant me no harm; besides, my slippers would never fit you.'

A gush of relief escaped his lips and he closed his eyes. Apart from his sister, he had met few young women with a real sense of humour. A little strange though hers may be, Millie at least had the ability to laugh in an awkward situation.

'Have you really met a pirate?' he asked, intrigued.

She nodded her head. 'Yes, and he stole my gold bracelet, the swine.'

A rush of anger coursed through Alex's body. Wherever the pirate was now, he had better be dead. He felt a sudden and overwhelming need to leap on to the nearest ship and sail the seas to hunt down the brute who had taken Millie's bracelet.

'What did your father do? Did he have him flogged?' he asked as he fought to control his rage.

Her face turned bright red and her eyes widened with horror. She grabbed hold of his arm and pulled him close. 'You must never mention it to my father; he would kill me. Please Alex, swear you will never speak a word of this to anyone. Ever,' she pleaded.

'Why not?' he asked, sensing there was more to the tale than she had told him.

She screwed her eyes shut and confessed. 'You can never tell anyone, because I lost the bracelet in a game of cards. If my parents or brother ever found out it would be very bad for several of our current household servants. It was not their fault; they tried to prevent me, but I was too stubborn and stupid to listen. Believe me, I learnt my lesson and never went to a dockside tavern ever again.'

Alex nodded his agreement and she let go of his arm.

'Now, can we please have that cup of tea before someone notices we are missing?' she said.

Alex pointed toward an open door across the entrance. 'The kitchen is downstairs through there.'

Millie followed behind as he stepped into the small kitchen. He quickly checked the stove. Fortunately, Mrs Phillips had remembered to add an extra log to the fire and so the water in the pot on the stovetop was hot.

'The Phillipses will have already retired for the night, but thankfully they left us with hot water. We should have tea in no time,' he announced. He turned to see Millie removing her gloves and taking a seat at the wooden kitchen table.

'David and I normally eat in here or in our rooms. We don't use the dining room that much as we don't have the need for it. If we want to entertain friends, we go out to our club. Otherwise we dine with the family at Strathmore House,' he said.

She smiled at him. 'I spend half my life downstairs at home; our cook has been with the family since I was born so she knows exactly what I like to eat. She can tell from the look on my face what sort of mood I am in and what food will make me happy.'

Alex turned back to the stove and after locating the tea canister, he took it down from the shelf and brought it over to her. He lifted the lid and waved the tin under Millie's nose. 'Marsala chai, Miss Ashton,' he announced with a certain degree of smugness.

Her eyes lit up with delight and she eagerly took hold of the canister. She held one finger up to signal that she had yet to judge his offering. Then she put her face over the opening of the tin and took a deep breath. She sat back in the chair, still clutching the tea canister and closed her eyes.

'Oh Alex, you have no idea what that aroma does to me and how much it reminds me of home,' she murmured. 'I had forgotten how wonderful it feels when the sharp edge of the tea finds its way to the back of your throat. I have missed it so much.'

She might have been passing judgement on his tea, but Alex only heard the first two words she said. He quickly turned back to the cupboards and after taking several deep breaths, he began to search for the teapot. He located it in a far corner of the kitchen bench and filled it with hot water before placing it in the middle of the table. He took a seat in the chair opposite Millie. 'We shall have to make do without the pot being warmed. May I have the tea now, Miss Ashton? It will need some time to steep.'

Her eyes opened and she looked first to him and then to the white china teapot. She sat up and removed the lid from the pot. With a careful move of her hand she reached into the tea canister and drew out a handful of black tea.

'Exactly five minutes before you pour the first cup and not a moment sooner, Lord Brooke,' she announced with great authority, and placed the tea in the teapot. 'That should give you time enough to find some biscuits. You must have a large store of them hidden away for all the girls you invite here to partake of tea,' she teased. She placed the lid back on the teapot.

Alex laughed.

Oh Millie, if only you knew what your eyes do to me, and your lips.

'The only "girl" who gets to drink tea here is Mrs Phillips and she is rather partial to a ginger stem biscuit. Many a time I have had to fight her for the last one,' he quipped as he headed to the doorway.

'Lately I have taken to hiding a spare packet from Fortnum and Mason in my room; back in a minute.' He walked across the front entrance and upstairs into his bedroom.

Once inside his room, he took the opportunity to catch his

breath. Would it always be like this with her? He shook his head, unable to understand why this girl had such an effect on him. He had danced with a number of beautiful girls at the party, using the occasion to see if he could force himself to fall in love with them. But only she could bring a secret smile to his lips.

'Have you found them?' Millie's voice drifted up from downstairs.

'Still looking,' he lied.

'Need a hand?'

A sultry smile found its way to his lips. 'Not tonight, my love, but soon,' he chuckled.

He soon found the biscuits, still wrapped in their paper at the back of the wardrobe. He laughed at the notion of having to hide food from the servants, especially when Mrs Phillips usually did the shopping. She could have simply bought extra biscuits each week, but of course that would have taken the fun out of making her search high and low for the hidden treasure.

'Well, I shall have to find a new hiding spot for the next lot,' he murmured as he noticed that several biscuits were missing from what should have been a full packet. 'You are good, Mrs Phillips, I will give you that.' He broke off part of a biscuit and stuffed the golden, crunchy morsel in his mouth.

'Here they are,' he said, stepping back into the kitchen and placing the biscuits on the table.

Millie opened the already raided packet, saw the broken biscuit and shook her head. He wiped a stray crumb from the corner of his mouth. She took two biscuits out and handed the broken one to him. They shared a happy smile, while Alex secretly wished time would stop and they could spend eternity just enjoying this simple moment together.

'Tea?' she asked.

Alex the love-struck fool nodded.

She poured them both a cup and they sat in silence, sipping the dark flavoursome brew as the aroma of far-off India filled the small room.

'Alex?' Millie said a few moments later as she swirled the last of her tea leaves around the bottom of her cup.

'Millie,' he replied.

'May I ask you about David?'

'Just as long as it is not about why he and I aren't on speaking terms,' he replied.

'Actually, I meant about his status within your family.'

He nodded his head; he had been wondering when that particular subject would be broached.

'You mean how is it that he is older than me and yet I am my father's heir?' he replied.

'Yes, if it is not too personal or painful. If it is, I am sorry to have asked and I won't mention it again,' she replied.

Alex slurped his tea. 'This is really good, you know; I had not thought to put spice into my tea, but since I started drinking chai of late, I find I can barely stomach the normal English stuff. Anyway, you wanted to know about David.'

He put the cup down and sat with his hands softly clasped together on the table as he explained the circumstances of David's birth: how David's mother had been engaged to their father and how after having consummated their relationship, she had inexplicably called off the engagement and run away.

His father and his former fiancée's sister had searched for her for months, unaware that she was pregnant, and when they finally received word of her whereabouts they had raced to Manchester, only to discover she had tragically died in childbirth.

'My father and aunt took David home, raised him, and somewhere along the way they fell in love and married. Then I came along, then Lucy, Stephen and Emma. So, you see, David is both my half-brother and my cousin if you wish to go into the detail.'

He picked up the teapot and poured some more tea into both of their cups, quietly musing over the fact that Millie had asked him about David when she would have had ample opportunity over the past weeks to pose the same question to Lucy. For some unknown reason she was more comfortable asking him that delicate question. He liked that Millie trusted him.

'Anyway, he carries my father's name and will inherit his own estate when the time comes, though I think father will pass something on to him before then. Hopefully a solid fortune in his pocket will somewhat help to overcome the circumstances of his birth. So that's all there is to tell; he is my brother and always has been.'

'But not at the top of your most popular relative list at present?' Millie replied.

'No.'

He was not about to go into the how and why of the dispute with anyone; especially not with Millie. He let out a sigh and drained his cup. 'We had better get back. It must be nearly time for our next dance. If we don't, Lucy and Charles will be certain to notice our absence.'

He started out the kitchen door, and Millie followed him. As she reached the entrance, she stopped and quickly raced back downstairs into the kitchen. Alex followed her and, in the doorway, they collided as she returned.

'Ooh,' she cried as her head hit his chest.

She took a step back and held up her evening gloves. 'Mustn't forget these, otherwise we would both have a lot to explain.'

As she started to put her gloves back on, Alex took hold of her hands and stopped her. He slowly pulled off the glove she had placed on her left hand and after taking the other glove he put them both into his coat pocket. He took her hands in his. With his hands placed over hers, his signet ring with the Strathmore family crest formed a crown at the top. The gold horse and stars set in black onyx a representation of the wealth and power his family wielded. They both stood and stared at the ring.

Neither of them spoke.

He raised her hands to his lips and placed a tender kiss on the end of her fingertips. She shuddered and he felt her fingers tremble. As she lifted her head, he waited for the moment when their eyes would meet.

When they did, he found himself staring into two magnificent deep blue gems. Framed by long, dark black lashes, Millie's eyes drew him inexorably in. He cupped his hand under her chin, bent his head and placed a tentative kiss on her lips.

He felt the soft warmth of her lips in the brief moment that his touched hers. His heart pounded strongly in his chest. He had kissed his fair share of women before, but never had his heart been involved. This was a new and heady experience, for which he had waited his whole life.

He pulled away, just enough to break the bond and, seeing that she had her eyes closed, decided to risk a second kiss. This time, as he took her lips, he concentrated all his efforts on remembering the rules of kissing a young miss.

First, find a willing girl. He gave his imaginary checklist a tick. He appeared to have that sorted. Then find somewhere where you won't be disturbed; these things required patience and absolute attention. Besides, if you got caught with the wrong girl, you might find yourself before her angry father, followed swiftly by a march up the aisle. Discretion was of the utmost importance.

He was pleased that they were alone for their first kiss and unlikely to be disturbed. To woo Millie properly would take time. He had to be certain he had won her heart before he offered for her.

The spectre of her desire to return to India still loomed over him. She had to want to stay with him in England, not be forced by circumstance or have pressure brought to bear by others. If they were discovered and forced to marry, she would never forgive him. Life would be impossible for him if Millie became his wife and she regretted their marriage.

He had to win her, heart and soul. By kissing her now, he was making his intent clear. From this moment on he would begin his campaign and court her openly. A visit to her father would be the first thing in order for tomorrow morning.

He deepened the kiss, placing more pressure on her lips. When her lips parted slightly, he took her top lip and kissed it. She moaned. His whole body hardened. Then, emboldened by her response, he speared his hand into her hair, pulling her closer to him.

She let out a gasp of surprise as he took her mouth more fiercely.

His body began to wrestle with his mind for control of the encounter. This was so much more than anything he had ever experienced before.

His tongue swept past her lips and into her mouth. He felt Millie's hands on his chest and he steeled himself for the moment when she pushed him away. But, to his immense relief, she took hold of the lapels of his coat and pulled him in closer. He groaned.

She wants this as much as I do, thank god.

Her response was just as he had always hoped it would be; she held nothing back as she gave her mouth up to him. Holding tightly on to his coat, her lips soft and pliant, she demanded everything he could give.

His right hand drifted down to her hip and settled on the curve which had filled his dreams for so many nights. His mind and body fought with one another as he struggled not to step forward and press himself hard against her. If he did there would be no mistaking the rock-hard erection that was throbbing beneath his coat.

She was an innocent. He knew if she suspected she was in any real danger from him, the evening would end badly and his campaign to win her would have suffered a major setback.

The time would come that she would understand what happened between a man and a woman, but that was not now. That moment would be planned down to the last intimate and minute detail. She would have willingly accepted his marriage proposal and an engagement ring would be sparkling on her hand when he first took her to his bed.

The clock in the front hall chimed.

They slowly drew apart. Millie brought a finger to her swollen, red lips. The stamp of his passion was there for all to see. Alex reached into his pocket and handed Millie her gloves. She smiled and with obvious effort put them on.

'I love you,' he said.

She shook her head. 'No, you don't,' she whispered. She took a step back.

The moment was over.

His heart sank. She didn't take him seriously. He could see that to her mind, she was just another of his sister's friends he had toyed with, just one more. All those stupid, thoughtless games he had played last season with Lucy's friends now came back to haunt him.

She pushed past him and climbed the stairs. Alex followed, and as they reached the front entrance he took hold of her arm.

'Millie, I am serious with regard to my affections for you, I—'

He stopped. Angry voices were at the front door.

As the door flew open, Alex let go of Millie and stepped back. He caught her eye and shook his head. 'Nothing happened,' he whispered.

They both turned to see Charles, David and Lucy standing on the threshold. Charles stormed into the room and took Millie by the arm. 'What the devil are you playing at?' he roared at her.

David stepped between Alex and Millie and gave his younger brother a hard shove in the chest. Alex staggered backwards.

Millie began to cry. 'Nothing, nothing happened,' she wailed.

Alex attempted to take a step forward, but David held him by the shoulders.

'We came to have a cup of tea, nothing else. We were just about to head back to the ball,' Alex said.

Charles looked to his sister, who stood shaking her head. 'Nothing happened, Lord Brooke had some chai tea and he offered to share some with me. You can check the pot in the kitchen if you like,' she pointed downstairs. 'I'm not lying.'

'Stay there,' Charles ordered her. He returned a moment later holding the teapot in his hand, and showed it to the others. 'It's still hot; she's telling the truth, or at least that part of it.'

David nodded. He grabbed Alex by the arm and began to drag him towards the main staircase. Alex pulled away and reached for Charles. He tugged on Charles's jacket sleeve.

'Please, you must understand, nothing happened, I would never do anything to risk your sister's reputation. I know what we did was a bit rash, but it was only a cup of tea.'

Charles pushed Alex's hand away with a violent swing of his

arm. 'David, you had better take him away this instant, or I shall not be held accountable for the bloody thrashing I give your brother,' he bellowed.

Charles turned and held out his hand to Millie. 'We are leaving. I shall deal with you when we get home. In the meantime, you might think of twenty reasons why I should not tell Mama and Papa what you did tonight.'

'But you promised,' stammered Lucy.

Charles took a deep breath and glared at Millie. 'Yes, Lady Lucy, forgive me. Millie, do you know what I promised?'

'No,' his sister replied, as she continued to sob.

'I promised not to beat Lord Brooke to a pulp if you came quietly and did not make a fuss. I also agreed not to tell anyone about this evening and your foolish little expedition to the house of an unmarried man. Though right now I am so angry that I would quite happily give Brooke a pounding and then go home and wake Papa to tell him the reason why.'

Millie dried her tears on the back of her glove and gave a silent nod. She would go quietly.

'Millie,' Alex said, but she refused to look at him. He knew she would think him a coward, one who used his sister's friends and then bolted at the first sign of trouble.

If she had not thought him a cad before tonight, then this evening's events would have left her in no doubt as to his lack of character. The kiss and its aftermath had been bad enough, but now all he could see was the almost insurmountable task he faced of trying to win Millie's trust, let alone her heart.

As the Ashton siblings headed for the door, he watched with a sinking heart as Lucy stepped forward and faced Millie.

'I thought you were different,' she said, tears filling her eyes. 'I thought you liked me for me, but you are just like *all* the others. I should have known it when the two of you spent the dance lesson giggling and whispering to each other. You used me to get to my brother.'

She shot Alex a look of despair before turning back to Millie. 'I shall ask Mr Roberts to send his card to your mother; she can arrange for you to have your future dance lessons elsewhere. Please do not bother to call on me at the house anymore; I shall not be at home to you. I wish you success with the forthcoming season.'

'Lucy,' Alex pleaded. 'It's not her fault, she did nothing wrong.'

Lucy shook her head, and held up her hand refusing to hear his words. 'You know the effect you have on vulnerable girls and yet you still play your pathetic little games with them.' She turned to David. 'When you are ready would you please take me home?'

Charles thanked David for helping to locate his sister and they shook hands. He took Millie firmly by the arm and ushered her out the front door.

It took only until the end of the first block for Charles to start in on Millie. After pushing her roughly into the carriage and slamming the door loudly behind him, Charles threw himself down on the bench opposite her. He seethed with rage.

'Nothing happened,' Millie said.

Her brother closed his eyes and held a hand to his forehead. 'Nothing needs to have happened, as you well know. If anyone finds out, you will be ruined. You don't seem to understand that a young woman's reputation is the only thing she has of value within the *haute ton*. If you lose that, you might as well go and live in a nunnery,' he replied.

He began to suck deep breaths in and out of his lungs at a furious rate. Millie could see he was trying to control his temper.

'The only reason why you are not currently betrothed to Lord Brooke is because I agreed with his brother that we should not have to be continually reminded of how reckless the two of you were. You should be sitting there quietly counting your blessings that your older brother takes care of you. Others would have seized the opportunity to push their sister into marriage with a lunatic who will one day inherit a title and a sizeable fortune.'

'He is not mad.'

'Then pray tell me, Millie, what rational man invites a girl of your social standing out into the night and expects no repercussions? I would suggest only one who is destined for Bedlam would think that way. Besides, I have seen him ride. He is seriously lacking in common sense.'

She would get nowhere arguing with Charles this night. The worst thing was he was right. She had risked everything by going with Alex to his house. She also knew that if anyone found out about their kiss, she would be the Marchioness of Brooke in no time. And no matter whose fault it was, she couldn't face the prospect that if they were forced to marry, Alex would be humiliated and she would bear the blame.

At least they had got their story straight, and both had held to it fast. The first thing she would do when she got home would be to retire to her bedroom to hide her face. She sat back into the darkened corner of the carriage so Charles could not see the obvious marks of Alex's passion on her lips.

In the panicked hope that Charles would not look closely at her face, she had forced herself to cry when confronted by her brother. Having to lie to him only made things worse.

'You are not going to tell anyone, are you?' she ventured.

Charles' temper flared once more. 'Your behaviour has been scandalous. If you don't see the game the Marquess of Brooke is playing then that much-vaunted intelligence of yours has deserted you.'

Millie took a breath and tried to respond, but she couldn't find the words.

One moment she had been held fast in Alex's arms, revelling in a kiss far more passionate than anything she had ever imagined; the next she had been faced with her worst nightmare. Now as she sat in the carriage, her hand touching her bruised lips, she could still smell the trace of his cologne on her skin.

'Well?' Charles continued, stirring Millie from her thoughts.

'Don't you care about Lucy? Could you not see how upset she was, how devastated she is to have found out that you are the same as all the other girls who have used her to get to her brother? As for me, and my position in society, you could not give a fig, could you? You care only for yourself: woe poor Millie.'

He sat back in his seat and pulling up the window blind, looked out into the night.

'I shall conceal your behaviour this evening Millie, but if you ever do anything so foolish again, I shall stand back and leave you to your fate.'

Chapter Twelve

A shamed.

There was no other word to describe how Millie felt the following morning as she sat glum-faced at the breakfast table, staring at her plate.

Adding to her discomfort was the presence of her brother and father at the now-regular morning meal. After the welcome home ball at Ashton House, her mother had decided it was vital that they spend time together to maintain their familial ties, so she had decreed that, until the start of the season proper, the whole family would share the same table for at least one meal a day. Now, instead of being able to stay in bed until mid-morning each day, Millie was compelled to rise early and sit down to breakfast long before she could face the prospect of food.

Most mornings her brother would hastily make a sandwich on his plate, wrap it in a clean handkerchief and head out the door to go riding in Hyde Park. This morning Charles sat at the table, a large plate piled high with toast, black pudding and eggs before him. It was clear he was not going anywhere early this morning, and Millie was not foolish enough to ask him why. Another consequence of the previous night had been the end of his daily rides with Alex.

When Charles asked her to pass a plate of kippers, she handed them to him without meeting his gaze. She was afraid to look at him, worried that he would still wear the angry look of disapproval he had worn all the way home in the carriage last night. His wrath had been truly frightening.

By the time they finally reached home, he had worked himself up into such a lather that when the carriage slowed to a halt, he had flung the door open, jumped out on to the pavement and gone inside the house before Millie had time to rise from her seat.

At least he had kept his word about not revealing the events of last night to their parents. After the embarrassing situation she had placed her brother in she had to be grateful for any small mercies.

She could not bring herself to imagine the scene which must have followed their departure from the house in Bird Street. With Lucy present, the brothers would not dare to have come to blows, but the possibilities of what might have occurred after David had returned from Strathmore House now preyed on her mind.

As for poor Lucy, Millie had proved beyond a doubt that her now former friend had had every reason to be worried.

What a mess.

Last night had been a complete disaster and it was all her fault. She should have said no to Alex, no matter how much he pleaded, but she had yielded to temptation. Now her brother was furious with her, David Radley more than likely thought her a loose woman and Lucy was left to mourn the loss of yet another friendship.

She picked up a piece of toast from the rack and slowly buttered it, then placed it on her plate. She shook her head and pushed the plate away; the mere sight of food made her feel nauseous.

'You haven't eaten a thing, Millie darling. Are you feeling a little off-colour? I did tell you to have a care as to what you eat at other people's parties,' her mother said.

'I am fine, Mama; it's just a little early for food,' she muttered. She blinked hard and let out a sigh.

'You don't sound fine at all my dear. What is the matter?' Violet pressed.

'Leave her be,' her father interjected.

Across the table his gaze met his wife's and he shook his head; James could not abide tears at the breakfast table. Violet would have to wait until after he had left for East India House to speak privately with their daughter.

'So, what are your plans for the day, Charles?' James asked, changing the subject.

Millie gave a silent prayer of thanks to her father and his sensitivity. He would sense she was holding on tight to her emotions. One careless word and she would dissolve in a flood of tears.

'I thought I might pay a visit to Tattersalls today, and have a look at a pair of horses Uncle has recommended for me. They come up for auction later this week, so I will take the stable master from Ashton House with me and get him to look them over. Uncle said he will purchase them for me and stable them until my handling of English roads is up to scratch,' Charles replied.

James finished off the last of his tea and wiped his lips with a napkin. Then, placing it on the table, he stood up and prepared to leave.

'That is a very generous gift. But you know he does not have to buy them for you; I am happy to give you the money to buy them yourself.' He walked around to his wife and, bending down, gave her a farewell kiss. She gave him a warm smile and her eyes sparkled when he whispered something in her ear which no one else could hear.

Charles nodded his head. 'I have to admit that while it is exciting for him to offer such lavish gifts, I am a tad uncomfortable with the whole business.'

His father planted a brief kiss on Millie's head, but otherwise left her alone. 'I shall have a word with him. You might inherit the title someday, but you are my son and heir, so if anyone is going to buy you a horse it should be me. I didn't spend all those years in India salvaging the family fortunes only to be relegated to a secondary role upon my return. I shall drop by and see your uncle later today.'

After Mr Ashton had departed for the office, Charles helped his mother hobble down to the main sitting room, where she planned to spend the day resting her swollen ankle and catching up on correspondence. Millie knew eventually her mother would send for her and begin to ask awkward questions.

Charles soon returned and after dismissing the footman, closed the hallway door behind him. Millie picked up her teacup and took a small sip. As she held her breath he walked around the table and took the seat next to her. He took hold of her trembling hand and, leaning over, planted a kiss on her cheek.

'It will be all right, Millie; we have managed to avoid a public scandal. The Radley siblings are as anxious as we are to keep this quiet. Just don't tell Mama anything of last night,' he said.

Millie nodded her head. 'I was thinking what to tell Mama, and I think a version of the truth is the best,' she replied sadly.

Charles gripped her hand. 'No. You cannot tell her you were alone with Alex; she would make you marry him.'

She turned and gave him a weary look. 'I am not that stupid.'

Her brother raised his eyebrows.

'Granted, I did some foolish things last night, but I am not about to tell Mama that I was alone with Alex in his house and that you and David discovered us. I am simply going to tell her that Lucy and I have had a falling out, which, sadly, is the truth.'

Charles sat back in his chair and ran his hands through his hair; she hoped it was a look of relief which now appeared on his face, but she sensed there was still lingering frustration on his part. After last night, things had changed between them. She suspected he no longer trusted her. It pained her to have disappointed him in such a careless way.

'I am sorry about last night, Charles; I had no right to do as I did; you have every reason to be angry with me. You were right, I was stupid and selfish and I let my girlish infatuation for Lord Brooke cloud my judgement. It will not happen again, I promise.'

He raised his eyebrows once more and she let out a little giggle. She reached across and gave him a punch on the arm.

'Stop it, this is serious,' she said.

He rolled his eyes. 'I know it is; why do you think I was so riled up last night? I am glad you finally realise how close to ruin you came. Of course, the biggest problem at the moment is how you are going to make amends with Lady Lucy. She was dreadfully upset when we left. You must speak to her this morning and try to put things right.'

Millie slowly nodded her head. While a major catastrophe had been narrowly averted, there were still injured bystanders.

'I don't know if she will see me; she made it clear our friendship was at an end. Will you accompany me to Strathmore House this morning? I may get further if you are in tow.'

Charles pursed his lips and then let out a long, tired sigh. 'Yes, the longer you leave it the worse things will be. I have a couple of errands to run this morning – you can come with me. When they are done, we will call in at Strathmore House and see if we can repair the damage.'

'Thank you,' Millie replied. She reached over, retrieved her plate, took a bite of the cold buttered toast and sat quietly chewing on it while Charles picked at the cold beef left on Violet's breakfast plate.

'What is it about cold breakfast meat that makes it taste so good?' he wondered aloud, taking a large slice of the beef and stuffing it into his mouth.

'I don't know, but I still cannot face eating beef at any hour,' she replied, turning her nose up. 'All I can think of is how offended our Hindu neighbours in India would be if they found out you were eating cow.'

Charles laughed. He wiped his hands on his mother's discarded napkin and excused himself from the table. 'Don't be long; the sooner we get around to Strathmore House to see Lucy, the better.' He reached over and ruffled her hair, before making a beeline for the door, leaving Millie sitting alone in the breakfast room, still chewing on her toast.

❧

Charles' little errands took a lot longer than expected, and it was close to noon before brother and sister reached the steps of Strathmore House.

The first sign that something was amiss was when a footman answered the front door, rather than Hargreaves, the Radley family butler. The young man was not wearing a coat and the sleeves of his shirt were rolled up. It was not exactly how one would expect a servant to answer the front door of a major house.

He looked rather surprised to see anyone calling at the front door and gave them both a quizzical look before asking, 'Yes, may I help you?'

Charles looked at Millie and raised his eyebrows.

'Charles and Millie Ashton to see Lady Lucy Radley, if you please,' he replied, and offered his card.

The footman took the card, gave it a quick glance and screwed up his face. 'They are gone.' He offered the card back to Charles, who refused to take it.

'What do you mean gone? Gone where?' Millie asked.

The footman looked from brother to sister, then appeared to remember what he was supposed to tell visitors to the house. He straightened his back and announced, 'The Duke and Duchess of Strathmore are not in residence in London at present. They and their family have adjourned to their country estate in Scotland.'

Millie's mouth fell open and an involuntary gasp escaped. She took hold of Charles's hand and squeezed it tight.

The footman started to close the large black door. Having delivered his message, he evidently expected the visitors would silently nod their heads and go away, leaving him to get back to whatever task involved him wearing his shirtsleeves above the elbow.

Charles stepped forward and placed his boot in the doorway. 'The entire Radley family has quit London for their estate in Scotland?' he asked.

'Yes, I just hadn't got around to taking off the front door knocker yet,' the footman replied, nonplussed.

'The whole family, including all their children?'

'Yes.'

'When will they return?' Charles pressed. Millie was grateful that her brother was determined not to leave until he got the full story.

The put-upon footman took a deep breath and replied slowly, 'The Radley family, including Lord Brooke, Mr Radley, Lord Stephen, Lady Lucy and Lady Emma have gone to Scotland and will not be back for another six weeks. As such they are not receiving visitors at Strathmore House at present. Is there anything else I can tell you, Sir?'

Six weeks!

Millie bit down hard on her lip and tasted blood. Last night had been bad enough, but this was utter humiliation. Here she was, standing in full public view on the front steps of one of London's grandest houses, discovering just how insignificant she really was in the lives of the Radley family. They had left London without a word.

Any other young miss would likely have dissolved into tears by now and fled, but Millie stood unmoved, her back ramrod straight. The only outward sign of her struggle to maintain her composure was how tightly she held on to her brother's hand. If she squeezed any harder, she feared she might break one of his bones.

'I see. Thank you. We shall call again when the family has returned,' Charles replied.

Charles removed his foot from the door and the footman let out a sigh of relief. The door closed. He turned to Millie with a relaxed smile plastered on his face, then gently prised her fingers from his hand and kissed the back of her glove.

As he bent over her hand, he whispered. 'Smile, Millie, smile. If anyone is looking out from the other houses, they must see that we are laughing off our mistake. Come on, let us walk home; I for one could do with a stiff drink.'

She did as he asked and managed a half-smile and a nod of her head.

'Well done my girl, and don't you worry, I shall make Lord

Brooke pay for this,' Charles vowed, as Millie took his arm. 'No one nearly ruins my sister and then disappears without a word. I knew I should have given him a thrashing last night.'

They had reached the street and were preparing to turn for home when the front door of Strathmore House opened once more and Hargreaves raced down the front steps after them. When he got halfway down the stairs, and had their attention, he slowed his pace to a walk. Reaching Charles's side, he offered him his hand. Charles shook it and then casually put his hand in his pocket.

'I am so sorry that you were received in such a poor manner. Marshall is a good boy, but he can be a little vague at times. Fortunately for us all, he did find me and give me your card,' Hargreaves said.

'The family leaves for Scotland at this time every year. They were due to depart later in the week, but his Grace announced to the staff late last night that they were to leave early this morning. The whole house has been up all night packing, ready for a pre-dawn departure. The first thing that some members of the family knew of the change of plans was when they were roused from their beds early this morning. His Grace likes to get a full day's journey in on the first day so the family is able to stay overnight at the Earl of Wiltmore's estate.'

Hargreaves gave Millie a sympathetic smile. 'I am sure Lady Lucy would have sent a message to you, Miss Ashton, but since they left in such a hurry, it probably slipped her mind. She did seem terribly distracted this morning.'

Charles smiled at the obvious lie. Nothing happened in the great houses without the head butler knowing of it. Hargreaves would have been well aware that Lady Lucy had returned home from the party with only one brother escorting her. Her lady's maid would have filled Hargreaves in on any other pertinent details.

'I am surprised you have not made the long trip north yourself, or are you following later?' Charles enquired. The longer this pleasant little exchange lasted, the less likely prying eyes would find anything of interest to note.

The butler shook his head. 'No, I shall be overseeing the closure of the house this week. A few days before the family returns, I shall reopen the house and the staff will make it ready for the season.'

Millie gave a nod. 'Thank you, Hargreaves. I do recall Lady Lucy had made mention of the trip,' she replied, her voice a little shaky. Hargreaves gave a polite bow and bade the Ashton siblings a good morning. As the butler disappeared back inside the house Charles whispered to Millie. 'Well done sis, nearly out of here. Fortunately, Hargreaves is a good stick and he knew exactly what we needed.'

She creased her brow.

He patted his pocket and gave her a wink. 'He wrote the address of the Strathmore estate in Scotland on my card. Now at least you can write to Lucy and apologise. Six weeks might be long enough to exchange a few letters and win her back.'

Millie nodded. With her lips remaining tightly locked in a forced smile, it was clear she was not prepared to mention the other member of the Radley family who was on her mind. Only her sad eyes betrayed the depth of her disappointment.

Charles gave her a happy smile for the benefit of any audience, and arm in arm they strode off toward Park Street and in the direction of home.

Chapter Thirteen

As he woke, Alex pulled the blanket down from over his head and looked around the carriage. His father was busy reading papers while his younger brother Stephen had his head inside a large brown book with strange letters on its spine.

He squinted and thought he could make out a Greek letter. He shook his head, Stephen was all of fourteen and could read five languages, whereas Alex struggled to read more than two words of English and so avoided reading at all costs. As a child he had believed that since he could not master a simple task such as learning to read, then he must be a simpleton. How could a boy who was unable to read or write one day become one of the most powerful men in all of England?

The hours spent in tearful frustration, trying to get his brain to decipher the swirling letters, had left their mark on his psyche. He considered his lack of ability to read a deep flaw in his character, a weakness of which he should be ashamed. He had not gone up to Eton with the other boys of his age; instead his father had hired tutor after tutor to 'fix the problem'.

At the age of twelve his luck finally changed; his father found a tutor who taught Alex to memorise everything he learnt. Still apprehensive that his secret would be revealed and he would be mocked by the other boys, Alex refused to go until the school agreed that he could bring his *special valet* with him. Every Radley son had attended the school since its inception and now he would get the chance to have his name recorded alongside theirs as having been a pupil. With a great sense of fear and trepidation he joined his brother in the hallowed halls at Eton.

To his surprise he performed exceedingly well. Long after class had been dismissed for the day, Alex would sit with his tutor *cum* valet and learn his lessons by rote. As his father was on the board of governors, Alex was able to gain a dispensation and take his exams orally. He would stand before a panel of examiners at the end of each term and answer the questions they put to him. He passed every exam this way, and with ease.

Once Alex realised that he was not a fool, his brain just worked differently, he began to come out of his shell. From the shy, unsure young man who had arrived at the beginning of the year, he soon became the most popular boy in the entire school.

His ability to remember everything meant he often won bets about obscure dates and events in history. He also had a long list of ribald jokes at the ready. As his confidence grew, so did his legend. The other boys thought his ability to sit and draw pictures throughout classes and still excel at exams was a sign of his true genius. None of his classmates or friends knew the truth.

With his brother David continually keeping watch over him, Alex shone. Alone at night in their shared room in the halls of residence, they would sit and laugh over the fact that the Eton school yard was ruled by a duke's bastard and his younger brother who couldn't even read. The years the brothers spent together at Eton had been the happiest days of Alex's life.

At least, he'd thought they were until he met Millie Ashton, who managed to turn his whole life upside down in an instant. When he had held her in his arms in his house the previous evening, he had felt so overcome with joy, he thought his heart would burst. If he could make a life with her, he knew his days at Eton would pale in comparison. Together they could overcome any obstacles which his inability to read and write posed. Millie was not the sort of girl to judge a man for his weaknesses, not when she loved him. Or was she?

A cold chill crept up his spine at the thought and he shuddered. What if she didn't understand? What if he had truly misjudged her and she did not love him? She had dismissed his declaration of love with a gentle but firm denial. He rubbed his face and sighed.

He knew he should not have taken her away from the ball, that her reputation could have been destroyed because of his reckless behaviour, but he had not cared. He had been brave last night, but now with the morning came a creeping sense of uncertainty.

With Millie many miles away in London, there was little he could do. When she woke this morning and found he had left for Scotland without sending her so much as a note, it would only confirm her perception of the depth of his feelings for her. He could hardly blame her if she thought last night had simply been a bit of lark on his part. Honourable men did not profess their love to a young woman, then suddenly decamp overnight. After the way he had kissed her, she would think he was nothing more than a heartless rogue.

He looked over into the corner of the carriage and saw David stir under his grey woollen blankets. Alex shot him a filthy look. David shook his head and looked away. Alex was on the verge of saying something unpleasant when he remembered his father and youngest brother were also in the carriage. He gave a silent prayer of thanks that Lucy was travelling in the ladies carriage. Being in no mood to make polite conversation, he roughly pulled his blanket up over his head and tried to sleep.

In the early hours of the morning he had been fast asleep, lost deep inside a dream in which he had been continually running after Millie. Every time he caught up with her and reached out his hand, she would laugh at him and sprint away. Alex tossed and turned until Millie stopped and spoke to him. 'Get up, Alex,' she said, holding a lamp and shining it in his face. The light was so bright it stirred him from his sleep.

When he opened his eyes, he saw his father standing over his bed with a large lamp in his hand. He sat up and tried to focus his eyes. He rubbed his face and stared as two burly footmen brought his travel trunk into the bedroom and deposited it with a thump in the middle of the floor.

'Come on, up you get, lad. We are off to Scotland within the hour, so get a move on, and make sure you pack warm; I hear it is bloody freezing up there at the moment. You can bring your blanket with you; there will be plenty of time to sleep in the carriage,' his father commanded.

"But why are we leaving today, I thought we weren't travelling to Scotland until early next week?" Alex replied.

The duke gave him a stern look. "I have a daughter who came home from the ball last night in tears and my two eldest sons are at each other's throats. At the rate things are going, if I wait until next week, I won't have any family left to take to Scotland. Now get dressed."

As soon as his father left, Alex dragged himself from under the blankets and stood staring at the clothes laid out on his bed. The timing of the annual Radley family pilgrimage north could not have been worse.

When the Strathmore travel party stopped at a coach inn at first light, Alex took the opportunity to find a washroom at the rear of the inn. After scraping the sleep from his eyes, he dipped his head into a bowl of ice-cold water in an attempt to wake himself up.

He strode back into the inn, his face still numb from the freezing water. In the main dining room, he saw his family had taken up a spot in the corner of the room and were tucking in to coffee and a selection of cold meats.

All except Lucy. His sister sat in the far corner of one of two booths and nursed a small cup. Her eyes were red and swollen; she looked as if she had been crying all night. Emma offered Lucy a piece of buttered bread, but she shook her head. Alex sighed. This was going to be a long and weary trip to Scotland.

Six more days of this, bloody hell. I wonder how long it would take me to walk back to London.

He caught his father's eye. 'Alex, come over and have some

breakfast,' his father ordered. 'We won't be staying here long. I want to make Wiltmore's estate by late afternoon; your mother and the girls will need time to recover from the journey.'

Alex took a seat in the next booth and, hoping that at least one member of the family was still on speaking terms with him, tried to strike up a conversation with Stephen. After managing to extract only a few grunts and hums out of his brother, he realised he faced an uphill battle. In between wolfing down large mouthfuls of eggs and bacon, the youngest Radley had his nose firmly stuck inside his book.

Alex felt inside his great coat and pulled out a small purse. After excusing himself from the table, he headed over to the bar and purchased a small bottle of whisky. He took his hip flask out from his coat and filled it with the pale liquid. Since he was not able to sit and while away the long hours with a book, he decided to resort to his favourite pastime of sitting up on top of the carriage with the driver and his mate. Taking in the view of the passing countryside and sharing some dirty jokes with them was far more preferable than sitting inside the carriage staring daggers at David all day.

It wouldn't be too long before their father decided enough was enough and made them have it out on the roadside somewhere, and he was in no mood to be making amends with anyone this morning. A row with his father would see him receive a dressing down in front of the entire family and staff. The prospect of walking back to London became even more appealing.

Returning to the table, he picked up a sharp knife from the breakfast tray and sliced off a large piece of pickled pork. Provisioned with a sandwich made from thick bread, the pork and a generous slice of cheese, Alex was ready for the ride up on top of the travelling coach. He took a large bite of the sandwich, nodded his approval of his own culinary skills and headed out the door of the inn.

Out in the yard he whistled to the head driver of his father's coach and pointed to an empty seat just behind the driver's mate. The driver nodded and Alex rubbed his gloved hands together with glee. After a morning of silence and filthy looks in the carriage, he was making his escape.

As he climbed up on to the top of the coach, he sent a silent prayer of gratitude to Phillips for having set out extra undergarments. If things with David did not improve, Alex planned to spend the greater part of the journey to Scotland sitting up here with the icy wind blowing in his face. Time which he could put to good use, thinking about Millie and how he could win her heart.

As Alex settled into the seat, he exchanged a friendly grin with the driver. He had finally found a friendly face among the travel party. His father looked up at him and shook his head as he opened the coach door and climbed inside. Shortly afterwards, the convoy of coaches pulled out of the yard, with the ladies' carriage taking the lead.

The Great North Road was surprisingly clear of snow and ice, but the side road which they turned on to two hours after lunch, heading toward Henlow, was a different story. It was only five miles to Lord Wiltmore's country estate, but it took most of the afternoon to complete the journey. Several times on the road, both drivers and their mates had to climb down and shovel the snow away to clear a path.

They were a mile and a half from the end of the day's journey when the lead carriage, with the Radley women in it, gave a sudden lurch to the right. One of the wheels had hit a rut in the road and the carriage swerved dangerously toward a snow-covered embankment. The driver pulled the coach away at the last minute, but the rear right wheel lost traction and disappeared into a deep hole by the edge of the road. Alex watched with bated breath as the coach slid back and tilted sickeningly to one side, before coming to a complete stop.

Fortunately, the driver of Alex's coach was an old hand and managed to pull up his team before they ran into the back of the lead coach. 'Whoa!' the driver cried, as Alex and the driver's mate waved frantically to the luggage cart, which was bringing up the rear. All three carriages now stopped in the middle of the road.

Alex gave the driver a pat on the shoulder and climbed down

from the carriage. His father opened the door and Alex poked his head inside. 'The ladies' carriage has hit a hole in the road and they look like they are stuck fast,' he said.

He marched up to the lead carriage and tapped on the left side door. His mother opened it. 'You might need to come out while they try and get you unstuck,' he said, offering his mother his hand.

A large pair of arms appeared on the right side of him; and he stepped back as his father took hold of Lady Caroline and lifted her down from the carriage. The Duke whispered something in her ear at which she smiled and shook her head.

In no time, the Duke had his wife and both daughters out and standing on the road. Lucy hugged her sister Emma. The youngest Radley child was nursing a sore head from having it hit hard on the wooden window frame of the carriage as it came to a sudden halt.

'If you ladies would like to go and keep warm in the other coach, I am sure the boys will make room. Some fresh air will do them all good,' his father said, after checking that Emma was all right. He lifted his daughter and carried her to the carriage. David and Stephen climbed out and stood looking concerned as their father settled Emma into the carriage.

'She's just had a bump on the head. Please go and fetch some snow for your sister.' He handed Stephen a clean handkerchief and pointed to a pile of fresh snow further back down the road.

As the drivers and hands from the three coaches set about freeing the stricken coach, Alex and David stood on the roadside silently watching them, their offers to assist the Strathmore staff having been declined with good humour.

David stamped his feet. 'It's freezing out here. I was having a lovely nap inside when Father dragged me out here.'

Alex took a swig from his hip flask and ignored him.

'Are you going to share that?' David asked, nodding toward the flask.

'No.'

David sighed and shook his head in disgust.

'Anyone would think that I was the fool last night, from the stinking mood you have been in all morning. Remind me again who was it that lured the Ashton girl to our house? I am sure as the devil it wasn't me.'

'Shut up, David,' Alex replied.

David took a step sideways and stood shoulder to shoulder with Alex. 'You have been in a foul temper with me since the night we went out two weeks ago. It's not my fault if you cannot take a joke. Anyone would think you were the first and only chap to have had to deal with an unwelcome erection. You made a complete ass of yourself in reacting the way you did,' David said.

Alex grabbed hold of David's arm and gripped it tightly. He felt him flinch. Good. He would be disappointed if his brother did not have bruises to show for his troubles tomorrow.

'That hurts, Alex. If you don't want the servants to see you dropped to your knees on the roadside, you had better release me,' he said through gritted teeth.

Alex eased his grip. His brother was a master of the single-punch fight. David stepped away and turned on him. 'Do you intend to behave like this the whole time we are in Scotland? Because I can tell you one thing: Papa will not stand for it. So, you and I had better have out here and now. I saved your precious Miss Ashton's reputation last night but anyone would have thought you didn't want to be rescued, the way you are carrying on.'

Alex stood silently staring at his brother. He took another swig of his whisky and handed David the flask.

'Thank you,' David said and took a nip of the fiery liquid before handing the flask back to Alex.

'You were the highlight of the club that night. Long after you had stormed out, the other lads were still laughing about you getting your cock hard over Millie Ashton. To be fair, she is a perfectly lovely girl, but—'

Before he could finish what he was saying, Alex let out a mighty roar and rushed at him. David had no time to react. When he hit the ground, Alex stepped forward and landed a heavy leather boot on his chest. With the whisky flask clenched in his hand, he leaned over his stricken brother, watching as a look of fear replaced the surprise on David's face.

'Alex!' bellowed their father, storming across the road to his two eldest sons. 'What the hell is going on?' he demanded.

Alex gave David a look of disdain and spat on the ground just wide of where his brother lay. He dragged his boot from David's chest and started to walk away. 'Ask him,' he snapped.

David struggled to his feet and began brushing the wet snow off his greatcoat.

'Well?' the Duke asked. 'We are not going anywhere until the two of you explain yourselves. And if I don't get a satisfactory answer, you can both bloody well walk the rest of the way to Felix's estate.'

David closed his eyes and let out a sigh. 'It's my fault, Papa I had a bit too much to drink and told some of our friends the truth about Alex's embarrassing predicament at Viscount Ashton's ball. Clearly Alex did not see the humour in my remarks.'

The roar of anger continued unabated in Alex's ears. He had been on the verge of forgiving his brother, and then David had insulted Millie. Now he was possessed of such a murderous rage that if their father had not intervened, he feared what he might have done.

'Is that what this spat is all about? You two are fighting because Alex's precious pride got hurt? You need to grow some thicker skin, my lad,' the Duke replied, angrily pointing a finger toward Alex.

Alex shook his head. 'Thank you for your timely advice, Papa, but the injury to my reputation is only the half of it.' He lifted the flask of whisky to his lips and drained the rest of its contents. He stuffed the flask back in his pocket and stared hard at his father.

'If you wish to know the real reason why my stupid brother's arse is soaked from a roll in the snow, it is because he sullied Miss Ashton's good name in front of our friends and then had the temerity to repeat it to my face just now. That offence shall not be tolerated, nor go unpunished.'

His father nodded and put an arm around him. They walked

together to where David stood and the Duke pulled David to his other side. With their backs to the coaches, no one could hear the ensuing conversation.

'We are on the road, as a family, heading to our ancestral home in Scotland. I am not going to have the two of you fighting with each other the whole time we are away from London, and especially not in front of the women or the servants. Now, David, apologise for what you said about Miss Ashton, as Alex has clearly taken offence. Alex, you in turn will apologise for attacking your brother and shoving him to the ground.'

The brothers exchanged looks. Alex could see David was still stunned by the sudden assault.

David shrugged his shoulders. 'I don't understand what it is between you and Miss Ashton, but clearly she is a valued friend about whom I have made inappropriate remarks. I offer my unreserved apology and ask that you and I talk further about the young lady so that I may better understand the situation.'

'Alex?' Ewan asked.

Alex felt his father's arm tighten about his shoulder. He looked at his brother and then dropped his gaze to the road. 'I'm sorry,' he replied, without emotion.

David offered his hand and Alex took it reluctantly. He was tired and the events of the previous night still lay unresolved between them.

Their father placed one arm around Alex and the other around David. 'My boys,' he murmured. 'Never let anything or anyone come between you. Family comes first, always.'

Alex heard a sniff and, turning, saw Stephen standing, on the verge of tears, beside him. The young lad had witnessed the violent altercation between his two brothers. Alex reached out and put an arm around his younger brother, pulling him into the all-male Radley embrace.

What the servants leaning against the now-freed carriage thought of the touching scene mattered little. The Radley family had held the Strathmore dukedom together for nearly 600 years by being united in both their purpose and support of one another. Brother always standing for brother.

When the group finally drew apart, it was with much slapping of shoulders and smiles. Stephen attempted to fight Alex, but he was easily overcome and found himself with a shirt full of snow before he returned to the warmth of their carriage.

With the ladies returned safely to their own coach, the family continued to Lord Wiltmore's estate and the end of their first night on the road.

Chapter Fourteen

W hen Millie and Charles returned home, Millie went up to
her room. Charles had offered to sit with her in the
upstairs drawing room, but she had declined his kind offer. At this
moment, a sympathetic ear was the last thing she needed.

'I am fine. It was just a bit of a shock to discover that the
Radleys had left town in such a hurry this morning,' she said, as
she gave his tortured hand one last squeeze.

She dismissed Grace as soon as she was able, telling her that she
needed to rest. As soon as her maid's footsteps retreated down the
hallway, Millie closed the door to her bedroom. With hands gently
clasped together, she stood in the middle of her room and waited
for the tears to come. The sense of utter disappointment and embarrassment she had felt, standing out in the cold outside Strathmore
House, had shaken her to the core. How little had she truly meant
to Lucy?

And to Alex?

She would ever be in her brother's debt for having saved her at
that moment.

Thank you, Charles.

Standing in the silence of her bedroom, a sense of calm slowly came over her and took hold. Things could have been much worse. The events of the previous evening and this afternoon had taught her a number of valuable lessons.

Six weeks without seeing either Lucy or Alex would be a blessing. She had allowed her world to consist of a small, select circle of friends; now it was time to strike out and make some new ones. 'This will teach me not to put all my eggs in one basket.'

She pulled Charles' card out from her reticule and looked at the address written on the back. Hargreaves had said it would take six days for the Radley family to reach their home in Scotland, so she had ample time to compose a suitable letter to Lucy.

There was no doubt that Lucy deserved an apology, but it would not be written today. Last night was still too raw. Millie needed time to assimilate the facts and put matters into perspective; only then would she put pen to paper. If Alex kept to his word, then all she would be apologising for was her disappearance from the ball.

What had begun as a harmless moment of indulging her fantasy had become all too real. One minute they were sharing an innocent cup of tea, the next he was kissing her. What on earth had possessed him to do such a thing? If it were madness, then she had suffered from the same malady. She had kissed him back.

'Nothing happened,' she whispered, recalling Alex's words. She touched a finger to her lips and sighed. 'Nothing other than you stupidly falling in love with him and then letting him kiss you.'

By lying to the others, he had surely saved their skins, but to have Alex's true nature confirmed still hurt deeply. To know that the very morning after he had declared he loved her, he had left London without a word.

Millie had seen a look in his eye which had tempted her for the briefest of moments to believe his words. The kiss had been a bold enough move, but when he tried to tell her he was serious in his affections, the moment had descended into farce. Her response had been entirely appropriate; he had no right to speak to her of love. By passing the encounter off as a bit of a lark, she had treated his declaration with the gravity it deserved.

Last night she had been gracious, but the next time she met him he would understand the depth of her contempt for his behaviour. How many other girls had heard those words of love, taken them seriously and then had their hearts broken, not to mention the cost which Lucy had borne?

She looked at herself in the mirror and smiled. There was the bitter sting of disappointment in her heart, but she understood that no girl was truly immune to the charms of Lord Brooke. She took a deep breath and gave a prayer of thanks. She had escaped with her reputation and heart mostly intact, and now it was time to move on.

There was life after Alex Radley. The loss of Lucy's friendship would be a blow if she were unable to repair the damage, but Millie now had over a month to form some new friendships before Lucy returned to London. A spark of hope flared in her. If she prepared a contingency plan, then at least there would be time to decide if she wanted to stay in England or go back to India. Things were looking a lot brighter than they had been only an hour earlier.

'Who knows, maybe I shall find someone who will make me want to stay.'

Deciding there was no time like the present, she opened the bedroom door and went to find her mother. While Violet would still be laid up with her damaged ankle for the next few days, once she knew that Millie was serious about making new friends, a miraculous recovery would no doubt ensue.

Two weeks later, David had begun to regret that he and Alex were on speaking terms once more. Somewhere in the days after they had arrived in Scotland, his brother had decided he needed to write to Millie and once Alex got an idea into his head, there was no stopping him.

The morning after one of his and Alex's regular evenings at the local village tavern, David sat at breakfast feeling rather less than ordinary. After the third time he had looked at the salted pork and bread on his plate and felt his stomach churn, he gave up and pushed the plate away. A mug of hot sweet tea looked a safer option.

He heard Alex approaching long before his brother reached the breakfast room. Whistling as he strode into the room, Alex picked up a plate and proceeded to pile it high with food.

'Good morning to you, brother dear. What a refreshing night's sleep I've had. I feel marvellous, and I'm absolutely starving,' Alex announced. With his plate crowded with bacon, white pudding and roast beef, he scooped up several greasy fried eggs and balanced them on the top of the bacon, before banging the silver cover back down over the serving dish.

If David had been feeling better, he would have shaken his head. Instead, he just closed his eyes and tried to concentrate on keeping his tea down. Alex threw himself into the chair opposite and rubbed his hands with glee.

'Today is going to be a good day. Fancy a ride up to the top of the valley? Papa says the main trail is clear most of the way. I can't wait to get on a horse and just ride somewhere. No carriages and no people, just the wilds of Scotland. What do you think?' Alex stuffed a large piece of white pudding into his mouth and happily chewed away.

The previous night Alex had drunk his brother under the table, yet here he was, bright and early and looking none the worse for wear.

David picked up his tea and took a sip. The thought of bouncing up and down on the back of a horse, coupled with the smell of the bacon, edged him ever closer to being physically ill. 'No, I think I might just spend the day doing a spot of reading and perhaps write some letters,' he replied.

Alex loudly clapped his hands together. David winced.

'Excellent, just what I wanted to hear,' Alex said, and stabbed his fork into his breakfast again. He leaned in over the table while brandishing a piece of bacon, dripping with egg yolk, on the end of his fork. 'I need you to write a letter for me.'

David stared at Alex. In his entire life Alex had never once written a letter, nor had he ever asked David to scribe one for him. The whole time they had been at Eton together, he would wait for David to write his weekly letter home and then add his own initials at the bottom.

Alex was up to something.

'Who would this letter be going to, may I ask?' David replied.

'Millie Ashton,' Alex replied.

David looked at Alex with concern. 'Are you sure about this?' he finally asked.

The smile disappeared from Alex's face. 'Adamant,' he replied, as he put his knife and fork down in the middle of his plate and sat back in his chair.

Silence hung in the room, while David searched for the right words.

'So, what do you want this letter to say, apart from a sincere apology for risking her reputation? May I suggest a nice friendly letter, telling her of your journey to Scotland? Add in a bit about the weather and perhaps finish it by saying you miss her smile. Nothing too serious,' David replied.

Alex scratched his ear. 'I need you to write a love letter.'

'Why?' David asked warily.

Alex sighed. 'Because the night I took Millie back to our house, I kissed her and told her I loved her. That's why. And the more I think about it, the more certain I am that it is love. So, you see, I have to do something about it. I want to marry her. I want her to be my duchess someday; I think she would be perfect in this place.'

David's heart sank. The poor girl had probably spent every day since that night convinced that Alex was a heartless cad who had used her. If Alex was to stand any chance of wooing Millie, there was nothing else to be done; David had to do as he asked.

"So, do you have the words in mind you wish me to write?" David asked.

Alex screwed up his nose. "Actually no. You know how hopeless I am with composing sentences in my head. I'm sure you could come up with something appropriate far quicker than I could."

'You could go back to London,' David replied. That option was far more preferable to him, in fact anything was better than having to pen a love letter to a girl he barely knew.

Alex shook his head. 'I already asked Papa this morning. He said no. I told him that it was urgent. He said I needed to take my responsibilities as the future leader of this valley more seriously and I couldn't just flit off back to London on some whim.'

Alex pushed his half-eaten plate of food away, while David pricked up his ears. If there was one thing his brother never did, it was leave food uneaten.

'He was the one who suggested I get someone to write to Millie; he said he was not convinced that I am serious about her and I shouldn't rush into anything. He thinks I should take things slowly and establish an understanding of her mind before I make any formal approach to her father. As he sees it, if she doesn't want me then at least I will have a few weeks to nurse my wounds before we return. Please, David, I really need your help.'

David wiped his face with his napkin and stood to leave. He turned to Alex and held up a hand in surrender. 'All right, but I will need time to think it. As long as you don't nag me I will try and get something down on paper in the next day or so,' David said.

'Thank you; this means everything to me and I won't forget it,' Alex replied.

David winced. 'Actually, you will forget about it. If I write this letter, I never want to hear another word about it. If you so much as whisper a word of my involvement to anyone, I shall never speak to you again. Are we clear?'

Faced with little choice, Alex nodded.

With his hands stuffed into his jacket pockets, David headed back to his room, hoping that with any luck Alex would come to his senses and forget about it. If he did not mention it to Alex, then maybe the whole foolish notion of writing to Miss Ashton would die a natural death.

But by supper he knew he was in for no such luck. Alex had taken to stalking his every move. His friendly offers of tea every half an hour was driving David mad. He had even made a special trip into the next town to procure David's favourite butter tablet. A four-hour return trip on horseback in the bitter cold and Alex was still smiling upon his return.

Finally, having begged off from the family's evening entertainment, David took to the private parlour reserved for his and Alex's personal use. 'I can't believe I allowed myself to be talked into doing this; I must be insane,' he muttered as he pushed open the door to the cosy parlour. He closed the door behind him and leaned against it, quietly surveying the room. The fire had been lit since early afternoon, allowing the room to become comfortably warm. The whisky cabinet was fully stocked, while a selection of cigars sat neatly arranged on its top.

'Let's get this done, and then hopefully he will leave me in peace,' he said to himself.

He crossed the floor to the large desk situated in front of the window and took a seat. A couple of lines about flowers and the stars in the sky, followed by a sentimental declaration of love, and his job would be done. He picked up the pen, dipped it in the ink pot and leaned over the desk. It would only take a few minutes to write a simple love note.

Ten minutes later, he was still staring at the virginal white paper, the pen gently rolling between his middle and index fingers. He swore and put the pen down.

'Come on, just get something down on the page, it doesn't have to be Wordsworth,' he grumbled in frustration.

His gaze drifted across the room to the whisky cabinet, where it fell upon his favourite aged malt. The light from the fire played magically across the front of the crystal decanter. He smiled. 'All right my love, I hear your siren's call.'

With a tumbler of the golden glory in his hand, David returned to the desk and sat down once more. He took a swig of the whisky, tasting the smooth malt as it slid over his tongue. He immediately decided he would be more comfortable by the fire. Armed with paper, ink and pen, he settled himself into a large leather armchair.

He looked hard at the paper and prayed for inspiration. How could he write a love letter to a girl he hardly knew? 'A-ha!' he said waving the pen around as if it were a conductor's baton. If he had to write a love letter, he needed to find his muse.

An image of Lady Clarice Langham eased its way into his mind. He had loved her from afar for many years, but she had always politely refused to dance with him. Her father had made it patently clear that the illegitimate son of a duke would never be good enough for his daughter. He knew pursuing her would be a waste of his time, but his heart belonged to her. As long as she remained unmarried, the faintest flicker of hope still burned.

While his heart's desire lived beyond his reach, he could at least use what he felt for Clarice when he was penning a love letter for his brother. All he had to do was imagine she was the one reading the letter.

He dipped the pen in the ink and began to write.

An hour or so later, Alex quietly opened the parlour door and found David fast asleep in the chair. Several sheets of crumpled-up, partly burnt paper lay at the edge of the fireplace. He shook his head as he picked them up and placed them into the burning embers. David had a terribly bad throwing arm.

On the floor, a few feet in front of David's chair, lay a folded piece of paper. It had been addressed, but not yet sealed. Alex picked it up and turned it over. He couldn't make out the words of the address, as David's handwriting was worse than his throw. But he could just make out the large printed L of London on the bottom. Relief swept over him. His brother had not let him down.

He took the paper and placed it on the desk. Taking out a stick of black wax from the desk drawer, he crossed to the fire and after heating the wax, he returned and sealed the letter with his own personal coat of arms.

Alex stood looking at the letter while the wax slowly cooled. Rather than a declaration of love upon which all his future happiness depended, it looked like any other business letter his father would have sent.

It doesn't look like a letter from me. There is nothing to show that I wrote it, which of course is because I didn't, but I need to make it more personal.

David stirred in his sleep and as Alex looked over toward him, he noticed the ink and pen sitting on the table next to the armchair in which his brother dozed.

'Fortune favours the brave,' he muttered.

Alex retrieved the pen and ink pot and placed them on the desk, making sure not to spill any ink on the precious letter. He then set about painstakingly adding his initials to the back of the letter, just below the seal. Once his task was complete he sat back and looked at his handiwork, happy in the knowledge that when Millie received the letter she would know it was from him before she even opened it.

With the letter in his hand, he left David still sleeping and went in search of the castle's head footman. By morning's first light the most important piece of correspondence he would ever send would be on its way to London.

After handing the letter over, he went back to the parlour, intent on rousing his brother so they could enjoy a nightcap and a cigar together, but when he opened the door he found the room empty. David must have woken while he was gone and headed up to bed.

Pity.

Alex looked at the fire; if he intended to stay up for a while longer, he knew he should add some more wood. Instead he pushed the largest log to the back of the fire and scattered the embers, allowing the fire to die down low. He picked up a small cigar from the tray and using one of the mantelpiece candles he lit the cigar.

After returning to his room and putting on his greatcoat, Alex left the private family apartments of the castle. With the blanket he had brought with him from London tossed over his shoulder and a thick woollen scarf wrapped around his neck, Alex climbed the large stone steps leading up to the castle ramparts. As luck would have it, the snow had stopped and he was able to keep warm in one of his favourite childhood hiding spots. Looking out through one of the arrow loops cut into the stone wall, he was afforded a view over the darkened valley, past the head of the nearby loch. By lifting his head, he could just make out the lights in the village below the castle.

He couldn't wait to bring Millie up to Scotland and show her the castle and its surrounds. He was certain she would love the estate, and once they met her the tenants would love her too. With a special place in her heart for Scotland, he hoped the pain she felt at the loss of her home in India would ease.

Sitting with his coat buttoned up and the scarf now wrapped around his head, he blew smoke rings into the cold, still air while he tried to imagine Millie's reaction to his love letter. He counted the days it would take for his declaration to reach her and how long it would take for her hurried reply to find its way back to him. In little over a week and a half he should have her precious words.

He was confident that with the exchange of letters, they would have an understanding. As soon as he got back to London, he would call upon her father and ask for Millie's hand.

'A June wedding would be good.'

He made a mental note to book St George's church the moment he had Mr Ashton's approval. Once word got out that his wedding was to take place on the second Saturday in June, no one else in the *ton* would be foolish enough to book their wedding for that day.

Alex drew back on his cigar. A smile found its way to his lips. His marriage to Millie would be the defining moment in his transition from party lad Alex to future duke. No longer would he be sharing digs with his brother and out drinking and carousing until all hours of the night. Instead, he would have a loving wife and a warm bed to come home to every evening.

'We will need somewhere to live,' he said, addressing the stone walls.

He began to compose a list of things he needed to do once he got back to London. As the list grew, he realised it would take all the time up to the wedding just to get his affairs in order. There was a lot of work involved in taking on a wife.

In the morning he would talk to his father; there had to be a way for the family to cut short their stay in Scotland. He stood, and threw the cigar down on the cold stone rampart. A whisper of smoke escaped the rolled leaf as he crushed it with his boot. As he turned toward the door, intent on heading to bed, he saw the door open and Lucy stepped out into the frigid night.

She gave him a smile. 'I hoping to find you up here; everyone else has gone to bed,' she said, closing the door behind her.

'I was just about to turn in myself,' Alex replied.

Lucy took her hand out from her fur muff and withdrew two large oatcakes. 'Could I tempt you to perhaps stay for a few more minutes?'

Alex nodded.

They settled back into the nook where Alex been sitting and he lay the blanket over their legs. Lucy handed him an oatcake and they sat in companionable silence while they ate.

'I've been meaning to speak to you for a couple of days, but it has been difficult to find a private moment. I thought you might like to know I received a letter from Millie the day before yesterday,' Lucy said.

Alex felt his breath catch in his throat.

Lucy gave his hand a squeeze. 'While it was short in length, I was pleased to see that it was a note of apology. She accepted that she had been foolish to run away from the ball with you and that by doing so she had hurt my feelings. She explained that our friendship was of great importance to her and she asked for my forgiveness.'

A breath of relief escaped Alex's lips.

'What I want to know is: should I accept her apology or was this yet another friendship that only existed because someone wanted to get closer to you? Tell me, Alex, should I forgive her or should I let Millie go as I did with all the others?'

Alex put an arm around Lucy's shoulder and gave her a hug. 'I wish with all my heart that you would accept Millie's apology and remain friends. Millie didn't use you to get to me; it was the other way around.'

Lucy gave him a quizzical look and he smiled. 'Please keep this a secret, Lucy because there are still matters to be resolved. But I do want you to be friends with Millie, because I intend to ask for her hand in marriage once we get back to London.'

Lucy gasped with surprise. 'Alex, I had no idea you felt that way about her. It would be lovely to have Millie as a sister. I shall write to her this week and ensure that we are reconciled.' She turned and fixed Alex with a gorgon's stare. 'You do love her, don't you? Marriage isn't something to be considered lightly.'

Throwing the blanket off, he stood and, taking Lucy's hand, pulled her swiftly to her feet. She put her arms around his waist and they shared a hug.

'Yes, I do love her. I am not that much of a rogue,' he chuckled, sliding a hand up to Lucy's hair and giving it a brotherly ruffle. With Lucy and Millie friends once more and his declaration of love on its way to London, Alex felt certain of his future. With a favourable response from Millie only a matter of days away, he could afford to remain in Scotland and stay in his father's good graces.

≈

The following afternoon, Alex and David took the opportunity to take a ride to the top of the valley.

As they reached just below the rocky valley peak, Alex stopped his horse and leapt down. The crunch of ice under his heavy leather boots made him smile.

'I love it up here, it's so good to be out of London and breathing the fresh air,' he said, watching as David dismounted from his horse.

'Nothing better than freezing Scottish air when it hits your lungs," David replied.

'Life is good.'

David reached into his pocket and took out a small folded piece of paper. He handed it to Alex.

'What's this?' Alex asked.

'The letter I said I would write; don't tell me you have already given up on the idea. I spent hours last night trying to pen something, but ended up burning them all. So, rather than break my promise, I got up early this morning and wrote that,' David replied pointing to the letter.

A cold chill raced down Alex's spine.

What did I send to London?

'What was wrong with all the letters you wrote last night?' he cautiously ventured.

David shrugged his shoulders. 'I made a few failed attempts, before I finally managed to scratch out something of substance. But after I had addressed the letter, I came to the realisation, it was too much. There is only so much heartfelt passion which can safely be written in a letter to an unmarried woman.'

'So, you burned it along with the others?' Alex replied, as his toes curled up in his boots.

'Yes.'

Alex looked down at the letter in his hand and made an instant decision. The letter, which David thought he had burned, was well on its way to London, and there was nothing either of them could do about it. Telling David would only serve to put the two of them at loggerheads once more.

He smiled and gave his brother a nod of gratitude.

If the letter currently bound for London was indeed full of heat and passion, his brother had unknowingly given Alex exactly what he needed to convince Millie he truly loved her.

Later, after having returned to the castle, Alex burned the second letter.

Chapter Fifteen

'Beautiful; absolutely stunning, my dear,' Violet said as Millie stepped out from behind the screen in the fitting room at Madame de Feuillide's salon. The new deep pink gown Millie had chosen sat perfectly on her hips and showed her new figure to perfection.

'Can you tell if I have lost weight?' Millie asked anxiously. She stared into the long glass mirror, twisting and turning as she examined her new gown. She did not expect miracles, but something, anything to show for all her hard work would be a godsend.

A smiling Madame de Feuillide held up her thumb and forefinger, to show how much she had taken the dress in from Millie's last fitting. Another inch. A whole two and a half inches had now come off Millie's waist in the days since she had begun her daily walks. Violet raised her eyebrows and smiled.

Millie would never be slender, it was not in her make-up, but she was beginning to like what she saw in the mirror. Perhaps she could be the woman her mother had described. A woman with the sort of curves men appreciated and women envied. With her hands on her hips, she did a little dance.

'Is this the moment when you make a remark about watching

the butterfly emerging from its cocoon?' Millie teased. Violet nodded and wiped a tear from her eye.

'The colour is magnificent. I did not think you could wear that dark a shade and get away with it, but it really does work with the colour of your hair,' Violet said. 'Though it is still not exactly the correct form of attire for a young debutante; you should be in something like a pale cream or white.'

Millie smiled, knowing she would not take the bait. In the days since she had told her mother of her falling-out with Lucy, the two Ashton women had begun a campaign for Millie to find new friends. A sticking point in their plans had been coming to agreement on Millie's status within the *ton*. Violet had argued that her daughter should have a formal coming-out and be presented at court, whereas Millie had said that at nearly one and twenty she was far too old to be making her debut.

The disagreement had continued until they finally settled on a solution. If anyone asked whether Millie had been presented to society, they were to be told she had made her debut in Calcutta. 'A little white lie for a summer of peace' was how Millie had sold the idea to her mother.

An accord had been reached, but Millie knew she was on a short leash. She could not regale anyone with stories of the wonderful night of her coming-out ball, nor was her dress to be described in great detail. She was out in society, and the rest was history.

It was the week after Easter, and more invitations to parties and gatherings were starting to arrive at the Ashtons' home each day.

'I think I might wear this to the ball on Tuesday, Mama; what do you think? I know it's not the season for a few more weeks, but I would love to wear this gown to Lord Langham's ball. I think it would be just the thing,' Millie said.

The ball at the home of the Earl of Langham was marked in her diary as an important event. It would be the perfect opportunity for the Ashton family to meet more of their neighbours. As for Millie, it would be a chance for her to show some of the other girls that she offered them more competition than simply a sizeable dowry.

Who knows? I may meet some young man who finds me irresistible and begs me to run off with him to Gretna Green.

'Please, Mama? I have been so looking forward to the ball. I promise I won't go near the supper table and I shall fill my dance card only with suitable gentlemen,' Millie pleaded.

Violet nodded. 'But only if the gown is ready by then. I won't have Madame's girls working till all hours just to get it finished.'

The modiste waved her hand in Violet's direction. 'It is not a problem, Mrs Ashton. We only have to finish the last of the hem this afternoon and the gown will be ready. I shall have it sent to your home this evening. Miss Ashton shall wear the gown to the ball.'

Millie smiled and gave the old woman a kiss on the cheek. Unlike many other dressmakers in London, Madame was not hiding a Cockney accent beneath her impeccable French one.

Millie's gaze fell sadly upon the small cameo of a man which Madame de Feuillide wore pinned to her dress. England had afforded a place of refuge for many fleeing the terror of revolutionary France, but some, like Monsieur de Feuillide, had never made it.

The modiste placed her hands over both of Millie's and gave a gentle squeeze. 'Merçi, my dear; you look so beautiful, I am sure you will make the young men take notice. I hope that by the end of the summer I shall be making your wedding dress. Now, off you go and change while I check to see if your slippers have arrived from the shoemaker.'

With her gown for the ball now organised, Millie and Violet returned home and sat in the sitting room planning out the rest of the upcoming week's social events.

'Your father and I have a dinner at your aunt and uncle's this Thursday, so that will allow you to have a day's rest at home after the ball on Tuesday. It is not good form for young ladies to be out every night at the start of the season. It says that you are too frivolous and not sensible enough to consider the serious business of marriage. We have to plan the nights when you are at home carefully, to create just the right impression within the *ton*,' Violet explained.

'Yes Mama,' Millie replied, absentmindedly. She was only half listening to her mother, her mind firmly fixed on the grand entrance and stunning evening she had planned for the Tuesday night. She reached up and her fingers unconsciously searched her face for her nose ring. She wriggled her fingers, remembering how she had taken the ring out the morning after the Earl of Shale's ball and had not put it back in.

Maybe it's for the best; at least people won't stare at me. I shall do everything I can to make it a success. I must come home having made at least one, no, two new friends at the ball.

'Millie?'

'Mm-mm?'

She felt a hand on her knee and she jumped in surprise. Her head whipped up and she saw her mother looking at her with concern. 'Are you all right, my darling?' her mother asked.

Millie nodded. 'Sorry, I was busy thinking of the ball. It occurred to me this morning as I was preparing to go out just how important this ball is in our plans. This will be the first major event I have attended since Lady Lucy left for Scotland.'

'Speaking of which, did you write to her?' Violet replied.

'Yes, I sent a letter early last week. I thought I had told you, but it must have slipped my mind. She should have received it by now.'

Millie had led Violet to believe that the argument between the girls had been a simple misunderstanding at the early Easter ball, one which required a polite letter of apology to smooth things over. Millie penned the note as best she could, stating the facts and arguing her case. The visit to Alex and David's house, while a foolish endeavour, had been purely in order to share a decent cup of tea. Nothing more. She had secretly sent the letter off to Scotland, ensuring that Violet did not see its contents.

She hated lying to both Lucy and her mother, but if either of them knew the whole truth of that evening, she and Alex would be in serious trouble. Which made it all the more important to make the forthcoming party a successful venture in finding new friends. If Lucy did not accept her apology, then at least Millie would be able to distract her mother from knocking on the door of Strathmore House, demanding an answer.

'I didn't beg. I was honest with her. If she does not want me as a friend, then I shall accept her decision with good grace,' Millie said as she stared at her hands. She was not a good liar and she knew her mother could read her face like a book.

The Earl of Langham's home was only five doors from the Ashton family house on the same side of Mill Street. At eight o'clock on the night of the ball the Ashton family carriage was brought around to the front of number twenty-three and the family climbed aboard for the short trip.

Millie was still enjoying the look on her father's and brother's faces when they first caught sight of her as she descended the stairs a few minutes before they were due to leave for the ball. Mr Ashton had beamed with pride, while Charles stood wide-eyed and speechless as she reached the ground floor. Her father took her by the hand and spun her around, allowing the gown to catch the light from the front entrance chandelier.

'Who is this divine creature and where did she come from?' her father said, his voice full of love for his daughter. Charles laughed. 'I don't know, but if you traded her for Millie, I think you got the better deal.'

Violet gave him a disapproving look and shook her head. 'Your sister looks absolutely beautiful, Charles. She has worked so hard over the past weeks, we should all be very proud of her.'

For her part, Millie could not care less what her brother thought or said at that moment. She felt as light as air; a goddess descended from heaven. Tonight, was her night. Miss Millicent Ashton was ready to set the *ton* alight.

When her father finally allowed her to stop spinning, she gave

Charles a small nod of her head. He took her hand and placed a tender kiss on her long white glove.

'Your carriage awaits, my lady,' he said, adding a deep bow.

As Charles assisted Millie with her cloak, he leaned in and whispered in her ear. 'Well done Millie; time to show London that the Ashton family are cut from quality cloth. You look fabulous.'

Upon the family's arrival a short time later at Langham House, Millie entered the ballroom on her father's arm. Charles and Violet walked a few steps behind. 'I want your sister to have her moment to shine,' Violet murmured to Charles, as she slowed her pace and allowed a suitable gap to form between them and the other members of their family.

After greeting their host, the widower Earl of Langham, the Ashton siblings were free to roam the party. If she thought that without Lucy or the Radley brothers she would feel lost, the success of her stunning gown soon put paid to her concerns. Within an hour, she had danced with several highly eligible young men, all of whom complimented her on her gown. And the green-eyed glances given by several other young ladies did not go unnoticed.

The world was Millie's oyster.

When she walked through the front door on her father's arm, Millie had felt as if she radiated light; now she was positively giddy with success. Every word which came from her lips seemed to be the perfect one. She laughed in all the right places in other people's jokes, and her dancing was so light of foot, she barely touched the floor.

'I just need a moment to catch up with Uncle Oscar, Millie. Are you all right to sit here until I return?' Charles asked, as they stopped in front of a row of chairs on their way from the dance floor to the supper area. Charles had managed to get a dance with his sister late in the evening, but only after he had exchanged firm words with one eager young man who was adamant about his name being on Millie's card for that particular dance.

She called Charles to task for his behaviour as soon as they were out of earshot of the offended dance partner. 'You didn't have the right to push in, Charles; Mr Banks' name was on my card.'

'I wanted to dance with my lovely sister; besides Banks is only interested in your dowry. You could have turned up in a sack tonight and he still would have begged to dance with you. His father has just dropped a fortune on a failed mining venture in Scotland and the son desperately needs cash. Don't go trading a mad rake like Lord Brooke for a gambler's son, Millie. At least Brooke knows how to handle his blunt,' he replied.

As Charles headed off to find their uncle, Millie took a welcome rest on one of the comfortably padded chairs. Being the centre of attention for the evening was giving her sore feet. Why did new slippers always have to pinch? She gave the supper table a brief glance and wisely settled on a cup of tea offered by one of the Langham household staff.

'He is so romantic, such a hero. I can't believe he would be too shy to speak to her, but when I saw the letter I knew it was from him. She is the luckiest of girls,' Millie's ears pricked up; someone had a secret admirer.

She sat quietly sipping on her tea, while straining to hear the conversation between two other young women who had sat down several chairs away from her.

'She received it yesterday, all the way from Scotland.'

Millie recognised one of the girls as being Lady Clarice Langham's friend, the one who had made such horrible comments about Millie at the Earl of Shale's Ball. Lady Susan something or other was her name. They had never been formally introduced, but she knew exactly the kind of girl Susan was: a spiteful gossip who took pleasure in other people's misery.

'So, do you think Clarice will have him?' the other girl asked.

Millie stared at her tea. Lucy had confided to her that David carried a flame for Lady Clarice Langham. Now it would appear he had finally mustered the courage, albeit from afar, to finally speak his heart. She smiled. After all that had happened, she still liked David and wished him happiness.

Lady Susan let out a large sigh of disgust and replied loudly.

'Don't be silly, of course she will have him. He is handsome and funny, and one day she will be a duchess. One does not get a love letter from Lord Brooke and put it in the top drawer, never to be read again. This is going to be the wedding of the season, and it's only April.'

A hot flush raced up Millie's neck and stopped to burn brightly on her face. The china teacup rattled as she gripped the edge of the saucer tightly in her hand. She wasn't sure if her breath had caught in her throat; she knew only that she couldn't breathe. She gritted her teeth and slowly lifted her head. As her eyes rose, she began to frantically survey the ballroom, searching for any sign of salvation.

'Isn't that Millie Ashton, Lady Lucy's friend?' the girl who was not Susan asked. 'Why yes, I do believe it is; though since the letter only arrived yesterday, chances are she has not heard about Lord Brooke and Clarice. More's the pity,' Lady Susan replied, in a voice too loud for what should have been a private conversation

The two girls stood and walked away; as they passed in front of Millie, Susan looked over her shoulder and gave Millie a self-satisfied smile, leaving no doubt as to why she had chosen that particular place, and that exact moment, to divulge Lady Clarice's good news. Susan had wished to see the results of her handiwork: to see the heartbreak written all over Millie's face.

With a brittle smile painted on her lips, Millie looked away and waved to an imaginary person across the room. She would rather die than give Susan any kind of satisfaction.

When Charles returned to his sister's side a little while later, she was white-faced and trembling. 'Millie?' Charles asked.

Without looking up, she offered him her hand. 'I need to leave, Charles,' she replied. 'Now, please, if you don't mind. I would walk home, but Mama paid a small fortune for these slippers and it wouldn't do to ruin a second pair. I need my outside shoes and my coat, please.' She pointed in the direction of the ladies' cloakroom.

Charles looked at her crestfallen face and took hold of both her hands.

'What has happened? You were all light and gay when I left, and now you look as if you are about to face the executioner.'

'He's getting married,' she said, without emotion.

'Who? Who is getting married?' he replied, perplexed

She closed her eyes and whispered. 'Alex'.

Charles sighed.

Millie sucked in a deep breath. 'He wrote a love letter to Lady Clarice Langham, and everyone knows. Or if they don't, that horrid Susan friend of hers will have it all around the room by the end of the night. Please Charles, I cannot bear to face Clarice; you have to take me home.'

Her brother let go of her hand. 'No,' he replied.

'What?'

He shook his head, and then to make certain she understood his meaning, he put an arm around her and steered her back toward the main ballroom. 'No, I am not taking you home, Millie. Nor am I going to allow you to sit and mope in a dark corner all evening. You have been the centre of fun and laughter tonight, and as far as I am concerned our work here is not yet done.'

'But—' Millie stammered.

'But nothing.' Charles waved his hand in the air. 'Don't tell me, because I can tell you the story myself. You, along with most other young women in London, allowed yourself to fall in love with Lord Brooke. He paid you some attention and you thought he was a gift sent especially from heaven just for you. Shall I go on?'

Millie shrugged her shoulders and Charles continued. 'As soon as he sensed you were getting in too deep, he took a large step backward. Or to be more accurate, fled to Scotland.'

Charles stopped a passing footman and took two glasses of champagne from a well-laden tray. He handed one of the glasses to Millie. 'Here's a toast to your bruised heart, Millie. Wear it with pride, and learn the lesson well.'

He downed the contents of his glass in one attempt and then pointed the empty glass in the direction of Millie's still full one. 'Come on, we have a long night of it ahead. It's time you saw your first London dawn while still in your evening clothes.'

Millie looked at the glass in her hand and gave a tentative laugh. If ever there was a defining moment in her quest to be accepted by the *ton*, this was it. The gown, exquisite though it was, served only as a thin layer of decoration; how she handled herself in the face of possible public humiliation was the true test of how far she had come in the past few weeks. If she did encounter Lady Clarice Langham, it would be with all the grace and humour she could muster.

She took one small sip of the champagne and pulled the glass from her lips. 'Just don't allow me to ruin this dress, Madame de Feuillide will kill me.'

'Deal,' Charles replied.

Millie put the glass to her lips once more and finished the rest in one large gulp. 'Time to find some interesting people to have fun with and while we are at it, see if we can find some more of this magnificent champagne,' she announced as she straightened her spine.

With their arms locked together, sister and brother headed back into the ballroom and Millie's coat and shoes stayed safely hanging in the cloakroom.

&

The day after the ball, Millie wrote to Lucy and ended their friendship.

In time her heart would mend, but she couldn't risk encountering Alex and his new bride when visiting at Strathmore House. The price of preserving her pride would unfortunately be her friendship with Alex's sister.

'I have not seen an engagement notice in the *Gazette*,' Violet noted as she and Millie went about their daily social planning later the following week.

'It is odd, the whole business. All I have heard is a rumour that Lord Langham's daughter received a love letter from Lord Brooke, but no one else seems to be able to shed any further light on the situation,' Violet added.

Millie continued to thumb through the latest copy of *La Belle Assemblée*, taking careful note of the newest hairstyles. She had considered cutting her hair short, but when she mentioned the change of hairstyle to her mother, Violet's eyes had grown wide with horror.

'Where on earth did you get such as foolish notion from, my dear? Short hair is not at all suitable for a young, innocent miss such as you,' her mother explained. 'Unless you have had a very public affair with someone fascinating and need to make a dramatic statement, the whole thing would be lost on society. You would just look silly.'

'Maybe he is waiting to make things more public when he returns to London,' Millie replied, trying to shake off the feelings of dread and guilt which were her current constant companions.

Her mother shook her head. 'That's what I don't understand.'

'Pardon?' Millie replied.

Violet leaned over Millie's shoulder and pointed to a gown with white ruffles and a high neckline. 'That's sweet,' she said. Millie closed the book and glared at her mother. 'What don't you understand?'

'Why the Radley family are still in Scotland, that's what. If Lord Brooke is getting married, then why did he write to that poor girl and then remain in Scotland? It makes absolutely no sense. By the way, have you written to Lucy again? Now that you two have made amends, if anyone has any idea as to what is going on with her brother, I would think she would be the best source of information. I am surprised she didn't mention it in the letter she wrote to you. Then again she may not be in her brother's confidence; men tend to be rather secretive creatures when it comes to their personal affairs.'

Millie puffed out her cheeks, thinking it might be time to tell her mother something of the truth. It was hard enough to mask the pain of a broken heart, but at least she could share the sadness she felt over the loss of Lucy's friendship.

'I have written to Lucy again, but I don't expect a reply. In light of Lord Brooke's impending nuptials, I have decided it would be prudent to end any association with the Radley family,' she replied.

She heard Violet sigh. An arm came around her waist and she was pulled in close. A gentle kiss was planted warmly on her cheek. 'Do you feel better, now that you have finally told me? I thought you might be nursing a little heartache, darling. You seemed very much out of sorts the day Lucy and her family left town. I thought at first it might have been disappointment at Lucy's departure, but it didn't take long for me to suspect there was more to it than that.'

Millie smiled and gave her mother a kiss in return.

'Thank you,' Millie said.

Violet smiled. 'Not to worry, my love, your special someone is out there, and I would not be surprised if you met him very soon. Over the next few months town is going to be full of charming young men.'

There was a knock on the sitting room door, and as the two women looked up, they saw Mr Ashton enter the room with a puzzled look on his face.

'You will never guess who I just had a visit from.'

Chapter Sixteen

Alex's back ached and he shifted uncomfortably on the leather bench. He would never again complain about the discomfort of travelling in the Strathmore family coach.

By the time he and David had reached Darlington he was ready to bribe the driver and take over the reins of the London-bound mail coach himself. He would give anything to get out of the cramped public coach and into the fresh air. He would swear on a holy bible that the man seated opposite him had decided that sniffing was an art form. He had been studiously practising it for at least the last thirty miles.

When the coach did stop to change horses and exchange mail, it was only for a few minutes. There was just time for a quick visit to the rear yard, followed by the hurried purchase of some provisions, before they got back into the cramped coach and ready for the next forty miles of road.

'We are making good time,' David noted as he handed Alex a slice of buttered fresh bread. 'This would normally have taken us two days.'

Alex nodded. They had made excellent time in the day and a half since leaving Edinburgh. He looked out the window at the countryside as it rolled past, grateful that the Great North Road was clear of snow. He could hardly believe his father had not stopped him from going back to London.

They had been in Scotland for just over two weeks of their intended stay, but Alex knew if he remained at the castle any longer he would go mad.

During that time, Lucy had received the letter of apology from Millie and penned her own letter of reconciliation. Within days of having sent his own letter to Millie, Alex had taken to pacing back and forth across the bailey and down to the castle gatehouse, waiting expectantly for the morning cart which brought supplies up from the village. But each morning he returned to the keep empty-handed and disappointed.

By Alex's reckoning, he should be an almost engaged man, but his intended fiancée had not deemed it necessary to pen him a reply. There had been more than ample time for Millie to respond to his heartfelt declaration, and her silence began to concern him.

Then one morning, Lucy received her second letter from Millie. She came into the breakfast room with a look of deep worry on her face, the letter clutched tightly in her hand.

'Alex, I need to speak with you,' she said. The hairs on the back of Alex's neck stood up when he saw the pained look on her face.

'This doesn't look good,' David muttered under his breath, and put his cup of coffee down.

'I don't know what has happened, but Millie has politely but firmly ended our friendship.' She walked over to David and handed him the letter. His brow furrowed as he read it and a sense of dread and foreboding gripped Alex as he watched.

Something had gone terribly wrong in London.

'She says that due to recent developments it is no longer possible for her to visit at Strathmore House, as she would not be comfortable knowing that you may also be in attendance,' David said.

As Lucy took the letter back from David, she looked sadly at Alex. 'I *knew* there was more to that evening at your house than you were prepared to admit; you were far too quick to protest your innocence. But that aside, it would appear that Millie is *not* in love with you after all and has decided you pose too great of a risk to her reputation to be seen in your company. I'm sorry, Alex, but it doesn't look like you are going to get your happily ever after.'

She folded the letter, and gave a quick glance at the food on the table. David pulled out a chair and offered her a seat, but she shook her head. 'I don't really feel like breakfast this morning; I might just take a cup of coffee and go for a stroll on the ramparts. The fresh air might help to clear my thoughts.'

David poured his sister a cup of coffee and showed her to the door, closing it after she had left. Alex meanwhile remained rooted to the spot, stunned by Lucy's revelation. When David returned to the table he came and sat by Alex's side. A cold chill rippled across his shoulders as David placed a firm hand on his arm and gave him a friendly pat.

'There was more in the letter, and you are not going to like it. After ending things with Lucy, Millie went on to say that she is going to marry the first man who offers to take her back to India.'

Alex shot to his feet. 'I need to leave,' he said.

'Father will not agree to you going; you know he won't.'

Alex nodded. 'I know, but I have to see Millie. If father won't agree to me leaving then I shall have to find my own way back to London. Let me try and talk to him as soon as he returns from the village. In the meantime, I will check my top drawer and see how much money I have. I might need to buy a coach ticket.'

He picked up a fresh plate from the table and upon reaching the sideboard, started piling it high with food. No matter the outcome of his discussions with his father, he could not be sure when he would next sit down to a hot meal. He sat back down at the table and started to eat, only looking up when David placed a tray containing a whole baked salmon on the table in front of him.

'You are going to need your strength to face him and the long cold road back to London,' David said, teasing some pink meat from the fish and placing it on to Alex's already overladen plate.

❦

The discussion between the Duke of Strathmore and his son went just as Alex had expected. As soon as his father had returned to the castle, Alex sought him out and demanded he be allowed to leave. A furious row had ensued, at the end of which Alex had packed a bag, bidden his mother and sisters farewell and started walking for Edinburgh.

Three hours later, his father sent a carriage. The Duke of Strathmore would not allow his son and heir to freeze to death just to prove a point.

As the carriage pulled up on the roadside, David leapt down and hailed Alex. 'Had enough?' he called out. Alex picked up a lump of snow from the road and threw it at him. 'About bloody time; did he expect me to walk the whole way?' Alex replied.

David dodged the snowball and made a rude sign with his hand. 'You did well getting this far, I'm impressed. I think Father expected you to hole up in the tavern for a few hours and sulk before coming back to the castle. He waited over an hour before he sent someone to look for you. The rest of the delay was my fault. I decided to take my time packing a bag when he asked me to go after you.'

Alex shook his head.

'I'm not going back to the castle; I'm going to London.'

David put an arm around him and pulled Alex toward the carriage. 'I know; that's why he sent me. He's worried that you are rushing off and making decisions without thinking them through. I'm supposed to be the voice of reason.'

They looked at one another and laughed.

'Father said we can take the carriage to Edinburgh and then get the mail coach to London. We should be back in town by Thursday. He even gave me money.' David pulled a wad of five-pound notes out of his pocket and gave them a sniff.

'Truth be told, I think he was pleased that you wouldn't take no for an answer. As I left the room, I swear I heard him mutter something about you finally showing some backbone.'

Smiling, David took hold of the carriage door handle. He turned to Alex, and all merriment disappeared from his countenance. 'Are you sure about this? You are not just condemning us both to a long trip because you cannot go back and face Papa?' he asked.

'Yes, I am certain about this; I have to see Millie. Something has happened to make her sever all ties with us and I will surely go insane if I am forced to stay in Scotland,' Alex replied.

The brothers exchanged a brief handshake. David climbed back into the carriage, while Alex threw his bag up to the driver's mate on top and climbed in after him. With a crack of his whip, the driver turned the horses' heads and they set off on the road to Edinburgh.

Later, huddled in the mail coach as it steadily ate up the miles between Edinburgh and London, Alex and David attempted to formulate a plan for Alex to successfully win the hand of Miss Millicent Ashton. Flowers and presents would only get him so far. Millie had seen through Alex's previous floral apologies and not been swayed. She was more than likely to send back any attempt on his part to buy her good favour.

After several days of discussion, and some valuable input from an old widow heading for Cambridge, they agreed the direct approach was the only one where Alex stood a remote chance of success. Upon their return to London, he would call on Millie's father and request permission to court his daughter.

'She couldn't refuse to see me, could she?' he asked the widow. She raised her eyebrows. David, meanwhile, slept on in the corner, having lost all interest in the conversation several hours previously. 'It will depend on how terrible a slight you have caused her. If it is only a trifling matter, then you should be able to make amends,' the lady replied.

Alex grimaced. He had told the old lady everything, all except his name. But if she was as perceptive as he suspected, she would have seen the family crest on his whisky flask and realised that the two young men in the coach were in fact the Duke of Strathmore's sons. What they were doing travelling in a common mail coach, he would leave to her imagination.

When the coach changed horses at Biggleswade, the widow departed from the London-bound journey. As they made their goodbyes, she placed her card in Alex's hand and shook his hand, saying 'Don't think about it too much, young man, just go with your heart.'

After he had escorted her across the yard and seen her safely on board the Cambridge-bound coach, Alex hurried back toward the inn to check on David and their food. If he was lucky this would be his last meal on the road. Tomorrow they would reach London and their own house.

As David handed him a hot meat pie, Alex gave him the old lady's card. David read the back and then turned it over. Alex saw a flush of red appear on his brother's cheek.

David smacked his lips. 'It says, "Good luck. Invite me to your wedding and give my regards to your mother. Caroline always was such a sweet girl."' He shook his head and looked at the Cambridge-bound coach as it rolled out the yard and down the road.

'That was Lady Margaret Sutton. What on earth was she doing travelling in the mail coach?' David said.

'I don't know, but she has reminded me that I need to book St George's as soon as we get back. Then I need to go and see James Ashton,' Alex replied.

Chapter Seventeen

Alex took the long way home. After the disastrous meeting with Millie's father, he badly needed to walk off his anger.

The Radley brothers had arrived back in London early the previous day and after catching up on some well-needed sleep, they set about re-establishing themselves. A bored Phillips had been delighted to see David and Alex on the doorstep, travel bags in hand, and had spent the following morning making sure both their wardrobes were up to the mark.

'Unfortunately, none of the other staff will be available for a few days,' Phillips noted. 'But I am sure between Mrs Phillips and myself we shall all manage.'

David screwed up his face in disgust, while Alex shrugged his shoulders. He had more important matters to consider.

The following afternoon, once Alex had managed to get some sleep and seen to a few urgent errands, he called in at Millie's house to see Mr Ashton. The reception he received from Millie's father was not at all what he had expected.

James Ashton had been polite but not overly friendly when he greeted Alex at his study door. He had shown Alex to a green leather club chair and then taken a seat in the matching chair opposite. Their discussion was brief and James's response to Alex's request to court Millie was curt, to say the least.

Now as he headed home, Alex focused his gaze on the pavement as he walked, hoping that it was just lack of sleep to blame for the surreal day he was having. It occurred to him that perhaps he had not heard Mr Ashton correctly when he had mentioned the Earl of Langham, but the fact that Millie's father had then swiftly shown him the door left him in no doubt as how unwelcome he was at the Ashton house.

He stopped in the middle of the street and looked back the way he had come. What had Millie's father said? 'I don't think the Earl of Langham or his daughter would think too highly of your suggestion, young man,' Alex muttered, recalling James Ashton's words. What was that supposed to mean?

He continued past Grosvenor Square and into Bird Street, finally arriving back at the house a little over an hour after he had left. The moment he stepped inside the front door, he was greeted by David, who wore a smile of great expectation.

'Well, how did it go?' his brother asked, attempting to give him a hearty congratulatory pat on the back. Alex stepped out of David's reach and held up a hand. 'Dreadful. He didn't exactly give me a welcome to the family speech. In fact, he didn't even offer me a cup of tea. He said no and then asked me to leave.' Alex pulled off his coat and after roughly tossing it on to the coat stand, stood shaking his head in disbelief.

'I have never been thrown out of a private home before,' he said, his voice edged with anger.

'Not a good time for a first. So, what happened; what did you do wrong?' David replied.

Alex screwed up his face. He had no idea why things had gone so awry. He sighed. 'It's got me completely at a loss. The only thing I am certain of at this point is that if I don't get a cup of hot tea in the next five minutes I am going to expire from thirst.'

'You go upstairs; I shall find Phillips and get him to bring us up a tray to the main sitting room. I will see you in a few minutes,' David said, patting Alex on the back.

Alex nodded in agreement and went up to his room. Alone in his bedroom, he stood staring at his own reflection in the mirror above the fireplace. He rubbed his temple and made himself a silent promise to stop scowling. 'When did I lose my charm?' he asked the mirror. He heard a knock on his bedroom door as David passed by. He gave his reflection one last look and shook his head.

Seated in the sitting room, with a cup of tea in his hand, David tried to help him make sense of the situation. 'So, you asked to see Millie, but Mr Ashton said no. Then you asked to court her, but he also said no, and then he said something about the Earl of Langham before throwing you out? Do I have it right?' David asked.

Alex nodded. 'That's about the sum of it. I was only in his study for all of perhaps five minutes. I consider myself fortunate that he offered me a seat.'

David drummed his fingers on the leather chair. 'So, if we add the strange letter Lucy received to your not-so-welcoming reception at the Ashtons', we can conclude that something is seriously amiss.'

Alex rubbed his eyes. 'And if that was not strange enough, I passed Viscount Lewis on the way back here and he offered me his congratulations.'

David raised his eyebrows. 'What for?'

Alex shook his head. 'I don't know, but the more I think about it, the only way we are going to get any answers is by getting out and talking to people. The season has kicked off so there must be more balls and parties starting to happen. With any luck I will be able to run Millie to ground at one of them and get an answer from her. Otherwise we are just guessing.' He held up a finger. 'I have an idea; I'll be back in a moment.'

He put down the cup and headed downstairs and into the front hall. On the small table inside the hall, Phillips had left a pile of letters and invitations. He picked them up and brought them back upstairs. After dumping them in the middle of the sitting room coffee table, he and David set about opening them all.

'Don't worry about any functions which have already taken place, just burn those. We only need concern ourselves with parties which happen this week,' Alex instructed as he tore open a large, heavy letter and handed it to David.

He watched as David's eyes quickly scanned the paper, then felt his heart leap as his brother's mouth opened and out came a loud. 'Yes! Oh well done Alex, you illiterate genius.'

'What is it?' he asked, ignoring the backhanded compliment.

'The East India Company Annual Reception. James Ashton is quite senior within the company, so there is no way he would miss something like this, especially when he has been away for all those years.'

He read a little further down the invitation and smiled. 'And a special presentation will be made to Mr James Ashton in celebration of his outstanding service to the company and his appointment as a principal. Brilliant; now we know the whole family will be there.'

'So, when is it?' Alex replied.

David gave a knowing smile as he shook his head, but said nothing. Alex leaned over and made an unsuccessful grab for the letter. David laughed. 'Relax, brother dear, the party is tonight. You have all afternoon to get yourself ready.'

Alex closed his eyes and sighed with relief. He would only have to wait a few more hours before he could speak to Millie. He was certain that by the end of the evening, everything would be sorted and any misunderstanding between them cleared away.

Finishing his cup of tea, he went back to his room, where he lay down on his bed. The soft, burgundy-coloured coverlet was a welcome comfort for his tortured mind, but within minutes, the confidence he had felt when speaking to David began to ebb away and the first signs of doubt slowly crept in.

What if Millie would not speak to him? No, he was sure she was not the sort to go in for the silent treatment. In fact, if anything was certain in this world, it was that Millie Ashton would die having the last word. He rolled over on to his side and tucked a pillow under his head.

'I know one thing I need and that is sleep,' he muttered as he closed his eyes. 'I might just take a small nap; at least I will look a little less haggard when she sets eyes on me.'

As sleep overcame him, Alex descended into a strange dream, where he found himself married to an angry woman who looked just like the Earl of Langham.

※

Millie sat quietly in the family carriage for the ride to East India House. She nursed a quiet, self-satisfied smile, knowing that the deep blue silk evening gown she wore matched her eyes perfectly. As soon as she had seen the fabric at Madame de Feuillide's salon, she knew she had to have it.

Any argument Millie might have anticipated from her mother soon evaporated when Millie held the sample of blue silk up to her face. 'Yes,' Violet had said, without hesitation.

Under her cloak, against her heated skin, lay a stunning sapphire necklace. Every so often Millie reached up and touched her throat, just to be sure it was still there. Aunt Beatrice had offered to loan her the family heirloom the moment she saw Millie's new gown. Mr Ashton had agreed to his daughter wearing it on the stipulation that she not leave the main reception room at East India House without being accompanied by one of the family.

'I don't have to tell you how priceless a piece that necklace is, Millie,' her father had explained, the afternoon he brought it back from Ashton House. 'If anything happened to it, your uncle would never speak to me again. It was one of the few items we agreed not to sell when we discovered how much of the family fortune your grandfather had lost.'

'Yes, Papa. I promise to guard it with my life,' she'd replied, holding the black velvet box in which the necklace lay.

A chill of excitement swept over her as she stepped out of the family carriage and into the glittering reception area. This was a special night for her father and she would do everything she could to make it a success for him. She had heard so much about East

India House growing up that it was a little surreal to finally stand within its hallowed walls.

On every wall of the room hung huge paintings showing the countries and trade routes which The East India Company controlled. Around the walls hung a series of six large canvases, each one depicting a location in the world which was a source of the company's wealth, she recognised a picture of Calcutta and smiled.

Closer to the doorway which lead to the main reception room she saw a large map of India with Calcutta marked out in the top right-hand corner. Gold silk tapestries bordered both sides of the painting of India, edged with tassels of pure gold and silver thread; they were priceless. A lump formed in her throat and she blinked away a tear. East India House was a small piece of home set right in the heart of London.

Entering the main reception room, Charles took a glass of champagne from a footman and handed it to her. She gave him a smile. 'Thank you, Charles. This shall be the first of only two champagnes I shall have for the evening.'

Her brother raised an eyebrow.

'Why?' he asked.

She looked past him, and into the elegant crowd. 'Because, Charles dearest, I intend to be sophisticated and sober this evening; I know how much this means to Papa,' she replied, taking a sip of the fine bubbles.

Charles stepped in close and whispered in her ear. 'And here I was thinking it was because father would skin you alive if you lost that necklace.' Millie gave him a serene nod of her head. 'That too.'

It was close to nine o'clock by the time Alex and David arrived. Alex had slept well into the evening, and it had taken all of Phillips' immense skills as a valet to get him washed, shaved and dressed in just under an hour.

'At least the bags have disappeared from under your eyes,'

David remarked as they climbed the stairs and joined the line of guests being received by the head of the company's London office.

'Thank god for that,' Alex replied, though he had a terrible feeling he would need more than his boyish good looks to get anywhere with Millie tonight. The letter Lucy had received from Millie had kept him awake for days. His greatest fear was that she had found someone else and that his hurried dash back to London had all been in vain.

Her father's outright rejection of his request to court Millie had rattled him to the core. He had to find her. 'I will take the left side of the room, you take the right. The sooner I find her and speak to her, the better things will be,' Alex said. He gave David a wave and began to work his way through the crowd.

Half an hour later and he was still searching. His progress was hampered by the sheer number of guests who wished him to pass their regards on to his father. At one point a slow panic began to creep into his mind: what if Millie was not at the reception? A quick check with the head footman confirmed that the Ashton family had arrived around eight o'clock and were somewhere within the main reception hall.

'Where are you?' he muttered, as he turned and headed toward a group of guests gathered near a large window.

Lord Gilbert was wickedly funny. He was also extremely wicked. The third son of the Duke of Lamberton had a reputation which stretched nearly all the way back to Scotland.

An unashamed rake, he was a cautionary tale for mothers to tell their unmarried daughters. Millie thought he was brilliant. And the fact that she was standing in a group listening to Lord Gilbert's latest exploits at the racetrack bore testament to how popular Millie had become during the preceding weeks.

The Millie of old would not have been able to come within ten feet of him, but with her new figure and confidence, she had gained entrance to his select group of friends.

'Well, of course the jockey went off and had two of the biggest pies he could find. The owner couldn't for the life of him understand why his steed ran last; and I swear it took all my strength to keep a straight face as I walked over to the bookmaker to collect my winnings,' Lord Gilbert announced to the enthralled gathering, which promptly fell about laughing.

A round of applause followed his story, at which Lord Gilbert gave an elegant bow. As Millie wiped the tears of laughter from her eyes, she gave Charles a grin. Finally, she had found a man in London who had a sense of humour she could appreciate. 'He is rather good at holding a crowd,' she said.

Her brother smiled and shook his head. 'Don't get too attached to our outrageous friend, Millie. If Mama or Papa start heading in this direction, you and I will have to make a quick exit.'

'I know, I know. I think he was the second person I was warned about when we stepped off the boat,' she replied. 'But it doesn't mean we can't have some fun in his company at a public gathering.'

'True, but—' Charles stopped mid-sentence. Something over Millie's right shoulder had caught his eye.

As she turned to see what it was, her brother caught her arm and pulled her back. 'Careful, you nearly made me spill my champagne,' she snapped, hurriedly checking her gown to ensure nothing had spoiled the fabric. Satisfied that her appearance was in order, she looked up at him and saw a look of deep concern on his face.

'What is it, Charles?'

'Lord Brooke just appeared and if I am not mistaken he is searching for someone.'

She blinked hard. Why had Alex chosen this of all nights to make his reappearance? And why did it have to be at a function he knew she would be certain to attend?

'He has a bloody cheek,' she replied, sotto voce.

'Yes, well, Lady Clarice Langham is here tonight, so it makes sense he would be looking for her,' Charles replied. She nodded; of course, he would be looking for his future wife.

It seemed Alex Radley had developed the unfortunate habit of attending functions and spoiling Millie's evening every time he did. She took a deep breath; this was one evening he was not going to ruin for her.

'Fine, let him come to every party for the rest of the season. We mean nothing to one another. He is merely an acquaintance.'

Charles ran his hand through his hair. 'I would be more inclined to believe you if I didn't happen to know who called on Papa today to ask if he could court you,' he replied. She watched his gaze as it tracked Alex's progress across the room. 'Yes. Well. Papa said no, and that's the end of it, he cannot court two women at the one time,' she replied. She took a large mouthful of champagne and swallowed it down. 'Let him come.'

Millie's firm resolve and disinterested veneer began to crumble the moment Charles drew in close and whispered. 'Be brave, my girl, he has seen me and is headed this way.'

She put her hand to the precious sapphire necklace, touching it as a talisman, while keeping her back facing the direction from which she knew Alex now approached.

'Ashton; I can't believe I finally found one of you. I was beginning to think you had come and gone and I had completely missed you,' Alex said, with obvious relief in his voice.

'Brooke, I heard you were back in town,' Charles replied.

Out of the corner of her eye, Millie saw Alex offer her brother his hand. Charles shook his head and put his right hand in his pocket, in an unmistakable snub.

'Oh,' Alex said, as a look of surprise appeared on his face. Millie clenched her left fist tight.

Good, let him know disappointment for a change.

A slight smile formed on her lips as she heard her brother address Alex in the most unfriendly of fashions. 'Don't bother, Brooke, save it for the well-wishers; I am sure there are plenty of them in the room tonight. Now if you don't mind, I think it best if you clear off and leave us alone, because if you don't, I might feel the need to rearrange your deceitful face.'

Millie bit her lip. Charles always did have a way with words, especially when he was in a fighting mood. She looked up at her brother, fiercely proud of her champion. She had a knight who not only defended his sister's honour but took a stand for her broken heart.

A spark of bravery found its way to her heart as she realised that after tonight she might never get another chance to speak honestly to Alex. 'I think you had better do what he says, Lord Brooke, my brother doesn't normally give his opponents a second chance to walk away,' she said, her gaze still firmly locked on Charles.

A long moment of silence followed before Alex spoke again. 'Millie?'

Before turning to face him, she allowed herself a brief second to compose her expression. She turned and stared Alex down. 'As we are no longer friends, Lord Brooke, you shall address me as Miss Ashton. Using my first name shows a lack of decorum, which I find personally distasteful.' She watched as his eyes grew wide with shock.

'What have you done to yourself?' he stammered. 'Where are all your beautiful curves?' He took a step forward and looked closely at her face. 'And where is your magical little nose ring? Oh Millie, please don't tell me you have become the same as the rest of them?'

Charles reached out and took a firm hold of Alex's evening jacket. He pulled Alex toward him, before giving him a hard shove. Alex staggered back, his gaze still fixed on Millie.

'As I said before, Brooke, you are not welcome in my sister's company. So, unless you want to find yourself sitting on the floor, wiping your own blood from your face, you had better make yourself scarce,' Charles ordered.

Millie laid a gentle hand on her brother's arm and steered him away, taking the opportunity to give a small backward glance toward Alex. The look of contempt she gave him was well worth the hours of practice she had spent in front of her bedroom mirror.

'Come Charles, I think he understands our position. Let us not create a scene; he is simply not worth it. Besides, we should be heading back to the dance floor; the orchestra will be starting up again soon. And since my dance card is full, I should hate to disappoint any of my gentlemen friends by lingering elsewhere and missing the fun,' she said.

Turning to Charles, she gave a nod of her head and allowed him to escort her away, leaving Alex standing in their wake.

As they walked away, Millie made a point of stopping and greeting other guests, smiling and shaking hands as they moved through the crowd toward the main ballroom.

Once they cleared the reception room, and Alex was out of sight, Charles let out a large sigh. 'Well done, Millie,' he said.

She didn't reply. The shock of seeing Alex after all those weeks had rapidly sunk in and drained her resolve. She gripped her brother's arm tightly and puffed out her cheeks.

I will not cry in the middle of a reception. I shall not give him the satisfaction of knowing how much he hurt me. I am not that girl any more. I will not cry.

'I think I shall have that second glass of champagne now, if you please, Charles,' she replied.

♨

Alex stood rooted to the spot as he watched Millie's progress through the throng, until she finally disappeared from view.

His chest hurt from where Charles Ashton had laid his fisted hand. Although he was not a strongly built man, Charles had a powerful boxer's arm. He gave silent thanks that Charles had not made good on his threat to rearrange Alex's face.

'Well, how did you go?' a familiar voice asked.

He turned to see David, who wore a worried look. 'I've had no luck with finding Millie or Charles, but I did manage to find their parents. You were right; something very odd is going on,' David explained.

'I found them, but they made it crystal-clear that I am no longer considered to be a friend. Ashton threatened physical violence if I came near his sister again,' Alex replied.

'Do you think Ashton knows about you kissing Millie?' David

asked. 'That could explain the extremely cool reception you received.'

Alex shook his head. 'If Millie's family suspected for one minute that I had so much as touched her, I wouldn't have been thrown out of their house by Mr Ashton. Instead, you would be reading our betrothal notice in the *Gazette* tomorrow morning. No, something else is amiss. I just can't put my finger on it.'

'Well, I don't think we are going to get much more out of anyone tonight. How about I call the carriage around and we head home and try to come up with another approach to the problem?' David said. 'You might have got some much-needed sleep this afternoon, but I still feel like I'm ready for the knacker's yard.'

Alex looked at his brother. He was in two minds as to whether he should do as David said, or try to talk to Millie again. 'All right, I will do one last turn of the room and see if I can find her. I shall meet you outside shortly,' Alex replied.

David gave a nod of his head and started toward the front door. As Alex watched him go, he saw his brother stop and greet some old friends. He smiled. Once David started talking, he would have to be dragged out of the party, so Alex knew he had plenty of time to try to track Millie down once more.

He found her on the dance floor. She was twirling through a waltz with a tall thin man he did not know, and she was laughing. The stunning blue gown she wore hugged tightly to her new, slimmed-down frame, her smaller breasts now gently peeking over the top of the neckline. The Millie of old would have spilled over the top of the bodice, if she had dared to wear that style of gown.

She moved gracefully through the turns of the dance, while he struggled to comprehend the sight before his eyes. Where was his Millie, with all her luscious curves? Who was this creature who now inhabited her body and regarded him as a mere acquaintance?

His breath caught as his body remembered who she was and how it still ached for her. As for his heart, nothing of what he felt for her had changed during their weeks apart. He was in love with her.

A tap on his shoulder roused him from his musings. He

turned to find Lady Clarice Langham standing staring at him with a bemused look. Clarice Langham, David's secret love. Tall, thin and absolutely nothing like Millie. While Millie had curves and inviting breasts, Clarice struggled to make any form of impression in her clothes. To Alex's mind, she bordered on dowdy. If David failed to understand Alex's attraction to the now slightly less chubby girl from across the other side of the world, his own choice of inamorata left his brother equally at a loss.

He gave her a bow. 'Lady Clarice, how nice to see you, I trust you are well.' She let out a snort. 'Is that it? You keep me waiting and all you can do is to ask after my health?'

He frowned. What on earth was she talking about?

Clarice took a step forward and brought her face close to his. 'Why haven't you called on me since you returned?' she asked. Having been friends with her for a number of years, Alex had exchanged enough silly banter with Clarice over the years to assume she was in jest. He gave a laugh.

'Well, we only arrived back in London yesterday. I was still working my way through the long list of young ladies I have to pay my respects to. Fear not, you were on top of the next page,' he chuckled. 'Of course, I can now tick your name off.'

Her face fell and he saw her bottom lip quiver.

A cold fear gripped him. Was there nothing he could do right this evening?

'I see. I didn't realise I was that far down on your list. Far be it for me to assume I was any sort of priority,' she replied. Tears were forming in her eyes and Alex had the sinking feeling Clarice Langham was about to cry all over him.

He shook his head, while his mouth opened and closed silently. With his mind in a whirl, he could think of nothing else to do. He reached out, took hold of Clarice's hand and gave her a gentle pat on the glove. There, there.

Not satisfied that Alex's evening was already a complete disaster, Fate then decided that the music should stop, and Millie and her dance partner would exit the dance floor right next to where he stood. He saw Millie take in the sight of him holding Lady Clarice's hand and his heart sank just that little bit more.

Their gazes met for an instant and he knew the situation was now hopeless, as Millie gave him the same look she had given him on the dance floor at Ashton House the moment before she had walked away. For the second time this evening he had failed in his efforts to talk to her.

'I am sorry if there has been some misunderstanding; I did not mean to speak out of turn,' Clarice said, withdrawing her hand. 'I should not have been so forward. Please excuse me.' Before Alex had a chance to say anything else, Clarice turned on her heel and disappeared back into the crowd.

'What on earth was that all about?' he whispered to no one in particular. 'This would have to be the strangest night of my life.'

His gaze swept back over the room, where it fell on Millie once more. She had her back turned to him, and Charles stood at her side. His arm was loosely draped around his sister's waist, while she leaned gently against him. When Charles dropped a tender kiss on the top of Millie's head, she looked up at him and smiled.

Alex would have given everything he owned at that moment to swap places with Charles Ashton. But it didn't take a genius to know the reason Charles needed to comfort his sister. Her show of bravery had lasted just long enough to see Alex off. He had hurt her, the woman he loved.

He closed his eyes and sighed. For the first time in his life he understood what it was to be unpopular and he certainly wasn't enjoying the strange prickly sensation. He was Alexander the Great, suave and debonair. Men did not threaten him with physical violence, and he didn't make women cry.

His conscience gave him a sharp dig in the ribs. He knew he had made his fair share of young ladies go home and cry over him. Until now, he had never had any reason to face the consequences of his silly, hurtful games.

Tonight, in the space of half an hour, he had watched two girls on the verge of tears and known it was his fault. His conscience dug a little deeper into his soul, and painfully drew his sense of shame to the surface. In the middle of a crowded London ballroom, Alex Radley faced the ugly truth that he was nothing more than a callous, selfish heartbreaker.

The orchestra struck up a tune and he watched as Millie took her brother's hand and allowed him to lead her to the dance floor.

Realising his cause would not be furthered any more tonight, he admitted defeat and went to find David and their ride home.

§⚫

After removing his key from the front door, Alex slammed the door loudly behind him.

The unexpected hour-long walk home had done nothing to improve his already sour mood. When he discovered David had abandoned him, he was too angry to hail a hack. Instead, he had buttoned up his coat and marched all the way back to Bird Street. Anyone foolish enough to have tried to rob him would have seriously regretted their decision.

'David!' he yelled from just inside the front door. 'She had better be the best damn courtesan in town for you to have up and left me like that.'

An upstairs door closed and David appeared at the top of the stairs. He had his heavy greatcoat on and his soft travel bag was slung over his shoulder.

'Where the blazes are you off to at this time of night?' Alex bellowed.

As he reached the bottom of the stairs, David threw the bag down on to the tiled floor. Opening the store cupboard, he withdrew two pairs of clean boots. He opened the bag and stuffed them inside. He picked up the bag and started for the front door.

Alex marched across the front entrance and stood in front of his brother, blocking David's exit. With his hands fisted at his side Alex stood his ground, ready to demand an answer.

As David made to step around him, Alex countered his move and the brothers stood toe to toe, angrily eyeing one another.

'Get out of the way, Alex. If you don't I shall beat you to a bloody pulp,' David replied. The calm in his voice sat on the thin edge of rage.

'Not until you tell me where you are going and why you left me at the reception,' Alex replied. 'You owe me that much, at least.'

David threw the bag down again, this time hitting Alex in the leg.

'I don't owe you a thing, you stupid ass. Not content with making a mess of your own life, you decided to ruin mine.'

'What are you talking about?' Alex replied.

David sucked in a deep breath and slowly let it out again. 'Let me ask you this: did you mail the letter I gave you to send to Millie Ashton?' he asked in a tone normally reserved for a recalcitrant child.

Alex screwed up his face. 'Well, yes and... no.'

'What the devil is that supposed to mean?'

'I didn't send the letter you handed to me; because I had already sent the other letter.'

'That much I now understand. But what I cannot comprehend is why you didn't bother to tell me,' David snapped.

Alex sighed. 'I found the original letter on the floor while you were asleep. I gave it to a footman to post. By the time you gave me the other letter the following day it was all too late. I reasoned that a passionate letter to Millie was better than a kind sweet one, so I told you a small white lie.'

'Which unfortunately has turned into a very large problem,' David ground out.

Alex felt his heart sinking further by the minute. 'What do you mean?'

'I mean that the first letter was not meant for Millie Ashton. I sat down to pen a love letter for you, but after a couple of pathetic attempts, I knew I couldn't do it. So, I had a couple of glasses of whisky and ended up writing a letter to the woman I love. A letter in which I poured out my heart.' He put a hand over his mouth and Alex saw tears form in his brother's eyes. David shook his head as he fought to keep his composure. 'I told her how much I love her and the hope I hold for a future with her as my wife. A letter filled with impossible dreams.'

David pinched his thumb and forefinger into the inner corners of his eyes. 'A letter I addressed, but never signed. A letter I thought had made its way into the fire along with all the other failed attempts.'

'Oh, David. Oh no,' Alex whispered. 'I picked it up off the floor, I thought it was—'

'NO! You never thought anything, Alex. You just took my letter, sealed it and sent it off without giving it a second thought. And then you had the audacity to lie to me about it,' David snapped. He drew his hand over his eyes, but when he took it away, more tears quickly replaced those he had wiped away.

'But the footman I showed the letter to said it was addressed to Millie. That's why I let him put it in the post,' Alex pleaded.

'Did he, Alex? Really? Tell me Alex, what did he say, exactly?'

Alex racked his brains, trying to recall the conversation of nearly three weeks earlier. After leaving David sleeping in the chair, he had found the head footman and handed him the letter to put in the morning's post. The young man had checked it and confirmed the address.

'Did he tell you it was addressed to a young lady in Mill Street?' David asked, taking in a deep breath.

'Yes,' Alex replied, feeling the ground shifting from under him.

David bent down and picked up his bag. 'You may recall the Earl of Langham and his daughter live in Mill Street, five doors from where the Ashton family live. Clarice was the *lady* the footman was referring to when he read the name on the letter. So, you signed my love letter, and then had it sent to the only woman I have ever loved. She now thinks you intend to marry her, and so does most of London society.'

Too stunned to respond, Alex could do nothing except watch, helpless, as David pushed past him. As he opened the front door, David looked back and said. 'There is nothing you could say right now that would make any difference. As far as I am concerned, you have made this mess, now you can lie in it. If anyone calls for me, I will be at Strathmore House.'

'But the house is closed up; the staff won't be expecting any of the family for another couple of weeks,' Alex stammered, in a vain attempt to stop his brother from leaving.

David nodded his head. 'Yes, I know, but I would rather sleep under the Holland covers at home than here under the same roof as you. To be honest, the way I am feeling at the moment, the temptation to murder you in your bed is too strong for me to remain. You are on your own from now on, Alex. Good luck with extracting yourself from this bloody disaster; you are going to need it.'

He began to go through the door, then stopped and marched quickly back to Alex. He brandished a clenched fist in Alex's face. 'And before you start to feel sorry for yourself, try standing in my boots for five minutes. Can you possibly begin to comprehend how this is for me? How soul-destroying it was for me to stand there and listen to our friends tell me how wonderful it was that my brother is about to marry the love of my life?'

He turned sharply on his heel, walked all the way through the door this time and slammed it loudly behind him as he went. Alex stood alone in the entrance and stared at the door.

He put his hands to his head. 'Oh, Alex, you idiot!' he whispered, sinking to his knees. He wrapped his arms around his body and hugged himself. With eyes tightly shut he rocked back and forth as the whole terrible reality of what he had done threatened to overwhelm him.

Everything now made perfect, horrible sense. Millie hated him for being a miserable two-faced liar. How could he claim to love her when he had declared himself to Clarice? He dared not think how she must have felt when she heard the news about the passionate love letter he had sent to another girl.

'Is it any wonder she doesn't want to know me?' he moaned.

And as for poor Lady Clarice, she thought she was about to become the Marchioness of Brooke. That at least explained the odd encounter he had had with her earlier in the evening. He had supposedly written a wonderful love letter declaring his feelings for her, but instead of calling on her at the first opportunity when he returned to London, he had, to her mind simply ignored her.

A cold emptiness formed in his stomach when he remembered how he had teased Clarice, and how the poor confused girl had walked away in tears. If she had been another of Lucy's false friends, he could almost scrape himself a feeble excuse for his behaviour, but he could not in Lady Clarice's case. Alex was one of only a handful of people David had trusted with the knowledge of his secret love, and now he had completely ruined everything for his brother. If he could not set this right, David would never forgive him.

He let out a cynical laugh. At least he now understood the cryptic comment Mr Ashton had made.

'How the hell am I going to get out of this?' he muttered.

He slowly got to his feet and unbuttoned his coat. There was no point in racing out into the night to chase after David; his brother had made it clear the last thing he needed from Alex right now was a heartfelt apology.

Coat in hand, he climbed the stairs and walked into the sitting room. The fire had been well stoked before they left and the room was warm and light in readiness for the Radley brothers to return and share their usual evening nightcap.

After throwing his coat over the back of a padded leather chair, he poured himself a large drink from the whisky decanter on the table beside the chair. He took a large swig of the drink and plopped down into the armchair. Staring into the fire, the enormity of what he had done washed over him as he felt ever-increasing waves of despair. The anguish was almost too much to bear. With the whisky bottle by his side, he proceeded to quietly drink himself into an unconscious state.

Chapter Eighteen

W hen Grace arrived early the next morning, she found Millie still fast asleep in bed.

Every morning for weeks now her mistress had made the trek across to Park Lane, and then all the way up to Oxford Street before returning home. But on this particular morning, nothing could rouse Millie from her bed.

'Go away,' was the first response Grace was able to evoke from Millie after several minutes of shaking the blankets. 'But miss, it's walking time. We are late,' Grace replied.

Millie threw the covers down from over her face. 'We are not walking this morning, Grace. I don't feel very well. Please go downstairs and see what breakfast you can scratch up from Mrs Knowles. I will send for you when I am ready to get dressed. If anyone asks, tell them I am feeling poorly this morning.' She pulled the blankets back up over face, leaving Grace to shrug her shoulders before leaving the room.

After the door closed, Millie pulled the blankets down to her neck and rolled over to face the window. It might have been heading toward summer, but London was still chilly first thing at daybreak. She leapt out of bed and hurried to her dresser. In the top drawer of her dresser, tucked inside a small bag, was a piece of paper on which were listed the departure dates for all India-bound ships for the next four months. She ran an eye over the list, wondering which of those ships she would board.

She folded the paper once more and put it securely away. The only thing she was missing was a husband prepared to give up England and take her home.

Climbing back into bed, she decided not to leave the house that morning. The risk of running into a certain young gentleman was too great. He might have made a tactical retreat at the reception, but she was under no illusion that Alex would suddenly give up and leave her alone.

She had managed to deal with him in a crowded ballroom with Charles by her side, but the prospect of encountering him on the street with only her maid and a footman to protect her filled her with dread. 'I don't know what he thinks he playing at; he has made it clear he wishes to marry Lady Clarice, so he can forget about trying to make amends with me,' she said to herself and snuggled further down in the bed.

The Ashton family had arrived home in the early hours of the morning, they had been among the last to leave the gala reception. Mr Ashton had refused to leave until company staff had found the portrait of him painted just before he left for India and had it hung on a hook by the front door.

'Stubborn man,' she muttered under the blankets.

Of course, her father would still have risen from his bed early for work this morning, late night or not.

Millie closed her eyes, and decided she would sleep the morning away. 'I will walk in the park this afternoon. If Alex comes near me, Charles can make good on his threat to punch him on the nose,' she murmured as she went back to sleep.

By late that afternoon Alex could not decide which Greek tragedy his life resembled the most. If it was *Medea*, then Millie would be perfect in the role of the scorned woman, plotting vengeance against him. 'I don't recall Medea having a brother who could box,' he muttered as he strolled through the main gate of Hyde Park and joined the other members of the *ton* out for the daily promenade.

With the season now underway, the park was a crush of people all vying to see and be seen by anyone who was anyone. It took a lot of handshakes and polite small talk before he could finally steal away from the crowd and begin looking for Millie.

The instant he spied Lady Clarice and her friends heading in his direction, he turned and made a hurried dash for a group of walnut trees. He moved as quickly as he could without drawing attention to himself. He did not need a repeat of the awkward encounter from the previous night. He still had no idea what he would say to Clarice now that he knew she had received the love letter.

As soon as he reached the trees, he hid behind a large one. Standing with his back to the tree trunk Alex tried to catch his breath. 'Definitely the Sword of Damocles,' he said aloud. 'One false move and I am surely a dead man.'

'That can be arranged,' a voice replied.

He turned and ducked as David swung a half-hearted punch towards his head. He was too quick now for David to successfully land a punch on him.

David took a spot next to him and leaned against the tree. 'Come to see how much more damage you can do, or are you content to rest on your laurels?' he asked.

Alex saw the grey bags under his brother's eyes. While he had slept the sleep of the inebriated, it was obvious David had found no such rest. 'Did you get any sleep last night?' Alex asked.

'No. As it turns out, Holland covers are not the warmest things to sleep under,' David replied with just the right touch of guilt-causing sarcasm. 'Have you managed to resolve anything, or are you just here for the flora?'

Alex shook his head. 'No, I was hoping to see Millie and try to talk to her. So far all I have done is shake hands with half of London and try to avoid your future intended.'

'Lady Clarice is here?'

'Who do you think I am hiding from behind this tree? Certainly not the Bishop of London,' Alex replied. He had slept late, but his black mood had not improved.

David harrumphed. 'No, but I couldn't blame you if you did. If his Grace got wind that his favourite nephew might be in the marriage market he would have you and the first unsuspecting girl in front of him bound together as man and wife. Alex poked his head around the side of the tree. Clarice and her gaggle of friends were heading toward the park gates. Finally, he hoped his luck was on the turn.

'The problem is, I am in the marriage market, but it has to be with the right girl. And unfortunately, at this moment, that particular girl appears to hold a fairly low opinion of me.'

David pushed off from the tree and began to walk away. Alex called out after him, 'Aren't you going to stay and help me?'

'I told you last night, Alex: you are on your own. My days of pulling your sorry backside out of every hole you get into are over,' David replied, waving his hand in farewell. 'But if you are looking for the Ashtons, you might want to try over near the rose-bordered lawn.'

He turned and called out over his shoulder. 'Oh, and by the way I have stolen Mrs Phillips, so you will have to fend for yourself for breakfast. Most of the main household servants are not due back until the end of the week. And before you complain, just be grateful I didn't take the rest of the servants. You couldn't blame me if I did.'

Alex's stomach rumbled as he stood and watched David walk away. He prayed his older brother would turn around and come back. After the mess he had made of things, he counted himself lucky that David had bothered to seek him out and exchange a few civil words. With David's dreams in tatters, Alex certainly didn't deserve his brother's good favour.

David joined a group of their mutual friends, and after exchanging greetings, Alex saw him walk with them out of the park and on to Park Lane. David was keeping true to his word; Alex would have to sort this out for himself.

He leaned back against the tree and closed his eyes. 'Come on, Alex, you can do this, just find Millie and talk to her. Use the old Radley sweet smile and charm; girls have never been able to resist that combination,' he muttered to himself. He pumped his fist. 'Come on, Alexander the Great.' He pushed himself away from the tree and after a quick check of his clothing, and a small prayer, he set off to find Millie.

As he headed toward the lawn, Alex continued to talk to himself in this encouraging manner. By the time he finally reached the other side of the rose beds, he had convinced himself that he could win Millie over.

He caught sight of her sharing a laugh with Charles and a quartet of well-dressed young men. He bridled, feeling a twinge of something he recognised as jealousy. He had competition.

As he neared the merry gathering, she turned and the smile died on her lips. Their gazes locked together for a moment, before she tore hers away and turned her back on him.

'What part of "push off" don't you understand, Brooke?' Charles Ashton sneered, as he stepped away from the group and stopped dead in front of Alex.

Alex gave a nod. 'I would like to request a short audience with Miss Ashton. There has been a misunderstanding and I wish to clarify matters with her,' he replied.

'The only misunderstanding I am aware of is you thinking that I'm not serious about making good on my threat,' Charles bit back.

Alex swallowed. 'No, I understand perfectly well that you are an excellent pugilist and mean to harm me if given half the chance. That said, it does not change the fact that it is imperative for me to speak to your sister, and I will not leave until I have done so,' he replied as calmly as the precarious situation he was in allowed.

Charles snorted. 'All right, I shall ask my sister if she will speak with you. But if the answer is no, you must leave her in peace. Agreed?'

'Agreed.'

Alex hoped Millie knew he would not take no for an answer, but still he was relieved to see Charles walk over to Millie and speak to her. As Charles put the case to his sister, she glanced in his direction and said in a loud enough voice for Alex to hear. 'All right, I shall speak with him. I have a feeling that it is the only way he will get the message and leave me alone. I thought I had made my position perfectly clear last night, but some people obviously need to hear things twice.'

She left the group and walked slowly over to where Alex stood. He gave her what he hoped was his most charming smile, as she approached. Millie just scowled at him.

'Millie,' Alex said as she came to a stop several feet away. He bowed. She gave him half a nod in return.

'Miss Ashton to you, Lord Brooke. You will address me in the correct social manner or this conversation is at an end. Am I clear?' she snapped. She turned to leave, but as she did Alex reached out and took hold of her arm.

'How can I call you Miss Ashton, when my nights are filled with thoughts of whispering your name as I look into your eyes?' he replied.

She laughed and pulled her arm from his grasp. 'What a silver-tongued snake you are Lord Brooke. But you can save your lies for your future bride; your words are wasted on me.'

He blinked. This did not sound like the Millie he knew and loved. Something approaching a self-satisfied smile crossed her face.

'But I came back for you,' he finally replied. 'I wasn't lying to you that night when we kissed. I love you. I want to marry you.'

The smile vanished and Millie shook her head. Her lip quivered as she said in a low, menacing voice, full of venom, 'Liar.'

He let out a frustrated sigh. 'I am not lying to you, Millie, I know you didn't take me seriously when I first told you how I felt, but I promise you I am telling the truth,' he pleaded.

Millie stiffened and her nostrils flared. 'As far as I am concerned, Lord Brooke, I think you are incapable of loving anyone other than yourself. You flirt and play games, but you would never seriously put your heart in any form of jeopardy.'

She took a deep breath and continued. 'I must admit I was

shocked and somewhat distressed to discover that you had sent a love letter to Clarice Langham, but of course it makes sense. She is a family friend, someone who can be relied upon to be a solid, uncomplicated wife for you.'

She looked down at her fingers as they twisted the cords of her reticule. 'Though I think sending her that letter was the cruellest and most selfish thing you could have ever done. Giving her hope like that, all the while knowing that you will dash them to pieces once you are married.'

Alex stared at his boots.

Millie clenched her fists and as Alex raised his head, he saw the look of disdain in her eyes. 'You don't have an answer for that? Why am I not surprised that you hadn't thought about anyone else's feelings? I don't suppose you saw Lady Clarice in tears late last evening? No, I expect you were off having fun with some other poor gullible girl.'

Millie bent down and picked up a stone from the driveway. 'Here is your answer, Lord Brooke,' she replied as she threw the stone hard at him, hitting him in the chest. He barely felt it; the pain in his heart greater than anything physical she could inflict.

'You are a cad of the worst kind, Alex Radley,' she continued, a hint of tears in her voice. 'I feel nothing but utter pity for Clarice. Her days will be spent living her life at your beck and call, while at night she will lie awake wondering where you are and with whom. It gives me no satisfaction to know that your sister Lucy was right about you. She did try to warn me, but did I listen? No, I was like every other foolish girl in London; I allowed you to flirt with me and then fell in love with you. To quote the hymn, "I was blind but now I see."'

She swallowed and stepped closer to Alex. When they were only mere inches apart, she looked up into his face. Only a fool could mistake her look for anything other than bitter disappointment, thought Alex miserably. He searched her face and took in the deep blue of her eyes, which shimmered with tears. Her luscious lips, which he had so lovingly kissed, were set in a thin harsh line.

'I think I have said all I need to at this juncture. As to what you might have to say to me, you can save your breath, because I am not interested.'

She took a deep breath. 'Good day, Lord Brooke. I hope for your health's sake you take this as a final warning. In future I shall allow my brother's fists to do the talking for me.'

She turned and strode back to the small group who stood watching and waiting for her to return. Taking Charles's arm, she led her select group of friends toward the main gate of the park.

Alex shook his head and sighed. His efforts to speak to Millie were getting him nowhere. She didn't want to hear him out, and if he were honest, apart from asking her forgiveness, he didn't know what else he could say to her. Telling her the truth was a gamble he was not prepared to make. And then there was the problem of Lady Clarice.

'There has to be another way,' he muttered.

With his hands in his pockets he followed Millie and her admirers out of the park. Once they were out on to Park Lane, Millie and her friends headed in the direction of the nearby cafés, while Alex crossed over and made his way toward Duke Street.

He prayed his cousin would be home. If any man in London had more than one lifetime's experience in getting himself out of tight spots, it was the Earl of Shale.

'What did they call the baby?' he muttered to himself as he climbed the front steps of the Earl's home. He remembered his cousin's wife had been delivered of a boy a few weeks after the Easter Ball.

After exchanging the obligatory congratulations and holding the newborn for two minutes, Alex was finally ushered into his cousin's study. 'We won't be long, darling,' Lord Shale called out to his wife as he closed the door behind him and pointed Alex in the direction of a chair beside the fire. The Countess of Shale said something which Alex did not quite catch, but his cousin let out a hearty laugh.

'I thought she might have mellowed with the arrival of the baby, but I should have known better,' Lord Shale said, taking a seat in the club chair opposite Alex. 'She will be the death of me, but I shall die a happy man. Drink?'

'Just tea, please. That's a fine-looking lad you've got yourself,' Alex replied.

The earl grinned. 'That's what comes from good bloodlines. Heard you might be starting your own family shortly, my dear boy. Kept that one close to your chest.' He gave Alex a friendly punch on the arm.

Alex sighed.

'That is not the look of a man heading happily into the parson's noose,' the Earl said.

'No, it is not,' Alex replied sadly.

Lord Shale chuckled and Alex looked up. Seeing the knowing look and the grin on his cousin's face, he realised his cousin knew the whole story. 'David's been here, hasn't he? You know all about the mess I've gotten myself into, you grinning gargoyle,' Alex replied.

The Earl raised his hands in surrender, while continuing to laugh. 'Yes, he came this morning and *he*, being his usual caring and generous self, bought a present for my son and heir. Unlike you, you lovestruck ninny.'

'Well, at least someone manages to find the humour in all this,' Alex replied, shaking his head.

The Earl poured himself a glass of claret and then rang the bell to order Alex a pot of tea. 'The good thing is, Rosemary and I have had all afternoon to think up a solution to your problem.'

As spies during the war against Napoleon, the Earl and his wife had faced enough close calls for Alex to be certain they already had a well-planned solution to his problem. He would simply have to follow their instructions and all would be right with the world.

'All right, tell me slowly and I shall commit it to memory,' Alex said, grateful that his cousin was privy to the secret that he could not read or write.

The Earl put his glass down on the table next to his chair. He sat forward in his chair, clasped his hands together and took a deep breath. He pursed his lips and Alex leaned forward, listening with all intent.

'Beg.'

The only sound in the room for the next minute was the crackle of the logs in the fire place.

Slowly Alex let out the breath he had been holding. 'You fought half the French secret police and that is all you can recommend?'

'Actually, it was Rosemary's idea. I spent hours racking my brains, and all I could think of was suggesting you take the first ship to Italy. Then I realised your father might not think too highly of me if he discovered that I had suggested his heir flee the country.' He sat back in his chair and viewed Alex from over steepled fingers.

'This is how we see it, Alex. If you tell Lady Clarice the whole truth, both you and David will be the next meal for Langham's biggest dog. You, for being stupid enough to send that letter, and David for having the cheek to fall in love with his daughter. That man will only settle for Lady Clarice marrying a duke or, in your case, a duke in waiting.'

Alex nodded in agreement. The Earl of Langham currently posed the greatest threat to his personal safety. Charles Ashton was a mere babe in the wood compared to the reputation Clarice's father wielded as a dangerous man.

'Tell Lady Clarice you cannot marry her, and then get on your knees and offer her anything, just as long as she will give you the letter back and forget about the whole sorry mess. As for the Ashton girl, we have come to the conclusion that we cannot help you.'

'What?' Alex stammered.

His cousin shifted in his chair. 'The only thing we can suggest is that you tell her the whole truth if you want any chance of her accepting your suit. Sorry, Alex, but honesty is the only weapon you have at your disposal in that fight. If she thinks you are a liar, she will never marry you.'

A knock at the door saw the arrival of a footman carrying a tray with a welcome pot of tea, and one cup. After pouring Alex a cup, the footman set the pot down on the table and left.

'Still not drinking tea? I don't think there are any French spies in your kitchen plotting to poison you,' Alex said, sipping his hot tea.

His cousin shook his head. 'One can never be too careful.'

Alex put his cup down, having suddenly lost his appetite for tea. He got to his feet and stood for a moment quietly absorbing his cousin's advice. 'All right,' he finally said. 'I shall do it. I shall throw myself on Lady Clarice's mercy and do whatever it takes to get her to jilt me.'

'Good lad,' the Earl replied and offered his hand. Alex waved it away. 'You can shake my hand when I have got things sorted; until then I am a man on an unfinished mission.'

The Earl downed the rest of his wine and laughed. 'Far more dangerous than any I ever undertook. At the worst, I could have been killed. You, however, young Brooke, could find yourself with the Earl of Langham as your father-in-law. I would much rather face a French firing squad, thank you very much.'

᪣

It was dark by the time Alex left Duke Street, only slightly the wiser for the experience. His next stop should be Mill Street and the Earl of Langham's house, but the thought of seeing Lady Clarice so soon after the berating he had received from Millie filled him with dread.

Was it possible to die twice in one night?

As he walked the short distance back home, his stomach began to rumble. With Mrs Phillips now in residence at Strathmore House, there would be no hot breakfast at home for the next week. He swore. The prospect of waking to an empty house was bad enough, but with only hot tea for breakfast it would be purgatory.

I can't exactly write the footman a shopping list.

David certainly knew how to punish a man in the cruellest of ways.

He could, of course, head to White's and get a hot meal there, but the thought of having to shake hands with more well-wishers put paid to that idea. There was also the real danger that he might run into Clarice's father.

'Time for an evening stroll, methinks,' he murmured to himself, as he stuffed his hands in his coat pockets and headed in search of an onion pie from the bakery around the corner. Alex had a sinking feeling he'd be a regular customer over the next week, or at least until he could steal Mrs Phillips back from his brother.

By the time he arrived in Oxford Street, he had a long list compiled in his head. Man could not live by bread alone, but add some cheese, a jar of pickled herrings and some apples and he could manage quite well.

❧

'For someone who was desperate to get to the tea shop and have a bun, you barely touched any of it,' Charles said as he and Millie made their way home from their visit to the park.

She shrugged her shoulders. The visit to the tea shop should have been her victory meal; instead all she could taste were ashes in her mouth. For days, as she and the two family servants went for their early morning walk, she had rehearsed just what she would say to Alex when they finally met once more.

Last night, she had conducted herself with dignity. Today, when she'd had the chance, she had let Alex know exactly what she thought of him.

But not how I feel. How can you tell a consummate liar that he has broken your heart? And that for the briefest of moments, he let you believe you could be happy in this place? That you thought he saw more in you than others did?

There was so much more she had wanted to say to him, but now as she trudged silently beside her brother, she realised how pointless it would all have been.

'Millie?' Charles said.

She stopped and hurriedly turned her back to the other people in the street. Charles took a step closer and, putting an arm around her, pulled her close to him. He pointed out several items in the window of the milliner's, while Millie wiped the tears from her face. 'Are you all fixed?' he asked a moment or two later. 'Brooke really did hurt you; I never realised how much until now.'

She straightened her bonnet and gave him a smile. 'Yes, thank you. For some silly reason you always know exactly what to do in a moment of crisis.'

'Remind me of that when I am out searching for a wife this season, I can add it to my long list of admirable qualities,' he replied.

Millie shook her head. 'Come on, let's go home.'

Chapter Nineteen

The following afternoon Alex was standing on the street
corner opposite the main entrance to Hyde Park.

Waiting.

If Lady Clarice Langham stuck to her usual daily routine, she
would pass by this spot before heading into the park to join the
fashionable hour.

Soon after he woke, Alex and Phillips left Bird Street and spent
most of the day downstairs in the kitchen at Strathmore House.
Alex hid there from David while Phillips helped his wife prepare
batches of freshly baked biscuits to keep Alex fed.

Around four o'clock, Mrs Phillips sent Alex on his way, with a
full stomach and a small bag of fresh oaten biscuits. 'Mind you
don't crush them in your coat pocket, Master Alex,' she said. He
smiled. He would one day be the Duke of Strathmore, but to Mrs
Phillips he would always be young Master Alex.

'Thank you, Mrs P; I would have starved without you,' he
replied as he headed up the kitchen steps. 'I just hope I live long
enough to enjoy them.'

As he waited for Lady Clarice to pass by, he leaned against a gas lamp and watched as the cream of London society made its way down Park Lane. Putting a hand into his pocket, he found the wrapped, still-warm biscuits sitting deep inside.

He pulled a biscuit out and slowly ate it, savouring every crunchy bite. Then he pulled out another one and ate that too. By the time Clarice and her friends finally appeared, Alex had eaten all six of the biscuits and was feeling rather ill.

He brushed the crumbs from his fingers and straightened his clothing. This would be the hardest thing he had ever done. If he couldn't pull it off, he would be honour-bound to marry Lady Clarice. He would gain a wife, but lose his brother in the process.

And Millie.

As the group of well-dressed young women approached he puffed out his cheeks and tapped the side of the lamp post for good luck. With his best nonchalant smile on display he walked toward Lady Clarice and her friends.

'Good afternoon, Lady Clarice, I trust you are well? Ladies,' Alex said, giving a bow.

Clarice stopped and gave him a dirty look. 'Lord Brooke,' she replied coolly, while her friends giggled into their gloves. Inside his boots, Alex curled his toes.

'Are you and your friends heading for the park?' he asked. It was an obvious and stupid question, but just talking helped to calm his nerves.

'We are,' replied one of the other girls. 'You should come with us; you could walk with Lady Clarice and whisper sweet nothings in her ear.' The girl turned and smiled smugly at her companions.

Clarice rolled her eyes. While he could not understand what David saw in her, Alex could appreciate that she had little patience with the behaviour of her insipid friends.

'Yes, Susan, that is a wonderful idea. How about the rest of you go on ahead and I shall walk with Lord Brooke? My maid can accompany us. I am certain we have many things to discuss. Off you go.' She waved her friends away. Lady Susan's face fell at being dismissed, but she quickly laughed it off.

Alex and Clarice stood and watched as her friends crossed over Park Lane and out of earshot.

'You have them on a tight rein,' he said.

She shook her head. 'And sometimes I would love to strangle the lot of them with it.' Alex offered her his arm, but she ignored the gesture and instead reached inside her reticule and pulled out a folded piece of paper. As soon as he saw the broken wax seal, he knew it was the letter he had mistakenly sent to her from Scotland. His heart began to pound heavily in his chest.

'I think you ought to have this,' she said, handing him the letter. 'I don't know what must have come over you to write it, but it was clear last night that you no longer hold those sentiments. If ever you did.'

A large gush of relief escaped Alex's lips before he could stop it. 'Well, I—' A flash of anger crossed Clarice's face.

He grabbed her by the arm. 'I'm sorry, I'm so sorry; believe me, I didn't mean for it to come out like that. It's just that I have been so worried about seeing you and trying to sort things out. This should never have happened. None of it.'

'But it did,' she replied sadly. 'And I stand to be held up to public ridicule as a result.'

'I know, and I hate myself for doing this to you,' he replied. He looked across the street and saw Lady Susan and her cronies waiting. They waved at Alex and Clarice. Clarice ignored them.

'Is there somewhere we can talk in private? There are a few things we need to discuss, and I don't need a Greek chorus standing by,' she said.

'I would appreciate the opportunity to talk. You deserve to know how this whole mess came about,' he replied.

Or at least as much of it as I can tell you without making things worse.

Clarice waved half-heartedly to the girls across the road, before taking Alex's arm. 'We had better follow them. If we are alone together for too long, it will only make matters worse.'

Once inside the park, Clarice and Alex continued to walk together, just out of earshot of her friends.

'I am sorry, Lady Clarice, but I cannot marry you,' Alex finally said, feeling like an utter heel.

'I know,' she replied.

'Why?'

'Why am I certain that you cannot marry me? Well, for a start, you have never shown the slightest bit of romantic interest in me in all the time we have known one another. When the letter arrived, I thought perhaps you were being made to choose a bride, and so you had thought better the devil you know.'

'I would never do that to you,' he replied.

'Before you sent me that letter,' she said, pointing to Alex's coat, where the letter now resided. 'I would have said the same, but now I don't think I know you at all.'

Alex sighed. At least he could be grateful that David wasn't hearing this conversation.

'What can I tell you?'

'The truth would be a good start,' she replied.

He stopped, ignoring the fact that they were now falling well behind Clarice's group of friends. Summoning his courage, he told Clarice as much as he could without revealing the whole shameful truth. He did not once mention David's name.

After quietly listening to his explanation of how a letter which was never meant to be mailed got sent to her by mistake, Clarice opened her reticule and took out a pencil and a piece of paper. She scrawled something on it and then handed it to him. He glanced at the paper, pretended to read it, and then stuck it in his pocket alongside the letter.

'This is what you are going to do Alex, without question. Any deviation from my plan and I shall go straight to my father and tell him you have ruined me. He will have us bound together as man and wife before this day is over. I only have to say the right word in his ear and you shall have yourself a blushing bride.'

She checked around quickly, ensuring there was no one else nearby. 'Do I make myself clear?' she asked, her anger still obvious.

He nodded, as a sinking feeling began to form in the pit of his stomach.

Clarice took a deep breath and clicked her tongue. 'Good; since the whole of the *ton* expects to hear an announcement regarding our betrothal, we need to do something to kill that speculation stone dead. So, we shall stage a very public argument at a very public event. At the end of which, I shall jilt you, making it clear to all and sundry that you are not suitable husband material.'

'But—'

'Be quiet, Alex; I'm not finished. I might be allowing you off the hook, but I did not say it would leave you without scars. You have no idea what the past few weeks have been like for me. From the moment that ridiculous letter arrived, my life has been turned upside down. If it isn't my father asking when our engagement is to be announced, it is infuriating Lady Susan gloating over the fact that she was there when I received it. I have felt sick every day since then, wondering when you were going to arrive at my father's door and tell me exactly what on earth you were playing at!'

'Oh,' Alex sighed, dropping his head and staring at the ground. The full reality of his careless efforts to communicate with Millie was truly hitting home. He had hurt David and Millie; that much he understood and accepted, but it had never occurred to him that his one act of random stupidity had caused so much chaos in other people's lives.

He now added self-loathing to the growing list of miserable emotions he had recently experienced for the first time in his life.

'Clarice, what can I say?'

'You can say yes to my next demand,' she replied.

'Which is?'

'I want to meet whoever wrote that letter, because I know you didn't. No one could pen those words and then greet me the way you did last night. I have known you long enough to be sure you don't understand the meaning of half those emotions. I don't even think you read the letter Alex, let alone wrote it. And don't go thinking that just because I have given you back the letter, I don't recall every single word of it. I have studied it long and hard and can recite it word for word. So can Susan.'

'The number I wrote on that piece of paper is the amount of money you will pay me, in cash if you don't reveal the identity of the letter's author. The amount is non-negotiable, and if you don't hand it to me by midday on the morning of your wedding, if of course the girl in question will still have you, I shall make your life totally unbearable.'

Under less trying circumstances he would have laughed at that moment; he had never been blackmailed before, least of all by the daughter of an earl. But when he saw the look on Clarice's face, he knew it would be the worst thing he could do.

As soon as he could find David, he would have his brother tell him just how much this disaster was going to cost him financially. He had a sinking feeling it was more than the price of a dress or two. At this point he had little option but to agree to pay up.

'All right, I accept the need for you to save face, so tell me where and when my public denouncement is to occur and I shall be there. But as for telling you who did write that letter, I cannot agree to that demand. You are right in assuming that it was not me, and I would dearly love to tell you, but if I did, it would cost me far more than anything for which I could write you a promissory note.'

Clarice held out her hand. 'Give me the paper back, Alex,' she demanded. When he handed it to her, she hurriedly struck a line through the number and wrote something else before handing it back to Alex. He glanced at it before putting it back into his pocket.

'As you can see, I have doubled the amount you shall pay me. Now would you like to continue to refuse me? I know your father's pockets are deep and I expect you are in receipt of a handsome allowance, but I doubt even you will be able to hide that much money from him.'

Alex heard the huff as it escaped Clarice's lips. She was clearly beginning to lose patience with him.

'As I said, the payment is to be in cash; no promissory notes or letters of instruction. Come on, Alex, what is it to be? My patience is beginning to run out,' she said.

He shook his head. 'I'm sorry, Clarice, you didn't deserve any of this, and I am truly ashamed of the pain I have caused you. It was never intended. I just wanted to send a letter to the woman I love; instead I sent the wrong letter to the wrong girl and you got hurt. Do whatever you have to do to me publicly; I will take it, but I beg of you, leave everyone else out of it.'

He sighed and fumbled with the papers in his pocket. He pulled out Clarice's blackmail note and held it up. 'You shall have your moment of revenge, and your money, but the author of that letter shall remain secret. I have done enough damage already. If I am successful in securing the hand of the woman I love, I shall gladly pay you the money.'

He offered her his arm. She stood and stared at it for a moment, before shrugging her shoulders and accepting his offer.

'Oh well, two out of three isn't bad. But don't think I won't discover who did pen that letter,' she replied.

They hurried to catch up with Clarice's friends. Alex stayed long enough to make polite conversation with them, and to be seen publicly in Lady Clarice's company. He briefly caught sight of Millie and gave her a wave. She stared at him and then turned away.

After taking his leave of Lady Clarice, and following a fruitless search for David, he decided it was time to head back to Strathmore House. He might still have been in David's bad books, but things would surely get worse if his brother found out about the meeting with Clarice from anyone other than him.

A low whistle escaped David's lips as he read the note on which Clarice had written her demand for money. 'I had always hoped she had a wicked side to her, but this is absolutely brilliant,' he said with a smile.

'How much?' Alex asked, his nerves on edge. He wondered how little would be left in his bank account after Lady Clarice's demands had been met.

His brother screwed up his nose. 'Well it looks as if she had originally written five hundred pounds, then changed her mind and made it a thousand. What on earth did you say to make her double it?'

Alex took the paper and folded it in half. 'I told her I would not give up the identity of the person who wrote the letter. She knew it was not from me.'

David closed his eyes and whispered, 'Thank you.'

'Though it did occur to me that this might be the perfect opportunity for you to come clean and tell her how you feel,' Alex said. 'Perhaps it is time to approach her father and ask for her hand. You have a lot to offer.'

'But not my father's name or title,' David replied.

Over the years, the brothers had discussed the impact of David's illegitimacy on his future and agreed to do all they could together to overcome the impediments it caused. However, they both knew that no amount of money could change the mind of those who saw David Radley as only a bastard son.

'Alex, the only time the Earl of Langham acknowledges me is when I am standing right next to our father; other than that, I don't exist. He would never consider me worthy enough for his daughter. As far as he is concerned I am a by-blow and earls do not allow their daughters to marry bastards.'

In his hands he held the love letter he had written to Lady Clarice and which Alex had now retrieved. He smiled at it before sighing and placing it on the table next to him. 'You did the right thing by not revealing my name to Clarice. To be spurned by her after she had learned the way I feel would be the worst humiliation of my life.'

It was nearly three in the morning, and the Radley brothers were sitting in their father's study, warming their feet by the fire. Alex had arrived at Strathmore House in the early evening, only to discover David had gone to a party somewhere out near Highgate and wasn't expected back until tomorrow.

Fortunately, the party had died an early death and David had made the trip back to London. More heartfelt words of apology had come from Alex, followed by a solid punch on the arm in return from David, after which they had declared a truce. A second bottle of the duke's favourite red from Italy was nicely taking the edge off the long evening.

'So, when is this scene to be played out?' David asked.

Alex sat staring at the wine as he swirled it around in his glass. The light from the fire turned the wine into the colour of a late summer sunset. 'I don't know; I am leaving the details up to Lady Clarice, but I hope she doesn't intend to make me wait. One, because the suspense is killing me, and two, the quicker she puts me out of my misery, the sooner I can get back to the real task at hand, which is Millie.'

David's eyebrows lifted slowly.

Alex took a sip of wine from his glass. 'Believe me, I have done all I can to make things right with Clarice. With any luck, she will come out of this with her reputation intact, if not enhanced. As for me, I will be lucky if I get invited to any social functions for the rest of my life.'

'And thoroughly deserved it would be if you became a social outcast,' David remarked.

'Thanks.'

David raised his glass, but stopped short of putting it to his lips. 'You are heir to one of the largest fortunes in the country, so give over on the "woe is me", will you? There will always be plenty of title-hunting mamas ready to shove their daughters at you, so I doubt you are in any danger of dying alone, Alex.'

They both laughed. 'And I wonder why I missed you these past few days,' Alex said.

'Well, you can miss me for another few hours, dear brother. I am off to bed.' David emptied his glass and placed it on his father's desk. Alex stood and for a moment they stared silently at one another.

'I am a complete idiot who does not deserve a brother like you, so once again let me tell you how sorry I am,' Alex said. They both blinked hard as they slapped each other roughly on the arm.

'I know, but someone has to save us from you, and Stephen is not yet old enough to be hauling you out of tavern brawls, so it comes down to me,' David smiled.

He put his arm around Alex and led him to the door. 'Come on, Hargreaves has had a bed made up for you in your old room; it's too late for you to be walking home. Let's both get some sleep, and see what tomorrow brings.'

Chapter Twenty

I t was with an odd mix of excitement and fear coursing through his body that Alex set out for the ball, knowing full well that he had willingly agreed to be publicly humiliated. Only a matter of weeks ago he would have cut his own throat rather than even consider what he was about to do.

The note from Lady Clarice had arrived earlier that afternoon; and after consulting with David, he had decided to let her take the lead and dish out whatever punishment she felt was warranted.

She had only made him wait two days before sending word of when the axe would fall. Sitting in the back of the carriage, with David opposite, he counted his blessings. 'At least the odour of this scandal will have lessened by the time the season is at its height. Not everyone is back in London. Mama and Papa won't be back for another few days,' he said.

David leaned over and poked Alex in the ribs. 'Good chap, keep telling yourself all the lies you need. As long as we get through this evening without being set upon by a murderous horde, anything else is a minor detail.'

His brother was attempting to be his usual jovial self, but Alex could hear the grinding of David's teeth from across the other side of the carriage. It wasn't only Alex's future which was at stake this night. Much as David denied the possibility of ever being allowed to marry Lady Clarice, he still lived in hope.

'I won't foul this up,' Alex replied. The consequences if he did were too dire to consider.

The carriage slowed to a halt in front of an imposing medieval building in Bishops Avenue. As he walked under the brick archway which covered the entrance to Fulham Palace, Alex turned to David. 'Why do I suddenly wish I had been stricken with some terrible malady?'

'Yes well, uncle's ball is one of the social highlights of the season, and as the only members of the family currently in London it would have looked odd to say the least had we not made an appearance,' replied David walking up the front steps.

Alex's blood ran cold as he saw the Bishop of London standing at the top of the stairs.

'Alex my boy, come to set a date?'

&

'You do know that the Bishop is related to the Duke of Strathmore, and therefore to the one person in London I am attempting to avoid?' Millie remarked as she scanned the ballroom.

'Yes, I do,' Charles replied.

'Then why the devil are we here?' she snapped.

Charles shook his head. 'Blasphemy? May I suggest that if you intend to use that sort of language in the palace of a bishop, you might want to get yourself off to church first thing? I am sure they will excommunicate you if you don't'

She gave him a look of disgust. 'They can bring on the Spanish Inquisition for all I care, just as long as I don't have to speak to Lord Brooke,' Millie replied.

Over the past few days she had managed to turn Alex's title into a form of insult. If she found anything distasteful, she made a point of thinking of him. By associating unpleasant things with Alex, she hoped to build a high and wide wall between them.

Avoiding him wherever possible also helped. She had seen him two days earlier in Hyde Park late in the afternoon, standing with Lady Clarice Langham and her friends. For two people who were supposedly in love, they both looked thoroughly miserable. From where Millie had stood, hidden at the back of a group of her new friends, she could see they barely exchanged a word.

Alex occasionally gave a nod of his head, as Clarice's friends flittered around him like a flock of pigeons. Horrid Susan, as Millie had named her, spent all her time laughing and grabbing at Alex's arm. Seeing the look of pained discomfort on his face had, she admitted to herself with some shame, made her day.

Good. You thoroughly deserve to spend the rest of your days surrounded by brainless harpies. Such a pity Lady Clarice does not see how suited to them you are, Lord Brooke.

At that moment, one of her new gentlemen admirers had told a particularly amusing joke, and Millie had roared with the most unladylike laughter. After several social outings with her new group, she realised they appreciated her openness and candour. With Millie they were able to relax, knowing she did not have a secret agenda. She was not interested in hurrying any of the men down the church aisle.

As she composed herself and wiped the tears of amusement away, her gaze had once more fallen on where Alex and his harem stood. While Lady Clarice and the other girls were busy fixing their bonnets and taking no notice of their surroundings, Alex stood staring straight at Millie.

For the first time since she had met him, he appeared unable to muster a smile. His shoulders were slumped, and the look of annoyance which appeared on his face every time Lady Susan let out a laugh did not give the impression of him being a happy man. Before she turned back to her friends, Alex gave her a small wave of his hand. Millie had never seen him so despondent.

She could barely remember the hour she and Charles had just spent in the park, nor the walk home. If Alex now had what he wanted, why did he seem so sad? It made no sense.

Perhaps now that he was about to settle down, he had been

forced to face the reality of being a married man: that he would no longer be able to openly play the field. She prayed he would take his marriage vows seriously, and try to be a good husband to Lady Clarice. He could be an utter charmer when the mood took him, but he also knew how to break a heart.

'Millie,' Charles whispered. 'Stop staring into space.'

She shook her head, roused herself from her musings and gave her brother a hard stare. 'I was thinking, you dolt. You might want to try it some time.'

'Not if it makes my face look like yours when you are deep in thought,' he replied with a laugh.

'Be quiet, or I shall make you dance with dreadful Lady Susan; I know she is here tonight, I can feel it in my bones,' Millie replied.

Charles clapped his hands together. 'Blasphemy and now witchcraft; keep it up, my girl and you shall have us both burned alive at the stake. Though if it warmed us up a bit, I wouldn't complain. No one in this country has decent heating; I am always cold.'

'Have you heard?' David asked.

'What?' Alex replied, as his gaze roamed the room.

'The Earl of Langham is here tonight, and he is looking for you.'

Alex swore, and then sucked in a deep breath. Lady Clarice had better have a bulletproof plan, or he was in serious trouble. If his uncle and the earl got hold of him, he would have a glass of champagne in one hand and a fiancée in the other. Knowing his uncle, the Bishop would not care who she was as long as she was from a good family, and breathing.

'More importantly, have you seen Lady Clarice? If she is going to jilt me, it had better be soon. If not, I am off. I will not stand around here waiting for someone else to decide my fate,' Alex replied, his nerves on edge.

David placed a firm hand on Alex's shoulder. 'Fear not, little brother, I have managed to locate your jilter; she awaits you in the library.'

Alex shook his head, sensing a trap. 'I'm not going into any library or any other room with an unmarried miss. She can speak to me in the hallway, or I am leaving right now.'

'Come on, then. I shall chaperone you, and I will not leave you alone with Clarice for one minute,' David replied. 'The last thing I wish is a forced marriage between the two of you.'

They headed down a nearby hallway and stopped outside a closed door. David knocked on the door and Lady Clarice quickly opened it. A brief exchange followed, and Clarice came out and closed the door behind her. From the look on her face, it was apparent she was not happy.

'Seriously, Alex, if I were intent on trapping you into marriage, I would have done it days ago and saved us all a lot of trouble,' she snapped. 'But if you are such a hothouse flower, then we will have to discuss our plans out here.'

From where she stood at the other end of the hall, Millie watched as Alex, David and Clarice put their heads together. Deeply engrossed in their discussion, they were oblivious to their surroundings. Every so often one of them would pull away and shake their head, the others would then wave their arms around and the dissenting party would rejoin the group.

At first, she thought it was an argument, but from the amount of nodding they were all doing she was beginning to have her doubts. She stood watching the proceedings for several minutes, until Charles took her by the arm and led her away to join their friends.

'What do you suppose all that was about?' she asked, turning her head to get one final glance of the threesome.

Charles shrugged his shoulders. 'No idea. Probably trying to work out how they will announce the engagement while the duke and duchess are still out of town. A brave move if you ask me; I certainly wouldn't do it, but I'm sure her father must be urging them to make it public. We shall find out soon enough; in the meantime, you and I need to go and have some fun.'

Millie gave her brother a quick smile. He was right: Alex was no longer a part of her life. What did it matter to her what he did?

'Yes, let's go have a fine, fun and frivolity-filled...' She screwed her nose up, trying to think of a word to complete the sentence.

'Function?' Charles offered.

Millie gave the back of Charles's hand a solicitous pat. 'It will have to do, young man.'

❦

Alex decided that attempting to appear nonchalant while waiting to have one's face torn off in public was an art form he could not master.

A slow trickle of nervous sweat was working its way down his back, when out of the corner of his eye he saw Lady Clarice.

For years afterwards, the look on her face at that moment would haunt his dreams. He would wake at night in cold sweats, having dreamt that the hounds of hell had appeared and screamed his name. The hounds all bore the look of Lady Clarice Langham at the Bishop of London's 1817 early summer ball.

'ALEX RADLEY, YOU BLACKGUARD! How could you do this to me?' she bellowed as she pushed her way through the crowd which mingled around the dance floor.

'Strength, Alex, just remember it will all be over soon,' David muttered, as he walked away and left Alex standing alone to face his fate.

'Lady Clarice?' Alex replied as his heart began to race.

Clarice came to a halt several feet away. Her hands were placed firmly on her hips.

'Don't you "Lady Clarice" me, you swine. I know full well where you were last night AND this afternoon. I may not know their names, but I know what those women are, and if you think I am naive enough to accept you in these circumstances you are a bigger fool than I ever thought.'

Alex shook his head, trying to remember his lines. 'Now, now,

Clarice don't go jumping to any conclusions or saying anything you might regret, especially not in the present company.'

He stepped forward and tried to take her arm, but she pulled away. 'Don't you dare touch me, you filthy disgusting brute.'

'But darling,' he replied.

The slap, when it landed, nearly knocked him off his feet. His teeth rattled in his mouth and tears sprang to his eyes. The sound of it echoed throughout the room, closely followed by a collective gasp from the gathering.

'I am not your darling; I never was and never will be, Lord Brooke. When I choose to marry, it shall be to a man who respects and values me, not some...some cad like you,' Clarice cried. She let out a wail of distress, and with her hands covering the sides of her face, she ran from the room. A more consummate actress had never set foot on the stage.

David came to his brother's side and whispered into his ear. 'Time to move, Alex; I can see the earl headed this way.'

Alex blinked back the tears, and quickly followed David towards the front door. Fortunately for the Radley brothers, the gathering was a large one, and Clarice's irate father struggled to make his way through the crowd to reach them.

Once outside, they hurried down the stairs, across the yard and took refuge on the far side of the palace gatehouse.

'That was close; I thought he had us there for a moment,' David said, catching his breath.

Alex stood leaning against the high brick wall of the gatehouse. His face hurt like the devil. 'I didn't realise girls could pack that much into a slap. I almost bit my tongue.' He rubbed the offended cheek; it was still hot.

David put his hand over his mouth, but Alex could see he was laughing. 'That was absolutely priceless, Alex; we could not have rehearsed that better. Mind you, I don't recall us discussing Clarice giving you a good old slap to the chops – not that you didn't deserve it. After all you have put her through, just be grateful she didn't have a pistol.'

Poking his head out from behind the wall, Alex ventured a

quick look back toward the front entrance of the palace. 'Let's get out of here before the earl sends some of his lads to look for us,' he said as he turned and trotted further down the driveway. 'The sooner we are in the carriage and away from here, the better I will feel.'

A few hundred yards further on, an unmarked black carriage awaited them. As the Earl of Langham was not a man renowned for his charitable nature, a quick, discreet departure had always been part of their plan. As the carriage slowly made its way back to Bird Street, Alex reflected on the evening's events. Apart from having had his face slapped in public, he had to admit he had managed to get out of a dire situation rather lightly. He was now free of the expectation to marry Lady Clarice, while her reputation had remained solidly intact.

He hoped she had thoroughly enjoyed her improvised, theatrical exit from the ballroom, as Lady Clarice Langham would no doubt be the talk of most *ton* breakfast tables in the morning.

'Well, at least that part of your loosely thrown together plan went well. Now you just have to convince Millie Ashton that you are serious and get her to agree to marry you,' David noted as they climbed the front steps of their townhouse the following afternoon.

'Yes, I have managed to achieve the highly unlikely; now I just have to pull off the near-impossible,' Alex replied. 'I am going to give it a couple of days before I attempt to speak to her. I would suggest it might seem a little uncouth to be jilted on one night by one young lady, only to try to woo another the next day.'

David nodded in agreement.

As he closed the front door behind him Alex removed his coat and handed it to Phillips. 'It's nice to have you back, David.'

His brother shook his head. 'I'm not staying. I had a footman pick up some more clothes for me from here this morning. 'But, I thought you would be staying here now; why are you going back home?' Alex replied.

'Because, dear boy, you need to sort the rest of this out for yourself, and besides that, I quite like being at home by myself. I've never had the whole place to lord over on my own before, and I don't expect I will ever have the opportunity again, so I am making the most of it,' David replied.

Alex shook his head. 'Playing duke, are we?'

'Yes, well, I shall never get the chance for real,' David replied with a wry smile.

The idea of David disappearing back to Strathmore House and leaving him on his own disappointed Alex. He puffed out his cheeks and tried to shrug off his obvious disappointment. 'Fine, I will do this without your help. But just remember, when I do get Millie to agree to be my wife I shall expect you to stand up for me.'

David gave him a mischievous wink. 'Just let me know when you want me to give you some pointers for your wedding night.' He received a slap on the side of his head for his impertinence.

He started up the stairs and Alex heard him whistling as he went into his room. He appeared a moment later with a small pile of books in his hand. 'I don't expect to see you at the club tonight, because if I were you I would make myself scarce from the social scene until you have something concrete planned for your pursuit of Miss Ashton,' David said.

With a cheery wave of his hand, and still whistling a happy tune, David went out the front door.

Chapter Twenty-One

'Finally, a proper summer's day; isn't it wonderful, miss?' Grace gushed as she pulled a brush through Millie's long tresses and pinned them up into a stylish chignon.

Millie sat admiring her beautiful summer dress; it had a small blue floral print through the skirt, matched with a pale blue bodice. The flowers were then repeated around the cuffs of her sleeves, which were finished with white broderie anglaise to match the petticoat under the skirt. It was so markedly different from any dress she had ever owned; so very English in its design and construction.

When the dress first arrived from Madame de Feuillide, she had stood and stared lovingly at it for nearly ten minutes before finally taking it out of the box. Whereas the evening gowns the French modiste had designed for Millie spoke of elegance and champagne, this dress promised sunshine and afternoon walks by the river.

She stood up and gave it a little twirl. 'This cotton is so light and I don't have to have four layers of clothing on to stay warm. I just hope the rain holds off for the garden party,' she said.

Millie was under no illusions about the weather in England. It could suddenly turn again for the worse, and tomorrow she would be back in heavy gowns and a coat. In Calcutta if it was hot and dry it would remain that way, day in and day out, for months.

She was determined that today would be a good day. One of her newly acquired friends had invited her and Charles to a garden party out of the city near Richmond. It was the perfect opportunity to continue cultivating her new friends, as well as widening her growing social circle.

Charles was impatiently pacing back and forth across the front entrance when Millie came downstairs. 'Oh, finally; do you have any idea how long it will take us to get to Richmond? We will be lucky if we are in time for the party at all,' her brother complained.

Millie rolled her eyes and checked her gloves. 'We have plenty of time; the garden party does not start for another three hours, and I am certain all the early arrivals are going to talk about is the scene from the other evening,' she replied.

In the days following the ugly public spat between the Marquess of Brooke and Lady Clarice Langham, it had become the *only* thing people talked about. It wasn't every day that the heir to a dukedom was jilted, and slapped, by an earl's only daughter in the ballroom of a bishop. The standard for scandals of the season had been set early and high.

As they had stood among the crowd, Millie and Charles had watched, along with the cream of London society, as the whole unfortunate and most unforgettable scene had played itself out. However, unlike the rest of the stunned party guests, Millie knew there was more to the exchange than first appeared.

As soon as Clarice had dashed tearfully from the room, she turned to Charles and murmured. 'Now I know what the three of them were discussing in the hallway. That little scene was planned.'

She had wisely kept this information to herself when discussing the matter with other people. It was enough that she had been at the now-infamous ball without adding to the constantly changing rumours as to why Lady Clarice Langham had jilted Alexander the Great.

She looked at Charles and raised her eyebrows in expectation. His brow furrowed before an expression of enlightenment appeared on his face and he smiled. 'You look lovely, Millie and, dare I say it, almost happy?' he said. She smiled in return. While it was against her nature to fish for compliments, Millie decided it was the least Charles could do if he expected her to sit and listen to him tell her how magnificent his new high-flyer phaeton and pair of horses were all the way to Richmond.

'Today is going to be an excellent day; I won't have it any other way,' she said as Charles opened the front door and escorted her outside to where his new statement of speed and elegance stood awaiting them. Millie silently praised herself for having the good sense to wear a light coat and scarf. A footman handed her a fine green cashmere shawl, which she draped over her skirts once seated in the phaeton.

As it was, they had little opportunity to talk on the trip, because as soon as they had left the narrow city streets and Charles had given the horses their heads, the phaeton began to speed along at a cracking pace. In between Charles swearing as he struggled to regain control of his horses and Millie's squeals of delight, they exchanged few real words of conversation.

'Well, that took less time than I expected,' Charles said as they came to a halt out the front of the stately country house. A dozen or so other carriages sat parked in the drive, while a group of footmen and ostlers from the host's household attended to the horses.

'Yes, but it was such fun; I can't remember the last time I laughed so much,' Millie replied. Charles handed the reins over to an attendant footman and then helped Millie down from the dust-coated phaeton. She brushed the dust off her coat and removed her scarf before they went inside.

Having made such good time on the journey, they arrived earlier at the party than the friends they were planning to meet.

'I might just go and dust myself off before the others arrive, if that's all right, Millie? I knew I should have worn a coat,' Charles said, watching as a maid took Millie's coat and scarf.

She nodded her head and chuckled. 'Yes, considering how red in the face you are and the state of your hair, I think it wise, dear brother. Meanwhile I might go and stretch my legs in the garden.'

Charles' eyes lit up. 'Did you know they have a maze?'

She wrinkled her nose in annoyance; she had been hoping to keep the existence of the maze a secret and then surprise him. 'Yes, and I can't wait to lose you in it,' she replied with a laugh.

'Hah! Not a chance. I tell you what; you go and find the entrance while I clean myself up and then we shall see who the master of the maze is,' Charles replied, before dashing off. Millie wandered outside.

Out in the garden she stopped and offered her face to the sun's warm rays.

I was beginning to think the sun never shone in this country.

A few other early guests mingled on the lawn. Millie was pleased to see that she didn't know any of them, so she wasn't obliged to go and make small talk. She and Charles could have some fun in the maze before the rest of the guests arrived.

She looked back toward the house, but Charles had still not reappeared. She decided to go and have a quick look in the maze first, convincing herself that it wasn't cheating, but rather seeking a strategic advantage. She reached the two enormous grey stone pillars which stood either side of the path, marking the entrance to the maze.

She gave one last glance over her shoulder to look for Charles before taking a few tentative steps inside the maze. The towering yew hedge walls immediately cut out all sound from outside and enveloped her in an eerie green world. She kept walking, while an evil plan to lie in wait for Charles and surprise him began to form in her mind.

As she rounded the second corner, she came across a man kneeling over another who was lying sprawled out upon the ground. His back was turned, so she could not see the face of the kneeling man, but as soon as he spoke, her lungs seized.

'Come on Alex, don't you dare die on me.'

Millie let out a cry and raced over to where David knelt beside his brother.

David raised his head, his face registered who she was and then he went still. 'Please, Miss Ashton, go and find help; my brother has been assaulted,' he said.

One look at the bloodied mess that was Alex's face and Millie turned and ran as fast as she could back to the entrance of the maze. Charles had realised she had already gone into the maze and as she reached the entrance, she narrowly avoided a heavy collision with him.

'Ooof! Steady on, Millie,' he groaned as she glanced off the side of his shoulder and staggered around to face him.

She waved her hands and tried unsuccessfully to stem the flood of tears which poured down her face. 'It's Alex, he's been hurt. Oh, Charles you must come and help. There is blood everywhere,' she sobbed.

He grabbed her by the arm and led her quickly back inside the maze. When they got to where she had left Alex and David, they found Alex had begun to come to. David was trying to help him sit upright.

Charles put an arm around Alex's waist and hauled him to his feet in one swift move. 'Bloody hell, Brooke, what happened to you?' Alex swayed unsteadily on his feet, prompting David to put an arm under his shoulder.

'I don't think the Earl of Langham is quite as forgiving as his daughter, and has decided to make his displeasure known,' David replied.

Alex mumbled something which Millie did not catch.

David nodded. 'A couple of heavily built ruffians were waiting for him when we got here. While I was greeting some friends, they dragged him into the maze and set to work on him. Fortunately, I arrived not long after and they cleared out when they saw me.' Alex lifted his hands and Millie could see they were covered in blood and had several large, ugly cuts.

Charles raised his eyebrows and gave a small approving nod of his head. 'Looks like you went down fighting. The fact that you are still alive shows you must have got in a few good punches.'

'Alex,' Millie whispered as she gulped down air.

David and Charles helped him over to a small wooden bench in the corner at the turn of the maze. As they sat him down, Millie heard Alex mutter to Charles. 'Please take your sister away; I cannot bear for her to see me like this.'

Charles nodded. 'All right, but I shall be back. We need to get this blood cleaned up as best as possible before trying to get you into the house. Millie and I will get some clean cloths and fresh water.'

'No!' Alex cried, and he winced in obvious pain. 'No one must know about this. Lady Clarice has suffered enough. If anyone sees me it won't take them long to realise what has happened. I don't want her to know.' He screwed his eyes closed and sat back on the bench. His breath was coming in short sharp gasps.

David looked at Charles. 'This maze comes out on the other side of the garden. If you can help me with Alex we should be able to leave without anyone seeing him,' David said.

Charles looked at Millie and she shook her head. 'I am not leaving.'

She reached into her reticule and pulled out a clean white handkerchief. She walked over to the bench and bent down, lifting Alex's face gently with one hand. With slow and careful pressure, she tried to stem the blood from a vicious cut about his eye.

'Just a minute,' she said, standing once more. 'If we can't get help from the house, I have something else.'

She slipped around the corner and quickly lifted her skirts. Taking her cotton underskirt in her hands, she pulled it down and stepped out. Then with one hand on either side of the seam, she tore the skirt open.

When she came back, Charles had a small knife ready. 'Well done, Millie; always the resourceful one. Sorry about the new outfit,' he said as he cut her underskirt into more manageable pieces.

'I shall buy you a new one,' Alex said, through gritted teeth.

Millie shook her head, and began to bandage the cotton strips around his badly cut hands. 'That won't be necessary, Lord Brooke. Seeing you fully recovered will be payment enough.'

He attempted to brush a hand against her face, but she pulled away.

'Don't,' she whispered.

Charles and David exchanged a brief look, before David gave a nod of his head. 'Right; give me a few minutes to find the carriage and our driver, and then I will be back. Will you wait with him?'

'Of course,' Charles replied. 'Millie can continue to clean Brooke up and I will keep watch for any unwanted visitors to the maze. Wouldn't want those blackguards thinking they had not done a good enough job and deciding to come back for another go.'

David headed through to the other side of the maze, while Charles took a position at the entrance. Millie opened Alex's shirt and wiped away the blood pooling at the top of his cravat. Taking the seat next to him, she cleaned his face as best she could.

'There; I think you shall pass inspection, from a distance,' she said. With a piece of her petticoat folded into a pad, she placed it over the large cut on the top of Alex's left eyebrow. 'You may need to get that stitched. It is quite a deep gash.'

'I miss you,' Alex murmured.

Millie looked down at the pile of bloodstained rags in her hands and blinked hard. She had never thought to be this close to him ever again. His cologne reminded her of that fateful night at his house. At a distance, she could summon her resolve and push him away. Being so close to him now left her soul naked and vulnerable.

Bloodied and beaten, he was still the most handsome man she had ever laid eyes upon. The one man she had ever loved. She watched as one of his bandaged hands took hold of hers and held it.

'Don't,' she pleaded, her voice breaking. 'I beg of you, please don't.'

He cleared his throat and with longing in his voice replied. 'I love you.'

She dug her teeth into her bottom lip and screwed her eyes shut as she fought to maintain her composure. She sucked in a deep breath. 'No. No you don't Alex, and if this afternoon has not shown you the error of your ways, then you had better choose the next miss you cross in love more carefully. Because I can tell you, there are some men who would risk the hangman's noose for the sake of their family's honour.' She lifted his hand and pulled hers away.

'You are a liar and a fool, Lord Brooke, and I don't know which of those is worse. But, for what it's worth, I gave you my heart and you crushed it, without mercy. So, apart from the shreds of my underskirt, I have nothing else to give you.'

A weak smile came to his lips, and he leaned in close so only she could hear. 'You are everything that I want, Millie, and I will never be done with you,' he replied.

She turned to check on her brother, but Charles still stood with his back to them at the end of the path, keeping watch. 'What else could I possibly give you?' she replied, staring at her brother's back.

'Your nights and your babes,' Alex murmured, his voice full of longing.

A trickle of blood escaped from under the cotton pad and began to run down Alex's cheek. Millie replaced it with the last clean folded cloth she had. Placing it in Alex's hand, she made him hold it to his head. She bundled up the rest of the rags, and stood.

Turning to face him, she shook her head. 'You tell me I am yours and want me for your wife, and yet you wrote a love letter to another woman. A fact you cannot deny. If you really did love me, Alex, it would have been sent to me, not to Clarice. As I said, you may be a fool, but I most certainly am not.'

She screwed up the sodden rags and dumped them in a pile next to him on the bench. 'I wish you a speedy and full recovery Lord Brooke, but as far as I am concerned, we are estranged and shall remain so. Goodbye Alex.'

'I didn't write the letter,' she heard him utter as she walked away. But with her heart so close to breaking again, she couldn't bear to turn around and go back to face him. By sheer force of will, she managed to keep going until she reached Charles' side.

'As soon as David returns we shall have to leave. My outfit is no longer presentable,' she said, and took hold of her brother's hand.

𖠌

With Alex laid low from the events of the garden party, Millie felt it safe to venture out for her walk the following morning. It was only on the return leg, that she realised how much she had missed the exercise. Upon her return she handed her coat and gloves to Grace. Standing in the front entrance of her home she considered the quandary which had kept her from sleep nearly all of last night. Should she confide in Charles what Alex had said in the maze, or simply go and buy a passage back to India?

Still in two minds as to what she should do, Millie walked toward the staircase. As she passed the door of her father's downstairs study, she noticed it was open. She poked her head inside and was surprised to see her both her parents sitting on the small leather couch which faced the window.

'Hello,' she said, giving them a cheery greeting.

Her father turned to her. 'Good; I am glad you're finally home. Close the door and come and sit with us,' he said.

Millie closed the door behind her and came around to face her parents. The first thing she noticed was the distressed state Violet was in. Tears poured down her mother's cheeks and she shook all over.

'Mama, what's wrong?' she said, kneeling before her mother and taking her hands. She had never seen her mother so distraught and it frightened her. 'You are not ill, are you?'

Violet shook her head as her bottom lip quivered.

Millie looked to her father, seeking an answer. 'Your mother is not ill, Millie, she is heartbroken. I have told her what I have long suspected, and which has kept me up many a night. That you intend to leave England and return to India,' James replied.

In his hand he held the list of scheduled departures for India Millie thought she had hidden so well. The breath caught in Millie's throat and her face crumpled as she burst into tears. How foolish had she been not to realise her father would have known. James reached out and lifted his daughter on to his lap on the couch. She flung her arms around her father's waist.

'I'm sorry; I never meant to hurt you. I just wanted to go home,' she sobbed into the lapel of his jacket. Violet stroked Millie's hair as both mother and daughter continued to cry. 'You are home, darling; this is where your family and your friends are, and where your future lies,' Violet whispered.

Millie screwed her eyes closed and shook her head. 'I just wanted to get away; I just wanted to be happy again. As I was in India. Every time I think I might be able to live here, it all comes crashing down on me.'

Her father held her tightly. 'I will not lose my daughter,' he replied, his voice full of conviction. 'I stood by once and nearly lost you; I will not do that again.'

Millie pulled away and sat staring at him, searching his face. 'What do you mean, you nearly lost me?' she asked.

James looked at Violet, who nodded her head.

Her father sighed. 'We have never told you this before, but as it seems pertinent to the current situation, it is only right that you should now know. The year after we arrived in Calcutta, your mother told me she was leaving me and going back to England. She intended to take Charles with her.'

Millie gasped and looked at her mother, who held her hand over her eyes as she sobbed quietly.

'I didn't argue with her. I just stood and let her go. Ours was an arranged marriage and I knew she didn't love me. That no matter what I said, it wouldn't make a difference. The morning she was due to take the ship to England, I left for work and we didn't even say goodbye,' James continued. He bowed his head in silence and Violet took hold of his hand.

'I was a shrew, Millie, so full of anger and resentment at being made to go to India. I couldn't see what I had. That my husband loved me and I would destroy him by leaving,' Violet said. She reached over and gave her husband a gentle kiss on the lips.

Millie looked at her parents, stunned by the shock revelation that her parents' marriage had not always been a happy one. 'But you didn't leave him, you didn't go back to England,' Millie replied. 'Why?'

Violet took hold of Millie's hand and placed it within James' hand. She then laid her own hand on top. 'I actually got as far as the dockside, but when I saw the ship I knew I couldn't do it. I couldn't take Charles from his father; they were devoted to one another. I also couldn't take the child he didn't yet know existed within my womb and keep it from him. A child he would likely never see. You.'

'So, what did you do?' Millie replied.

Her father raised his head and looked lovingly at his wife. 'She made an incredibly brave decision and decided to give happiness a chance. Millie, I cannot begin to describe the despair I felt when I returned home that evening, expecting to find an empty house.

'But from the moment I opened the bedroom door and saw your mother's things on the dresser and her standing in the evening light, I knew I would never let anything so precious escape again. I'm sorry, Millie, but you are going to have to make a life here in England; you cannot go back to India. I will not allow you to marry anyone who takes you from us.'

Millie bit her lip and nodded. She had known in her heart she couldn't ever leave her family; that a life in India was only a faraway dream. A fantasy that was not real.

'Promise me you won't ever go back. I couldn't bear to know we would never see you again. Charles would be crushed to lose you, as would we,' her father said, as he put an arm around Violet and pulled her into his embrace.

'Yes, Papa, I promise I shall stay,' Millie replied, and gave both her mother and father a kiss. She shook her head and wiped away her tears. How could she have ever entertained the thought of leaving her parents and brother?

'May I go now?' she said. She needed to be alone.

Her parents both nodded. She stood up and took a deep breath. It was liberating to finally have the air clear with her parents; for them to know how she truly felt.

As she reached the door, Violet rose from the couch and came to her side.

'I don't fully understand what has happened between you and

Lord Brooke, but as one who nearly walked away from the love of her life, I would counsel you not to be too hasty in pushing him away. There are things which don't make sense here, and I suspect Lord Brooke is in a purgatory of his own creation, but you may wish to give him one more chance to make matters right,' Violet said.

Millie nodded. After Alex had returned to London he had made repeated attempts to speak to her, but she had refused to hear him out. Once his injuries were healed and he was back in society, she would give him the chance to explain himself.

'Sort it out with Brooke, or I shall pay his father a visit when he returns to London,' Mr Ashton added.

Millie smiled, her mind now clear on what she had to do. 'Thank you, I will, and thank you both for understanding how hard this has been for me. I appreciate everything you have done for me, and Mama, I am especially grateful you didn't get on that ship back to England. We would have all lost so very much if you had.'

After leaving her father's study, Millie went up to her room, where she sat on her bed and tried to recall every word Alex had said to her in the maze. She went to her desk and pulled out a piece of paper, writing down her recollections of their conversation.

'One more chance, Alex,' she whispered, as she put down her pen and stared at the written words.

Chapter Twenty-Two

A lex's late-night dream was of a squirrel.

A tall one, which for reasons unknown kept throwing stones at his window and calling his name. He rolled over on to his back and tried to find a new dream. The insistent squirrel, however, would not go away.

Finally, he opened his eyes and stared up at the ceiling. The low-burning embers in the fireplace danced shadows across the ornate plasterwork.

Thunk.

A real stone hit his window, followed by a voice which called out 'Alex.'

Some fool was in the laneway at the back of his house, tossing stones against his bedroom window. 'Go away, whoever you are; I am not in the mood,' he moaned, running his hands over his face and touching where the stitches still held his eyebrow together.

Another stone hit the window and he heard the glass crack. He was out of bed in a flash, grabbing a woollen blanket from the fire-side chair and wrapping it around his shoulders as he crossed the icy bedroom floor.

'Steady on,' he yelled angrily at the stranger in the darkness as he threw up the window sash and looked down. 'You nearly broke the glass.'

'Thank god; I thought I was going to run out of stones before I found the right window. Let me in, it's freezing out here,' came a distinctly female voice from below.

He pinched himself; surely, he was still dreaming. There was no way on God's green earth that Millie Ashton was standing under his bedroom window in the middle of the night.

'Millie?'

She let out a frustrated growl.

'I don't see any other girls down here. Well, except for the orange-seller back on the corner, but I am certain she doesn't make house calls. Now, will you please come downstairs and let me in at the kitchen door before I freeze to death?'

Alex let the window drop back down and hurriedly began searching for some clothes. In the days since the attack in the maze, he had stayed at home and mostly slept. Naked. He pulled open the top drawer of his tallboy and quickly put on the shirt and trousers he found inside. With Millie waiting outside in the dark, he didn't stop to consider shoes or a jacket.

'Finally; I was beginning to think you had gone back to bed,' she grumbled as he opened the door and let her inside. 'There's certainly no such thing as a balmy English night.'

She was wearing a black greatcoat which must have belonged to her brother and had a gentlemen's tall hat pulled down low to hide her face. With pair of ladies' boots and a skirt on underneath, she would only pass for a young man at the first glance.

'Millie?'

She rolled her eyes. 'Don't start that again, or I shall go straight out the front door and hail the nearest hack.'

He laughed. She was such a tiger when she was angry, and so bloody sexy. He felt his manhood go hard. Luckily his shirt was long enough to cover the evidence of his desire. He closed the door.

'You do know it is the middle of the night?' he asked.

'Actually, it's around one o'clock,' she replied.

'And yet you have come unaccompanied to visit a single man

while he is still abed?'

The frustration in her voice lifted a notch higher. 'Yes. I couldn't wait any longer.'

He scowled and shook his head in disapproval. Millie raised her head and stared hard back at him. As he followed her gaze, he saw her making a careful study of his bruised and cut face. When she got to the large cut above his left eye, her hand began to reach out. His breath caught as she stopped, curled her fingers back into a gentle fist and let her arm drop to her side.

'Nice stitches. I do hope you have been putting a cold compress on those bruises. I'm not surprised I haven't seen you in the park these past few days. You may be interested to know Lady Clarice and her father are not on speaking terms, so I think word of what he had done to you must have got back to her,' Millie said.

Alex attempted to raise his eyebrows, but a sharp sting above his eye made him think the better of it. 'To be honest, I have pretty much slept since David brought me home from Richmond. Fortunately, the face is the worst of it. Whether by design or good luck, the earl's thugs only managed to wind me, rather than break my ribs. And by the way, thank you for coming to my rescue. I still owe you for your ruined clothes,' he replied.

They walked into the hallway and Alex motioned toward the kitchen door. 'Can I make you some tea?' he offered, remembering the cosy evening they had shared in the warmth of the tiny kitchen.

She shook her head. 'Thank you, no. I have not come for tea, I have come for answers. And I would rather we were not disturbed by any of your household staff.'

Before he could stop her, Millie had climbed the stairs, and when she reached the front hall, she continued on up the main staircase, turning left toward his bedroom. The room where he dreamed nightly of her.

'Corner window, corner bedroom,' she muttered.

He caught up with her at the top of the stairs and taking hold of her arm he attempted to steer her away from the bedroom door. 'I think we should go into one of the sitting rooms, I don't think you want to end up in my bedroom.'

'Really?' she replied, with a grin. 'Are you certain?'

His breathing faltered once more. Who was this girl, who looked just like the new Millie, but was standing in his house in the middle of the night, making suggestive remarks?

'I think your bedroom is perfect for talking, and also for when we are done with talking,' she added. She pulled out of his grasp and with a confident wag of her hips she strolled into his bedroom. He followed behind, his mind in a whirl. In the centre of the room, she stopped and turned to face him.

He closed the bedroom door behind him and locked it. He doubted very much that anyone would come looking for him at such an hour, but he wasn't taking any chances. He pointed toward the locked door and Millie nodded her assent.

'We won't be disturbed that way,' she said.

'All right, what do you want to talk about?' Alex said, as their gazes met and he fought an inner battle with the most private of his sexual fantasies. Any moment now, it would win and he would be powerless to stop. He wondered if she realised the danger she had placed herself in by coming to his room, and if she did, did she care?

She put a gloved hand inside the pocket of the greatcoat and after digging deeply, she pulled out a piece of paper and unfolded it. Then holding it in her hand, she gave a flick of her wrist and the paper opened fully. 'Do you know what this is?' she asked, waving the paper towards him.

Alex shook his head, and prayed she would not ask him to read it.

'It's a passage to India on the merchant ship Apollo, which sails from London a week on Sunday. If you look closely, you will see the ticket bears my name,' she said, her expression suddenly turning grim.

A thunderbolt of shock hit him and coursed violently through his body. He swayed on his feet.

Millie was leaving!

While she remained in London, he still had a chance to repair their relationship, but if she took her place on board the ship, all was lost.

'No, you cannot leave! I won't let you,' he shouted, not caring whom he might wake.

A wicked smile appeared on her lips. He had not seen this coming, and she knew it. She wagged a finger at him and stuffed the ticket back into her coat pocket. 'I thought that might get your attention. Now listen, Alex Radley, and listen well, for this is the very last chance you shall ever get with me. You are going to tell me the whole truth about you and Lady Clarice. The moment I suspect you are lying to me or have left out an important detail, I shall walk out that door and you will never see me again.'

Alex immediately regretted leaving the key in the door. 'Yes,' he replied, as his mind went completely blank.

'Good; finally, we agree on something.' She pulled her gloves off and stood slapping them against the side of her coat.

'First things first, when I left you in the maze, you said you didn't write the love letter to her. I think that comment alone deserves its own full explanation.'

Alex closed his eyes and let out a tired sigh. The time had finally come to tell her the truth, to reveal his humiliating secret and watch as she walked out of his life forever. Of all the places he had imagined this scene would be played out, he had never considered it would be here in the privacy of his own bedroom.

'I didn't think you heard me,' he replied.

She pulled the tall hat from her head, and with no pins or ribbons to bind her hair, her long brown tresses fell freely down. Wherever her maid was, it was clear she was unaware of Millie's secret late-night ramble. She threw the hat on a nearby chair.

'I heard it; I just didn't understand it. I have run so many different possible explanations through my head since then and it has taken me until today to make sense of everything and come up with a plausible answer. But before I tell you what I think, it is only fair that I let you give your version of events.'

'All right,' he replied.

Everything hinged on what he was about to tell her. His whole future would be defined by her response. He tried to paint a mental picture of her, a memory of what she looked like the moment before he told her the awful truth. Alex took a deep breath and summoned his courage.

'I didn't write the letter to Clarice; David did. I asked him to write a love letter to you and I mistakenly thought he had. I then mailed it. Lady Clarice received it and the rest of the unholy disaster you know as well as I do.'

Millie raised an eyebrow, but stayed where she was. 'Except for the obvious question as to why you got your brother to write the letter in the first place. Your prose couldn't be that bad. And you most certainly are no wallflower when it comes to women.'

'I asked him to write a letter because I could not. Why couldn't I write a letter to the woman I love?' He stammered as he struggled to find the right words. 'Because I cannot read or write.' He closed his eyes. If Millie left now, he could not bear to watch her go.

He heard her footsteps as she crossed the hard-wooden floor. Her skirts brushed against his leg as she came to his side. He opened his eyes and watched with wonder as she took hold of both his hands. 'Was that so hard?' she whispered as her deep sapphire-blue eyes looked up at him.

She smiled and Alex lived again.

'You put us both through weeks of misery and torture, simply because you cannot read? I don't know whether I should be relieved that you have finally told me, or if I should kill you.' She squeezed his hands.

Alex swallowed deeply. How could she be so calm? He was astonished to find her still standing in his bedroom, let alone so close. In all the versions of this encounter he had imagined never once had she stayed. 'The words on the page, they dance around when I look at them. I can never make head or tail of them. I can barely write my own initials; I cannot even read a street sign,' he replied.

She stepped in closer and standing on her tiptoes she murmured in his ear. 'Or the fables on a ceiling, or even a dance card. It all makes perfect sense now, but why Alex, why didn't you tell me? Did you really think I would see you as less of a man just because you cannot read or write?'

He searched her eyes for the slightest sign of insincerity, but they shone with a blinding honesty. She now knew his darkest secret and it didn't seem to make the slightest difference to how she saw him.

'You don't think I am some sort of village idiot because of it?' he said.

A warm kiss was planted on his ear and Alex chuckled as it tickled him. 'I said you were a fool, I never said you were stupid. You must have a brilliant mind to be able to recall all that knowledge of ancient Greece. I was impressed beyond words with your performance at the museum.'

He winced. 'You don't think me a terrible brother because I pressganged Stephen into telling me all he knew of the Elgin marbles and then dragged him out in the cold to come to the museum?'

She smiled. 'No, I thought it was rather sweet. You should have seen your brother's face when you gave your informative lecture to the assembled crowd; he was positively beaming with pride,' she replied.

Alex unlocked Millie's fingers and withdrew his hands. Reaching out, he put his arms around her and pulled her close. At the same time, her arms wrapped tightly around him. Her head came to rest against his chest and as he bent down to kiss her hair, he took in a deep breath. The heady scent of Millie filled his lungs.

Memories of the night he had first kissed her came flooding back. From now on there would be no need to steal away from ballrooms to be alone with her. He knew she would not let go. 'You have no idea what this means to me,' he murmured.

She gave him a playful punch on the back. 'It means you won't ever lie to me again.'

'And you won't be going back to India,' his replied with conviction. Before she could stop him, he had pulled the ticket out of her coat pocket, screwed it up into a ball and tossed it into the fireplace. It landed in the embers and burst into flames.

'Oh,' Millie said. 'It took me all afternoon to handwrite that ticket.'

Alex laughed. Whether from relief or joy, he didn't care. Millie was here with him and that was all that mattered. She wasn't going anywhere without him. 'I promise to pay you double for the cost of the ticket,' he replied with a smile.

She shook her head. 'Considering how hurt my parents were when they realised I was planning to book a passage back to India, if it had been a real ticket I would consider it an act of karma. I cannot believe I was foolish enough not to realise my father would have known the moment I decided on that particular course of action.'

'You did once tell me he could read your mind, and here I was thinking I was about to take on an intelligent wife,' Alex murmured.

Millie gasped, but Alex held her tightly. She would not be getting a second punch in.

'You haven't actually asked me to marry you,' she replied.

'Yet.'

She pulled out of his embrace and took a step backward. Alex congratulated himself for the second time on having had the good sense to lock the bedroom door.

'Only if you are sure, and only if I am your first choice,' she replied. All the humour in her voice was gone and he could tell she was still in need of some convincing. He could not blame her for having her doubts. His behaviour over the previous weeks would give anyone reason to have second thoughts.

'Yes,' he said, taking her by the hand and walking her over to the tallboy. Opening the top drawer, he took out a small black box. He sank down on one bended knee and placed a tender kiss on her fingers before finally speaking his heart's desire.

'Millie, it was only ever you, and I am sorry I made such a hash of things. But if you would do me the greatest honour possible and become my wife, I shall endeavour to spend the rest of my life trying to make amends.'

Chapter Twenty-Three

'Yes.'

Such a simple word and yet it meant so much to Millie. All the misunderstandings and false hopes were gone. A life's journey together now beckoned.

Millie blew the air out of her cheeks and tried not to cry as Alex placed the diamond ring on her finger.

She failed.

'It was going to be a sapphire, but I knew it would always pale against the colour of your eyes.' He came to his feet. 'There is something else for you to wear. It matches the ring.' He reached back into the ring box and took out a small diamond nose ring. Smiling, she took the ring and as she hooked it into place, she felt complete once more.

'Don't ever change, Millie; to me you are perfect the way you are,' Alex said, as he took her face in his hands. 'You are mine now, forever,' he whispered as he lowered his head and his lips met hers.

The kiss was slow at first, tender and uncertain, but as it continued, Millie sensed a change. Alex ran his tongue along her bottom lip and she found her mouth opening in response. His tongue swept past her lips and into her mouth, where it met her tongue and gently stroked.

She let out a low groan and gave herself up to the kiss. Softening her lips, she allowed him to possess her completely. Willing in her submission, she knew she had won.

Alex's hand glided down the side of Millie's waist and clutching her hip, he pulled her firmly to him. She felt the hard evidence of his desire press up against her stomach.

She gasped and stiffened; this was where his kiss had been heading that fateful night.

All the colourful images she had carefully studied in the *Kama Sutra* had not prepared her for the intimacy of this moment. The pictures failed to convey the heat and desire she knew both their bodies felt. The man she loved was holding and kissing her. And there was no doubt he wanted her.

She had risked travelling the dangerous streets of London on her own in order to get to the truth, but if she were honest with herself, beyond confronting Alex she had not planned for the aftermath.

He lightened the kiss and drew back. When Millie looked into his eyes, she could see they were still clouded with passion.

'Sorry I got a bit carried away then. I didn't mean to frighten you,' he said, clearing his throat. 'I had better take you home. If you are sure of your decision, then I shall call on your father in the morning.'

Millie felt her lips begin to cool as the heat of Alex's kiss faded on them. She looked down at the diamond ring newly placed on her finger. 'No,' she replied.

Alex winced and slowly nodded his head. 'I understand. Of course, it was too much to expect you to commit your life to an imbecile,' he replied. 'Rest assured, no one shall ever know you were here.'

A giggle found its way to her mouth as she raised her head. 'Oh, you should see your face right now, Alex; it's absolutely priceless,' she said.

He blinked at her, and then a look of relieved realisation

appeared on his face. 'You don't mean no to me speaking to your father, do you?'

She shook her head.

'You mean no to going home.'

She nodded her head.

'And I am Alexander the Completely Pathetic?' he laughed.

They both nodded in agreement.

She ran her hand over his chest, until it came to rest over his heart. 'This is why I must stay tonight. I know my own heart, but I am not convinced you are certain of it or that I love you as well as I should. Until am I completely yours I believe that uncertainty will remain,' she said.

Her fingers drifted to the collar of his shirt and after undoing the first of his shirt buttons, they slowly worked their way down his shirtfront until the four remaining buttons were undone. He quickly pulled the shirt over his head, and Millie offered up her mouth once more to him.

He took and then feasted upon her pliant lips. A true lover's kiss.

Millie reached out and found herself touching a man's bare skin for the first time in her adult life. She felt the light brush of hair on Alex's chest. He let out a needy groan when her fingers found a nipple and she gently squeezed.

'Minx,' he whispered into her mouth.

It was now his turn to tackle her buttons, and a shiver of antici- pation slid down her spine as he eased her out of her coat. He threw it and the gloves on the chair, where it landed on his recently removed shirt and the oversized hat. The coat was quickly followed by the rest of their clothes.

'I suppose we are a little past the point where I ask you if you are still sure about this?' Alex said, as he removed the last piece of Millie's clothing.

She nodded quickly and prayed he knew what he was doing. He took her by the hand and led her over to the fireplace. All the while she kept her eyes on his upper torso, fearful that if she looked any lower, all her courage would desert her. She didn't need to look to understand the state of his arousal.

He bent down and hurriedly stacked some more logs on the dying embers. Then, pulling the blanket off the end of the bed where he had loosely tossed it, he pulled her close and wrapped it around them both.

He brushed a stray hair from her face and placed a tender kiss on her nose. 'Before we go any further, there is something else you need to know,' he said.

She gave a quick glance at the fireplace; her homemade ticket to India was well beyond redemption.

'No, it's nothing that will result in you having to flee England. It's what you do to me,' he said.

She raised her eyebrows. 'Yes?'

'The first time we met, you thought I was horrid to you. Which, thinking back on that night, I was.'

Millie nodded. 'Go on,' she replied.

Alex bit his lip. 'Do you know what happens between a man and woman? I mean in the sexual sense?'

She chuckled. 'Yes, I understand the bits and where things go; I have not lived that much of a sheltered life. They do have animals in India, you know.' At some point she would share her special picture book with him, and she couldn't wait to see his face when she did.

'Good. I take it then you understand the effect you are having on me right at this moment?' he asked.

She smiled as she rubbed her body against his manhood. Alex closed his eyes and groaned. It was a wonderful, heady feeling to know she wielded such power over him.

He kissed her lips again.

'The thing is, the moment I laid eyes upon you at your uncle's ball, you had this effect on me. I thought I was going to faint from the lack of blood to my brain. My father was understandably furious. An experienced gentleman should be able to control his base desires in mixed company,' he explained.

'Oh,' she replied, remembering the look of anger she had seen on the Duke of Strathmore's face as he listened to Lord Ashton's speech.

'And the disagreement with David was because he got very drunk the next evening and revealed my embarrassing predicament to a number of our friends. As you can understand, I was utterly humiliated and we nearly came to blows. Of course, he has since apologised and we are reconciled.'

She gave him a sultry smile and murmured, 'I hope to test the limits of your control on a regular basis, Lord Brooke.' She gave the door a quick glance. 'I have a feeling we are going to be in need of a large set of keys with which to lock doors.'

Alex let out a growl and swiftly took her mouth with his, rendering her incapable of any further speech. His hands came around her waist and he lifted her up off the floor. 'Wrap your legs around me,' he ordered, before they went back to kissing.

Her breasts were now pressed hard against his chest. She brushed them to and fro, enjoying the exquisite sensation that this gave her. Heat pooled between her legs and she found herself becoming breathless.

He pulled his lips away and whispered. 'Come to bed, my love.'

In a grand declaration of intent, she tore the blanket from their bodies and threw it on the end of the bed.

Alex gently lowered her on to the bed and covered her naked body with his.

She looked up into his eyes, and saw they shone with joy and wonder. 'I love you,' she said. It was the first time she had openly admitted her love for him to anyone. It had taken the realisation of her truly loving him to gamble with her future and come here tonight.

'You had better love me, because I am about to completely ruin you,' he chuckled. As Alex began to gently knead her breast with his hand, she closed her eyes and lay back in the bed. When he took her nipple into his mouth and began to suckle, she put a hand over her mouth and stifled a scream.

The bed shook with his laughter as he continued to tease her sensitive nipple. With her body becoming more heated and flushed by the second, there was little else she could do but lie back and let him ravish her. When he turned and gave her other breast the same attention with his mouth she groaned.

'Make that seduced, ravished and ruined,' he murmured, as he playfully rolled her nipple between his tongue and his teeth.

The fingers of his right hand skimmed down the skin on the outside of her thigh, brushed over her knee and then began the journey up the inside of her leg. A single finger brushed over the soft curls of hair covering her most private place, setting her nerves alight.

As he slipped a finger inside her heat, she gasped. When a second finger followed and he began to stroke, Millie sobbed. 'Alex.' He shifted position and found her mouth again, taking it in a hard-passionate kiss. He continued to stroke her heat, calling forth her wet desire.

With the smouldering heat building in her body and threatening to burst into flames at any moment, she thought she would go mad. How much more of this could she take?

He removed his fingers from her heat and as he raised himself over her, his knees pushed her legs far enough apart for him to settle between them.

'You are ready for me now. You are so hot and so wet. Millie, I have wanted this from the first time I met you, I love you. I always will.'

His hard erection parted the lips of her womanhood and he pressed himself slowly into her. She felt her body begin to tense, and willed herself to relax. She had read enough of her brother's books to know that it only hurt the first time, and if the man was as considerate a lover as he should be it would barely sting. She placed her trust in Alex, knowing he would be skilled in the way of loving a woman's body.

From this night on, only she would be the judge of his sexual expertise.

When Alex reached the obstruction of her maidenhead, he stopped. She opened her eyes. Raised up on his arms above her, she saw he was drenched in sweat. His breathing was hard and laboured, as if he had run a hundred-mile race.

'Take me, make me yours,' she demanded, and grabbed hold of his buttocks. He bent and kissed her once more, and as he did, she felt his hips flex, followed quickly by the overwhelming sensation of taking him inside her as he took her innocence and buried himself deep within her willing body.

'*God*, Millie,' he growled.

The small sting she had felt as Alex entered her quickly faded as he partially withdrew and then slowly filled her body once more.

Her hands found a home on the side of his grinding hips as she quickly found the rhythm to the dance. Every time he thrust in deep, and his body ground against the opening of her sex, she dug her fingers in, spurring him on.

The bed creaked loudly as they met each other thrust for thrust and groan for groan.

Her breathing grew shallow as the pressure within her body built to a peak. Wherever he was taking her, she knew she was nearly there. She tore her lips away from his and looked at him, searching his face for an answer.

'Alex?' she gasped.

'Let go, let go and come for me,' he commanded, as his thrusts became more powerful and deep.

She fell back in the bed and as her world fractured she let out a sob-filled scream. Somewhere off in the distance, she heard Alex cry 'Oh my god, oh my god,' as he thrust deeply into her one last time. Soaked with sweat, he slumped on top of her, kissing her face and whispering her name over and over again.

'We will get better with practice,' Alex said, as he lifted from her several minutes later, and pulled the bedclothes over their rapidly cooling bodies.

Millie laughed. At this rate she would be dead in a week. She shuffled over in the bed and lay on his chest, her head resting where she could hear his heart beating strongly in his chest. 'I always knew you would be magnificent,' she murmured. 'But know this, Alex Radley: you are all mine from now on. I will not share.'

Strong arms wrapped around her and pulled her in close. 'I wouldn't dare do anything to lose you. When the woman a man loves screams as loudly as you did when you climaxed, he would have to be mad to stray from her bed.' He gave a deep sensual laugh. 'Though I expect to receive complaints from the neighbours in the morning.'

She slid her hand down and cupped Alex's balls, giving them a friendly squeeze. 'Well, they are just going to have to get used to it.'

'Hmm,' he replied. 'Fortunately for us, David is a heavy sleeper.'

'David!' she cried as she sat bolt upright in bed. 'I forgot about your brother. Don't tell me he is here? I thought he was back living at Strathmore House.'

Alex chuckled softly once more and pulled her back down on to the bed and into his arms. 'He moved back here to look after me after I was attacked. Besides, the rest of the family arrived home from Scotland late yesterday, and he didn't want Papa walking in on him while he was playing lord,' he replied.

How would she ever face David Radley again when she had just screamed half the house down? She felt her cheeks begin to burn.

'Don't worry, I once fired a pistol two feet away from his sleeping head and he didn't flinch. Though I think it prudent for me to ask him to move his things home after we are married, at least until he can find a new house in which to set up his own married life,' Alex said.

Millie turned and brought her face close to Alex. 'David is in love with Lady Clarice, isn't he? I hear the love letter was both beautiful and heartfelt.'

He nodded. 'I think he has been in love with her all his life. I just wish he would do something about it.'

'Even after her father had you assaulted? Would he want such a man as his father-in-law?' she replied.

He rubbed the tip of his nose against hers, sneaking a little kiss on the lips every so often. 'If the Earl of Langham had really wanted to hurt me, I would have received the last rites in the maze and we would not be lying here together now.'

He ran a finger along the healing wound above his eye. 'This is going to scar. So, every day for the rest of my life, I shall look in the mirror and be reminded why I should not act without thought for the consequences of my actions. The earl has taught me a timely, though painful, lesson in humility. And since this is what has finally brought you to me and we are now to be married, I am in no position to complain.'

Married life.

She would soon be a wife; Alex's wife. A tear found its way to the corner of her eye; and when it fell it landed on his naked chest. Another tear soon joined the first.

He lifted her up and placed her so she sat with her legs straddling his waist. In the pale firelight she saw the look of concern on his face as he thumbed her tears away.

'Did I hurt you? I tried not to be too rough, but I know I lost control toward the end,' he said, lifting his head and planting butterfly kisses on her breasts.

She shook her head.

'No, I just hadn't really thought about being married until you mentioned the word. It's humbling to think I will soon be your wife,' she replied.

'Marchioness,' he gently corrected her. 'You will be the Marchioness of Brooke, my love, and some day my Duchess, but hopefully not for many years to come.'

Her heart swelled with joy, she looked forward to the day when she could call him husband. 'I am so relieved this has all been sorted out, and I won't have to spend the rest of my life wondering what it would have been like to have spent it with you. My mother was right.'

'What do you mean?'

'After my parents confronted me over my foolish plan to go back to India, my mother advised me to give you one final chance.

Though I don't expect she had quite this manner of reconciliation in mind,' she said.

She gave him a swift but passionate kiss on the lips and climbed off him and the bed. After gathering up her clothes from the floor she began to get dressed.

A scowl appeared on Alex's face.

Millie picked up her coat. 'I had better go home or Charles might feel the need to give you some fresh bruises.'

Alex sat up and swung his legs over the side of the bed. He scrambled around in the poorly lit room and picked up his clothes. He took a jacket and a pair of boots from the cupboard and put them on. Millie finished buttoning her coat and retrieved her hat from under the fireside chair.

'What are you doing?' she asked, as she tucked her hair up under the hat. 'I can hail a hack from out the front; you don't need to get dressed. I can slip back into the house easily enough, and back into bed. Our night footman is a sound sleeper. Then you can come and see Papa this afternoon when he gets home.'

Alex took hold of her hand and placed a deep kiss on her palm. 'I shall take you home; I will not have you travelling the streets of London on your own at such an hour. You can steal back into your father's house if you like, but it will be under my watchful eye. I protect what is mine.'

She smiled at him and handed him his coat. 'Promise me we won't ever stop sneaking around together.'

Alex took his coat and placed another kiss on Millie's lips.

'Fear not, my lover; I have an inexhaustible list of places in which I intend to make love to you,' he murmured, as he put his coat on.

'Wicked man,' she replied and unlocked the bedroom door.

Epilogue

Millie and Lucy exchanged excited grins; in little over an hour they would be sisters. Seated on a chair in the upstairs sitting room of her soon-to-be-former home, Millie watched as the Ashton family's Indian cook painstakingly made the final touches to the intricate patterns of *mehndi* on Millie's feet.

Lucy, kneeling on the floor beside her, leaned over and gasped.

'You have the Strathmore Crest on your feet! That is amazing!'

Millie smiled. 'I thought it would be a nice surprise for your brother when we are alone. If you look closely you can see I have the initials AR also painted within the swirls on the side of my ankle.'

Lucy looked closely and smiled. 'So, what is the paint made of?'

'It is henna paste, made from the henna leaf. I painted it on Miss Millie's feet last night and overnight the colour has darkened to a beautiful *naringee*,' Mrs Knowles replied.

'It's orange,' Lucy said.

'Yes,' Millie replied. 'It will darken over the next few days, and if I continue to rub oil on to it, it should last for a few weeks. Or until I get sick of it and scrub it off.'

Mrs Knowles clicked her tongue in disgust. 'A bride does not wash off her *mehndi* that is for her husband when he bathes with her in the river.'

Lucy blushed, and Mrs Knowles gave a knowing chuckle.

Millie yawned. She had been out of bed since before dawn, checking and rechecking everything. Her beloved travel trunks had left home for the last time the previous afternoon and their contents were now unpacked at Bird Street, awaiting her arrival as the new Marchioness of Brooke.

'I wonder where Alex and David spent last night?' she pondered.

'Well, I can tell you they were not out drinking last night, if that is your concern. We had a lovely family dinner at home and all my brothers, including Stephen, spent the evening holed up with Papa in Papa's study going over paperwork,' Lucy replied.

Millie raised her eyebrows. 'And I expect the paperwork consisted of your father reading the labels on several bottles of wine, before deciding which one to open first,' she replied.

The Duke of Strathmore had made a promise to her that he would ensure Alex arrived at the church on time and in a suitable state to be married.

'So, have you decided on where you will take your honeymoon trip?' Lucy asked.

'We have talked about a tour of the Lake District later in the summer, but Alex wishes to remain in London for at least the next month,' Millie replied.

Alex had been adamant in his decision that they remain in London after the wedding. There were too many people ready to assume he had married Millie because of the scandal surrounding Lady Clarice Langham for his liking. That somehow Millie had been compromised and he had been compelled to marry her.

'I won't have it. I want the rest of the *ton* to be in absolutely no doubt that this is a love match and I have willingly chosen you as my future duchess,' he had said several days earlier.

As Millie was at that very moment lying naked in his arms after another afternoon of lovemaking in his bedroom, she had neither the strength nor the desire to argue with him.

Millie smiled a secret smile.

Mrs Knowles completed her work and stood. 'It is a pity you would not let me paint your hands, Miss Millie.'

Lucy's eyes widened in consternation, but Millie shook her head. 'No thank you, Mrs Knowles; Mama and I agreed that my feet would be enough of an acknowledgement of my Indian birth. Besides, the Bishop was clear in his stipulation that as this is a Church of England wedding service, I have to respect the customs of my new home as well as my old one.'

§

An hour later she stood in front of the Bishop of London as her father placed her hand in Alex's. As she looked up at him, she saw his gaze take in the garland of love-in-the-mist which she wore in her hair, a sapphire-blue ribbon threaded between the delicate buds.

He took a deep breath and the most incredible and joyous smile appeared on his face. If there had ever been a trace of uncertainty among the assembled guests as to how the Marquess of Brooke felt about his bride, the look on his face dispelled all doubts. No happier bridegroom in England existed.

Alex recited his vows and Millie mirrored his. Taking the ring from the Bishop, Alex placed it on Millie's left hand. He spoke clearly and loudly. 'With this ring I thee wed, and with all my worldly goods I thee endow. In the name of the Father, the Son and the Holy Ghost, amen.'

His uncle smiled and leaned in close to Millie. 'Welcome to the family, my dear; I think my nephew has met his match.' He turned to Alex and chuckled. 'You can kiss her now.'

Alex needed no second prompting.

§

When the wedding service was finally over and the newly wedded couple were being congratulated by their guests, Lady Clarice

Langham stood on the steps of St George's church, Hanover Square, enjoying the morning sun.

'It is a beautiful sight, is it not?'

She turned and saw David Radley standing several feet away. He smiled and gave her a bow.

'Yes, it is a magnificent sight. I do so love the weather in June, especially when it is coupled with a happy wedding, I am honoured that your brother invited me,' she replied. Clarice fiddled with her gloves and decided it was time to be brave. 'Mr Radley, I believe you have something for me?' she said, holding out her hand.

'Yes, I have,' said a voice from close behind her.

She turned to see Lord Stephen Radley, looking very pensive and holding out a small parcel. 'My brother Alex has asked that I give this to you. He begs for your forgiveness on this, his wedding day, but he is unable to comply with your final demand.'

The youngest Radley male handed her the parcel and then beat a hasty retreat. Clarice looked down at the parcel in her hand and sadly shook her head. 'I cannot accept this; it wouldn't be right.' She handed it to David, who gave her a nod of approval in return.

'Would you please give this back to your brother and give him and his new wife my very best wishes for the future?'

David tucked the parcel inside his coat. 'On behalf of my brother and new sister I thank you.' He patted the side of his coat. 'I hope I shall remember to return this to Alex. But perhaps I may not.'

She scowled and then came and stood by his side, her face pointed toward the sun.

'I will find out who wrote that letter and I just hope that when the time comes he will have the courage to stand and fight for me,' she said.

They stood in silence for a minute before David gave her a short bow. 'Good day to you, Lady Clarice; I hope to see you again at the wedding ball next week. Perhaps you will dance with me,' he replied.

She watched as he climbed back up the steps of the church and warmly greeted Millie's family. From a distance he looked as self-assured as any other son of society.

Clarice touched the side of her reticule. Before giving the original letter back to Alex, she had copied every loving and passion-filled word into her private diary, which she now carried with her constantly.

'You cannot live all your life in the shadows, Mr Radley,' she whispered after him.

*

Thank you so much for reading this story and I hope you loved it as much as I did when I wrote it.

Sasha xxx

Newsletter
Join my mailing list to receive news of new releases, special giveaways and other exciting news at www.sashacottman.com.

Bookbub
You can also follow me on Bookbub https://www.bookbub.com/authors/sasha-cottman

Other places I hang out.

Facebook https://www.facebook.com/SashaCottmanAuthor
Goodreads https://www.goodreads.com/author/show/713610 8.Sasha_Cottman

For a full list of books by Sasha Cottman
https://www.sashacottman.com/books/

The Duke of Strathmore Series
Book 1. Letter from a Rake
Book 2. An Unsuitable Match
Book 3. The Duke's Daughter
Book 4. A Scottish Duke for Christmas (novella)
Book 5. My Gentleman Spy
Book 6. Lord of Mischief
Book 7. The Ice Queen (coming 2019)

London Lords Series
Book 1. An Italian Count for Christmas.

Did you know that every review a reader leaves for a book is like gold to the author?

If you enjoy any author's book please consider leaving a short review on the book retailer site from where you purchased the book. My fellow authors and I thank you so much for all your wonderful support.

xxx

Sasha

Turn the page to read the first chapter of An Unsuitable Match

When all the world is against their love.

Award-Winning Series
The *Duke* of
Strathmore
Book 2

Sasha
Cottman

Romantic Book of the Year Finalist

An Unsuitable Match

An Unsuitable Match

CHAPTER ONE

I dream of the hours when you and I can finally be alone.
Softly sharing whispered words of love.

As the carriage slowly snaked its way up Park Lane, Clarice picked at a loose piece of thread on her gown. No matter how hard she pulled, it refused to come free.

She sighed, dreading that this was a sign of things to come. Tonight was going to be a trial, no matter what.

And I have no-one to blame but myself. You could have done it all in private, but no, you had to go and make a huge public scene. Well done, Clarice. Well done.

'At this rate we shall have to get out and walk if we are to arrive at the dinner on time,' Lord Langham grumbled.

Stirred from her thoughts, she looked across the carriage to her father. Everyone, it would appear, was headed to Strathmore House for the wedding celebrations of the Marquess and Marchioness of Brooke. It had taken them nearly an hour to get this far in the slow-crawling line of carriages.

'We could turn the horses around and go home,' she offered.

He shook his head. Reaching out, he took hold of her hand and gave it a gentle squeeze.

'We have to do this, my dear. We must show the rest of society that you are not crushed by the unfortunate event of your failed betrothal to the groom,' he replied.

She mustered a hopeful smile for him. Her father was right, of course. If she stayed away from the wedding celebrations it would only confirm what the rest of the *ton* no doubt thought of her. She was Lord Langham's poor little broken bird. An object of pity.

'Yes, of course, Papa,' she replied.

The truth was, she didn't particularly mind what the rest of London thought of her. In fact, she rather preferred they didn't think of her at all. Being unremarkable was at times a blessing.

She shifted in her seat and forced herself to sit upright. As she straightened her back, the tight garments under her gown shifted and eased. She took in a shallow breath. The discomfort meant little. For her father's sake she would endure far worse.

Tonight she would stoically bear all the whispers and sly looks that came her way. This evening was for her father. London's elite would know Henry Langham was a man capable of forgiveness. But Clarice knew there was a limit to her father's magnanimity.

She knew she could never confess her terrible crime against him. To have him know that she had stolen from him the thing he had held most dear. Earl Langham might forgive others for their sins against him, but Clarice knew there could be no forgiveness for what she had done.

Her wish to remain invisible for the evening was not to be granted. Within minutes of their arrival at Strathmore House, she had been discovered.

'Clarice!'

A mass of hair and a smiling face filled her field of vision and she was caught up in a warm embrace.

Lucy Radley.

'We were so worried you would cry off,' Lucy exclaimed, when she finally released Clarice from the heartfelt hug. She stepped back and Clarice could see the smile which stretched across Lucy's face.

'Yes, Papa and I were delighted to accept your parents' invitation; it just took a little longer than expected to get here,' she replied.

Lucy looked at the earl.

'Lord Langham, I'm so pleased you came,' she said, dipping into an elegant curtsy.

'Lady Lucy,' he replied, with a formal bow.

Lucy looked at the other guests mingling around them in the enormous entrance to Strathmore House. She wrinkled her nose and leaned in close.

'Lord Langham, would it be acceptable for me to take Clarice away at this moment? I am sure there are plenty of your friends and business partners here tonight whom you would like to greet. I promise to take good care of her.'

Clarice looked at her father, and breathed an audible sigh of relief when he nodded his head.

'Thank you,' she whispered as Lucy took hold of her hand and quickly spirited her away. Lucy made a beeline for the nearest footman bearing a drinks tray and returned to Clarice's side with a glass of champagne in either hand.

'I hope it didn't take too long for you to travel here tonight. From what I hear all streets west of Grosvenor Square are at a standstill,' Lucy remarked.

Clarice gave a gentle shake of her head. She was going to be anything but disagreeable this evening. Besides, it wasn't every day that the heir to one of the most important titles in England got married. A crush of carriages was to be expected.

'Tonight is a night for champagne. Here's to a wonderful dinner and a magnificent ball,' Lucy said, raising her glass.

Clarice took a sip of her champagne, holding the bubbles in her mouth for a moment as she savoured the excellent French wine.

'Good evening, Lady Clarice,' a deep male voice murmured.

She turned and her gaze fell upon him.

David Radley.

Tall. Dark. When had he become so handsome?

Author of a passionate love letter which had recently gone

astray and accidentally fallen into Clarice's hands. Hour after hour she had spent poring over the words of his letter. Words she knew had been written with her in mind. Words which meant she could never marry his brother. His declaration of love burned deeply within her soul.

'Mr Radley,' she replied, willing herself to remain calm.

He stepped forward and as he did, the light from the chandelier hanging overhead reflected in his eyes. The blue and green hues turned momentarily to a dazzling emerald, forcing her to blink.

He bowed deeply.

For the first time in the many years she had known him, Clarice was at a loss as to what she should do or say. At such proximity, she found herself decidedly uncomfortable.

How does one react to a long-time friend who has unexpectedly and most passionately declared that he loves you?

You have me at sixes and sevens.

Lucy cleared her throat. 'So how are the dinner preparations, David; did you spend the last hour polishing silver? I hear the downstairs servants were beginning to complain.'

He shot his sister a sideways glance and growled. Clarice spied the edge of a grin on his lips.

Lucy chuckled. 'Such an easy target, it's almost unsportsmanlike.'

'Ignore my darling sister, would you please Clarice; she is determined to make me a laughing stock this evening,' David replied.

A gasp escaped Lucy's lips and she placed a hand on his arm.

'Oh no, I would never do that to you. Especially not in present company.'

Clarice smiled, suppressing the familiar twinge of envy which came from being an only child. A gong sounded and dinner was announced.

'Saved by the bell,' David replied. He shot a forgiving smile in Lucy's direction.

How she managed it, Clarice was not entirely sure, but Lucy suddenly vanished into the crowd of other dinner guests, leaving her and David standing facing one another. As the other guests found partners for the procession into the dining room, the reason for her friend's disappearance soon became apparent.

'Since I suspect your father may have been waylaid by my sister in order for you and I to spend a brief moment together, Lady Clarice, would you do me the honour of allowing me to escort you into dinner?' David said.

She hesitated briefly before taking his arm. Lucy's less than subtle attempt at playing Cupid was the last thing she needed this evening.

Strathmore House, home of the Radley family, was one of the largest private residences in the whole of London. Over fifty people were seated on either side of the two tables which lined the length of the dining room. The head table seated another dozen guests as well as the hosts.

Enormous chandeliers hung overhead from the ornate ceiling. At intervals along the long, elegantly carved oak tables, towering three-armed silver candelabra were set, giving enough light for the guests to see each other clearly.

Clarice's gaze followed the seemingly never-ending line of huge, food-laden platters and dishes which covered the tables. All manner of delicacies beckoned to her.

'How many are coming for the wedding ball?' she asked, as David escorted her through the room.

'I understand it's somewhere in the vicinity of a thousand. Mama sealed the guest list at eight hundred, but my father kept inviting more. You should have seen her face when he told her he had invited another thirty guests only yesterday'.

As they reached her chair, he stopped.

'Since it is unlikely that I will get an opportunity to speak with you privately later, Clarice, may I say now how delighted I am that you are here tonight.'

She gave him a non-committal nod of the head. With her father present, it seemed unwise to offer him any further sign of encouragement. Earl Langham did not approve of David Radley.

At dinner, she was seated across from David. While he remained standing, she could see him clearly, but as soon as he took his seat, only the top of his black hair remained in view. He picked up the silver candelabra which sat in the middle of the table and moved it to one side.

He raised a single eyebrow and a titter escaped Clarice's lips. She briefly closed her eyes. 'You are incorrigible.'

'True, but now I have an uninterrupted view,' he replied. A wolfish smile appeared on his face.

Clarice was pleased to see that whoever had devised the seating plan had managed to put most of the younger members of the gathering at one end of the table. They were far enough away from the senior members to be able to relax and share the latest *on dit*.

Lucy, having slipped away from Lord Langham, took a seat to the left of Clarice. Close by, Millie and Alex, the newlyweds, sat across the table from one another. Every so often they would share a love-struck glance.

'You should have heard the row Mama and Alex had when he said he wasn't going to sit at the head table. I tell you she was fit to be tied,' Lucy said.

'Yes, I did think it rather odd that they did not sit in the place of honour,' Clarice replied, picking up her wine glass and taking a sip. She leaned forward in her chair and peered down the long table, smiling with pride when she saw her father was many seats further down the line of guests, almost at the head of the table.

She sat back in her seat, sensing that his presence tonight was more than just a last-minute change of heart. He had flatly refused to attend the wedding. Now it would appear that the rift caused between the two families over Clarice and Alex's failed betrothal was being publicly smoothed over.

Thank you, Papa.

The dinner was far more enjoyable than she had expected. It was full of laughter and friendly banter. Her earlier concerns that she would feel awkward in the presence of the Marquess and Marchioness of Brooke were quickly swept from her mind. At one point she and Alex shared a knowing smile. All was right between them once more.

She made a point not to stare long at the still-healing scars which dotted Alex's face. They were reputedly from a pre-wedding horse riding accident, but Clarice had her doubts. Her father had sworn retribution against the Marquess and she could only pray he had not followed through with his threat.

She picked at several of the early courses when they were served, eating little. When a large platter containing a sliced piece of roast beef surrounded by roast potatoes was placed in the centre of the table, she knew her patience was about to be rewarded. While David regaled the gathering with a slightly risqué story, the guests all hanging on his every word, Clarice took the time to savour her favourite meal.

She cut a piece of roast potato in half and put it into her mouth. Cooked long in goose fat, it was delicious. She sat chewing, savouring the caramelised crust while listening to the buzzing conversation which continued unabated around her. Was there anything better than a well-cooked potato?

'How are you enjoying this evening, Lady Clarice?' David asked from across the table.

With a mouth full of roasted vegetable she was unable to respond politely. She picked up her glass of wine and took a sip, hoping to quickly wash down the potato and reply.

The instant the potato and the wine met in her throat, she began to choke.

Doing her best not to make a scene, she pulled her napkin from her lap and tried to hide her face. Shudders wracked her body as she coughed and struggled to breathe. No matter how hard she tried to dislodge it, the potato remained firmly lodged in the back of her throat.

On her fourth attempt to take a breath of air, a hard thump landed between her shoulder blades. The offending potato dislodged from her throat and she spat it into her napkin.

Sitting back in her chair, she sucked in air, relieved when she felt the colour go back into her face. Lucy handed her a handkerchief and Clarice wiped away the tears in her eyes.

'Clarice, are you all right?'

The hand which had helped to dislodge the potato now began

to gently rub her back. She looked up over her shoulder and saw David standing behind her.

In the blink of an eye, he had leapt up from his chair, dashed around the end of the table and gallantly rescued her.

'Yes, yes I am fine. I was in too much of a hurry to speak, and failed to chew my food properly. Please forgive my dreadful lack of manners.'

David knelt down next to her chair, and she looked at him. His worried gaze searched her face. She placed a reassuring hand on his arm. 'I am fine; thank you so much for coming to my aid.'

He smiled. 'Think nothing of it, Clarice.'

As David stood and walked back to his chair, she brushed a stray lock of hair back behind her ear. She tried not to stare at him.

You are rather lovely. Not only did you just save my life, but you called me Clarice. In public.

A footman quickly replaced her soiled napkin and she calmly reassured the other concerned guests that she was fine.

She politely excused herself from the table and sought refuge in the ladies' retiring room. Needing a moment alone, she asked the maid to fetch some fresh warm water.

Slipping into one of the small private stalls, she stood with her back against the wall.

'Breathe slowly and remain calm,' she whispered to herself.

She had managed to get through dinner mostly intact, now she just had to find a way to endure the wedding ball. To make her father proud.

'I must stay away from David Radley,' she vowed.

Click here to keep reading An Unsuitable Match.

https://www.sashacottman.com/books/

About the Author

Born in England, but raised in Australia, Sasha has a love for both countries. Having her heart in two places has created a love for travel, which at last count was to over 55 countries. A travel guide is always on her pile of new books to read.

Her first published novel, *Letter from a Rake* was a finalist for the 2014 Romantic Book of the Year.

Sasha lives with her husband, teenage daughter and a cat who demands a starring role in the next book. She has found new hiding spots for her secret chocolate stash. On the weekends Sasha loves walking on the beach while trying to deal with her bad knee and current Fitbit obsession.

Follow Sasha and find out more about her and her books on Goodreads and Pinterest or her website:

www.sashacottman.com

Manufactured by Amazon.ca
Bolton, ON